THE INVERTED MASK

A Science-Fiction Story

IZZY DOROSKI

"The world that we see and feel is just an illusion. It really doesn't exist at all, at least not in the way we think it does."

Existence Wave Media

www.theinvertedmask.com

Disclaimer: This book is a fictional book. Any fictional depictions are not meant to represent any person living or dead. The characters, activities, and events that take place in the book are an artifact of my imagination and are not to be taken as factual in any way. Any physical location in the book is merely a pretended creation that was produced to enhance the overall story and texture of the narrative. Any references to scientific activities, products, or building structures are fictional and have no association to actual locations.

ISBN 978-0-9908045-0-5 (pbk.)
ISBN 978-0-9908045-1-2 (ebk.)

Developmental editor: Denise Schnittman
Book editor: Lourdes Venard
Cover designer: Gabrielle Prendergast
Book designer: Jennifer Zaczek

To my wife Jeanne, who helped me in every way possible in creating this book.

Visit the official website for the book at:

THEINVERTEDMASK.COM

For information, updates, preview, reviews, where to purchase, contact the author, blog and media

This book is dedicated to Hugh Everett III

Hugh Everett was an American physicist who first proposed the many-worlds interpretation of quantum physics in 1954. Everett's remarkable insight and research into the realm of quantum mechanics provided modern physics with the radical viewpoint that we live in a universe where parallel worlds exist outside of our own. This theory has now become an increasingly accepted premise in the modern physics community. Hugh Everett passed away in 1982 at the age of 51.

Contents

Acknowledgments

It's a complex and time-consuming process writing a book, a labor of love, from the initial step of thinking up an interesting story to the process of getting it down on paper and refining it into a beautifully designed novel. All this would not have been possible without the help and services of several people who assisted me along the way. Some of these people deserve to be noted.

Early on in my project I realized I needed someone to help me refine my ideas and verbiage into the best that it could be. Denise Schnittman fulfilled that task as my writing consultant, proofreader, and developmental editor. Denise and I had a fantastic push-pull relationship throughout the book development and she helped me get my story skillfully designed and laid out. I am totally in gratitude for Denise's assistance.

As good as the manuscript was, I knew I had to find a great final review editor to look over the completed draft and see what then needed to be done with the document at that point. Luckily, I found Lourdes Venard. Lourdes has been employed by a major newspaper for nearly two decades and came highly recommended by a friend who had also written a recent sci-fi novel. Lourdes went right to work editing the manuscript and I was amazed at how skillful and proficient her work was. Of course, after spending two years writing and refining a manuscript you are worried about any changes to your document. But after I saw what Lourdes recognized and recommended I was totally astonished. She truly helped me refine and sculpt the document into a professionally laid out sci-fi novel that everyone would enjoy reading. Lourdes was also helpful in assisting me in finding a cover designer and a book formatter.

I wanted the cover design to reflect the abstract and surreal texture that was projected throughout the story and even a little romance, too. Luckily, I discovered graphics designer Gabrielle Prendergast. Gabrielle and I worked together back and forth with possible designs and we settled on two designs that totally reflected the feel and aura I sought. She also designed my website and assisted me in developing designs for other book promotional materials.

When you open a book it should give an appearance that stimulates your interest and looks great too. I was glad to have signed on Jennifer Zaczek as my book formatter. Jennifer did a great job in designing the book interior and helped get special graphics laid out in some sections. Jennifer also assisted tremendously in getting my manuscript formatted into the publishing company's required setup.

There are always unforeseen issues that can develop when trying to publish a book. One of these is possible legal issues. I was lucky to have found Thomas O'Rourke, attorney at law, who assisted me in resolving any potential legal conflicts. Tom was totally professional and immensely knowledgeable in the field of copyrights and related matters. I sincerely thank Tom for contributing his time to my book.

Lastly, I would like to thank the family members and friends who encouraged me during the entire process of the book development. That always helped me continue on the long adventure of actually getting a book published. Thanks to you all!

Prelude

For thousands of years, philosophers and scientists have pondered the nature of our existence. Some have questioned whether the reality we all experience and share is real or an illusion. Most have settled on the conviction that our lives are real and that they are part of a fundamentally predictable universe.

Reality has actually kept her secrets from us, her innermost mysteries unrevealed. The realities within our being and consciousness are actually not so certain or predictable as we might have thought. Mother Nature, after all, has her own direction to flow and follow within her own formation and being.

At the most distant outer edges of our universe in every direction, unrealized by humanity, there lies a magnificent structure of information and formation. A shimmering enigma that flows and coalesces with unity and purpose—ever-reaching with influence, and flowing dynamically with infinite force. In this timeless fluid domain, various images are revealed to a consciousness with awareness. A mass of ethereal fabric is perceived and accreted throughout the infinity there—the realm of that entity. Multitudes of brilliant light are formed with movement toward inner regions so large that human perception has no valid comparison. This meta-structure is glimmering with motion—broadcast ever so far into the infinitude—radiating the formation of thoughts.

THE INVERTED MASK

[1]

The Devil's Path

I had always felt a deep connection into the future. Ever since I was a small boy I could feel it from time to time.

My mother sensed too there was something different about me. I knew that there was more to life than just what seemed to be in front of us.

I cannot fathom infinity. I cannot comprehend forever . . . and I am certainly not capable of understanding the mind of God! What is it out there that we see in our experiments? Why is it so dammed intrinsic to this abstract construct and everything it reaches? So that's it . . . we continue to live on, don't we, not comprehending our own thoughts? The world is just a damn dream. It doesn't exist at all, at least the way we think it does.

"Jon? Jon! Wake up! You're daydreaming again, aren't you?" Marta shook Jon by the shoulder as she sat next to him on the huge boulder. "Come on! We're not too far from the top, just a little more to go! I knew you stayed up too late last night. No wonder you're so tired today. Maybe next time you'll listen to me when I tell you to get to bed instead of staying up half the night to obsess over your work."

"Yeah, you're right, Marta. I did stay up too late looking over the data . . . that and a few glasses of wine. VG sent me some more of those images from our latest QUEST run, and I just had to check them out."

Marta put her arms around Jon's waist and pulled him toward her. "Maybe I'll have to think of some way to get you to bed earlier tonight," she whispered.

"Uh . . . Oh, that sounds like fun! I can't wait, Doctor."

Suddenly, they heard the faint noise of an approaching hiker coming up the trail. They released each other, and turned to look in the direction of the oncoming trekker. Through the balsam firs and small spruces that lined the trail they watched an older man approach.

"Hello, there. Nice day, isn't it?" called the hiker.

"Yeah, it really is. How is your hike going today?" answered Jon.

"Great. Just another beautiful day here in the Catskills today, isn't it?"

"It sure is. Have you ever been to Slide Mountain before?" Jon asked.

"I come here quite a bit. I've been to the top of just about every mountain here in the Catskills."

"Wow, that's quite an accomplishment."

"I'm semi-retired now, so I have a lot of time, and the Catskills are a very special place to me."

"Where are you from?" asked Marta.

"About twenty miles from here, so I guess you could say I'm a local."

"We'd love to have a place up here. I'm Jon, and this is my fiancée, Marta. We love coming up here. So, what did you do for a living?"

"Well, I worked as a scientist some years ago."

"Really? I'm a scientist, too. What field were you in? Where'd you work?"

"I worked at several places. I just did basic scientific research. What about you?"

"I'm a physicist. I work at Ridgewood National Laboratory—on Long Island."

"Ridgewood!"

"Yup, Ridgewood. Have you ever been there, or did you know someone there? You seem familiar with it."

The man stared at Jon for a moment, and then said slowly, "Yeah, I did know someone from there, but that was a long time ago."

"So, what's your name?" Jon asked.

The hiker held out his hand, "My name is Evan. It's nice to meet you both."

"The pleasure is ours," Marta said.

"There is something about you . . . have we ever met before? Somehow you seem familiar to me and I don't know why." Jon looked at the older man's timeworn features and deep blue eyes. The man looked to be in his seventies, but was in fit shape.

"Funny, I've experienced that feeling myself several times. It's the way our minds work. Our perceptions aren't what they seem."

"Now that's an interesting thought. What do you mean by that?"

"Well, maybe it could be that what we perceive as the past, that which is in our memory, is actually something that's a little different than what really happened in the past. We're locked into our memories but we live in the present. Our minds kind of trick us sometimes."

Jon stood quietly, contemplating Evan's deeply lined face, and considered his words for several seconds. "I think about exactly that quite a bit. It's really amazing that we're thinking some of the same things. What a coincidence!"

Jon looked out beyond, to the forest, and then back to Evan, and said, "So Evan, what are you doing these days? Are you still working?"

"Yeah, I'm still working, but only part time now. My son's running an electronics firm and I work for him some days. I stay busy by helping him out, but I like to take it easy these days. I get in a lot of hiking throughout the Catskills. It's my passion. There's nothing that I'd rather do, and it keeps me active, especially at my age. Just being here in these mountains, hiking and thinking about this beautiful world and the universe, that's what inspires me and makes life so wonderful."

"Wow. That's something else we have in common. I love these mountains, and can't imagine a better way to spend my days," Jon said.

Their conversation was interrupted by the clamor of more hikers approaching down the trail.

"Well, it was very nice meeting both of you," the older man said. He looked deeply into Jon's eyes and, with a slight smile, he patted Jon's shoulder. "Good luck with your research project, Jon. I know it will all work out fine for you. Oh, and one other thing."

"What's that, Evan?"

"Ridgewood's always had a reputation for tragic incidents. Be careful there."

Jon noticed the awkward focus that Evan projected and the serious tone he conveyed. For a moment, he thought over those last words Evan had spoken and their intended meaning. Then Evan shook Marta's hand and continued on his way to the mountain peak.

Jon called after him, "Very nice meeting you, Evan! Maybe we'll see each other again at the top."

"Enjoy your hike!" shouted Marta, as Evan marched on toward the top of the mountain.

They watched Evan continue on up the rugged rocky trail. For a short while they could hear the noise of the loose stones he dislodged, and the soft sounds he made brushing up against the dense firs and spruces lining the trail. They watched until he disappeared from view.

A cool gust of wind swept by them. "What an interesting guy!" Jon said.

"He seemed like a really nice soul," Marta added.

"When we retire, we should try to hike up all the mountain trails here in the Catskills."

"I would so love to do that. Let's put that on our list of things to do in retirement," said Marta, with a smile.

Just then, the group of hikers they had heard approaching passed by on their way to the top. Marta and Jon greeted them, and nodded hello to a few of them as the group quickly passed them by. A few minutes later Jon and Marta picked up their hiking poles and continued back up the mountain trail toward the summit.

"We have this last steep part, then it levels out for a while, and then we'll be on the summit."

"Good! I feel like we've been hiking all day! I'm getting a bit tired. It's quite a long trail," Marta said.

"This is the longer of the trails going up Slide Mountain. We usually go up the old Burroughs Range Trail from the west, which is easier and shorter. This is the Curtis-Ormsbee Trail. It's about seven miles long. I haven't been on this trail in about ten years."

"It certainly had some great views along the way up. I can't wait to see the view from the top."

"This is one of my favorites. Slide is the first mountain that I ever climbed in the Catskills with my college buddies. When I got to the top I fell in love with the views and the Catskills."

After several more minutes of hiking several steep rises through thick boreal forest filled with plush balsam firs, and dotted by the occasional sugar maple, they finally reached a flatter area. They followed the last remaining yards of the trail, taking in all the rich aromatic scents of the mountain ridge. Then suddenly, directly in front of them, the woods opened up, offering them the magnificent sight of a raised rock base, highlighting a sweeping view of the eastern and northern Catskills.

They walked out onto the rocks, took in that panoramic view before them, and were both overwhelmed with emotion. The eastern vista revealed a striking array of mountain peaks.

"Oh, my God. What beautiful views we have here today. This is totally breathtaking!" Marta said.

"They are magnificent. And all the fall colors are just tremendous. So vivid and brilliant, they seem to be bursting out today in their full glory—just the way the sun is."

"Jon, let's sit and eat. I'm hungry, and I could use a rest. How about you?"

"Sounds great!"

They sat down and enjoyed their lunch while taking in the beautiful sight of the Catskill ridgelines in the distant background.

"Jon, what mountain ranges are those in front of us?"

Jon gestured with his peanut butter sandwich in hand. "Over to the left, we are looking out north toward the Devil's Path ridgeline of the Central Catskills. That area includes Plateau, Sugarloaf, and Indian Head Mountains. Over to our center here, closest to us, we can see Wittenberg and Cornell Mountains to the northeast. And over to the east, you can make out Kaaterskill High Peak. That's quite a ways back, along with several others."

"Wow. They all look so beautiful and majestic. They're almost like gigantic green living statues."

"Actually, from here we can see thirty-three of the thirty-four high peaks that are part of the Catskill Forest Preserve. The only high peak that is not visible from here is Thomas Cole Mountain."

"Amazing! What's that large body of water that's in back of that mountain there in front of us?"

"That's the Ashokan Reservoir, which is one of New York City's reservoirs. When it was constructed in 1910 it was the largest reservoir in the world."

"It looks like a large lake," Marta said.

"How are you feeling now that you got some rest and some food?" Jon asked.

"Great. My legs are a bit tired, but since we're heading down after this rest, it'll be easy and I'll be fine. Where is the mountain we've climbed several times, Giant Ledge Mountain, from here?"

"Oh, Giant Ledge is just over to the west of Slide. We can't see it from here, but it's not too far away. It's right next to Panther Mountain. Did I ever tell you that Panther Mountain is the site of an ancient asteroid impact?"

"No!"

"Yeah. Years ago some geologists realized that the creeks that flow around the entire mountain base form a circular structure. They're pretty sure that only a massive asteroid strike could have caused that to happen."

"How long ago?"

"About three hundred seventy-five million years ago during the Devonian Period, when this was all a large shallow sea."

"It's incredible. Maybe that is why these mountains are so enchanting."

"Maybe so, Marta. They certainly are special, aren't they?"

They stood up and embraced warmly while looking into the beautiful views of the glorious mountains in front of them. As they enjoyed that moment and contemplated the dreamlike panorama, a frigid breeze blew by, forcing Marta to put on her sweatshirt.

As Marta turned she noticed Jon staring down toward the bottom of the rocky base area they were on.

"Jon, what do you see down there? What are you looking at?"

"I could have sworn that I saw Evan down the trail leaving this side of the mountain, looking back at me."

"I don't see anyone there. There's no one around here now but us."

Shaking his head slightly, Jon muttered, "I guess I'm a little worn out from the hike we did today."

"I'd say you're a bit tired. Come on, let's get going down. We're going to have a great time at the inn tonight."

"Yeah . . . let's get going. It'll be a great hike down and I can't wait to have a cold draft when we get to the inn!"

They packed up their provisions, drank in the magnificent mountainous landscape once more, and then started their trek down Slide Mountain. As Marta turned to leave, she called out, "Good-bye, Old Friend!" Her salutation was answered by the sounds of birds chirping in the dense balsam firs.

The energetic ramble down the mountain was as beautiful and peaceful as it was on the way up. Much to their delight, they did not pass anyone on the way down, and had the mountain and its spirits all to themselves. By midafternoon they arrived back at the car. Happy, satisfied, and exhausted from their forty-two-hundred-foot climb to the top of Slide Mountain, they threw their packs into the back seat and rested for a little while, each silently reflecting on the majestic wilderness they had witnessed.

[2]

Unusual Clouds

Jon and Marta passed the small hamlet of Oliverea as they drove down Slide Mountain Road toward the main highway that traversed the southern Catskills. They drove alongside a creek bed swollen with rainwater.

"Boy, this creek looks like it's close to flooding. Sometimes they are so dry up here," Marta said.

"There's been a decent amount of rain these past few months. You can see some erosion at the creek's edges. I heard that a few of the houses alongside of the creek have even flooded this year."

"I noticed that. I'm glad that the road is leveling out here in Oliverea. That last part of Slide Mountain Road was really steep! It's a little nerve-wracking."

"It's definitely a steep, rugged road. Many of the back roads here are pretty rugged, and the rain and snow do a number on them."

"It's all very beautiful here. I love traveling on these back mountain roads, even when they're a little intense. There's a special boundlessness in this mountain forest. The shapes of the mountains, the colors of the trees and rock faces . . . it's hard to describe, but it feels like they cast a spell on me."

"They are beautiful. There's something mystical here, too. I noticed it the first time I ever came up here, when I was in college. I know this might sound odd, but I've felt called back here ever since."

Jon navigated onto Route 28 and pulled into the post office parking lot. "I'm just going to stop at the Big Indian Post Office to mail something out," he said. "I'll be right back."

"What do you have to mail?"

"It's just a postcard to an old friend. It shouldn't take more than a few minutes."

Marta's gaze followed Jon into the lonely, little post office, and then wandered to the surrounding mountain ridges. A strong gust of wind rattled the car. She grabbed her sweatshirt, wrapped it around her shoulders, and stepped out of the car, noting the chill in the air; she reflected that it would soon be Thanksgiving.

The cool, clean air was refreshing, and it helped her relax. She stretched out her muscles, tired after the day's activities. Scanning the horizon, she noticed some very peculiar cloud shapes just over a mountain ridge to the southwest. The odd, murky, fast-moving clouds were thickening quickly. An eerie feeling swept over her. She shivered and climbed back into the car, slamming the door shut. She rested her head on the headrest, reclined her seat back, and closed her eyes. Tired from the day's exertions, her mind drifted. In a sort of dream, she saw a strange object off in the distance. It was familiar to her . . . something she had recently come across while researching certain test subjects who were participating in a psychiatric study. In her reverie, the image of the unusual object drifted toward her, until it was within a few feet. The object seemed to be somehow distorted and grotesque. Shocked out of her drowsy daydream, Marta came fully awake, gasping in terror at the evil apparition.

Jon jerked open the car door, pausing to notice the unusual darkening cloud formation in the sky to the southwest. He stared at it for several seconds, thinking he'd never seen anything like it before.

"Nice people here, very friendly. Are you okay? You look a bit flustered."

"I dozed off for a minute. I had a bizarre mini-dream with a sort of flashback from work. I guess I'm just tired and worn out from the great hike we did today. I'm fine now."

They stared quietly at each other, each sensing something strange in the moment that had just passed by. Something they had felt before.

Jon smiled. "Well, darling, a few glasses of wine and a great dinner at the inn tonight will definitely be good therapy for your hiking ailments."

"That sounds like just what I need," Marta said, smiling brightly.

"It's starting to get cold. There's a real chill in the air," he said.

"I noticed that when I got out to stretch my legs."

Jon swung the car onto Route 28. At that exact moment in time, a huge tractor-trailer truck was also barreling down Route 28 a few miles further to the east. Ahead of Jon and Marta's car, it was traveling in the opposite direction. The truck was traveling very fast, and the driver of the truck was very tired, finding it hard to concentrate on the road.

"Marta, could you put on the radio and try and get us a weather report?"

"Sure, just a minute," said Marta, fumbling with the controls to the car radio.

"You can try News 77 out of Kingston. They give a weather report on the sevens, so one should be coming up soon."

As Marta searched for the station, a brief musical jingle caught their attention. It was followed by a commercial, and then the very clear voice of a female radio anchor announced, "This is the Weather Watch Forecast now with 77 Radio chief forecaster Mike Thomas. Mike, what do we have coming up this afternoon? Can you give us a picture of what's going on out there?"

"Right now, Stacy, it's about forty-six in our eastern suburbs, forty-four in Kingston, and around forty-one degrees in the central sections of the Catskills. These temperatures are a bit cooler than normal for this time of the year. This afternoon we will have a continuation of the nice cool, dry conditions. Some increasing clouds come into the picture later in the evening, along with a few possible stray showers. Tonight, expect continued colder-than-normal conditions, along with a bit of a breeze and lows dipping down near the freezing mark. It's going to be a chilly Sunday, with some clouds and sunshine in the forecast. Monday looks to be a mix of sun and clouds along with cooler weather. We'll see increasing clouds over here on Tuesday as a weather disturbance tries to move in and we may even get some of the first snow showers of the season in the mountains to our west. There you have it, Stacy. We'll have more about the coming week's weather later in the broadcast. Now go on everyone, get out there and enjoy the cool brisk weather for the rest of the day!"

"Thank you, Mike. Now in other news around Kingston today, there's a murder mystery in Ulster County concerning a forty-seven-year-old woman who was found dead in her home in Kingston."

Marta turned down the broadcast. “It looks like it’s going to be cold tonight with a possible shower.”

“Yeah. It’s a little nippy, but it feels good. Maybe after dinner we’ll bundle up and go for a little walk around Pine Hill. We can check out the stars if it’s not too cloudy tonight.”

“That sounds good, but let’s not stay up too late after that hike we did today! It’s amazing how much clearer the stars are up here in the mountains than what we can see on Long Island.”

The massive tractor-trailer truck was fast approaching Jon’s car, picking up speed, heading downhill as it neared them. The truck wandered into the oncoming lane slightly, and was now less than a mile away, rounding a curve in the highway and coming on fast.

With a sultry gaze, Marta said, “Oh, Jon, I forgot to tell you that I packed something very special that you are going to love. You’d better not fall asleep until I put it on later. I picked it out especially for you, and I do know that you love to—”

Suddenly, without warning, the massive tractor-trailer appeared in front of them. It was traveling remarkably fast, and mostly in their lane—oncoming.

Marta screamed. “Oh, my God! Jon!”

Jon had no time to react.

Even from far above and away, the view of the crash was both surrealistic and horrifying. All of the birds in the nearby trees instantly flew away from the immense noise and reverberation of the crash. The mountain peaks echoed the ghostly sounds of the catastrophe.

Moments passed by with no movement or activity except for the thrown pieces of metal and glass that had shattered and were flung out onto the roadway, finally releasing their energy from the immense crash and coming to a rest.

Shortly, a family traveling east came upon the horrific scene. The driver pulled over. For a few seconds they were all stunned into silence. The driver suddenly vaulted into action. He yelled, "Call 911 and stay in the car!" He flung his door open, and ran toward the crash, looking to help in any way possible. He surveyed the carnage of the disaster. His head dropped, and he returned to his car. The faces of his wife and child mirrored his own despair. He got in and rested his head on the steering wheel. They remained there in utter stillness, until the sounds of emergency vehicles broke the silence.

[3]

Target Practice

Jon was enjoying his morning jog out by the bay near the county park. He energetically ran over a small sand dune and brushed by some of the lovely cedar trees that decorated the barrier beach of the Peconic Bay shoreline. He kept up his jogging pace as he trudged over the thick sand mixed with stones, but his mind started to drift toward his work and his to-do list. After all, as leader of the world-renowned QUEST research project, he really couldn't drop the ball. He remembered that he should call VG, his assistant and friend, concerning the insertion of a new dipole magnet section that was to be installed in the near future. The installation itself would be no small task, since the magnet weighed several tons. He glanced at his watch and started to head back to his Aquebogue beach house. His cell phone rang with its distinctive *space echo* ringtone.

"Hello?"

"Jon, is that you?"

Catching his breath, he answered, "Yes, this is Jon."

"Good morning, Jon! This is Marta!"

"Hello, Sweetie! I couldn't make out your voice too well with all that noise in the background. Where are you?"

"I'm at the North Hampton shooting range right now with Lois. We're taking our shooting practice here with our ladies' shooting team."

"Oh, I was wondering what all those loud noises were. It sounds like you're in the middle of a war zone."

"We like to come to the shooting range early because it's not crowded, and we can set up our targets without too much interference."

"I guess that makes sense."

"So, the reason I called this early is to remind you that you're giving a talk to my Cognitive Psych class about your QUEST project today. It's at Bowers Hall at ten. You didn't forget, did you?"

"What me? Forget? Of course not! I'll be there, don't worry."

"Good, because my students are really looking forward to your presentation. I already filled them in about who you are, and I told them all about your work at QUEST. I told them that you're a big shot in the field of theoretical physics."

"I can't wait to meet them. It will be fun."

"Great! I'm so glad you don't mind doing this for me. I know they'll love your presentation. Oh, one other thing. I stopped by your house yesterday to get something, and when I brought in your mail I saw that you got a postcard from someone that had something really strange written on it. I don't know if you saw it already but I put it on your kitchen counter by your phone."

"No, I didn't see it yet, but I'll check it out. Thanks for bringing in the mail."

"I've got to go now. We're ready to start our shooting practice. Lois is signaling to me to get off the phone. I'll see you at about ten."

"You've got it, Marta. I'll try to get to your class early to see some of your presentation."

"Good! Remember this class will be attended by other groups here at Ridgewood so it may be crowded when you come."

"No problem. I'll be there. Oh, wait, just one more question."

"What's that, Jon?"

"Are you moving in with me?"

"Yes. I'm moving in with you for good now. We'll be together from now on. Just you try and get out of it!"

"Great! See you later then. Bye!"

"Bye!"

At the shooting range, Lois Aldmann saw Marta pocket her cell phone. She walked over to her, holding her rifle up in the air with both hands.

"Hey, Marta! How's Jon doing?" she yelled. Lois Aldmann was Marta's friend and work associate.

"He's doing well. He's coming to my Cognitive Psych class later today to give my students a talk about QUEST."

"Sounds cool. I'd love to hear about that."

"Why don't you come? It will be at Bowers Hall at ten."

"I'll try to get there!"

Their conversation was interrupted by the loud sounds of rapid repeating shots. They turned quickly and saw several men in dark blue uniforms shooting an assortment of guns at the general targets set up at the range.

"Oh, no!" exclaimed Marta, visibly dismayed.

"Great. The Ridgewood cops are doing their handgun training. Just great!" complained Lois, frowning.

"I hate it when they come here to shoot. They disrupt everything."

"Egotistical assholes. They couldn't shoot the side of a barn from ten feet away!"

Marta chuckled. "Let's get started with our target practice. I have to be out of here by nine."

They headed over to the group of women who were already starting their target shooting practice. They put on their specialized shooting vests and eyewear, grabbed their professional rifles, and began to practice hitting their targets, which were placed fifty yards away.

Lois banged away at her target using her competition-style .22-caliber Ruger 22, a weapon which was elegantly designed in a custom aqua blue color.

Marta used a similar Ruger professional quality rifle. After they discharged several clips of bullets, they took a break and used binoculars to see how well they had come to the bull's-eye.

"Wow, Lois, you blew me away with these last rounds. You have all bull's-eyes except for two shots in the number eight ring. Very well done!"

"Thanks, Marta! Yeah, I beat you now, but you keep improving your accuracy as we keep shooting, and I seem to go down in accuracy the longer the session goes on."

All of a sudden, Lois and Marta were mystified to see that someone else was shooting at their targets! Looking around for the source of the shots they spotted one of the Ridgewood cops intentionally aiming at their targets.

"It looks like Reynolds, that idiot Ridgewood cop, is shooting at our targets. He must be trying to piss us off."

"What do you think we should do?" asked Marta.

"I know how to handle this. Just watch and see!"

Lois walked over to her stock of guns and chose a large, imposing black rifle. Holding her M-16 semi-automatic upright, she walked back to Marta.

"I think this will get his attention," she said.

"Hey, Lois! Don't do anything crazy!"

Lois stared Reynolds down, positioned the M-16 slightly toward the group of Ridgewood cops, and then redirected her weapon to aim at the target that Reynolds had been using over on the right side of the shooting range. The shots from her semi-automatic rang out in such a rapid fashion that everyone at the shooting range stopped to take note. Reynolds and his fellow officers had frozen, and were watching Lois shoot.

One of the officers smirked, yelling, "Christ, Reynolds, she's shooting that M-16 so fast it sounds like a fully automatic rifle!"

The gunfire stopped. For a moment all was silent, and then one of the officers yelled out, "Goddamn, Reynolds Just checked out her shots at your target. She got nearly all bull's-eyes. What a hell of a shooter!"

Frustrated, Reynolds shoved his rifle at his assistant officer, and stormed over toward Lois and Marta, looking both mean and agitated.

"It looks like we've got trouble," said Marta, uncertainly.

Lois flashed a confident grin at Marta, and then turned to Reynolds, and said sweetly, "How can we help you, Lieutenant?"

"Where the hell did you learn to shoot like that?"

"Practice, practice, practice, Lieutenant! That's what our ladies' rifle team does here. We practice all the time. You know that."

"You shoot better than most cops."

"Yes. I do. My uncle taught me to shoot when I was a little girl. He's a state trooper." There was no doubt, from Lois' tone, on how she felt about Ridgewood security cops compared to state troopers.

"You're a good shot, but you have lousy judgment, acting like that. You ought to be more careful or something very bad could happen to you in the future."

"Don't worry, Lieutenant Reynolds, Lois and I know how to handle ourselves, and deal effectively with any trouble that comes our way!" said Marta. She looked quite valiant, and held her rifle boldly, clearly ready to use it when necessary.

Reynolds stepped toward them, leering at them and purposely challenging their personal space. "You ladies enjoy the rest of your shooting practice. I'm sure we'll be seeing each other sometime in the future."

As Lieutenant Reynolds walked away, Marta said, "What a jerk!"

"Yup. All of those Ridgewood cops have bad attitudes. They seem to specialize in hiring arrogant assholes with superiority complexes. I have a feeling that one day Reynolds is going to get what's coming to him."

"Well, let's just hope that we don't run into him too often."

"Unfortunately, he works where we work. We'll probably bump into him every now and then."

Marta checked her watch. "It's getting late! Let's get on with our target practice. I have to get going pretty soon."

"Yeah, hopefully those jerks will be leaving soon."

Lois put the M-16 back in her car and grabbed her target practice gun. They continued their practice, and Marta continued to improve her aim. Lois looked at Marta through her tinted-yellow safety glasses, and yelled, "Good shooting, girl! Damned good shooting!"

* * *

A few hours later, out in the middle of a large grass field located west of the Ridgewood Police Headquarters building, Officer Donald Lutz patiently awaited the landing of a transport helicopter. Standing near his truck, he felt the wind of the rotor blades increase as the large modern sleek chopper slowly descended. The white chopper with blue stripes landed on a square paved landing area marked out by large white lines, and a tall black man stepped out. He slammed the door shut and waved at the pilot as the chopper ascended into the blue sky. The man was well-dressed and carried an expensive suitcase. Lutz opened the door for him as he approached the police vehicle.

"Hello, Dr. Kenyatta. It's very nice to see you, sir. How was your trip?"

"Smooth traveling today, hardly any wind at all up there in the sky. Thank you for picking me up, Officer Lutz."

"No problem at all. Where am I taking you, sir?"

"I need to be at Bowers Hall right now. It looks like I'm late. Dr. Padlo is teaching her class there today, and I'd like to see some of it. I also have to meet with a few people there after her lecture, so if you can get me there as fast as possible I'd appreciate it."

"No problem at all. I can get you there in about three minutes."

"Excellent, Officer Lutz. Thanks again."

"Dr. Kenyatta, what will Dr. Padlo be lecturing on today?"

"I believe she will be exploring some new theories about human cognition—the way the mind works. There will be visiting students from Europe attending, too, so I'd like to be there to meet them."

"Sounds very interesting, sir. I wish I could attend."

"It really is fascinating. We know so little about how the mind actually works. The things we're learning now about the brain are truly stunning!"

The midnight blue police cruiser soon pulled up to the front of the large, modern-looking, multi-angled, concrete building. Tabu Kenyatta rushed into the enormous lecture hall. He found the lecture hall packed to near capacity with students and professors. Making his way toward the front of the room, he found a seat next to Jon Sanborne. Jon nodded to

Kenyatta, welcoming him silently, as he continued to listen to the lecture, already in progress.

Marta directed her laser pointer toward the screen, "Striving to unlock the secrets of the universe is a fundamental part of our human experience. Humans have evolved over millions of years, and we have survived, at least in part, because we are naturally curious. That process of evolution has produced a brain that is both complex and adaptable enough to help us survive in this challenging world. Here, in this next slide, you see a brain structure that contains thoughts, memories, and dreams. Over time, it processes the perceptions of reality, of what you feel, and what you see. Each time you listen to music, or observe a beautiful painting, those experiences are converted into information and that information is processed and stored by the brain for future use. There are more nerve cells in the brain than there are stars in our galaxy, and there are more connections within the brain cells than galaxies in the universe. That, my friends, is an amazingly powerful system. We are only now at the very beginning of trying to understand just how this consciousness system works."

Jon loved listening to Marta. He was thrilled she would soon be moving in with him, and still somewhat bemused by her beauty. He couldn't take his eyes off her shiny dark hair, her lovely figure, and her long legs, and, no matter how much time they spent together, he was still struck by how elegant and attractive she was in her tight black skirt. And then there was her voice, and the way she spoke. Smart as a whip, her words were clear and methodical, and he was still charmed by her mild Slavic accent. A shiver of pleasure ran down his spine as a memory of that voice whispering sweet nothings drifted through his mind.

"Now I am going to review the theory on how the brain system functions during the perception process, and then we will wrap up this discussion today," Marta continued. "In this next slide, you can see that as our five senses take in the information, it is received by the brain and the neuron cells. The neurons take in the information that is correlated with the level of input. That information is assimilated and passed on to other neurons. Perception and learning is accomplished by the altering of the strengths of the connections between the neuron cells in the brain.

"What is important is that the perception process in the brain is essentially an electro-biochemical molecular process that causes changes to the brain cells. These changes also affect the neurotransmitters and other biochemical entities that coexist in the brain structure. Okay. I think that we have gone over a lot of information today about human cognition, so I'll end here. This is really important material, and it will be on the next test, so please make sure to study it well.

"I think most of you are eagerly awaiting our very special guest today. Dr. Jon Sanborne will be discussing research that he is conducting here at Ridgewood. For our visiting students from Sweden and Norway, you are welcome to stay for this next short discussion, and then Dr. Kenyatta will meet with you to arrange for your visit to see our cute little Komodo dragon friend, Ayu, who is now on display at our Science Museum. She is one of our research animals here at the Lab, and you should not miss it! Just don't get too close, though. She'd loved to eat you all. But don't worry too much, she's in a cage."

Marta's words brought the expected laughter, during which Jon came up and got ready to speak.

"It is with great pleasure that I introduce our very special guest, Dr. Jon Sanborne. Dr. Sanborne is a theoretical physicist who has been conducting advanced physics research here at Ridgewood National

Lab for the past eleven years. Dr. Sanborne previously spent some time at CERN, in Europe, and at Fermi Labs, near Chicago, studying particle wave fields. Dr. Sanborne has received numerous awards in physics. These include the Warwick Award for pioneering work in quantum mechanics. Over the past ten years, Dr. Sanborne and his team of scientists have designed and built the QUEST project, which is one of the largest physics research projects in the world. This massive experiment is located nine hundred feet below the ground here at Ridgewood, near another huge underground physics research experiment named HITS. Now I am going to turn your attention over to Dr. Jon Sanborne. Thank you for coming today!"

Slightly nervous, Jon moved into place and took in the full auditorium in front of him. "Good morning, everyone, and welcome to Ridgewood National Lab. I am going to give you all a brief overview of the unique experiment that my teams of physicists have constructed here below ground at Ridgewood. But before I begin, I want to thank Dr. Padlo for that gracious introduction. I hope you all realize how lucky you are to have a professor like Dr. Padlo. She is a leader in the field of cognitive science. We are good friends, and have many fascinating discussions about the places where our very different fields of study intersect. You see, since Dr. Padlo is a psychiatrist and I am a theoretical physicist, we have some very divergent perspectives in terms of making sense of our world. Of course, we often kid each other about which perspective is the more accurate one, and which branch of science is more relevant. I distinctly remember Dr. Padlo asking me a paradoxical question which had a significant impact on my way of thinking. She asked me to think of absolutely nothing. I sat there trying to think of nothing for a while. Finally, she smiled at me and said, 'No matter how hard you try to think of nothing, you are actually thinking of something. You see in your mind you are always thinking of something even if that something is nothing.'

"And that thought was very much related to the research that we are doing in the field of quantum mechanics with our QUEST project. You see, she brought up an essential question that is of interest to both of our scientific studies. That question is *'What is the nature of nothing or something?'* It's not an easy thing to think about, even if you are a psychiatrist or a physicist. But we both crossed paths here on this fundamental concept of the nature of our reality.

"Now, the research that we are working on at our QUEST project is primarily in the field of science known as quantum mechanics. Quantum mechanics is a very strange field of science that still confuses most scientists who have studied it. You see, it involves the study of what is really happening at the very small level of the universe inside the atom. At that very small level, scientists have found that the particles that compose the atom can do very weird things. Things like travel through walls, or seem to be waves. They can also stay strangely connected even over very large distances. For example, two particles seem to be able to communicate with each other over the entire length of the universe. But perhaps the strangest thing that particles seem to be able to do is to exist in many places at once. But there is even more to this story. We have even now found that this quantum weirdness in not just confined to the small particles inside the atom, but to larger entities like molecules and even larger items like baseballs, cars, or trees.

"Our QUEST research is focused primarily on the quantum weirdness at the larger scale. We focus on how large things in life are affected by these mysterious forces of nature. Incidentally, this field of study first got a boost by the pioneering work of a famous scientist who once worked right here at Ridgewood. He postulated many principles that are the foundation of our QUEST project. I only wish he could be here now to see how far we have come with his ideas into this field of research."

A woman's voice called out from the audience, "Is that scientist Dr. Emery Hilcraft?"

Jon walked up toward the front of the stage and scanned the audience, "Who is asking about Dr. Hilcraft?"

"I am, Dr. Sanborne." A student waved from the front rows.

"You are correct. That scientist was Dr. Emery Hilcraft."

Jon moved back and indicated the large screen. "I am going to show you some pictures of our QUEST research facility. In this first slide, you see an aerial photo of the site where our QUEST facility is located. Those buildings may seem too small to house the project. Well, that's because our QUEST facility is located nine hundred feet below the ground. QUEST is also adjacent to HITS, the Heavy Ion Target Supercollider, which is the second-largest particle accelerator in the world. HITS provides a stream of protons which our QUEST facility requires for our research, so we always coordinate our work with the folks at HITS. The HITS accelerator was built prior to our QUEST facility, and the location of QUEST is no accident.

"In this next slide, you can see just what it looks like to be in the HITS facility, four hundred fifty feet below ground. Notice the long, blue, tube-like structure. That structure carries the stream of protons to QUEST. The proton beam is contained by a powerful magnetic field.

"And this is QUEST, nine hundred feet below the ground, twice the distance underground as the HITS facility. You're probably wondering why we would want to devote so much time and money to constructing these two facilities hundreds of feet below the surface of the earth. The depth is necessary for two reasons. First of all, these experiments create tremendous amounts of radiation, so the depth is a safety measure. But we also need to shield the sensitive detectors inside the research facilities from the cosmic rays that bombard the Earth every second.

"This next, strange-looking picture is taken from inside the heart of QUEST. This is the place where we generate tremendous magnetic forces and use them to manipulate the proton particles that are from HITS. It's known as the Macro-STARR chamber, and it is the only one of its kind in the world ever constructed. This facility is very large, larger than two domed stadiums combined, as a matter of fact. It uses more electricity than a small city. Visitors who tour the place often tell me that it looks like something out of a science-fiction movie.

"Now this last slide was taken inside the QUEST control room. This is where the experimental data is processed. You can see that it is a very complex control room. You can see there are many high-resolution monitors and instruments that are staffed by a large team of scientists. We use the latest quantum computer technology in processing the data generated by our experiments. These computers are specially built for us by a pioneering computer company. Our work would not be possible without this latest quantum computer technology.

"I'll be in the back handing out informational brochures about QUEST and HITS if anyone is interested. Also, if you have any questions, you can ask me them there. It was a pleasure meeting you all today. Good luck with your studies. And I just want to say that whatever you do in life, follow your passions. They'll lead you to your destiny, and to success in life. And remember that life goes by fast, so work hard and enjoy the ride!"

Enthusiastic applause filled the room, and Jon headed back to a table near the exit, where he had set up a box of the informational packets he had brought with him. He handed out information and was greeted by several students as they left the room. Some students remained to ask questions before they left, packets in hand. The stream of students stopped, and Jon began to organize his materials and get ready to leave.

"Hello, Dr. Sanborne!"

Jon looked up, and recognized the attractive young woman from the audience who had asked about Hilcraft.

"You're the one who asked about Dr. Hilcraft! How do you know about him?"

"I've heard a lot about him and his theories from my father."

"Really? How does your father know about him?"

"My father worked with him when he was a research scientist here at Ridgewood. He told me that Hilcraft apparently just disappeared one day and they couldn't find him anywhere."

"Wow, that's very interesting! He did disappear mysteriously. Who is your father?"

"My father is Ben Carson. He's a physicist here at Ridgewood."

"Ben Carson is your father! I know Ben well. We're good friends. Your dad is working with us on our QUEST project now. I was able to get him on loan from the Accelerating Energy Synchrotron (AES). He's helping us straighten out some problems that we're having with our dipole magnets. I can't believe he's your dad. He's a great guy, and he really knows his stuff."

"Yeah. He's a good guy, my dad. He told me all about QUEST, and about you. He said you're very smart, and kind of weird, but he likes you, and he's enjoying working with your staff, too."

"What's your name, Ben's daughter?"

"I'm Brenda. Brenda Carson."

"Well, it was nice to meet you, Brenda. I'll mention it to Ben when I see him later today."

As they shook hands, Marta called to Jon from the lobby, "Jon, Dr. Kenyatta wants to discuss something with you before he escorts the visiting students to the Science Museum."

Jon called back, "Okay, Marta." He saw Dr. Kenyatta approaching, and handed Brenda one of his info packets, saying, "Here you go, Brenda. Again, it was nice meeting you. Take care."

"So long, Dr. Sanborne. I'll tell my dad that I met you. Bye!"

Kenyatta hurried over from the side of the auditorium toward Jon and called out. "Hello, Jon!"

"Hello, Dr. Kenyatta! I hear you're taking the visiting students to the Science Museum."

"Yes, so I can't talk long, but I just want to give you a heads-up. The environmental officials from the state and county will be here tomorrow to inspect the old graphite reactor with our environmental coordinators. Since you and Ben are on the Environmental Review Committee you will be needed to accompany them and assist them in their inspection. Ben can probably answer any questions that they may have. Is that alright with you? They're meeting at nine tomorrow morning, at the north side of the reactor, near the old entrance. Make sure that you and Ben have your personal dosimeters with you when you go."

"Okay, I'll be there. I'll talk to Ben, too."

"Great, Jon! Just be there by nine, that's when they'll start the inspection."

"No problem! Ben and I will be there. Oh, by the way, that girl I was just talking with was Ben's daughter.

She's in Marta's Cognitive Psychology class."

"It's a small world, isn't it? Especially around here. I have to get back to our visitors now, but I'll meet up with you, Ben, and the Environmental Review Committee after your joint inspection tomorrow. Maybe on Wednesday we'll review the committee findings in my office. Oh, and Dr. Tonner's going to be there, so be prepared for some questions about the unfortunate incident that occurred at QUEST."

"Very well, Dr. Kenyatta."

Kenyatta turned and headed off toward the visiting Scandinavian students.

Marta had walked up as Kenyatta left. "Jon," she said, "if you're going into that reactor tomorrow, you and Ben need to be extra careful. That old reactor had significant radioactive contamination inside."

"Marta, it's been totally decontaminated over the past decades and Health Physics has certified it as safe."

"I've been told by someone in Health Physics that they found trace amounts of plutonium inside the containment area last year. You know that, theoretically, one atom of plutonium is enough to kill you."

"Don't worry, Marta, we won't be in there long, and I promise you I'll be careful."

"Thanks for your talk today. The students really seemed interested."

"They seemed like a nice bunch of students. Oh, my phone is going off. It's probably VG. I better get going now. We got stuff going on at QUEST."

"Okay, Jon, you be careful tomorrow. I'll see you tomorrow night at your place."

"Great, Marta! I'll make a nice dinner for us."

"Be careful down there!" she shouted after him.

[4]

The Graphite Reactor

The Ridgewood Graphite Reactor loomed large as Jon and Ben drove up toward it. Jon was struck by enormity of the large structure and of the huge red and white striped vent stack that was present along its side.

"Damn, Ben, I never realized this place was so humongous. Now that we're near it I can see that it is truly an amazing place. It must have taken years to build this complex."

"Yeah . . . It took a number of years and a lot of workers to construct it during the late 1940s. Oh look, Matt Richter and his team are here already in the parking lot."

Ben and Jon parked the car and walked over to the gathering of the members of the Environmental Review Committee and introduced themselves.

Matt began, "Welcome everyone. My name is Matt Richter and I work here at Ridgewood National Lab, in Dr. Tonner's office, as most of you know. I'll be assisting the director's office with this environmental site inspection. I am glad that you could all make it here today to conduct this important final inspection of the long-defunct Ridgewood Graphite Reactor. I have worked with some of you over the past years in environmental matters here at the Lab, so you may know me. Feel free to ask any questions that you may have concerning this reactor inspection. At this point, I am going to turn the discussion of the Ridgewood Graphite Reactor over to Ben Carson. Ben is a physicist here at Ridgewood and has many decades of experience here at the Lab. He worked at the RGR for some years."

Ben began with a bit of the historical background of the facility, pointedly including the fact that the reactor had been through a series of thorough inspections and remediations ever since it was shut down in 1968. He informed them the RGR was an air-cooled graphite reactor pile consisting of a 900-ton, 45-foot cube of graphite fueled by uranium. Reactor power was controlled by the insertion and removal of boron steel control rods. Cooling was supplied by one or more of six-drive fan units which provided airflow through the core.

Kyle Evans, the state inspector interrupted, "Wow! Those cooling fan units must have been very large—it certainly would have taken a heck of a lot of air to cool that pile down, compared to a liquid-cooled system."

"Yeah, the fan units were huge. We can show them to you later if you want," Ben said. "By the way, these fan units are also slated to be completely removed in the near future because they are also contaminated with radiation on the inside."

"What was the purpose of the reactor?" Kyle asked.

"Researchers used the neutrons from the RGR as tools for studying atomic nuclei and the structure of molecular systems. They investigated many physical, chemical, and biological systems," Ben said.

"Biological research!" Clair Parsons, the county's environmental inspector, jumped in. "Why would you be using a reactor structure like this to study a biological system?"

"Just after World War II, there was massive concern about just what the nuclear age had brought to the world," Ben said. "We were in a severe Cold War at the time, and there was a great call for research into just what the nuclear age could do for us—and against us. At this reactor, as far as the biological research program is concerned, it was used to specifically irradiate biological systems to study the effects of radiation—and just exactly what happens at the molecular level of cells, and to the genetic material within the cell nucleus."

"Can you give us an example of what kind of biological material was irradiated?" Clair asked.

"Well, sure . . ." Ben hesitated a bit, careful not to reveal anything that might be classified. "I do recall that many types of plant seeds were irradiated, planted, and brought to maturity to observe what changes occurred to the plant expression." He continued with discretion. "As far as materials and molecules go, the reactor was used to irradiate engine parts, metal and material compositions, and even art treasures. Among other things, all this research contributed to many new findings, and led to the development of several products—for example, 10W-30, a multigrade motor oil that is now commonly used in automobiles."

But before he could go any further, Richter interjected rather forcefully. "Look, we have a limited amount of time to complete this inspection. I'll be handing out a packet that has a lot of historical and functional information on the RGR. I believe that will answer any remaining questions you may have. Now, when we go through the reactor building we must follow all the proper rules and procedures. Even though this building is totally secured, both environmentally and in terms of any personal health concerns, RNL has a policy of constant quality assurance. For your own protection, we require that you each put on a personal digital radiation dosimeter before you enter the building. You must wear the dosimeter throughout your visit, both inside and outside of the RGR. Ben and Jon always wear them because they work in exposure areas, but I do not think that all the other members of the team have them. If you do not already have an assigned radiation dosimeter I will issue a temporary one now."

Clair Parsons and Kyle Evans already had permanent digital radiation dosimeters. After Matt issued the dosimeters to the remaining ERC members, the group walked up the walkway toward the large reactor building. Curiosity, shadowed by concern, was evident on several faces. Stopping the group from entering, Clair confronted Richter, "Matt, is this place safe for us to conduct an inspection without wearing self-contained Level C personal protection gear? I personally know this reactor was used extensively for a few decades, and that during its operation transuranic elements including plutonium were generated here. I think most of us are concerned there may be some traces of those radionuclides remaining."

"It's absolutely safe. This facility has been totally decommissioned according to the Department of Energy procedures. Furthermore, our Health Physics Department and the Department of Energy have independently tested for all contaminants several times," Matt assured her. "I wouldn't hesitate to escort my own family through this facility if I could. Personally, I do not have one single concern. Now, let's proceed. We have a lot to do here and time is limited."

The group left the parking area and walked up the long sloped sidewalk toward the reactor. Sitting atop a small hill at higher ground from the other RNL buildings, the reactor commanded an interesting view of the Lab grounds. Walking together, Kyle commented to Clair, "This building is enormous, and it kind of looks like a bank and a prison all rolled into one."

Laughing, she replied, "It does look strange! I couldn't imagine working in this place."

The entire Environmental Review Committee approached the main entryway. Ascending a long series of stairs, they were greeted by big bold black letters proclaiming: RIDGEWOOD GRAPHITE REACTOR—and just below those words: BUILDING 700. A series of large brass doors with thick glass led them into a large empty lobby. This lobby once held a reception area, a security area with a phalanx of armed agents, and an information display area. Devoid of these past services, the large lobby had an unusual, eerie feel to it. The cold silence was penetrated by echoes. There was also an odd odor in the area.

Looking around in wonder, Clair noticed—on each side of the balcony—a large glass booth with holes in the glass. The glass was very green, and extremely thick. "Ben," she asked, "what were these areas for? They look like they belong in a bank."

"Clair, if you were a terrorist who thought it was a good idea to harm the reactor, several men in each booth would have their 30-caliber machine guns squarely focused on you—with their gun sights probably marking your chest right where your heart is located. Let's not go anymore into detail than that."

"Oh, no! Were these really for that purpose?" Clair said.

"*Everything* at this facility was taken very, very seriously. If someone had the opportunity to get into the reactor, and knew how to cause a runaway reaction, which actually isn't all that difficult, the reactor would immediately go on fire. And since it was a graphite reactor, most of Long Island, New York City, and some of Connecticut would have to be evacuated," Ben said, giving Clair a long, cold stare.

"Okay! Let's get on with this inspection. Be very careful not to brush up against anything," Matt said. They entered a hallway that led to a balcony with several stairwells. From there, they looked out over the balcony into a gigantic open space—a vast, mostly empty cavern with numbered squares all over the floor, walls, and ceiling.

"Attention everyone," Ben called out. "Over this balcony you are looking at the inside of the RGR graphite containment area. The graphite reactor used to occupy the area over to the west side of this entire area here. It has been removed, of course, and the entire area is clean."

"Ben, why are these numbers labeled onto all the surfaces throughout the building?" Kyle asked.

"The Department of Energy requires that after the shutdown of a licensed reactor, which this reactor was, the reactor must be completely dismantled, cleaned, decontaminated, and then surveyed in every indoor area. Every area of a reactor interior must be assigned a number, and that area must have periodic radiation surveys that are recorded and noted for future reference. I know they look alarming, but it's just standard compliance with DOE reactor decommissioning procedures."

Ben led the team into a long hallway. "We are now entering the managerial section of the reactor. This is where the operators and management had their offices. There are approximately fifty to sixty offices here for office and design work. Nothing took place in this section that would create any kind of environmental concerns."

Next, he led them into a stairwell and down four flights of stairs. The door at the bottom of the stairs opened into a large concrete and steel cavern—the heart of the old graphite reactor. Nothing was left of the reactor pile. It had been completely removed several years before. The team examined the monstrous room.

"Wow, you could probably hold a nice-sized rock concert here," said Kyle.

"Yeah," said Jon, "I could definitely see Pink Floyd doing a gig here, and really getting off on being in what once was a nuclear reactor."

"Hey, they could record the concert live and call the album 'Radioactive Journey'," said Clair. Some of the ERC members let out a small laugh.

Matt Richter, unamused by their humor, stared down the team members. "Let's not get distracted here! We must complete our work in a safe manner, and we should not stay inside this place any longer then we have to."

Ben looked around at the group. "There are so many places here that I could take you all, but since we have limited time I'll concentrate on the most important areas."

"Definitely," Jon said.

Ben explained that most of the rooms off to the side had no activity of an environmental concern. "Okay, group, if you will all turn around and observe the outside edges of this room, you will notice that there are a lot of doors that lead off this room. These are assorted offices and workshops. One of these entryways leads to the former reactor maintenance division. We are going to proceed there now."

As they walked to the former site of the reactor maintenance department they saw many side offices which stood silent and empty, with doors wide open. They entered a large open room. "This is where the maintenance staff would work on items at the reactor that needed repair. They worked on all kinds of things, including electric motors, pumps, and reactor measurement and monitoring equipment," Ben said.

"Did they use any chemicals here—such as chemical solvents? And did they generate any radioactive waste here?" Clair asked.

"Well, I really don't know about any chemical waste generated here, but I can tell you that it is possible. I have no idea what they would have done with such waste. As far as any radioactive waste, I definitely know that any radioactive waste was collected and taken to Building Number 800 for storage and removal according to Department of Energy guidelines," Ben said. "It was standard procedure that any part that was brought into, or removed from, the reactor was surveyed for radiation. If any part was found to contain any radioactivity it was removed to Building 800, the official radioactive contamination processing area."

Ben escorted the group out of the reactor maintenance room and back into the hallway. As he led the group into another large room, he said, "This was the main reactor control room. This is where the associate plant operators operated all the equipment that controlled the reactor." Pointing to several very large, thick glass windows, he continued, "As you can see, these windows provide a complete view of the large reactor containment area. This allowed the plant operators to view the graphite reactor pile while monitoring all the equipment instruments. There is nothing here now—and all the plant operation equipment has been removed, tested for contamination, and disposed of or recycled properly. This room was shielded by four-foot thick walls from the reactor. The walls were made of lead and concrete. The room also had its own environmental control system, including a separate isolated air/oxygen supply, and a special air-filtering system that would remove any airborne contaminants rather quickly. Finally, there is also an escape tunnel just below the room. The escape tunnel would allow the operators to escape unharmed in the case of a Level 4 nuclear accident."

"Ben, where was the escape tunnel located?" Kyle asked.

Ben led the group to the northwest side of the room and pointed to a hatch in the floor. "Here," he said.

The entire ERC group was astounded by this information, and examined the hatch in amazement.

"I had no idea that the designers of the reactor would go that far in their preparations for emergencies!" Clair said.

"This was the first peacetime reactor in the United States—and it was a graphite reactor—so they tried to prepare for any contingency possible. At that time, the science of nuclear fission was new and unknown. The designers knew that if the graphite pile went on fire it was all over. All hell would break loose—and then nothing mattered but getting out of the building as quickly as possible," Ben said. "There was another auxiliary control room located in an underground vault somewhere below this building. That control room was used as a backup in case there was a Level 3 system transient event which would have caused the evacuation of the entire reactor."

"I never thought that there would be a backup control room at a nuclear plant, but it makes sense," Clair said. "Did the operators here ever have to use that auxiliary control room?"

Glancing at Clair, Ben replied, "Sorry Clair, I can't answer that question because it's classified information. What I can tell you is that this reactor was the first of its kind in the world. The designers thought of every possible problem that the operators might have had to deal with—so they built every safeguard into it that they could think of. Overall, during its twenty-year plus lifespan, this reactor performed superbly. But from time to time, as in any dynamic system, things could go wrong."

Richter glared at Ben and then said, "Let's proceed and visit the next area."

Ben escorted the group out of the reactor control room and into the large hallway toward the east section of the building. They entered a large area where many stairwells converged. Several levels of the building could be viewed from here. "This area was used all the way into the early 1990s. It was used as a library and as an educational area for visitors. It is isolated from the main reactor section by a twelve-foot thick wall of concrete and lead, and was considered a safe area," Ben told the group.

As the team examined the area, Jon walked around to the northeast section of the building, becoming isolated from the rest of the joint inspection team. He entered an area which was also segmented from the large reactor area and near the stairwell from the balcony. This area was not considered a health risk. While the reactor had been in use it was used for staging equipment and for special experiments.

As he investigated, Jon found interesting displays, once part of a public science museum which had been established after the reactor was shut down and decommissioned. The museum displayed typical reactor parts, detectors, scientific instrumentation equipment, and mannequins that were used to demonstrate just how the reactor looked during its routine usage and how the personnel attended the operation of the systems. The out-of-date clothing on the mannequins, and the dust and the cobwebs that covered them, as well as the rest of the strange displays, gave Jon an eerie and mysterious feeling that ran through his senses.

Jon continued to search out the northeast section of the lower level. By the dim light provided by the windows, which were high up on the wall and made of extremely thick glass, Jon stumbled through the morass of displays toward a stairwell in the far right corner of the room. He descended to a subterranean level with too little natural light to distinguish much of his surroundings. He heard the environmental inspection team faintly, at a distance, and from an upper level somewhere.

Noticing a gleam from a heavy steel door located on the left side of the room, Jon walked toward it. He had to push aside some museum pieces to make his way through. Suddenly, a mannequin, dressed in a radiation suit and holding a radiation counter, leaned over and toppled to the ground in front of him. As the mannequin hit the ground, the head broke off and rolled toward him. Recovering from the shock, Jon looked down at the head of the lifeless mannequin. He noticed a large crack in the right cheek of the museum's loyal soldier. Jon flinched and shouted out in shock as a hand touched his shoulder.

"Ben, what the hell are you doing here?!" he barked.

"I was just about to ask you that," Ben said.

"Some of the antique science equipment caught my eye, and I wanted to see it close up," Jon said.

"Jon, we really should not be here. This is a restricted area, see the sign on the door!"

"This is a really heavy, impressive metal door. Have you ever gone through it into the next area?" Jon asked.

"That area is most likely a service area for the pneumatic tubes that were used in the RGR reactor research. The tubes carried experimental material from the reactor building to Building 720 for further research. I know that those pneumatic tubes were located there and tunneled through the ground there, but I've never been inside."

"Let's take a look!" Jon urged.

"I think we had better get back to the group. They have reports to complete, and some of those officials may get pissed off if they are delayed," Ben said.

"How about if we just open the door a bit and check it out?" Jon asked.

"Alright, but then we have to get right back to the others."

They cleared the area around the doorway together so they could open the door. The imposing door was made of finely worked steel and brass. The hinges on the door were huge, exposed, and a bit oxidized. The door barely budged.

"It did move a fraction, so the good news is it apparently is not locked," Jon said.

Ben and Jon both pulled with all their might. The door opened a few inches, but it was tough going.

"God, look at that biohazard sign on the door. What do you think it's there for?" Jon asked.

"I don't know, but we'd better get back now before we get in trouble."

"Yeah, I guess so," Jon said. They started to head up the stairwell and back to the group. At the top of the stairwell they were met by Richter.

"What were you fellows doing in that restricted area?" he said, with a flared red face and gesturing forcefully with his finger pointed at them.

"I didn't realize that area was restricted. We are required to perform a complete inspection of the building for environmental concerns, so I thought I should take a look around this area too," Jon said.

"The New York State and Suffolk County environmental officials have been looking for you and Ben. When we realized that you had wandered off, we stopped and waited for fifteen minutes. Then some of the Environmental Review Committee members went back to the reactor control room to look for you. When no one found you we all started searching other areas. Then we realized that Ben had gone looking for you in this direction," Matt said. "Remember, Ben, you must accompany this inspection in case anyone has any questions for you. I want your full cooperation on this, and I don't want to insult the group of officials any further. Now let's get going and continue our joint inspection with the others."

"Sorry about that, Matt! There is no problem here, and you can certainly count on old Ben and me to help you in any way we can!" Jon said as the three men rejoined the group.

The entire group headed toward a hallway on the east side of the reactor. As they entered the hallway, still feeling a bit unnerved from the last encounter with Matt, Ben looked at Jon and Jon read Ben's face. That look informed him there was something very odd and troublesome about the doorway they had just discovered. He felt that Lab Officials were hiding something and he wanted to learn more about it sometime in the future.

[5]

Radioactive Leaks

As the Environmental Review Committee approached the northeast exit of the graphite reactor, Clair suddenly stopped and abruptly asked Ben and Matt, "When did the staff at RNL first learn that there was an environmental issue with leaked rainwater that was contaminated with radiation?"

Matt Richter looked at Ben and Jon, took a deep breath, and said, hesitant and reluctant, "We first learned about the radioactive rainwater contamination sometime in the mid-nineties. When they first learned that the High Flux Linear Reactor had a leaking tritium problem from the spent rod storage pool, the management at RNL required a full review of the on-site reactors for environmental compliance and health and safety. Engineers and staff from our Health Physics unit performed a detailed inspection of the three reactor sites located at RNL and, at that point, we discovered that the rain contamination issue was present. Keep in mind that this was in addition to the leaked contamination from the spent fuel canal."

"Matt, can we do a quick review of all the radioactive contamination issues that have caused a leak into the ground and groundwater?" Kyle asked.

"Sure. Okay. There were several issues: The leakage from the spent fuel canal, the rainwater intrusion from the graphite fan sump, and the rainwater incursion from the bottom drainage sump were of concern. Additionally, the floor drains from the reactor machine shop that flowed to a dry well system were also an environmental concern. That is all that I know of. I also know that Clair made several inspections of this site years ago so she should be somewhat familiar with most of these."

"When the reactor was in operation what species of uranium did they use as the fuel source of the reactor?" Kyle asked.

"Originally, the plant physicists used Uranium 235 and then they used Uranium 238 later in its operation," Matt said.

"When the reactor was shut down in 1968, how extensive was the decommissioning and cleanup?" Clair asked.

"I was not present during most of its operation because I began my employment with the Department of Energy, which operated the RGR, in 1964," Ben answered her. "More recently, I witnessed the removal of the fuel rods and the total cleanup and stabilization process, which occurred in stages. Later in the life of the building some sections of the building were used as office space and a science museum. Then in the nineties all areas of the building were restricted from any normal public access, and all of the personnel using the building were moved to other locations on the RNL site. After some special testing, areas in the RGR showed lingering contamination, so a more extensive environmental cleanup was performed with the Nuclear Regulatory Commission and county and state officials present to witness the final cleanup process."

"Yes, indeed, I remember when our department was involved with the environmental cleanups back in the 1990s at RNL, but I only infrequently participated in them back then," Clair said. "But, anyway, thanks for that excellent primer on the RGR—and for all the other background information that you and Ben have provided. I certainly will note it in my reports."

The group exited at the northeast side of the RGR to tour some of the areas of interest located on the outside. From the much higher ground at the west side of the building, they noticed an outside structure that was once apparently part of the RGR complex.

"What on earth is that structure? It certainly is strange looking!" Clair said.

"That," Ben began, "was—"

But his attempt to answer was interrupted by Matt Richter.

"That area was just a normal part of the RGR that was used for additional cooling. It's nothing important, and had no environmental concerns at all."

They continued to the south and the east sides of the reactor.

"This is one of the areas which we were discussing," Clair said. "There was some leakage from the reactor into the groundwater from the spent fuel rod storage and transfer lagoon. Also, there was a problem with leakagc from the graphite fan sump that flooded from years of rainwater getting into the cooling system ducts. The leakage contained some radioactive elements, including Strontium-90."

"Well, yes, but that is now irrelevant. It's a dead issue. We did a complete groundwater remediation. The spent fuel rod storage, transfer lagoon, and the graphite fan sump were all removed too," Matt said.

"If you look around this area you will see several groundwater remediation and monitoring wells that are still active. These were installed in the 1990s and successfully remediated any significant groundwater contamination from radionuclide material."

Clair suddenly lowered her clipboard and glared at Matt with bulging eyes. She immediately challenged him vociferously, "Matt, you and I both know that there still is some radionuclide material present in the soil, and that it can never be completely removed because it is trapped in the soil by ionic molecular attraction."

"Some radioactive radionuclides are still present, but they do not present a danger to the groundwater or to human health," Matt insisted.

"I understand that it is no longer an issue as far as the groundwater contamination or health, but let's just get things straight," Clair said. "Yes, we were there to monitor the entire cleanup and we are now satisfied, along with the state officials, of the environmental condition of this site. However, I think it is important for the ERC group to understand just what the leakage issues were here."

Matt, ever the bureaucrat, snarled, "Well, thanks for making that clear to everyone."

It was obvious to all the members of the committee that Clair clearly had won that debate and made Matt look a bit foolish. She radiated a hidden smile as she looked up at Matt and said, "Matt, we have completed our inspection now. Is there anything else that you want to go over with us before we leave?"

Matt, still reeling, looked both at and away from Clair and said, "No, Clair. We don't have any other things to go over. This facility is one of the most environmentally secured and monitored areas on the entire site now."

Clair, speaking for the entourage of state and county environmental officials, thanked Matt, Ben, and Jon for taking them on the recap tour.

"If any of you have further questions, feel free to call me anytime. We will always be happy to answer any questions you have. Everything here at the Lab—and I mean everything—is out in the open for all to see. We believe in complete transparency, and we would never try to hide anything from the public," Matt said, giving his best impression of a Boy Scout.

"We do actually care about the environment and we take our jobs here seriously," Jon added.

As everyone began to leave the site, Jon walked back with Ben to his car. In the car, he reminded Ben, "Today is the last day for us to hand in our personal radiation dosimeters. I must get mine in or I'll get in trouble again with the RNL Health Physics Worker Safety monitoring staff. I already caught hell from Health Physics last month and they sent me a nasty email, which they also forwarded to Dr. Kenyatta. Dr. K had something to say to me about that."

"I have to get mine in too," said Ben. "We might as well go together now if you have time."

At Building 971, they headed over to the Dosimeter Monitoring Office. A woman called out to Jon.

"Jon, good to see you! It's been a while," Emily Collins said. She had worked with Jon a few years earlier at the Accelerating Energy Synchrotron.

"Hey, Emily great to see you—you look great," he said.

"I've been thinking of calling you to do lunch one of these days. We have to get together to do something, Jon," said Emily, her interest apparent. They had dated briefly, but drifted apart, and changes at work had meant they no longer ran into each other often. "I'll contact you next week, and drag you out of that concrete and magnet dungeon called QUEST."

"Sure, Em, that would be great," Jon said.

"You know, Jon, I've read all about the work that you guys are doing at QUEST—that is some really weird stuff. Last month, the RNL Isotope newsletter had a great article on that monstrosity of a machine called QUEST. What's going on with that Macro-STARR device? Are you guys really going to work that system up to 400 gigavolts? What the hell is that thing, Jon? It seems scary."

Jon smiled and said teasingly, "Em, you always get me hot when you talk gigavolts."

Emily laughed playfully. "Jon, you are too much! I miss being around you, and hanging out like we used to."

"Yeah, I miss those times together too," answered Jon, before resuming a less intimate tone, and continuing, "We are going to get over 400 gigavolts on the QUEST system just as long as that prick, Dr. Tonner, doesn't carry through with his threats and throw a monkey wrench into the funding."

Emily lectured sternly, "Jon, you know I want you to be very careful with all that new equipment that you have built. I wouldn't want anything to happen to you. Working with 400 gigavolts is extremely risky. Remember, I know because I spent time at CERN, and there were times we were very worried about safety issues—especially a quench event with the superconducting magnets. We were working with energy levels of over 450 gigavolts, and that place was in a lockdown safety mode."

Grabbing Jon's hand, she added more softly, "Let's get together sometime, okay, Jon?"

"You bet, Em. I'm looking forward to it. You take care of yourself too!"

As they walked toward the Worker Safety office, Ben inquired, "Does Emily know that you are kind of serious with Marta?"

"I guess she kind of knows that we are close, but she always does her own thing, you know. She's very intelligent and a little crazy and likes to get attention. You just have to give her personality a little room,"

Jon said, smiling and raising his eyebrow.

"Okay, Jon. I think I understand," Ben answered, smiling.

As they entered the monitoring office, Theresa Kelly greeted them, "Well, it looks like you are both getting your digital dosimeters in on time this month!"

"Yeah, we're getting tired of those nasty emails, so we're getting these babies in on time from now on," Ben said.

"Yeah," she replied, "you know how bureaucratic this place is. Even I get nasty emails sometimes."

Ben grinned in response and asked, "Is this box over here for the dosimeters for this next month?"

"Yes, that's the one, but let's just make sure that I assign the correct placement numbers on them so we don't get them mixed up. Here you go, Ben, and Jon, these are yours. I guess we'll see you about this time next month."

"Thanks, Theresa, we'll get these back on time again next month," Jon said.

[6]

The Environmental Experiment

As they approached his car, Ben asked, "Jon, do you mind stopping at my office so I can take care of a few pressing concerns with the AES?"

"Not at all—I have the rest of the day open, and I haven't seen the AES for quite a while."

As they headed there, Jon brought up the subject of Emery Hilcraft and the legendary research he had conducted at RNL decades before.

"Ben, I understand that you worked with Dr. Emery Hilcraft when he was here at Ridgewood."

"I worked with Emery early in my career here."

"I'd never heard of the guy until I came across his name when I started reading research papers on quantum field theory. What I read totally blew my mind. I got completely hooked. I searched through a lot of what he published about his research, and that's where I was first exposed to the many worlds theory. I think that pretty much changed the direction of my career—and my life."

"Yeah, Emery was way ahead of his time. He really shook things up, and caused quite a storm in the field of theoretical physics. We became pretty friendly. He had a significant impact on my career here. When we get to my office I'll show you a few things that I kept on Emery."

"Cool! He's a real legend in quantum theory. I'd love to learn more about the guy," Jon said.

"We won't be here too long, I just have to check on a few things and call someone," Ben said, as he parked the car.

"No problem, I'll just check in with QUEST to see how they are getting along with the setup for our experiment tomorrow. You're coming tomorrow, aren't you, Ben?"

"Yeah, I'm looking forward to helping you guys out! It's always neat working at QUEST. The Accelerating Energy Synchrotron housed beneath this building was one of the first high-energy accelerators in the world," Ben said, as he led Jon into his office.

"Yeah, I know. I worked here for a while. It's amazing that they still use it to feed protons into the Heavy Ion Target Supercollider, and that QUEST relies on it too."

"Considering that it was built in the 1960s and it's still in use today, I guess it was research money well spent," Ben said, leaving Jon to make his call.

Ben returned to his office to find Jon surveying the photos he had displayed on his walls.

"These are great photos of the old RGR, but I don't recognize some of these other locations. Do you have any pictures of Dr. Hilcraft around?"

"I think so. Let me take a look."

Ben searched through the drawers of his old desk. Opening a drawer, which held an assortment of photos, papers, and odds and ends, he sorted through the contents, pulling out the photos. He showed Jon a photo of Hilcraft and himself.

"Damn! I completely forgot about this photo—it was taken so long ago. This picture was taken in 1967, when the RGR was still operational. A friend attending that lecture took this photo of our RNL group. God, look how young we were then. We were attending a series of lectures together at Princeton. One of the lectures was on quarks. Boy! That was an exciting time in particle physics. We were breaking new ground in quantum physics. New discoveries were coming out almost every day. Amazing stuff—things that would have seemed crazy just a few years earlier. At that particular lecture, Dr. Hilcraft was asked by the lecture committee to discuss his new ideas on the multiple worlds interpretation of quantum physics."

"Wow, really—back then!" Jon said.

"Hilcraft had written a paper called 'Reality and Quantum Physics.' It was accepted by the Modern Physics Journal. It was one of the first attempts to use quantum physics as a guide to looking at the philosophy of our perceived reality. Nothing like that had ever been presented before. It was amazing.

"Hilcraft blew everyone away at the lecture. He got them to think about the possibility of everyone's existence as one of infinite possibilities—one where this universe is one of an infinite number of universes, each with their own unique outcomes.

"He confronted them. He said, 'Look at your equations! You know that they are telling you that one particle in the quantum realm is in several places at once. You are made of these quantum particles. Therefore, my friends, you are in several places at once also!'

"Hilcraft's ideas totally stirred them up—and many of them totally rejected his concepts. Some of the classical quantum physicists looked at Dr. Hilcraft as a heretic. They castigated him in discussion papers and presentations. Fierce debates always accompanied his presentations. Sometimes, it nearly came to blows!"

"Did he have any supporters?" asked Jon, fascinated by Ben's memories.

"Oh, yeah. He had a good number of supporters. Remember, Hilcraft was not the only one to promote this new multiple worlds idea. There were others, including a well-respected physicist who had obtained his PhD at Caltech back in the fifties."

"This is really fascinating stuff. I had no idea that the multiple worlds concept went all the way back to the fifties. What was Dr. Hilcraft doing here at RNL, and how did you guys cross paths?"

"I came to work at RNL back in '64. I was part of the team of physicists working on the operation of the graphite reactor. We also conducted experiments there. Dr. Hilcraft had joined the Lab somewhere in the late 1950s. I met him when I had to be trained in the control room of the graphite reactor. I was working the core cooling operation. Hilcraft was one of the associate operators. He showed me everything about the RGR. I learned it all pretty well. I also worked with Hilcraft on the environmental radiation experiment that RNL had going in the Pine Barrens wilderness on the northern section of the Lab."

"What the hell was the environmental radiation experiment?"

Laughing, Ben said, "It was a crazy experiment that was produced through the collaboration of a wacky biologist and physicist who got together. Basically, the purpose of the experiment was to better learn how radiation affects the natural environment. The experiment took a very strong radioactive source—in this case, Cesium 137—and placed it in the natural environment of the Pine Barrens for specific periods of time. We also placed radiation monitoring equipment throughout the experimental area, and allowed the radiation to interact with the natural flora and fauna. The area was then observed to see what effect the radiation had on the flora and fauna. Both short-term and long-term effects were monitored. There was quite a bit of damage."

"What was the longest period and accumulation of radiation exposure?"

"Well, the experiment went from 1962 to 1981, and the source was a very high curie source."

"Where on the site was this place located?"

Ben indicated an area near the facility wastewater treatment plant on his wall map of the Lab.

"Just to the northeast of the plant, down a dirt road, perhaps a third of a mile northeast of the wastewater treatment plant."

"What did they call the site?" asked Jon.

"Interestingly, it was one of the few places at RNL that does not have a building number. As you know, everything here has a building number. They just referred to the site as the Environmental Experiment."

"You're kidding me—the Environmental Experiment! What an oxymoron!"

"Yup, it's definitely an oxymoronic name for a place that basically radioactively fried out the life of a natural forest," Ben said.

"What about the animals that went into the area? Were they affected too?"

"The experiment was designed for as much as possible of the natural flora and fauna to come into contact with the radiation, so that the effects on them could be observed. A sampling of the animals in the area was sacrificed to the experiment so that body tissue surveys and biosamples could be taken. Deer, squirrels, rodents, rabbits and other animals were involved. It was a challenge, but they also got samples from many of the nocturnal flying squirrels that live there."

"What did you and Dr. Hilcraft have to do with the study?"

"We had to check on the high-level Cesium 137 radiation source equipment to make sure that it opened up automatically every day. It was in a specially built lead underground well. The source was raised automatically by a mechanical cable and pulley system. We also had to calibrate the radiation measuring equipment that recorded the dose of radiation emitted within a certain radius. Anyone present in the study area when the Cesium 137 was raised would get a dangerous dose of radiation. That actually happened to a few workers during the life of the experiment.

"Wow, that certainly brings back memories of my early days, Jon—I guess that's about all there is to say about the 'Environmental' Experiment. But getting back to Dr. Hilcraft, he had several work areas at RNL for various experiments. Most of them are now dismantled or renovated for newer projects, although there is one old workshop that Dr. Hilcraft used that might still be untouched. It's at a remote site that is now part of the AES metallurgy assembly shop. He loved to go there because he could get away from the bureaucrats and all the managerial crap he was responsible for."

"When was the last time you made a visit to that site?" Jon asked.

"I guess it wasn't all that long ago. I had to visit the metallurgy shop to pick up some fabrications for the HITS Collider project. I doubt anyone's been near the old workshop in years. It's pretty isolated and no one knows much about it, so it's not too disturbed. You have to go around the back of the building to get to it."

"Do you think that there is anything left there from the Dr. Hilcraft's days?"

"When I was at the shop I actually took a stroll over to that part of the old building and took a look at Hilcraft's old office area. It was kind of a mess with stuff that has just been stuck in there for storage. But I did notice that a good part of the old workshop is still there, including his old storage cabinets and files. I never went through them, so I can't tell you what's in there now, but it would be interesting to see."

"If you don't have anything pressing planned for the afternoon, would you mind showing it to me?" Jon asked.

"Sure, why not? We've been strolling down Memory Lane anyway!"

[7]

The Metallurgy Shop

As they headed toward Ben's car, Jon's cell phone rang. Glancing at the phone, Jon saw that it was VG calling.

"Excuse me, Ben, I hate to do this, but VG is calling, and I have to take this call."

"Hi, VG, how is the place running without me?"

"Things are going pretty well. I wanted to tell you that the Health Physics Management Office just left the QUEST research site."

"What were they doing there? They didn't let me know that they were coming for a visit," Jon said, somewhat annoyed.

"It wasn't a visit. It was a walk-through inspection of the entire area. They asked for you and I told them that you were working with Ben at the graphite reactor with the Environmental Review Committee team and you would be there most of the day," VG said.

"What exactly did they do there?"

"They were here all morning going through the entire area, looking for anything that could have caused the incident that involved Garrett."

"Yeah, I thought they might come down to check out the place. Did they find anything that they thought was an issue?" Jon asked.

"I really don't think so, but they didn't give me an indication either way. They did look at the beam lines that are coming from the Heavy Ion Target Supercollider all the way up to the crossing point. They also checked all the super-cooled magnet locations for damage and wear, but they found nothing wrong with the equipment."

"What else did they do?"

"Let's see . . . they went through the Macro-STARR system and found nothing wrong there. They took radiation readings throughout the entire facility, and they found no leakage from the shielding. They did ask what chemicals we use, and if they were toxic. For some reason, they specifically wanted to know if we used a penetrating solvent called Phosglow. I told them that we do use it, and I made sure to show them how the chemical storage lockers are properly grounded and vented. I explained exactly what we do with them, and how carefully we dispose of any waste chemicals. I also showed them our records on use and waste chemical removal, and how the workers use their personal protective chemical gear and respirators. Then I showed them that all the workers are certified and recertified as required by the Health Physics regulations."

"Great! It sounds like you did a good job dealing with them."

"Well, they did have a few questions about what happened to Garrett, and exactly what he was doing during the incident. They wanted to know if anyone had any idea what could have caused his death. All the personnel here basically said the same thing—

that we have no idea what could have happened, and that Garrett was a healthy guy—and then he just stopped breathing. We told them that he wasn't working on any particularly dangerous project at the time, and that when he was found unconscious we immediately notified Emergency Services and tried to perform CPR, but there was almost no pulse. We kept at it anyway until Emergency Services showed up and removed him, and that was the end of the story, as far as any of us knew."

"Yeah, VG, they're just doing their job, checking on what happened. Okay. Very good. I have to get going now. Ben and I are heading over to the metallurgy shop, so I'll see you tomorrow after I get out of the Environmental Review Committee meeting with Kenyatta and Tonner."

"Very good, Jon, I'll see you tomorrow. Everything is on track for our experiment tomorrow. Oh, and if you can please stop by Building 719 and pick up that package of interface connectors for the dipole magnets for the Macro-STARR. Jim there called me and told me they are ready for pickup."

"Okay, VG, will do."

He turned to Ben, pocketing his cell phone. "I'm ready to go now. I wonder what is over at that old office."

After a short ride toward the north side of the campus they drove by several of the older buildings that were first constructed at RNL—right after it was converted to a National Laboratory in the late 1940s. Ben parked at the old AES 112 building. Hilcraft's old workshop was dusty and dirty, and apparently had not been cleaned since Hilcraft disappeared nineteen years earlier.

Exploring the office, they found some water-damaged items on the floor. As they looked through the old file cabinets they were astonished to find many of Hilcraft's old documents. Jon and Ben each pulled out a ream of material and made room for it on the table, pushing away some of the dust, dead insects, and years of neglect.

Ben retrieved rags from his car and cleaned the table more thoroughly, while Jon wiped off a couple of chairs. They both sat down and started going through the documents. After several minutes, Jon found something that piqued his interest. He handed Ben several pages, discolored and affected by all the years of environmental exposure.

"Good find—this is very interesting, Jon. It has to do with RGR when it was operating in the later part of its life—when I was around."

"Did you see the handwritten comments . . . are those Hilcraft's?" Jon asked.

"Yes, I'd say this is Dr. Hilcraft's writing."

"What's this Hades Project that this is referring to?"

Ben stared up at Jon with a blank face and said nothing.

"Ben, do you know what this Hades Project was? Have you ever heard of it before?" Jon repeated.

Ben stopped reading. He looked at Jon, glanced around the room, and caught Jon's eye again. Slowly, maintaining eye contact, Ben replied, "Yes Jon, I do know something about the Hades Project." Just then, both men were startled by a noise outside the old building. Ben grabbed the ream of documents. "Jon, maybe we better get going. It's getting late and we both have a lot of our own work to do."

As they left the building they looked around to see what could have caused the noise. Nothing seemed out of place, but they heard a voice coming from somewhere near the building. It sounded like someone was working around the corner, near the active area of the metallurgy building.

As they walked toward the car they both noticed a midnight blue Yukon SUV drive by at an unusually slow speed on the normally deserted roadway adjacent to the isolated AES building.

"That's an RNL cop," Ben said.

"Before the big changes twenty years ago this was a much friendlier place. People were easy to work with. Everybody had a great time working here, and most importantly, everyone got along. But when the new management service provider brought in Dr. Tonner to oversee site operations things started going downhill.

"I miss the good old days when Dr. Hilcraft was still at RNL. It was incredible to be part of the exciting work that was done on our first particle accelerator. We nicknamed it the LINACK, and it was one of the first particle accelerators to explore the use of supermagnets, keeping the particles properly aligned while traveling at near light-speed."

Somehow, learning more about the background of the Lab left Jon with a vague feeling of apprehension. "Wow, it's sad that this place has taken such a downturn in terms of human relations. I guess I'd better get going. Marta is coming over and moving into my place for good, and I want to start off the visit by impressing her with a great dinner."

"Hey, Jon, make sure you tell Marta about everything going on with Emily!" Ben lectured.

"Oh, no! I can't do that," Jon said, laughing nervously.

As they drove to Ben's office, Jon asked, "Hey Ben, do you mind if I take some of these papers home with me?"

"What papers are you talking about?" Ben smirked, giving Jon a subtle wink.

"Can I also have that picture of you and Dr. Hilcraft—the one when you both were at the Princeton lecture back in 1967?"

"I definitely want that picture back, so I'll lend it to you. But I want it back soon. It's a great picture of

Hilcraft and me—and since I'll be retiring soon, I want to keep it to remember the good times I had here."

Jon walked back to Ben's office with him, and Ben put the picture into a manila folder and handed it to him.

"Bye, Ben. I'll see you tomorrow at the Environmental Review Committee meeting to go over the final report. I hope they don't have too many questions. Meanwhile, I'm going to look over these papers, and if I find out anything interesting I'll let you know."

"Okay, Jon, I'm always around. Give me a call if you find out anything. Just don't lose anything!"

[8]

Dinner at the Beach House

Jon stowed the photo, the writings, and the blueprints from Hilcraft's Lab in the trunk of his car, and reflected on his surprisingly interesting day as he turned onto Greenwood Road, headed south toward Planck Avenue, and then west, leaving RNL through the main entry guard gate. As Jon passed the guardhouse he waved good-bye to the two guards, who waved back, as usual.

Jon was always happy to head back to his beach house in Aquebogue. Driving through the Pine Barrens of Long Island was pleasant. As an avid hiker and backpacker, Jon frequently hiked in the backwoods of the Pine Barrens—either alone or with Marta. He was always renewed by the natural scenery, and would occasionally hop into his car to drive through one of the less populated areas of the pine forests. He always returned from these excursions more relaxed, and better able to concentrate on his work.

He continued to head east past Riverhead, and then turned onto Peconic Street, and into his neighborhood. Pulling onto Red Creek Drive, he took in the view of the bay framed by beautiful sand dunes in the distance. He drove up Shore Road and pulled into his driveway.

The beach house was one of several houses on Peconic Bay. Most of the houses in the area were modest and well cared for. Many had been renovated in the past fifteen years, and the majority were occupied by year-round residents. But more recently, there had been an influx of big money from the Hamptons, and several sizable estates had popped up nearby.

Jon walked around to the back of the house and paused to take in the peaceful, pickle-green bay at his feet. A sweet, brisk breeze carrying the unique blend of aromas from the estuary anointed him, washing away his stress and filling him with joy.

Finally relaxed and eager to call Marta, Jon took out his cell phone, "Hello, Sweetie! I had a long day with the ERC and the inspection, and some other adventures, and I am really tired. I'm at the house and I'm going to do a few things and then start dinner. When are you going to get home?"

Marta, in the Polish-English accent Jon found quite sexy, answered, "Hello, Jon! Good to hear your voice! I'm finishing up some employee medical review evaluations. I will be on my way as soon as I'm done."

"Great, Marta. I'll see you then!"

Jon stood for a time, looking out and breathing in the motion of the waves, marveling at the beauty of the natural inlet and the pristine beach to the west of his house. He was struck by a pleasant epiphany about the nature of the universe and his relationship to it. *It's amazing how I perceive this beautiful reality. Is this reality real? Which one is it? It's beautiful and it must be real because I feel the wind on my face. It's hard to imagine how my perceptions would be different had I not explored the science and philosophy of quantum physics—strange.* The shriek of a gull flying overhead was somehow reassuring as it blended with the ambient tones of the waves on the beach.

Jon redirected his thoughts to the more present reality and headed back to his house. As he walked up the back steps he could hear his best buddy, Onyx, yowling her customary greeting. He pulled out the cat food from the shelves under the stairwell and fed Onyx, petting her as she ate.

"Yes, Onyx, I know you own this house and I just work for you."

After a few routine chores Jon began to gather the ingredients for dinner. Remembering the box full of the papers and pictures in his car, he headed back out to retrieve it. Sitting down with a hot cup of tea, he examined the documents one by one. He savored each sip as he looked for something that piqued his interest. An old postcard to Ben, written by Hilcraft from some foreign location, caught his eye. The postcard featured exotic and unique rock formations, sharp pinnacles that reached into the sky from a magnificent mountain range. The card itself looked old, discolored, and edge-worn. Jon read Hilcraft's tiny lettering, *"Hello, Ben! I am having a great time with my friend here in Czechoslovakia. I am having an amazing experience here in the Carpathian Mountains. This is a beautiful, mystical place full of surprises. I'll tell you more when I get back to the Plutonium Asylum. All the best, Emery."*

Jon looked at the clock and realized that Marta would soon arrive for her visit. He began to prepare dinner and get the house ready for her, hoping to create a comfortable ambiance.

Marta arrived to a big welcome. She was impressed with Jon's beach house, and teased, "Jon, it looks like you spent all day cleaning up!"

"I did do a little bit of cleaning—and Onyx helped out too."

During dinner Jon asked Marta about her day. Then he told her all about his day—the inspection of the reactor, the interesting things that he had come across when he had done a little private exploring during the inspection tour, and his afternoon with Ben.

"Ben took me to one of Dr. Hilcraft's old workshops that still exists undisturbed at the Lab."

"I know Ben. He is a very nice man. I had to do a workplace physical exam of him and the other employees in his section. Now remind me, who is Dr. Hilcraft? I know you mentioned him to me a while ago, but please refresh my memory again."

"Everything I know about Dr. Hilcraft comes from my discussions with Ben Carson. Dr. Hilcraft was a famous quantum physics scientist who worked at RNL back in the sixties. Ben and Hilcraft became friends when they worked together on the same projects—one of which was the old graphite reactor. They worked together into the early nineties and then one day in 1992 Hilcraft did not show up for work. After a few days, the management tried to contact Hilcraft at his home, but they couldn't reach him. They contacted the police, who did an investigation, but apparently he was never located. He just disappeared!"

"What was Dr. Hilcraft's first name?"

"Emery. Well, anyway, when I was with Ben today we went searching through some of Hilcraft's old files cabinets and desks that seem to have remained completely undisturbed in his old workshop. We went poking around and we found some of Hilcraft's old papers. Then we went back to Ben's office and he lent me an old photograph of himself with Dr. Hilcraft. It was taken at a lecture they attended together at Princeton in 1967."

"Wow! That's amazing that Ben had that picture from that many years ago. Can I see it after dinner?"

Jon agreed, and they continued to enjoy the lovely dinner Jon had prepared to impress Marta.

"Jon, this chicken is excellent. How did you cook it?"

"I grilled it outside just before you came over. I used a marinade consisting of my personal top-secret blend of spices and beer, and barbecued the chicken slowly on low heat. The beer keeps the chicken moist and flavors it magnificently, don't you think?"

"It is delicious, and the chicken is so juicy! You're a great chef!"

"Well, the most important thing about barbecuing chicken is not to overcook it. If you overcook it, you might as well throw it out. Quality assurance is important, Marta!"

"I will have to show you a little of my quality assurance tonight," Marta said, with a dazzling smile and a suggestive look.

Jon, eyes open wide, looked at Marta. "Doctor—are you going to perform any procedures on me tonight?"

"Well, you will find out later."

After dinner, Jon brought out the box and placed it on the table in front of Marta. He apologized for the moldy smell, and pulled out the black and white photograph of Ben and Hilcraft.

"So, I was telling you about Dr. Hilcraft. He was an established research physicist at Ridgewood, and he was an associate operator of the graphite reactor too. When Ben started working at the RGR, Dr. Hilcraft took him in as a Reactor Operator trainee and trained him thoroughly in all aspects of the reactor. They also worked together on several other projects at Ridgewood, including the Environmental Experiment. That is also fascinating, and I'll have to tell you about it sometime."

"Didn't you say that Dr. Hilcraft disappeared from the Lab while he was working there with Ben?"

"Yes, about nineteen years ago. It is totally freaky. There was a major search, but he was never found."

Intrigued, Marta asked, "Were there any clues about what happened to him?"

"I asked Ben that. He said that there was speculation about what could have happened to him, but no indication of what really happened."

Marta looked at the photograph. "Who is this other person near Ben and Dr. Hilcraft in the photograph?"

Jon examined the photo carefully, and said, "I don't know who she is. I'll have to ask Ben."

"Look how young Ben looks in that photograph. Dr. Hilcraft was a handsome man. Look at that head of blond hair! He must have had a woman in his life. Was he married?"

"I don't really know anything about his personal life. I'll have to ask Ben."

Marta was already at the computer, searching the Internet for information about Emery Hilcraft. Despite his rather uncommon name several candidates turned up. She culled out the ones that were obviously not the Emery Hilcraft in question, and explored some of the more interesting hits.

"Look, Jon! I found some things about Dr. Hilcraft. Apparently, Dr. Hilcraft had a house here on Long Island, and a house in upstate New York, in a place called Pine Hill. It says here that the New York State Police also assisted in the search for Dr. Hilcraft in the Township of Shandaken, but they found no clue what happened to him."

"Let me see! Did you see this—the police searched that area in the Catskill Mountains for months, but stopped searching after turning up nothing."

Clicking on a different hit, Jon and Marta read an article in an old copy of The Isotope, the RNL newsletter, where they learned that Dr. Hilcraft had disappeared on or about March 22, 1992, and that there had been no trace of him since that date. The article also stated that Dr. Hilcraft was widowed and had two children but had lived alone at his time of the disappearance.

"I'm going to see Ben tomorrow morning—we're both meeting with the Environmental Review Committee—and then I will be at QUEST for most of the rest of the day. I'll ask Ben if he would like to have lunch with us at Bowers Hall. We can ask him about the other person in the photo, and some of these other things about Hilcraft."

"I'll be in the Medical Research building tomorrow morning doing some research on the baboon neurotransmitter study, so I think that I can meet for lunch with you guys after twelve thirty. If I won't be able to make it I will call you later in the morning."

"Tomorrow's a big day. The Heavy Ion Target Supercollider will be operating their particle beam. They'll be able to send some of their particle beam energy to QUEST, and it will be a good opportunity for us to get up some good energy level tests using the Macro-STARR."

"That device is very interesting, but somewhat frightening. I am scared that it may cause harm to someone working with it—and, by the way, it is even difficult to pronounce. I think you need a nickname name for it."

"Well, yeah, it is a beast of a machine, but it's amazing to think it may give us a good look at just what this universe is. Our team has come so far with its development, and I am determined to see it to completion! We're almost there. We have a lot of people counting on us. More than one billion dollars has been invested from many countries, and other entities, around the world. Don't worry about it being safe. If I didn't think it was safe I would not have any of my team of scientists working on it. I will admit that QUEST is using a hell of a lot of energy, but we have so many safety systems built into it, and we are taking the research slow because it is all new science looking into just what the quantum world is. Why don't you come down and visit with us tomorrow before we get QUEST running? You're our work team's official health physicist, so you're required to medically evaluate our workers at QUEST anyway."

"Well, Jon, that is correct, but if the Lab management found out that you and I are dating, I think that they would definitely get a replacement health physicist to evaluate your QUEST workers."

"I guess we just will keep that a secret, won't we?"

"Besides, Jon, I am going to medically evaluate you tonight."

Jon burst into laughter as Marta grabbed him by the waist and pulled him toward her. She tugged his shirt free, and caressed his back and chest.

"Jon, I think you are due for a physical now."

In the bedroom, Marta pushed Jon onto the bed, and they began removing each other's shirts.

"Marta, I hope you plan to keep this physical professional!"

"Absolutely, I am a psychiatrist. I know what I am doing. Now I'm going to find out what's in your mind . . . and elsewhere."

The next morning they ate breakfast as they watched the clear morning light play on the water of the bay.

"On my way home tonight I'll stop at Troyan's Seafood and pick up some Peconic Bay Cherrystone clams," Jon said. "Tonight I'll make you some of my famous clam casino."

"Where I come from in Europe we do not have any clams, and I have no idea what they taste like."

"They are one of my favorite things to make on the barbecue. I'm sure you'll like them."

"If they are anything like your barbecued chicken I'm sure I will love them."

"Thank you, Marta. Hey, some time we can get my kayaks out and you and I can kayak over to Red Cedar Point and go clamming there to get some really fresh Peconic Bay clams!"

"How do you catch clams?" asked Marta.

"You use your feet to find them, and then dig them out using your hands. You actually can get quite a few clams that way and it is fun it do."

"Sure, Jon, it sounds like fun, and I would love to try these clams, especially when they are so fresh."

Jon looked over at the clock. "Marta, I have to run. I have to meet with the Environmental Review Committee at the director's office and then go over the systems at QUEST with my research crew. I'll meet you for lunch, if that works out for you."

"Yes, I have to go too. I'm working with Lois this morning, and I have to be at the Medical Research building at eight thirty."

Jon and Marta left the house together and called out to each other.

"Love you, Marta!"

"Love you, too."

[9]

The Environmental Review Committee

Jon had an easy ride in, despite a slight delay on the Long Island Expressway. Approaching the Lab, he pulled out his ID card, complete with RFID encoding, and headed toward the main guard gate of Ridgewood. The attending officers glanced at Jon and checked their computer screens to verify his security clearance. After receiving the electromagnetic telemetry confirmation, the officers signaled to Jon to pass through the gate area. Recognizing Jon, one of the officers smiled, pointed a finger at him and waved, letting him know to have a nice day.

Jon noticed that it was already eight twenty-five, and realized that his meeting would start soon. He began to accelerate, then remembered that the speed limit for all roads at the Lab was strictly enforced at twenty miles per hour. He quickly slowed down, remembering the memos that he received from management that the speed limit would be strictly enforced. A visiting graduate student from Morocco had been killed while crossing Oppenheimer Road a few years back, and after that the Lab police had tightened up enforcement, including setting up radar traps.

Jon pulled into the parking lot of Building 124, where the Administration Office and the director's office were housed. He grabbed his notes and rushed to the conference room. Ben was already at the meeting, along with Dr. Kenyatta, Matt Richter, Clair Parsons, and Kyle Evans. The group was filled out by some of Matt Richter's assistants, and some representatives of the Building Maintenance department. They paused the meeting to greet Jon.

"Thank you for joining us, Jon," said Matt Richter, as Jon took a seat in the large, plush conference room.

Kenyatta continued the meeting, "I am very glad that we are all cooperating in improving the environmental quality here at Ridgewood. Clair, you were part of the county environmental inspection team that was invited here as part of our working agreement with Suffolk County in the 1980s. With the assistance of our staff, you and some of your associates conducted detailed inspections of the Lab decades ago in the 1980s and 1990s. In addition, you conducted an environmental sampling program of many of the building sites. Of course, we all know that in the past things were not always done in an environmentally proper manner, but as you can see we have made great strides in getting all of our Lab buildings into proper compliance with all federal, state, and county environmental regulations. We have also opened our Lab up for public review though the implementation of our Community Advisory Committee. We here at Ridgewood always strive to do the right thing, and we take every measure to do so. So, tell me, Clair, how do we stack up now?

What are your findings in this latest inspection?"

Clair Parsons was articulate and professional. Looking up at Dr. Kenyatta, she replied, "I have to tell you Dr. Kenyatta, I am very impressed with how well the Lab has performed in terms of environmental compliance. When we first inspected the Lab in the 1980s we identified various deficiencies with the handling, holding, and disposal of chemical wastes. At that time, we found various sites where waste chemicals had leaked into the soil and contaminated the groundwater. Radioactive materials had also contaminated both the ground and the groundwater." Clair paused as the door opened with a bang and Tonner entered the room.

Kenyatta stood up to greet him, "So glad you could make it here today, Dr. Tonner!" He then addressed the members of the committee, "For all of you who do not know, Dr. Hadley Tonner is the special liaison to the director's office. He is also the chairman of the RNL Site Security Committee, and a standing board member on the Health, Safety and Environment Committee. I invited Dr. Tonner to attend this meeting since we are completing this latest phase of our environmental improvement efforts."

Tonner, a tall, stiff-looking, older man with a slight British accent, apologized, "I am sorry that I was not able to join you earlier. I had a pressing matter to attend to. Thank you for inviting me. I am happy to offer your committee any assistance I can provide."

"We were just discussing the history of Ridgewood in terms of environmental compliance. Ms. Parsons was providing an update on the findings of the recent joint inspection," said Kenyatta. He gestured to Clair and Kyle and introduced them to Tonner, "Clair Parsons is from the county, and Kyle Evans, seated next to her, is from the state. They have recently completed their inspection."

Tonner replied, "Yes, of course, I am aware of Ms. Parsons' and Mr. Evans' work here. Pleased to meet you both. I'm eager to hear your findings. But first, let me say that I fully appreciate the assistance of all the members of the ERC in this cooperative project."

Kenyatta prompted Clair to continue.

"As I was saying, in the past we had identified improper handling, storage, and disposal of chemical waste at several sites here. More troubling, we also identified soil contamination and groundwater contamination from radioactive liquids leaked by the three previous reactors that were located on site. Your own environmental staff had identified these environmental concerns. They had also developed a site remediation program. This program took a long time to complete, but it now seems that most of the environmental concerns have been improved and remediated where necessary. I cannot speak for Kyle, but as far as the county is concerned we are pleased with your compliance thus far."

Kyle interjected, "Yes, we have come to the same conclusion in terms of compliance with New York State requirements."

Clair nodded and resumed. "We all know that there still are some lingering groundwater remediation wells still in operation—for example, the wells that are located near the RGR and the Beam Reactor, and at a few other chemical storage areas and service buildings. However, the groundwater samples near all the sites have shown significant and consistent improvement since we first identified the spill sites decades ago. The groundwater monitoring wells near the Glass Pits waste burial site are still showing some lingering chlorinated hydrocarbon solvent contamination, but we are encouraged that the levels of contamination have been falling for the last few years. That area will need to be continuously monitored and remediated if need be."

"Yes, that area has presented a challenge to our cleanup efforts," Matt said.

"Why is that, Matt?" Clair asked.

"This particular area of contamination was discovered in the late 1980s when random test wells were being installed around the Lab grounds. That area is one of the most ancient spill sites located on the Ridgewood site. It was probably a chemical dump site for the US Army when this area was a military training camp prior to World War I. We also know that during and after World War II, when the site was converted into a national lab, the Glass Pits area was used as a chemical dump for routine Lab waste, chemical wastes, possibly even some radioactive waste too. We believed our excavations of Glass Pits, and the chemical remediations of the contamination, were complete but—"

Matt was suddenly cut short by Tonner, "Matt, my good fellow. We can give any ERC member a written report of the history of the Glass Pits area, and a full report on the *extensive* remediations that have been performed at that site. That will do Matt, don't you think? We are short on time here and we don't want to get off track and bogged down on something rather inconsequential."

Clair ignored Tonner's attempt to change the focus of the conversation. "I did do some recon work on the Glass Pits area, and Kyle and I would both like to learn more about it. I do have a good concept of what is involved there, and although it is not an environmental priority, it should be continuously monitored on a long-term basis. I am sure that we will revisit the site further in the near future."

"I will have Matt issue each ERC member a full report on the Glass Pits site," Kenyatta said. "Also, if there is any other specific area at RNL that you would like to receive more information about just make a request to Matt, and he will include that too."

Closing her notepad, Clair said, "I really don't have anything else to add today. Kyle, do you have anything else to ask the ERC today?"

Kyle glanced around the room, and focused on Kenyatta. He shrugged his shoulders and said, "Not really. I am very satisfied with what the Lab has done. I am confident that the Lab is committed to complying with environmental regulations, and that they will continue their environmental improvement program."

Clair added, a bit sheepishly, "Well, I do have one other question to ask, but it really doesn't have anything to do with our work today."

Smiling, with a small shake of his head, Kenyatta asked, in his charming Nigerian accent, "Okay, Clair, what is your question?

"I have spent so much time here at Ridgewood over the past decades. I've been through the many buildings, and seen so many amazing research areas. I really consider myself lucky to have had the opportunity to experience this amazing facility. I have seen experiments ranging from things like irradiating rubber balls and metal parts, to the Environmental Experiment, to the medical reactor, and even the exotic animal holding pens at the Medical Research Building. There is an unusual area west of the Bowers Hall cafeteria, just south of the Ridgewood Fire Department Building; there is a unique forest of tall pitch pines. In the pitch pines there is a hiking trail system that kind of zigzags back and forth through the forest. I think there is a sign at the entrance that refers to it as the Park Course."

"Yes, Clair, that area that you refer to is named the Park Course. It has some stations for hikers or runners to stop and exercise at designated workout areas," Kenyatta said.

"Yes, that is it—that is the area."

"What is your interest in that area, Clair?"

"Well, as I said I have spent so much time here at Ridgewood that I actually stumbled across that area a while ago. I always look forward to hiking in that lovely pitch pine forest and I've always wondered about those large monolithic cement structures there. Some of them are really large, and they don't look new. I've often wondered how those large structures got into that very mature pitch pine forest."

"Aah . . . ," said Kenyatta, "I do know that area. I know exactly what you are referring to. This shows you how long I have been here at RNL. I have also walked there many times over the past decades. What you have noticed are the remnants of old World War I structures that were built around the Lab site sometime around 1911. This site was first established as a soldier training site for the military just after the turn of the century. The purpose of the cement structures is not certain, but many people familiar with them think that they were structures used for the very large guns that the soldiers used here when it was a military training site. There are some old pictures of them in documents at our RNL museum, and some of the documents state that the soldiers trained on large sixteen-inch guns. They used to fire live shells north into the Long Island Sound. As you know, that is located about six miles to the north of here. You may have also noticed there are some other brick structures in the ground, but we are not sure what those were used for. Some of them look like wells and others are very abstract and unique. Those may have been used during World War II but we are not sure. We do know that during World War II this site was expanded significantly. Many buildings were added. A few of those buildings are still standing. Some are still used to this day as part of the Lab. If you want to know more about the history of RNL, I definitely suggest that you make a visit to our Historical Museum—you will find very interesting information, pictures, and artifacts that shed light on the history of this site."

"Thank you so much for indulging my curiosity, Dr. Kenyatta. I think that this place is so fascinating. I love learning about the history here."

Tonner muttered, looking at Jon, "If people only knew what went on here, and what still goes on here at Ridgewood, they would truly be shocked and amazed."

Jon looked Tonner in the eye, sensing something abnormal about his tone. The puzzled look on his face reflected his thoughts about the recent pieces of information he had been mulling over. Lost in his thoughts, he suddenly realized Kenyatta was addressing him, "Jon, we are going to adjourn this meeting, but we would like you and Ben to stay for a short discussion. Dr. Tonner and I have a few questions for you concerning the recent incident at your QUEST facility."

[10]

The Hansen Incident

Kenyatta and Tonner thanked the committee for their work, and exchanged pleasantries as the ERC members began to leave the room. Tonner sat down and looked through his notes, apparently passing time until they had the room to themselves. Kenyatta closed the door and took his seat. Tonner looked up from his notes, and looked directly at Jon, asking, "How is all your work going on your QUEST project?"

"Things are going very well, overall. We are still getting the QUEST systems operational and properly networked. We still have some work to do to get the research more advanced but we are pleased with the experiments so far. Of course, since the incident in which Garrett Hansen passed away while working on the superconducting magnets, the managers at QUEST have instituted new health and security measures to minimize any health risks to the workers."

After a few moments of silence, Tonner said, "Jon, we have the medical report on what happened to Mr. Hansen. Dr. Kenyatta and I have reviewed it."

Garrett had been a healthy, active man in his thirties, with no apparent medical issues. Jon and his team had already conducted their own investigation and had found no evidence of any accidental radiation releases from the QUEST super-cooled magnet beam system and no traumatic injuries.

"The medical report came to no certain conclusion about what caused Garrett Hansen's death. They also found no evidence of any physical injuries; however, the report did find some biochemical abnormalities that were of undetermined origin. They speculate that those abnormalities may have contributed to his passing." After pausing, Tonner inquired, "Jon, are you and your team of scientists using any hazardous chemicals at QUEST?"

"No, nothing out of the ordinary . . . We use some incidental chemicals for our electronic systems. We use some epoxy glues and some readily available chemical solvents typically used for high-voltage electronics. We do use a special chemical flux for the soldiering of the high temperature platinum connectors used on the Macro-STARR device but I do not think that any of those solvents are particularly toxic."

Kenyatta interjected, "Jon, do you use Phosglow on any of your equipment?"

"Yes, we do use some Phosglow solvent. We use it to check the aluminum housings of the helium compressors for the super-cooling systems."

"What exactly is Phosglow?" asked Tonner.

"Phosglow is a special phosphorescing organic solvent that is used to find micro cracks in metal parts. We either dip the part into a Phosglow bath if it is small enough, or we brush some Phosglow solvent onto the metal area that we wish to check for cracks. Then we let it seep into the metal and examine the metal for cracks. When we use Phosglow we always use protective equipment. We use gloves and respirators, and we have special ventilation equipment to ventilate the whole testing area," Jon said.

"I know that the Health Physics staff has responded to a few reports of workers using Phosglow who were overcome by fumes and needed medical assistance," Kenyatta added.

"No, Dr. Kenyatta, we have not had one incident of any of our science and maintenance staff being overcome by Phosglow, or any of the other chemicals that we are using at QUEST," Jon said, adding more forcefully, "Everything that we do at QUEST, every chemical that we use, has been approved by the Health Physics staff. This was so well prior to Garrett's death, and just after the incident they came down and found no health or safety violations or any notable findings at all! Nothing! Furthermore, I personally know that Garrett Hansen did not work in any area where any of the solvent chemicals were being used. The only people who use those organic solvents are the special maintenance workers. They are routinely trained and checked by the Health Physics staff for proper protective equipment use, and their work areas are routinely checked for proper ventilation. They always use their protective equipment when working with any toxic or hazardous substance. By requirement, those workers attend training courses every year that are held by the Health Physics section. Garrett Hansen was not involved in any kind of work that would have exposed him to those materials."

Kenyatta commented, "I have to say that at this point there is no substantial evidence to indicate that Garrett's death had anything to do with his work at the QUEST site. His passing most likely had something to do with his own medical condition. These things can happen from time to time. Sometimes it can never be determined exactly why a person who seemed young and healthy just passes on."

"Is there anything else in the medical report that might indicate what the biochemical abnormalities could have come from?" asked Jon.

"Let me read that section to you," Kenyatta said. "According to the report, 'The subject's epidemiology findings show thrombocytopenia, abnormally low platelets, in serum blood. There are other indications of haemostatic failure as well, including anemia and proteinurea. Tissue samples found traces of an unidentified biotoxin in the blood and in nerve tissues.' That's it, Jon. That's all the pathology report says. I am not a medical doctor so I can't tell you anything more then what they reported."

"Can I get a copy of that pathology report, Dr. Kenyatta?" Jon asked.

"I do not see any reason why not."

"Jon, I personally do not think that your QUEST research had anything to do with the Garrett Hansen incident, but I am going to be frank with you all about what some of us think about the work that you are doing," said Tonner, his face flushing and attitude becoming more pronounced. "Several of us on the Lab Oversight Management Committee think that your project is a huge gamble of more than a billion dollars into an area of physics that is considered risky at best. It is probably a waste of funding money that could be used for more practical purposes. Some of us on the board are looking to reconsider the funding of your QUEST grant money. I personally do not think that it is a good use of taxpayer money, or private funding, and I am concerned that we here at the Lab have let this weird science project go too far. As far as I am concerned, it is now a very pink elephant in the making."

Ben noticed Jon's rising agitation, and gave Jon a pointed look. He carefully stepped on Jon's shoe under the table. Jon got the message, and refrained from losing his cool.

But Kenyatta also had noticed that Jon was very perturbed, and decided to head off Jon's response. "Dr. Tonner, I do not believe that we called this meeting here today with Jon with the intent of judging his entire research project. We all have our own opinions on the usefulness of certain activities here at Ridgewood, and we should not display any needless disrespect. I also know that Jon's research project has had much support from the members of the Research Funding Committee, and that several private funding consortiums representing some very large high-technology companies are interested in the science theory of the QUEST research. One of the companies committed to funding Jon's QUEST research is Q-Wave Computing Systems. They personally bankrolled a two hundred-million-dollar grant into the research that Jon is pursuing. As a matter of fact, the president of Q-Wave Computing Systems will be making a visit here at Ridgewood in the near future. He will be touring the QUEST project and plans dinner with the director of the Lab. Dr. Tonner, were you invited to attend this dinner with Jon and the director?"

That comment caught Tonner by surprise. He took a breath. "Well, I am sure that the QUEST project has some interesting technology aspects to it, and that there are some high-profile supporters to it, but we here at Ridgewood are facing real financial challenges with the new budget funding cuts. One way or another, some of the research at Ridgewood will have to be scaled back. I am sure that when the Funding Committee gets around to budget reductions QUEST will be on the list for cuts."

Jon was less perturbed, but still felt the need to speak. "Dr. Tonner, do you know what we are doing at QUEST? Do you have any idea just what kind of science we are working with? Why don't you come on down? I will be happy to give you a tour—it's really interesting, productive science. Some people have challenged our research because they don't want to know the answer to our questions. They are scared of what it implies. I can understand that they feel uncomfortable with what this research indicates. This is the same thing that past scientists like Copernicus and Galileo went through. Science wasn't ready to accept findings that challenged the status quo beliefs. Please come and take a look."

Tonner looked at Jon thoughtfully. "Perhaps I will have to make a visit to the QUEST project and see this strange system for myself."

"Very good," said Kenyatta. "Maybe I will go with you, Dr. Tonner. It really is a very interesting place to see. I do not think that there is anything else like it. Even though you are a molecular biologist I think that you will find the physics fascinating."

Tonner sighed and glanced at his watch. "I really have to get going."

Kenyatta rose from his chair and escorted Tonner into the hallway, while Jon waited in the conference room. When Kenyatta returned, he put his hand on Jon's shoulder. "Jon, do not get too upset over Dr. Tonner's inappropriate comments on the research you are doing. He is a political animal here in a bureaucratic system that is always looking for goats to sacrifice. You just have to accept it for what it is and try not to take it too seriously. I am very accustomed to this type of negative interaction. It is kind of like sand traps on an eighteen-hole golf course. You just have to try to avoid them, and if you find yourself in one you just have to pull out your pitching wedge and give it the right swing to get out of it. Dr. Tonner is not a physicist like you and I, and he is biased toward his molecular biology research."

"Well then, I have one question for you, Dr. Kenyatta. Was Dr. Tonner invited to your dinner with the president of Q-Wave Computing Systems and the director?"

Kenyatta laughed and said, "No, he was not, but you *are* invited to have dinner with us! Actually, the president of Q-Wave specifically requested that you come to the dinner. He really wants to meet you. He thinks very highly of you. You know, Jon, in the science world you are mentioned as being an up-and-coming notable person of interest."

"I never thought of myself as being all that important. I just like to do my research and stay out of the political crap," Jon said.

Kenyatta looked Jon in the eye. "You are lucky that the director of Ridgewood thinks very highly of you, and that he is very supportive of your research. Make sure you stay on his good side, and don't do anything foolish."

"I am just interested in getting my QUEST research to the next level—and we are getting close! We will be running some very important tests in the next few days because HITS will be able to send us the high-energy beams of particles that we need to do those tests. We don't want to waste the opportunity!"

"Interesting. Good luck with that. I hope that your tests all go well." Kenyatta paused, and added, "And, Jon, I forgot to tell you that we got a call from a local television station that is doing a news piece on the work here at Ridgewood. Apparently, they found out about your QUEST project, and they seem interested in interviewing you. They would like to bring their video equipment down into your facility and do a news story on you and the QUEST system. Is that okay with you? Would you be willing to do that? Publicity for QUEST could help get more money flowing into the project."

"That's great. Sure, I certainly would be willing to give them a tour of the system and show them some high-voltage particle physics in action!"

"Very good, Jon. I'll let you know when they want to come; it will probably be a while."

"Thanks for your support, Dr. Kenyatta. Ben and I should get going now. My staff at QUEST may need me. Just one more thing, I know that Dr. Tonner came to the Lab about twenty years ago. Do you know what he was doing before he came to Ridgewood?"

"Yes, I do know. Dr. Tonner worked for the United States Army. He was a high-ranking colonel, responsible for overseeing a military research facility in Utah or Nevada somewhere. He is a fairly smart man and has many political contacts, so we really don't want to get on his wrong side."

"I see. You are totally correct, Dr. Kenyatta; we certainly don't want any trouble from him."

"Okay, well, you guys take care! I do want to get you and Ben both on the golf course sometime in the future!"

"I haven't played golf in a few months. I would love to get out there—maybe at the Calverton Pines Golf Course. I love playing there," said Ben, heading for the door.

"Very good. We'll do eighteen at the Calverton Pines Golf Course in the next few weeks. I will let you and Jon know when I come up with a few possible dates for a golf outing."

[11]

Bowers Hall

Outside, Ben turned to Jon. "I am really glad that we didn't have to get all involved in the ERC discussions."

"Yeah, I'm glad that Matt and the management did all the talking. I don't like to get occupied in all that interlab stuff. We have enough going on without dealing with that stuff, too," Jon said, adding, "What are you doing today, Ben?"

"I'm on my way to the post office. You can come with me, if you want. I shouldn't be too long. After that we could grab lunch, and maybe Marta could join us?"

"Sure, it's almost noon anyway, so I may as well go with you. Hey, do you mind if we make a quick stop at Building 719? I need to pick up a package for QUEST."

"No, not at all. It's right around the corner."

They got into Ben's car, a white 1966 Corvette Stingray.

"Wow, what a great car! I've never seen a '66 before. Where did you get this thing?" Jon said.

"I picked it up a few years ago from an old guy in Westhampton Beach. I got it for a steal, and it was mint."

"It sure is, Ben! In this shape, you could get good money for it. Hey, I heard you're a surfer. I'll bet your board looks cool on this beauty."

Ben took off, revving the engine, showing off his car a bit. He pulled up in front of the Ridgewood Post Office, on the Lab grounds.

Jon entertained himself by people-watching. Several people went in and out of the post office. Then he pulled out his phone and called Marta.

"Hello, Jon. What's going on? Are we meeting for lunch today?"

"Yeah, Marta, I hope so! I just got out of a long meeting with Dr. Kenyatta, Dr. Tonner, and the ERC. Ben and I are heading over to Bowers Hall for lunch. We can meet you there in a short while."

"Great, Jon! Oh, Lois is coming too. So we will see you there in about thirty minutes or so."

"Great! We should be there first, so look for us."

Moments later, Ben returned to the car. "Okay, let's head over to 719 and pick up your package."

"I just talked to Marta. She's going to meet us at Bowers. Her friend Lois is coming too, so you'll get the chance to meet her."

Pulling into the lot at 719, Ben said, "This is the magnet shop. What are you picking up from here?"

"I'm picking up some magnet interface connectors for the Macro-STARR. Come on in with me and you can meet Jim Morris. He's our supermagnet fabricator expert. Without Jim and his team, our Macro-STARR system could not work. By the way, Jim is pretty impressive. He came from a poor black family in the South and got a scholarship to the University of Tennessee's Materials Science Center. After that, he went on to design supermagnets used around the world."

"Very impressive. I'll come along. I'd like to meet him."

Inside Jon greeted several other shop employees. "Hey Jim, how's it going?" he called out.

"Going well! Who's your friend here today?"

"This is Ben Carson. Ben is helping us out down at QUEST. I don't think you've met Ben before."

"No, I haven't. Very nice to meet you, Ben."

"Hey Ben, Jim and his team here produce many of the supermagnets for RNL and other high-energy physics research labs across the world, including CERN. They pioneered the neodymium supermagnets used in HITS and QUEST."

"That's very interesting. I know that the technology for the supermagnets has really advanced," Ben said.

"Jim, can you show Ben that little magnet pen gun that you invented?"

"Sure, follow me—just don't tell anyone about it, though."

They walked through the magnet research and manufacturing areas to a workbench with clear plastic cabinet doors. Jim reached inside one of the cabinets and pulled out several small metal rod-shaped devices.

"Okay, stand back a little."

"Wait till you see this, Ben!"

Jim pointed one of the devices at a cement wall nearby and pushed a small button, which caused a three-inch section of the rod to fly out with extreme force. It hit the wall and lodged several inches deep in the cement.

"Holy crap! What the hell! That thing just shot into the cement wall and made no sound at all! How is that possible?" Ben exclaimed.

"Jim, tell Ben how this thing works."

"Sure, we had invented a new magnet alloy containing a new form of neodymium blended with graphene. This created a very powerful magnet with new properties. The units contain two supermagnets with their positive poles placed near each other. This generates a repulsive force that increases over time," Jim explained.

"Here—you guys can take one of these mag-shooters. Just be careful with them! They can be deadly if you hit someone. To activate it, just push this button on the top of it here."

"Christ! It's only the size of a small pen and it can shoot like that!" Ben said.

"Thanks, Jim! I see you've been using that wall for target practice," Jon said, slipping one of the shooters into his pocket.

Jim looked a bit sheepish, "Yeah, we have shooting contests. We're all getting better with our aim."

"Oh, damn! We've got to get going now. We're meeting a few people for lunch shortly. But thanks again," said Jon, patting his pocket.

"Okay, guys! Don't forget to pick up your package by the front desk before you leave. I'll see you soon. Nice meeting you, Ben," said Jim.

"Nice meeting you too. Thanks again, Jim!"

As they drove down Tesla Drive toward Bowers Hall, Jon abruptly shouted out. "Look out, Ben, there's a speed trap up ahead!"

"Thanks! Good catch. Have you ever gotten a ticket here?"

"No. I never have and I don't intend to. I usually drive my car pretty responsibly, but the speed limit here at the Lab is so low in certain areas that you could easily exceed the limit without thinking."

"No kidding. I've gotten a few tickets over the past few decades. Once, I actually had to pay the fine."

"I guess it's best to slow down. The site is full of joggers, and lots of people walking around all the time anyway."

"Yeah, I know you're right. I should slow down. And the Lab security police are real pricks. They're just itching to give everyone a ticket and a hard time to go with it."

Jon laughed. Ben pulled into the Bowers Hall lot. As they walked to the main entrance, Jon asked, "Have you seen any interesting lectures or concerts in the auditorium here lately?"

"Yeah, I saw a sixties music band here a few months ago with my wife. I also went to that lecture by Dr. Harold Haslinger on the research that he's doing at the RNL Medical Building."

"Oh, you went to Haslinger's lecture. How was it?"

"It was pretty interesting, very worthwhile, actually."

"I wanted to attend that lecture but I had to work at QUEST that night. You know, Marta sometimes works with Dr. Haslinger and his staff on certain projects. One of the projects is using isomers of LSD as a treatment for pain management. Apparently, they are having some success."

"Dr. Haslinger discussed that research. He went into some detail about it. He said that LSD is actually an amazing chemical that is not fully understood. It seems that many of the effects on the brain are just now being realized," Ben said.

"Wow. I read about Haslinger's work in The Isotope. The article mentioned some of the LSD stuff. I also know that Marta and her colleagues have been working with baboons, and Haslinger has participated in that research. Marta told me that they have been testing several of the LSD isomer derivatives on the baboons. Then they do brain scans of the baboons. They've gotten some stunning results."

"Have you ever met Dr. Haslinger?" Ben asked.

"No, I haven't, but Marta offered to take me over to the Medical Research and Molecular Biology buildings to show me around."

"I heard the security at Molecular Biology is quite restrictive."

"Well, yeah, I hear that they are apparently doing some things there that are funded by the government that they don't wish the public to know about. I have no idea why they would have that policy, since here at Ridgewood almost everything is open to public scrutiny. I know because I'm on the Citizen Advisory Committee, and we openly discuss everything. Not only that, but ordinary citizens are permitted to attend and obtain research reports on anything at the facility."

They maneuvered through a well-dressed crowd chatting in front of the large space-age doors constructed of glass and brass. "I guess that explains the difficulty finding a parking spot," Jon said. "There must be a conference going on. By the way, Ben, do you know when Bowers Hall was built, and why it looks like a base station on another planet?"

"I believe that it was constructed back around 1976 when the Lab went through a significant buildup. That was when they built the Chemistry Research building, which is right to the east, and a few other buildings, including the site police building. The architect who designed Bowers Hall apparently wanted to give the building an ultramodern look to set a new tone for the Lab—moving it away from its old World War I and World War II look. The walls of the building are solid concrete and very thick, and they are angled, which makes it pretty abstract-looking."

After they scanned the lobby for Marta and her friend, Ben motioned for Jon to look over toward the entrance to the auditorium. "It looks like the director's office is having some kind of meeting."

"Yeah, I see the Lab director talking to some people over there, in front of the doorway to the auditorium. Tonner's next to him. I guess he was headed over here," Jon said.

"I wonder what those guys in military regalia are doing here, don't you?" said Ben.

"I have no idea, but I don't think that they're here for the good food—even though it is pretty good."

"Jon! We're over here!"

Jon and Ben looked around the crowded lobby and spotted Marta and her friend standing about ten feet to their left, between them and the cafeteria entrance.

The hum of voices and the clang of cutlery greeted them as they entered the large cafeteria, and they grabbed trays and utensils. Later, they found an empty table and started to enjoy their lunch together.

"Well, at least those huge, vibrant paintings make the place a little more attractive," Lois said.

Marta also appreciated the paintings. "They are very colorful and abstract. It seems like we are somewhere in the future because of the angles of the concrete walls, the art, and the view through the large window into the woods full of pine trees."

"Yes, exactly! It looks like a view into the future," Lois agreed.

Curious, Jon asked Lois, "What exactly do you do over in the Medical Building?"

Lois was a tall, attractive, well-dressed younger woman. Her blonde hair just covered her ears, and she somehow managed to display her jewelry and modest tattoos in a way that was stylish and tasteful, rather than tacky. "I work over in Medical Research, and sometimes also at the Molecular Biology Building. I'm a biochemistry research scientist, so I work on various medical and biochemistry research projects."

"Do you work with Marta often?" asked Jon.

"Well, sometimes we cross paths on some research projects but most of the time we are doing separate projects. I have been working with Marta for a while on the study of the LSD isomer derivatives that Dr. Haslinger has been studying."

"Wow! Jon and I were just talking about that," Ben said. "I heard Dr. Haslinger's last lecture here. That sounds like some very interesting work. It's hard to imagine how LSD could be used as a benefit to the medical field."

"Well, LSD is a very complex chemical that was first discovered in Switzerland in 1938 by accident. It has definitely had an impact in pharmacology," Lois said.

"Lois, have some of your food, you haven't eaten anything yet," Jon interrupted.

"Sorry, Lois, I didn't intend to keep you from your lunch," Ben said.

"No, that's okay, I like discussing the research. It is kind of fun to think about. It's exciting stuff," she said, digging her fork into her salad.

"Let me tell you, Lois is one of the most dedicated scientists I have ever met. She comes in early, stays late, and is a really hard worker," Marta said. "By the way, she is also an excellent shooter. She's on our ladies' shooting team."

"Shooting? What shooting team?" Ben asked.

"We both belong to the Eastern Women's Rifle Club. We participate in shooting competitions throughout Long Island, and sometimes we compete in other states too."

"That is so great. I haven't shot a gun in many years. Although I do have a few," Ben said.

"What kind of guns do you have, Ben?" Marta asked.

"I have a few shotguns that I use to go hunting with my brother and some friends."

"You'll have to come down to the range and shoot with us. We'll even get Jon to shoot too," Marta said.

"Jon, do you go shooting with Marta?" Ben asked.

"Yeah, Marta takes me out to the range every now and then to go shooting. It is a neat experience. Marta is really professional at it, but I can't get used to those loud noises at the shooting range. It's so crowded on weekends, and they have some very serious rifles out there. Marta, what are those semi-automatic rifles that we see there all the time? You know, the ones that guy Jack shoots?"

Marta replied between bites, "That is an M-16 rifle."

"Those M-16s are really loud and quite intimidating. They're used by the military, and they are really dangerous," Jon said.

Marta patted Jon on the back. "Jon is a good shooter, too. He is just a little scared when he goes to the North Hampton Range."

"Marta and I have shot M-16s a few times at some of our rifle club outings. Some of our members have M-16s, but they're all semi-automatic and not fully automatic like the military uses," Lois said.

Ben changed the subject. "Lois, you were telling us about the LSD isomer derivative that you were working on for Dr. Haslinger. Can you tell us some more about that? I really don't know much about LSD."

Lois put her fork down. "Sure, let me give you a bit of a background about LSD first. LSD is the acronym for the chemical substance Lysergic Acid Diethylamide. In 1938, a chemist named Albert Hoffman working for Sandoz Pharmaceuticals in Switzerland discovered LSD using a derivative of ergot. Ergot is a fungus which grows on wild grass. He used a derivative of ergot and the chemical diethylamide. While working with the mixture a small amount of it got on his skin and he experienced intoxication. Later when he took a bike ride home he experienced the first official LSD trip. Get it? Trip? Ha-ha."

"That must have been a memorable bike ride," Ben chuckled.

"It certainly was. Albert Hoffman realized then that LSD was big and had major potential. Sandoz patented and marketed LSD as Delysid. The "trip"—as we now know it—was then termed a 'psychedelic experience'."

"Do the derivative isomers of LSD that you are working with have intoxicating properties too?" Jon asked.

"Some of the ones that we are working with do indeed have highly intoxicating properties, others have mild intoxicating properties, and some have no intoxicating properties at all. One of the most intriguing isomers of LSD has mildly intoxicating properties. It consists of slightly altered molecules of LSD, and we are getting some very interesting results," Lois said.

"What are your research interests with that particular isomer of LSD?" Ben asked.

Lois took a sip of her coffee and put down her cup. "It's pretty interesting. This isomer is Species ND 0172. It's also called Pegasus. It turns out that Pegasus has very interesting chemical effects on the brain. It's a good candidate for pain research, and maybe even a candidate for migraine headache treatment. We also have several other LSD isomers species that we are researching because they seem to offer some promise."

"I've been collaborating with Lois on some of the research exploring the effects of some of these LSD isomers on baboons," Marta added.

"So," asked Ben, "Does Pegasus cause intoxicating effects in vivo?"

"Yes, but it's a pretty mild effect. It's like having a few glasses of wine, but with a little additional zing," Marta answered.

"Have you used human subjects in your research with Pegasus?" Ben asked.

Laughing, Lois replied, “Definitely Ben, we tested Pegasus on human subjects. I’m glad to report that they all are still alive and well. We’ll be conducting many more studies on humans in the future. In fact, we’ll need volunteers for some of our tests!”

“Ben, if you are interested, why don’t you come when I take Jon on a tour of our facilities?” Marta said. “I can show you the research animals, and some of our work. It will be very interesting to you, I think.”

“I’d like that very much,” Ben said. “I’d love to see the baboons and the Medical Research building in general. What other interesting research animals do you guys have down there?”

“We have many different animals! We even have a monster down there,” Marta said with a smile.

“A monster? What exactly do you have in there? I thought that it was impossible to get monsters anymore since they’ve all been recruited by Hollywood!” Ben said, grinning.

“You haven’t heard of our monster?” Marta asked.

“No, I must have missed the notice!” Ben quipped.

Marta giggled. “We have a special pet that we received a few months ago from the Honolulu Zoo. Her name is Ayu. She is ten feet long, and weighs three hundred pounds, and you do not want her to bite you! She is a Komodo dragon. I guess you did not hear about her yet, but she has been very popular ever since she arrived. There was an article in The Isotope a month ago about Ayu, and the research we are doing with her. Some local newspapers have even come here to take pictures of her.”

“Where did she come from originally?” Ben asked.

“She came from a small island near the island of Flores. It is part of Indonesia. She will remain here for approximately another year, and then she will return to the Honolulu Zoo.”

"What kind of research are you doing with the Komodo dragon?"

"We are very interested in the toxins and the microorganisms that are found in the venom and saliva of the Komodo dragon. They are very unique, and the toxins are powerful. The bite of a Komodo dragon is deadly. We want to explore the chemical properties of the saliva and venom. Since the discovery of Komodo dragons, which was about a hundred years ago, very few people who have been attacked by Komodo dragons have survived. Their bite is usually fatal within forty-eight hours. Even small bites are often fatal."

Ben shook his head and said, "Well, I would love to visit the Medical Research building to see the animals and your research, but I definitely do not want to get too close to the Komodo dragon."

"You don't have to worry, Ben," Lois said. "Ayu is kept in a special cage. She is very isolated and can't hurt anyone. We even use a special device to restrain her when we have to get blood samples from her. It takes five huge guys to restrain her and get her into it. I think that she is getting to like us a little better now. Having our own Komodo dragon to work with here makes it much easier for us to do our research. Previously, we had to obtain our Komodo dragon saliva and venom from other research facilitics. That was time-consuming and costly."

"Does the Honolulu Zoo charge a fee for loaning her to you?" Jon asked.

"Yes, Jon. There is a substantial fee, so technically it is more of a lease than a loan. But on the other hand, remember that the Honolulu Zoo had to pay a lot of money to the Indonesian government to get her, and Komodo dragons are a rare and endangered species," Lois said.

"Well, she must be something special to see," Ben said. "I'm looking forward to our visit."

"Ayu will be on display for the public to see at our science museum on certain weekends. The public loves her, and the kids go crazy over her," Marta said.

"Thanks for the invitation to visit you in Medical Research. I hope we can do that soon. As far as shooting at the Calverton Range—that one I'll have to think about a bit more," Ben said.

"So Ben, I would like to change the subject. Jon and I have a few questions we want to ask you."

"Sure, Marta. About what?"

"Ben, what exactly is the Plutonium Asylum?" Jon said.

"The Plutonium Asylum," said Ben, pausing to think for a few seconds. Grimacing, he repeated, "the Plutonium Asylum." Then he started to laugh, "Oh! The PLUTONIUM ASYLUM! I haven't heard that term in a very long while. Where did you come up with that, Jon?"

Marta handed the old tattered postcard to Jon. "This is a postcard Jon found in the box of items he brought home from Dr. Hilcraft's office yesterday."

Ben stared at the old postcard in Jon's hands. "Can that actually be an old postcard that was sent to me from Emery back in the 1960s? I can't believe it. I completely forgot about that! This is amazing! Let me see that, Jon."

Jon handed the old postcard to Ben, and Ben began to study it. He read aloud the words of his old friend who had disappeared so many years ago: *"Hello, Ben! Having a great time visiting my friend in Czechoslovakia. I'm having an amazing experience here in the Carpathian Mountains. This is a beautiful mystical place full of surprises. I'll tell you all about it when I get back to the Plutonium Asylum. All the best, Emery."*

Ben turned the postcard over and looked at the picture. "Yes, I remember now when I received it back in the 1960s. Emery had made friends with a research physicist who had worked here at Ridgewood for a while. I think his name was Peter Tomek. He was from Czechoslovakia. They played tennis together. They both had bikes here on site, so they often went biking together during lunch or after work. Emery was a very good tennis player and he even won the RNL employee tennis tournament once, back in the seventies. He played doubles with Peter. When they weren't on their bikes they could always be seen at the tennis courts after work or during lunch. I remember one summer back then Peter invited Emery to come and visit Czechoslovakia with him, and Emery went for about a month. When he got back he said that he had had a wonderful time, and that it had changed his philosophy on physics and life. After that, Emery modified some of his ideas. He developed a new way of thinking about the world and the quantum universe. The trip changed him. It was almost like he had a religious experience over there."

"So, what exactly is the Plutonium Asylum?" Jon asked.

"It was the uncomplimentary term that the workers at the graphite reactor used for the place. Since the reactor was a bizarre air-cooled fission reactor, it created quite a bit of spent radioactive material, including some plutonium. So we nicknamed the place the Plutonium Asylum. Everyone that worked there knew the risks of working in an environment where there might be some airborne plutonium. We knew that inhaling any plutonium at all could cause premature death. We kind of laughed about it. I guess it was gallows humor."

"Do you know where in Czechoslovakia this picture was taken?" Jon asked.

Looking at the picture of the strange mountain range with several pinnacle-like formations, Ben said, "Yes. I remember Emery telling me about his trip to the Tatra Mountains in northern Czechoslovakia. It sounded amazing. I remember him talking about spending time in a special area of the Tatra Mountains which the locals revere. They claim that it is an enchanted place which is especially suitable for worship and meditation. Emery seemed to think that there was truly something to their story about it being a mystical place. I don't remember what the place was called, though."

"You knew Dr. Hilcraft for quite a while, Ben. Do you think he changed much from the time you first met him in the sixties to later in your friendship when he disappeared?" asked Jon.

"What do you mean?"

"Well, what I am trying to ask is whether Dr. Hilcraft seemed different during the time just before he disappeared?"

"I think I see where you are going. Yes, he definitely did become a different person, in some ways. I guess he had started to become more isolated and disenchanted. He certainly didn't socialize as much as he had in his earlier days at Ridgewood. He was definitely very unhappy with the change in management and the redirection of the science research here at the Lab," said Ben, glancing around the cafeteria uneasily. "Let's just say he was frequently in conflict with certain people in management."

Marta pulled out a picture from her pocketbook and placed it in front of Ben. Pointing to a woman in the photo, she asked Ben, "Can you tell me who this person is?"

Ben picked up the photo. "This is the photo that I found in my desk drawer and gave to Jon." After studying the photo for a few seconds he continued, "That's Helen Dunne. Emery is to the left of me and Helen is to the right. This photo was taken at Princeton University in the sixties. We were attending a particle physics conference. Emery gave a presentation. Helen was a theoretical physicist who worked with our team of scientists at the graphite reactor, and later at AES with the new accelerator they constructed there. We were all good friends, and shared a lot of excitement about all the new breakthroughs in physics. Helen and Emery were very close friends. I think they were involved in a relationship for quite a while before Emery disappeared."

"Is Helen still working at Ridgewood?" asked Marta.

"No, she had a long career here. She started here in the sixties and retired from Ridgewood about five years ago. We had a really nice retirement party for her."

"Have you heard from her lately, Ben?"

"No, Marta. I haven't heard a thing from her for at least three years. She came back a few years ago for a Ridgewood alumni gathering. She was really enjoying her retirement. She was always a very healthy, active person, and a real intellect. I would not be surprised if she is still involved somehow in theoretical physics."

Making a few notes on her ever-present computer tablet, Marta asked, "How you spell Helen's last name?"

"It's spelled Dunne. D-U-N-N-E. But it's pronounced 'dune'—like a sand dune. I think it's an Irish name. If you ever meet her don't dare make the mistake of mispronouncing her name," he said with a chuckle.

Marta noted the pronunciation, and asked, "And how do you spell the name of Dr. Hilcraft's friend, the Czech physicist?"

"Oh, Peter Tomek. His name is spelled T-O-M-E-K. I don't know what happened to Peter after he left the Lab. He left sometime in the seventies, and we didn't stay in touch. I have no idea where he went with his career. I think Emery did stay in touch with him for a while."

After noting the additional information, Marta picked up the postcard again and looked at the picture of the mountain pinnacles for a long moment. "I would like to find out exactly where this place is. Obviously, it had an inspiring effect on Dr. Hilcraft." She drifted off into a private contemplation, and without taking her eyes off the photo she added, "These mountains are very beautiful. Even through the photo and all these years, I feel there is something special there." She broke out of her meditative state, turned to Lois, and asked, "Do you know anyone here at Ridgewood who is from the Czech or Slovak Republic? We could show them this postcard. Maybe we can find someone who will recognize this location."

"You know, I do know someone who I think is of Czech heritage. She works with the site security police, and plays in the Ridgewood volleyball intramural league. I'd be glad to ask her if she recognizes this place. If not, maybe she'll be able to give us a lead to someone who does!"

"That would be so great! If it's okay with Ben, I'll scan the card and email it to Marta. Marta can forward it to you," Jon said.

Ben nodded his agreement.

"It will be fun to solve this mystery! I feel like we're in a Sherlock Holmes movie!" said Lois, laughing.

"There are some Czech and Slovak people who go to my church. I could also ask them about these unusual pinnacles!" Marta added.

The ring of a cell phone intruded on their conversation. Jon pulled out his phone, excused himself, and walked away from the table. A stickler for good cell phone etiquette, he took the call in an area away from other tables.

"Hi, VG. How's it going at QUEST?"

"There's no emergency. Things are going well, but you may want to be here when we start up the power systems at the Macro-STARR and do the level three power tests. I got another call from Charlie Kenton at HITS. It looks like they are going to run it later tonight, so we want to test out all of our power line magnets and the Macro-STARR particle wave magnacasters before then."

"Okay, VG. Thanks for the call. Ben and I will be heading over soon." Jon walked back to the table. "We need to head over to QUEST now. VG called to tell me that everything is set for a power-up test of the Macro-STARR, and we want to be able to receive protons from HITS if they do get it going later tonight."

Rising, Ben said, "It was really great meeting you both, and learning about your work. It's really fascinating stuff, and I am looking forward to a visit some time!"

"It was very nice meeting you too, Ben!" Marta said.

"Nice meeting you, Ben," added Lois, with a friendly grin. "You really have quite a legacy of work here at Ridgewood, to say nothing of all those remarkable stories you can tell about this place. Be sure to come visit us in the Medical Building soon. We'll give you the grand tour!"

"Definitely, I really want to see Ayu the Komodo dragon. She sounds like a real interesting girl."

"Yes," said Marta, "she is a real character—she thinks she is the boss of the place."

Laughing, Ben said, "Well, a boss that has large venomous teeth is definitely the boss indeed! Okay, you two, take care and good luck with everything!"

"Jon, do you think it's okay if I take Lois down to see the QUEST project after we leave here? Will we disturb anybody there? We don't want to get in the way of your testing," Marta asked.

"Sure, come on over! We'll be a bit involved with our work, but you won't get in our way at all. I think Lois will find the place very fascinating."

"Cool," said Lois, "Marta has told me about QUEST and the Heavy Ion Target Supercollider, and how your research center gets proton beams from the HITS accelerator. It's hard to fathom that we are basically right on top of these huge, powerful contraptions! Is it true that they are nine hundred feet below the surface here?"

"Our QUEST system is nine hundred feet below the surface, but HITS is only down about four hundred feet," Jon said.

"Marvelous! It must have taken a long time to build them."

"Yup. It took about ten years of work, plus a lot of money and maybe even more acrimony!" Jon said.

"Jon, we'd better get going back to QUEST," Ben interrupted.

"Yes," said Marta, "VG will be getting upset with Jon."

"Well, I certainly don't want to get VG angry with me, so let's head back," Jon said, laughing.

"Jon, do you think it will be okay if I bring Lois into QUEST from the HITS line tunnel when we go in?"

"Sure, as long as they don't get the beam line running. But you won't have to worry because it would be closed from entry anyway. I'll give Charlie Kenton, the chief science director of HITS, a call to let him know that you are going through. We have to talk to each other several times a day anyway to coordinate our systems."

"Okay, well enjoy your tour of HITS, and maybe I will see you both later at QUEST."

"Thanks, Jon, very nice meeting you. Oh, and Marta is right. You are both handsome and smart."

"Marta told you that?" asked Jon, slightly flustered.

"Yes, she did."

"Well, I was only telling the truth," said Marta with mock defensiveness.

[12]

The Hades Project

Jon was laughing as he left the cafeteria with Ben. As they headed out of Bowers Hall, Jon said, "I was going to bring up something you and I were discussing yesterday, but I got sidetracked."

"What was that?" Ben asked, as they walked down the sidewalk that separated Bowers Hall and the parking lot. As people passed by, they paused near an appealing grassy area surrounded by large pitch pine trees.

"What went on with the Hades Project, Ben?"

Ben quickly scrutinized the surroundings, visibly agitated.

"Obviously, just mentioning this project has a distressing effect on you. Come on, Ben, what's up with the Hades experiment? What is it about that place that is so bad that it makes you look like you are stuck in the middle of a B-grade horror movie? When you and I were inspecting the reactor with the Environmental Review Committee a few days ago I noticed you dodged the topic of the Hades experiment completely. I could tell then that something about it is peculiar. So, how about coming clean on this? Get it off your chest."

As Jon finished talking, Ben grabbed him by the shoulder and pulled him off the sidewalk. "Let's take a detour, Jon. Let's go somewhere quieter." He led Jon toward the back of Bowers Hall, and into an area where quiet paths leading to a few other buildings were surrounded by large pitch pines and oaks. They walked further into the woods until they were fairly well isolated. Ben looked around carefully in all directions, making sure they were alone. "Jon, this is a very troubling issue. I am reluctant to discuss it with anyone."

"I hear you. Don't worry. I will keep anything you say completely to myself," Jon said, adding instinctively, "Ben, does this have anything to do with Hilcraft's disappearance?"

"I don't know, Jon. Maybe it does, but I really don't know."

Jon placed his hand on Ben's arm. "Go ahead, Ben, tell me what you can about the Hades Project."

"Very well. I will tell you what I know. Back in the sixties, I was an operator trainee along with some others who were working under Emery. We performed various operational procedures on the reactor, such as controlling the energy levels of the research reactor for various experiments. We also monitored the nuclear fission pile rods and associated equipment. Remember, this was the first peacetime reactor in the world. We also performed tests using the ancillary equipment that was connected to the reactor. One of these ancillary experimental systems was later codenamed the Hades Project and was kept from public access. It consisted of a number of specialized pneumatic tubes that went through the reactor core block and came out and then went to Building 720 through a conduit tunnel which is located directly northeast of the reactor. The Hades Project used several pneumatic tubes of varying diameters. Each one was used for carrying particles or materials through the reactor core for maximum radiation exposure. When I first got involved with the Hades Project, perhaps in 1964, there was no major security concern. We were passing the particles or materials through the core and then to Building 720, and I had no idea what the scientists there were doing with the materials that we sent. Then one day in November of '64 a bunch of military men in high command regalia visited the reactor. They met with several of the senior officials here, including Emery. During that meeting I saw Emery get visibly angry with the military personnel. He was different from that day on. Earlier that day, he had toured the reactor with a group of military officials. I believe they went over to Building 720. Emery was completely despondent after that. He seemed to lose interest in the research here, when previously he had been passionate about it."

"Have you ever been to Building 720?" asked Jon.

"I have been over to the first and second floors, but I have never seen the large subsurface complex where the pneumatic tubes which pass through the reactor core traveled. That basement complex was forbidden from most researchers. Only specially assigned personnel were permitted to go into what they called the 'carry Lab'."

"Did Dr. Hilcraft work in the carry Lab area?"

"He didn't officially work there, but as a senior operator at the reactor he worked with the researchers there all the time. It was necessary to coordinate their activities when the samples were inserted into the capsules and then shot pneumatically through the reactor core to the carry Lab. All the instrumental readings, such as the dose and duration of the radiation exposure that the capsule received as it passed through the reactor core, had to be meticulously recorded and documented. The carry Lab would then receive that information on the irradiated materials they were using in their experiments."

"Do you know what exactly they were sending through the reactor core?"

"No, I really don't know. But Emery must have, because whatever they were doing it really pissed him off royally."

"Well, thanks so much for filling me in. I would love to find out what they did at the carry Lab."

"Maybe one day we'll find out what they did there. Who knows, maybe that will give us a hint about what happened to Emery too."

"Yeah. Ben, we'd better get over to QUEST before VG ties me to the induction proton line beam while it is running!"

"That would be inhumane. I wouldn't want to see what you would look like after that megadose of radiation!" Ben said.

They laughed and the mood lightened as they approached Jon's car. Just as they reached the car, a large midnight blue Chevy Tahoe pulled up next to Jon.

"Hmm, it looks like we have company," Jon said.

"It's the site security police," Ben said. "I wonder what they're doing here."

The windows of the security vehicle were darkened, so they could not see inside. There were no emergency lights on the roof, as in most municipal emergency vehicles. Instead, the emergency lights were hidden in the grills. The Tahoe would have been indistinguishable from a civilian vehicle, except for the police emblem embedded on the sides of the doors. Engine running, the driver's-side window retracted, and the officer addressed Jon and Ben, "Hello, gentleman. I hope you had an enjoyable lunch here today."

"Yes indeed, officer. We had a very nutritious lunch today, and we did not have any alcoholic beverages, so you need not worry about a DUI," Jon said.

"Where are you two heading?" the officer asked.

"We're heading over to the QUEST project," Jon said.

"The QUEST project—well, I can definitely say that I have never had any business at the QUEST project, but I have read about it in the papers and heard about it from some of my friends. It seems to be in the news all the time. I'm Officer Donald Lutz and my partner here is Officer Adam Kendrick. We're members of the Ridgewood Lab Police force."

"Well, it's nice of you to stop by and wish us well after that great lunch. My name is Jon Sanborne. I'm a research scientist here. I work on various projects here at RNL, including the QUEST project."

"Yes, sir. I already knew your names and where you both work," Lutz said.

"That's amazing. Maybe you should enter one of those trivia game shows on TV. How on earth would you already know our names, if you don't mind me asking?"

"No problem. I ran identification on your vehicle and it determined that you were the owner."

"Officer Lutz, please tell me why you would run an ID check on my vehicle?"

"Did you realize that your vehicle inspection sticker is expired?"

"Damn! No, I hadn't. Thank you very much, Donald, for letting me know about that inspection date being overdue. I'll take care of it right away."

"No problem, sir."

"Am I in trouble with this now with you?" Jon asked.

"No, sir, not at this time. But take care of that right away. Next time will definitely earn you a ticket."

"Thank you. I'll get on it! By the way, Officer Lutz, you said before that you knew both of our names."

"Yes, your friend is Ben Carson. He works at the AES section, and is now working on a project with you at QUEST."

"So how the hell would you know Ben's name from just running an ID check on my vehicle?"

"We here at Ridgewood Police try to keep well informed as to what is going on here on site," Lutz said, making direct eye contact with Jon and holding it for longer than usual. "Have a good day, sir! And get that car inspection completed!"

Jon got into the car with Ben and they headed onto Tesla Drive, driving back toward QUEST.

* * *

Officer Donald Lutz closed his window as he pulled away from Jon's Prius. As he drove east onto Oppenheimer Road, Lutz glanced at the rearview mirror and said, "How did that go, Dr. Tonner?"

The man in the rear seat responded in a clipped British accent, "Very well, Donald. Very well. I want you to continue to monitor the activities of Dr. Sanborne and Ben Carson when they are on the Ridgewood site. If any of their activities seems suspicious I want to be notified immediately, day or night."

"Yes, sir. You will be notified immediately if we see anything unusual. We will keep a watchful eye on them. No worries. So Dr. Tonner, how was your meeting today at Bowers Hall? It seemed well attended."

"The meeting went rather well, Donald. We got quite a lot accomplished. Thank you for asking."

"Dr. Tonner, we are approaching the Molecular Biology Laboratory. Do you want us to drop you off at your car, or by the entrance?"

"Please let me off by the entrance."

"Here we are, sir," said Lutz, stopping the vehicle.

"Thank you, gentlemen. Remember, keep a sharp eye out day and night, and keep me informed of anything unusual—at any hour."

"You can count on us, sir!"

[13]

The Heavy Ion Target Supercollider

As they drove back to QUEST, Ben asked Jon, "What was that all about with the police?"

"I don't know really. I'm really puzzled. That officer knew both our names and what we do here. I can see him running a background check on my car and getting my name, because my inspection is expired. But how did he know your name? And why?"

"The police do surveillance of all the parking lots at Ridgewood's buildings from time to time. Sometimes they give tickets for infractions, but I have no idea how they got my name either. Maybe they were looking for you, and asked someone who happened to know we were having lunch together here today," said Ben, uneasily.

"That doesn't sound like a very likely scenario," said Jon, as he parked his car. "We'd better get to it. I hope we don't get VG and my staff annoyed that we took a rather long lunch!"

"I don't think VG will be upset."

"Yeah," said Jon, "VG is a pretty laid-back, philosophical Hindu dude—not really the type to get worked up over small things."

"You're lucky to work with people like him. Some of the people at AES are so hyper. They get their noses out of joint way too quickly," Ben said.

"There's no need for that kind of attitude. Life is too short. It should be enjoyed more, and realized more for what it is," Jon said.

"Realized more? What do you mean by that?"

Stopping for a moment to look at Ben directly, Jon paused and said, "That's what we are doing here at QUEST. We are studying the realization of existence. It's just what the hell this whole life thing is—all that we see and experience."

Ben's raised eyebrows and slight frown held unspoken questions, but he said nothing as they entered QUEST.

North of Bowers Hall, Marta and Lois approached the main entrance of the HITS facility.

"Marta, I'm so excited about getting to see this place! I really don't know what to expect. I've read about it in The Isotope and some local papers, but I've never seen it up close."

"Well, you're in for an experience. This place is unreal, and Jon's QUEST project is really extraordinary!" Marta said.

"So," said Lois, "We're going to get to the QUEST facility through the HITS facility? Right?"

"Yes, exactly. There are actually two ways to enter the QUEST facility. The most direct way to get access to QUEST is through the main entrance hall about two miles northeast of here. From the main entrance there are elevators that take workers and visitors down into the facility from the surface. But instead, we are going through the beam service tunnel that carries the proton beam line link from

HITS to QUEST," Marta said.

"I don't want to sound stupid but can you explain what HITS is anyway? I know it is a particle accelerator of some kind, but what is the significance of it? I mean why is it important, or why would anyone want to spend huge amounts of money on a project like this?"

"That's not a stupid question at all. These things are rather esoteric. HITS is the second-largest high-energy particle accelerator in the world. The largest one is CERN, in Switzerland. HITS stands for Heavy Ion Target Supercollider. Essentially, it is a massive machine that takes particles such as lead or gold atoms, accelerates them to almost the speed of light, and then collides them into other particles or substances. Scientists then study what happens when the collisions occur, and what other particles are formed during the collisions.

"Another benefit of HITS is that it is used as a source of accelerated protons for QUEST, which uses accelerated protons for its Macro-STARR device. Macro-STARR is the experimental system that Jon and his team are using to study the fundamentals of quantum physics and particle field theory."

"Wow, I had no idea you were so into this heavy physics theory. I took some physics as a biochemistry major, but how do you know all this stuff, Marta?"

"I first majored in physics at Jagiellonian University in Krakow. Then when my parents moved here I got my master's in physics."

"But you're an MD, a psychiatrist! What made you take your career in such a different direction?"

"I really liked physics, but after my master's program I got interested in medicine and the field of brain and neurotransmitter research—so I applied to medical school. They accepted me, and that is how I found my way to where I am today. I actually work with the QUEST project part time because I am their official Health Physics physician on staff," Marta added.

"What exactly do you have to do as their Health Physics physician?"

"I perform the medical evaluations which are required of all their employees because they all work in a high-radiation environment, use some hazardous chemicals, and work in dangerous high-voltage surroundings. Recently, a worker at QUEST died on the job, so now the director's office wants an improved medical evaluation program for all the workers in HITS, QUEST, and other research projects here at Ridgewood, too."

"What happened to the worker who died?" asked Lois, somewhat subdued.

"The postmortem report was uncertain, but there were apparently some unusual medical issues that are still under investigation. He may have died of an undiagnosed, pre-existing medical condition."

"That's too bad! How old was he?"

"He was young," answered Marta. "Thirty-six-years-old."

"Oh, my gosh, what a tragedy! That's way too young!"

"Yes, it is, Lois. I'm maintaining an extra careful medical watch over the QUEST workers now. I am even requiring them to come to the Medical Research building for complete physicals, including full blood test panels and brain scans."

"How do they feel about that?"

"They are much less reluctant than they were before their colleague died suddenly. Anyway, they really do not have a choice if they want to work at QUEST. If their physicals are not completed they don't get their paychecks."

Marta slowed down as they approached the parking lot. Lois read the sign, "Welcome to the

Ridgewood National Laboratory Heavy Ion Target Supercollider."

"Okay," Marta said, "we have to get you a pass, a personal radiation dosimeter unit, and clearance to go in with me as my assistant."

"Do you think there will be a problem with me getting in?"

"No, I don't think so. I personally know the chief science director of HITS. He and Jon are good friends. They work together all the time, so there should be no problem. And, besides, today you are my assistant on my Health Physics-related visit."

"Yes, yes . . . I am definitely your assistant. At your service, boss!"

They were both laughing as they got out of the car and walked up to the guard booth.

"Good afternoon. We need to visit HITS today," Marta said.

"Sure, I just need your ID badges."

Marta and Lois handed their badges to the guard, who scanned the barcodes and checked the display. He then handed the badges back to them.

"Thank you. You can proceed to the Visitors Center. Have a nice day."

Marta thanked the guard and led the way through the gate onto a sidewalk that led toward the Visitors Center. They approached an oddly jagged, sharply angled, large, four-story building made of glass and steel. The roof of the building angled higher toward the east, and the striking, abstract HITS logo was emblazoned on the building above the entrance.

"Marta, I don't see any evidence of an accelerator here."

"Didn't you know it is all underground? The entire sixteen miles of the accelerator ring is all underground."

Inside, three security guards maintained surveillance over the expansive, angular lobby. Here and there, several people were engaged in conversations.

"We have to get clearance now. We need to show our Ridgewood cards again, plus a second form of ID. Then we get an eye scan verification to get into the complex."

Marta and Lois approached the booth with identification in hand. Marta greeted the receptionist, who was behind a wall of glass, and said, "I am Dr. Marta Padlo, the site Health Physics physician, and this is my assistant, Lois Aldmann. We are here to do some monitoring of the staff at HITS and QUEST."

"Will you require access to the QUEST beam line junction tunnel also?" asked the receptionist.

"Yes, we will go in that way," replied Marta.

Looking up from her screen, the receptionist said, "Dr. Padlo, you have full access clearance here at HITS and QUEST, but Ms. Aldmann you will have to fill out some forms before you can be granted access."

Lois took the forms and thanked the receptionist, who directed her to a nearby desk where she could fill out the requisite paperwork.

Marta hung back and asked, "Would you happen to know if Dr. Kenton is here at HITS today?"

"Yes, actually, I saw him a little earlier. Would you like me to let him know you would like to see him?"

"That would be great. Thank you."

The receptionist entered some information into her computer, looked up and said, "Okay, Dr. Padlo, Dr. Kenton had been notified, so I'm sure he'll track you down when he is available."

Marta thanked the receptionist again, and Lois returned with her completed paperwork. The receptionist entered some information into her computer and directed Marta and Lois to the eye scanner. After running the scans, she asked to see their personal radiation dosimeters, and then directed them to walk through the security detectors.

"Is this a full-body scanner?" Lois asked.

"Yeah, sorry, it's required to gain access."

Lois sighed, "I don't like these things at all, but I'll go through."

A security specialist sitting near the scanner analyzed the scanned images and directed the women forward to the entrance of the secured area of the HITS administration building.

They were greeted by a HITS official. "Hi, Dr. Padlo, Ms. Aldmann, welcome to HITS. I'm Adam Eskola, one of the research scientists here. I'll help you get where you need to go today."

"Hi, Adam. We're here to perform some routine monitoring of the facility. I'm the resident Health Physics physician for QUEST."

"Dr. Padlo, I think I have seen you here at HITS before, is that not so?"

"Yes, I come here infrequently to do some work with the Health Physics inspection staff too. Anyway, Adam, there's no need to stand on ceremony. You can call me Marta, and this is Lois."

"Adam," asked Lois, "I detect a bit of an accent I'm not familiar with. Do you mind if I ask what country you came from originally?"

"No, of course not. I am French."

"Well, you certainly have a unique accent! It's kind of cute," said Lois, with a wink.

"Thank you, Lois. That is so funny. So, what can I help you two with today?"

"Lois is going to be helping me in the future with my health physics monitoring. I wanted to give her a tour of the facility so she will get to understand just what this place is and what to do."

"Sure, we can do that," Adam said.

"We have to go over to QUEST and the Macro-STARR too, so I thought we would head over to the east side of the accelerator section and go over into the QUEST beam line junction tunnel to get over there. I think it would be a good opportunity for Lois to get to know the facilities and where to go in the future if needed."

"Sure, no problem, but I will probably leave you when you get to the QUEST beam line junction tunnel."

"Great," said Marta. "Meanwhile, I'm sure Lois will have some questions for you since this is her first visit to this facility."

"At your service! I'll be glad to answer any of your questions."

"I know that HITS will be operating the accelerator sometime later today or tonight," Marta said. "I hope we won't be interfering with your accelerator schedule."

"No, not at all. We are not scheduled to operate the accelerator for several hours. We have time to take you through a portion of the HITS accelerator and then into the QUEST beam line junction tunnel before HITS is activated. Let's get started. We will start at the entrance into the HITS. We take the elevator down to the HITS ring. Follow me."

Adam led them through a series of hallways, down a flight of stairs, and into another lobby where the elevators were located.

In the elevator, Lois commented, "Marta told me that the HITS accelerator is four hundred feet below the surface."

"That is correct. It is actually four hundred twenty-seven feet below the surface of Long Island. The accelerator is located below the glacial aquifer here."

"How long did it take to build it?" Lois asked.

"It took about fifteen years to fully complete. It was started in 1998. At one time we had about seven hundred full and part time workers here constructing this facility and QUEST, which was completed a little later."

Just then the elevator vibrated oddly.

Concerned, Lois asked, "What was that, Adam?"

"Oh," said Adam, grinning, "that's just the interface where we pass through the glacial aquifer. There is a small anomaly in the elevator shaft that causes vibrations because special reinforcement is needed there to protect the shaft from the interface with the water in the aquifer. Don't worry. It's normal."

"Okay, Adam, I'll trust you on this. Underground, in a small box, may not be one of my favorite places," Lois said with a nervous laugh.

The elevator stopped, and the door opened.

"Right this way, if you please," said Adam, leading them through a short hallway into a room which featured a large door located on the forward wall. More security! We each need to do another eye scan to gain access to the accelerator ring."

"Wow!" Lois said, "I had no idea this facility would have this level of security."

"Yes, it's rated as a nuclear facility, so the level of security is very high," Adam said as he completed his eye scan. He pushed a button on the wall and the huge metal door slid into the wall.

"Why is the door so large?" Lois asked.

"Both for security reasons and for health safety. The accelerator generates a tremendous amount of radiation when it is operating. Exposure would be lethal."

Lois was clearly impressed.

"This is the actual accelerator tunnel," Adam said, as they approached the HITS accelerator tunnel.

Lois was stunned by the huge accelerator tunnel. She looked around in wonder. A tremendous steel pipe, about four feet in diameter, ran through the center of the tunnel. The pipe was mounted on cement and metal stanchions and painted a light royal blue. The blue monster was created of thirty foot-long segments, which were adjoined by metal collar rings. The outer tunnel was constructed of hardened clear-coated cement, and was well-lit by rows of LED lights above the accelerator beam tube. Inside the cement tunnel, to the right of the gigantic blue pipe, ran a roadway for small vehicles, and a monorail which was attached to the curved tunnel wall. Lois slowly explored the tunnel entrance, shaking her head in amazement. "Can this place truly be four hundred feet under Ridgewood National Lab? This is unbelievable."

Marta shared a smile with Adam. "I know. I remember how I felt the first time I saw it. This accelerator is in the shape of an oval. A sixteen-mile long oval."

"You mean," said Lois, "if I walk in that direction for sixteen miles then I will eventually come back to this exact place where we are now?"

"Yes, unless you veered off into the QUEST beam line junction tunnel. That tunnel carries the accelerator particles over to the QUEST facility, which is several miles from here."

"I just can't get over how big this place is!"

Adam interrupted, handing out small, self-contained breathing units. "Marta you know the drill. Lois, we need to carry these whenever we enter the tunnel. I'll show you how it works."

"Why do we need these?" Lois asked.

Marta answered her. "This is very important, Lois. Each of us has to have one of these units because the accelerator is composed of a number of dipole magnets that are super-cooled by liquid helium. If there is a leak of liquid helium while we are in the tunnel we would be asphyxiated by the released helium."

"Asphyxiated, as in dead?" Lois said, shuddering.

"Yes," said Adam, "this is of serious concern. There is the risk that we could be overcome by a helium gas leak. It takes more than one hundred tons of liquid helium to cool the eleven hundred super-cooled dipole magnets sections that make up the accelerator, and if there is a leak you need your breathing apparatus to have any chance of exiting the accelerator ring alive."

Adam demonstrated the use of the units, and showed them how to check the compressed air gauge. They ran through a simulation, and tested their units. He indicated that they could head into the tunnel, but Lois was still examining her device.

"So, Adam, how much time does this unit give you to get out of the beam line tunnel?"

"If you need to use your device you have about twenty minutes to find an emergency exit."

"Has there ever been a leak of helium down here in the accelerator tunnel?"

"Yes, there was one leak. Fortunately, everyone who was working down here got out in time. If you hear the pulsing buzz siren go off that's the emergency signal that a leak has occurred. At that point you must immediately put your emergency breathing device on as quickly as possible."

"I'm so glad to learn all these safety measures," remarked Lois, sounding somewhat less enthusiastic than she had earlier.

"Well, you know Ridgewood Lab takes health and safety concerns very seriously. That's exactly why you two are here today, isn't it?"

"Of course," said Marta. "That is one of the things that we always want to see—a complete health and safety program." She continued, "Lois, there are other health and safety issues we are concerned with that I'll go over with you later, but I want you to first experience this place as an observer."

"I'm really glad to have the opportunity to see this facility," Lois said, "and I'm looking forward to returning to work down here in the future."

"Okay, let's proceed," Adam said. "We'll walk in the HITS tunnel for a while, and then we'll get into the monorail to travel the several miles to the QUEST beam line tunnel junction. At that point, someone else will escort you through to the QUEST facility.

"Lois, while we're walking, I'll give you some background on what occurs in this beam line tube. These four-feet diameter beam tube sections travel the entire sixteen miles of this oval accelerator tunnel. The beam tube is made up of about eleven hundred dipole magnet segments. Each one is about thirty feet long, and each one had to be installed separately. Inside the dipole magnet sections there are actually two separate beam lines each traveling in opposite directions. Each beam line is carrying high-energy particles which travel to one of the four detector facilities at about 99.99 percent of the speed of light. At the detector facilities the beam lines cross into each other so the particles are interacting and colliding. That is what is so important about the physics going on here. When the particle collisions occur at extremely high energies other particles are generated. The detectors study exactly what happens when the new particles are formed. The physicists want to find out what those new particles are and why they were formed. This helps us to get a better understanding of what matter and energy are made of, and what the early universe was like when it was formed."

"When the two beam lines cross how many particles are actually colliding?" Lois asked.

"Actually, there are an amazing number of particle collision events per second. About six hundred million collisions events occur per second, and all the data from the collisions must be recorded and stored in huge supercomputers here at Ridgewood and other national laboratories throughout the world," replied Adam.

"How do you get the particles into the accelerator, and what are the actual particles anyway?"

"Well, the particles actually get into the HITS accelerator from a different smaller accelerator also located at Ridgewood. The AES, or Accelerating Energy Synchrotron, accelerates either protons, or ions of gold or lead, around their smaller accelerator ring. It then injects those particles into the HITS ring where the high-energy dipole magnets take the particles to near the speed of light."

"Is this accelerator completely underground?" asked Lois. "I mean it is so huge that it must be under a large part of Long Island."

"You're right," said Adam, "and most people on the surface have no idea that the accelerator is four hundred and twenty seven feet below them. Some of the accelerator is not really under Long Island. A significant part of it extends out under the Long Island Sound."

"Really—part of this tunnel travels under the Long Island Sound? What a construction project!"

"Yes, about twenty percent of the ring juts out under the Long Island Sound in the Shoreham and Wading River area. The accelerator actually passes almost directly underneath the now-defunct Shoreham Nuclear Power Station."

Lois chuckled, "Well, that is truly ironic. I've taken a look at the old nuke when I was in the area. It looks so freaky, rotting away empty, with weeds sprouting up through the pavement."

"I have never seen it, but we have some physicists here on staff who worked at the facility when it operated for a short time in the 1980s."

"Hang on, you two," Lois said. Adam and Marta stopped and turned to look at Lois. Lois looked intently at Adam and asked, "Do you guys do secret research of any kind here at HITS? I mean, are you trying to develop new types of weapons, or any of that sort of thing?"

Adam laughed. "No, no, everything we do here at HITS is open to the public for review. I will say that we do, however, do some very strange experiments here. Some of them are considered provocative enough to bring news crews here to interview us."

"What sorts of things do you do here that would be considered newsworthy?" Lois asked.

"We're researching some things that sound very strange—more like science-fiction than science! For example, we are looking for the possibility of extra dimensions in matter."

"Wow," said Lois, "that is strange!"

"Yes, it really is. We're also looking for the presence of dark matter and antimatter," Adam added.

"Huh, dark matter? I thought dark matter was confined to the outer reaches of the cosmos," Lois said.

"Actually, dark matter occurs everywhere in the universe, along with dark energy. So we are hoping to one day detect it right here in one of our own experiments. One of the most fascinating things that we are doing is learning how to further explore the Higgs Field that was confirmed at CERN years ago. We already have found it and we are trying to be able to use it in ways for further research."

"Yes," added Marta, "that is exactly what the QUEST project is all about."

"Yeah, that is one of the things the scientists at QUEST are trying to accomplish, along with their other research," said Adam, continuing, "Have you ever seen QUEST before, Lois?"

"No, today will be my first visit."

"Well, if you think that this place is amazing wait 'til you see QUEST. Dr. Sanborne is doing some of the most amazing research in the world there."

"Okay, meanwhile I have more questions for you. When you accelerate the particles of matter in the ring to near the speed of light, why do the particles not hit or interact with the sides of the accelerator tube? What keeps them in the beam line pipes? Why don't they go flying out?" asked Lois.

"I'll answer that by showing you one of the beam line segments that has been removed and is stored at the PIXX Detector, which is about two miles ahead in the tunnel. We'll take the monorail now, and ride over to the PIXX Detector."

They walked ahead a little further and entered a nearby monorail car. Adam closed the door to the car, checked the controls, and said, "Okay, we're on our way to the PIXX Detector, which is located ahead of us in the accelerator ring. This monorail only travels at a maximum speed of twenty-five miles per hour. It's a smooth ride so you should enjoy it. Seat belts on, please!"

"What happens if someone is coming from the other direction? Would we run into them?" asked Lois.

"Nope. That's impossible because the monorails only go in one direction—counterclockwise, and the cars can't back up either. So we're safe!"

The car accelerated slowly to a speed of fifteen miles per hour. Marta sat in one of the two seats directly behind Adam, and asked, "Adam, why did the designers of HITS include a monorail car for traveling the accelerator ring? I know at CERN they use bicycles and little electric carts to get around in the ring."

"We also use electric carts and bicycles, but we use the mini-monorail more often here. I think that the designers of HITS learned from CERN. Having a monorail is a more practical way of moving people around in the accelerator ring. There are also special transportation monorail carriers on the ring line that are built to take the beam line dipole magnet sections to locations where they are needed. Each thirty-foot-long dipole magnet section weighs more than thirty-two tons, so transporting the sections is extremely difficult. It's risky too, because any significant concussion of the magnet section could cause hundreds of thousands of dollars' worth of damage to it."

"How much does each dipole magnet section cost to manufacture?" Lois asked.

"Each section of the magnet costs over a million dollars."

"Oh, wow, big bucks! How much did it cost to build the entire HITS accelerator?"

"Everything, including all four accelerator detectors, but not including QUEST, cost about seven billion dollars total."

"That really is a lot of money," Marta said.

"Unreal," said Lois, "but I guess it's better to spend the taxpayer's money on studying the universe than on killing people in wars around the world."

Adam glanced at Lois and nodded in agreement, "Very true! We are discovering the secrets of the universe." He suddenly found himself noticing how attractive Lois was.

[14]

The PIXX Detector

The monorail car stopped. As they exited the monorail, Adam pointed out the emergency exits. "Here in the accelerator, the emergency exits are spaced every one thousand feet apart. The doors are always open. If there is ever any kind of emergency in the accelerator tunnel get to one of these emergency exits as quickly as possible. As well as the helium leak we discussed, fire is also a possibility. Either one would start at the top of the accelerator ceiling and then travel down. If you hear the alarm, you must immediately pull out your respirators, put them on, and then get down low. Proceed to an emergency exit as quickly as you can. I want to make sure you are clear on all this. There is always the possibility that we could be separated. If the tunnel suddenly filled with smoke it would be easy to become confused and frightened. Remember, there is an exit every thousand feet, so if you stay in contact with the wall and keep moving forward you will come to an exit. Later, I will point out some other hazards in the accelerator beam line tunnel, but if you don't have any questions, let's first do a quick tour of the PIXX Particle Detector."

They walked past several offices lining a hallway until they reached a large glass window that looked into the PIXX experiment control room. The room was filled with LED monitors, computers, and other electronic equipment associated with PIXX, as well as several workers who seemed to be intently focused on their research.

"Those are the first people we have seen since we came down here—more than four hundred feet below the surface of Long Island," Lois said.

"It's a very big place," Marta said, "you will see many people working down here if you stay long enough, and get around a bit."

"If you look over to the left, you will see the controls that are used to make adjustments to the particle detector," Adam said. "The equipment you see is monitoring equipment that the physicists use to observe and control the conditions of their experiments. They can adjust the incoming proton beams and the ion beams that will collide. This is the area where the two particle beams collide. The detector-sensing equipment tracks and records which new particles are formed, and their energy levels. It is kind of like a gigantic camera that focuses on the new particles."

"So is this the heart of the HITS facility?" Lois inquired.

"Oh, no," Adam said. "This is only the control area for the PIXX Detector. The main scientific control room is located on the surface, adjacent to the main administration building. We are about to enter the actual PIXX Detector facility. This is the space where the two particle beam lines actually collide, and where all of the sophisticated electronic detection structures are positioned."

They entered through the open door of the tunnel. The massive metal door was quite impressive.

"What does PIXX stand for?" Lois asked.

"PIXX stands for Particle Identification Xerographic Experiment. The scientists at PIXX are looking for the presence of the quark-gluon plasma. That is a state of matter where quarks and gluons at high temperatures and densities are no longer confined inside hadrons."

"Huh?" said Lois.

Marta explained enthusiastically, "They are recreating the conditions of the first few moments of the creation of the universe! Right after the Big Bang, the instant of the creation of our universe, there was an immense amount of energy formed. At that moment the infant universe was extremely hot and there were no defined particles—no protons, no neutrons, no atoms! The scientists here at HITS use the accelerator to collide protons or metal ions into each other. The collisions create immense heat and energy that replicate the condition of the Big Bang."

"Marta," said Adam, "that was a better description than I could have come up with. We could use someone like you here at PIXX and HITS—especially when we have visitors."

"Sorry, Adam, I already have a full-time position in Medical Research, and part time duties at QUEST, so I am booked. But thanks for the compliment."

Lois and Marta followed Adam into the PIXX unit by passing through a ten-foot containment area consisting of layers of lead and cement that encapsulated the unit.

"Why is such heavy-duty encasement needed here?" Lois asked.

Adam answered her. "There is a fantastic amount of radiation generated by the collisions. If the energy were not well contained, it would be lethal for anyone near PIXX when the particle collisions occur."

"When we were in the HITS accelerator, just outside the PIXX entrance, if the accelerator was in use with the particles traveling around the ring, and we were standing next to the beam line pipe, would we have been affected?"

"We would all be dead."

"Would we be vaporized?"

"No, not vaporized, but just about instantly dead due to the intense radiation."

"So is there any risk to our health from lingering radiation from the accelerator beam pipe now?"

"Good question, but no worries! When the accelerator is not running there is no radiation being generated, and no residual radiation remains. As a precaution, the entire HITS subsurface ring is cleared of any personnel anytime the accelerator is activated. I think we should get going now. The PIXX technicians are making adjustments to the sensing equipment in preparation for the next particle acceleration collision event."

"When will that be?"

"Some time in the next few days."

They walked up a series of metal stairways and onto a ramp that led alongside the tremendous, octagonal metal structure of the PIXX system.

"Wow, this thing is gigantic. How long is it?" asked Lois.

"Yeah, pretty big, isn't it? At one hundred and twenty feet long and sixty feet wide, it's one of the largest superconducting magnets in the entire world. It uses enough energy during its operation to melt eighteen tons of gold instantly."

"Was the detector built here in the tunnel?" Marta asked.

"No, it was constructed of modules which were built separately, lowered down into the tunnel, and then assembled. The PIXX Detector weighs about three thousand tons. It was constructed with more iron than an aircraft carrier."

"That is truly fantastic. I'm amazed at all the planning and design that went into this structure," Lois said.

"Yes," Adam agreed, "it took many years to design. And, remember, all this was built on the work that was done at the other pioneering accelerators around the world. In fact, much of the equipment for the HITS accelerator was constructed in the national labs of several countries around the world. The scientists from CERN, in Europe, and the Fermi Lab, here in the United States, gave us special assistance with the design and equipment for the Heavy Ion Target Supercollider. Their work was pioneering and paved the way for this new design."

"Adam," asked Marta, "has the PIXX Detector found any signs of antimatter or strangelets?"

"The supermagnets create enough magnetic force to isolate antimatter, and theoretically we can also find signs of strangelets. So far, there have been no confirmations of strangelets yet, but we are really close. I know that at QUEST they have been able to generate strangelets with the Macro-STARR."

"Yes, it's very exciting, isn't it?"

"What are strangelets?" inquired Lois.

Adam replied, "Strangelets are hypothetical small pieces of matter that are made of strange quarks—heavier and unstable relatives of the basic quarks that make up stable matter."

"Okay," laughed Lois, "I guess I'll have to research that one, but it's all very interesting anyway."

Marta said, "Don't worry Lois, I'll explain a little more, later—before we see QUEST."

They continued walking alongside the tremendous PIXX Detector, and headed toward the exit back into the HITS beam tunnel.

"How about a bathroom break? The restrooms are here," Adam said, indicating some doors. "I'll meet you in the break room across the hall. We can grab a cup of coffee to fortify us for the rest of the tour."

"Sounds good," said Marta.

A few minutes later, coffee in hand, they occupied a small seating area composed of a sofa and a couple of armchairs. "There are actually several of these break rooms along the HITS accelerator tunnel, and at all the detector locations," Adam said. "If you like, we can go over anything that you want to discuss about what we have seen at HITS today."

Looking around the room, Lois commented, "God, it is so damned quiet here. I don't hear one sound other than the hum of the refrigerator and the drip of the coffeemaker. It's almost scary. I am totally blown away by what I have seen today—this place is just so large and complex. It seems to go on forever. It's just like being in a movie. I was just thinking to myself, before, when we were at the PIXX Detector, 'What does all this mean to me? What is it here for?' Just how would you explain that to someone, Adam?"

Just as Lois finished her question, the quiet of the room was interrupted by the sound of approaching footsteps in the hallway. The cadence of the footsteps was so perfectly symmetrical that it seemed almost inhuman—as if generated by a sound synthesizer rather than a living being.

As the man who generated that perfect beat entered the room, Adam jumped up to greet him.

"Hello, Adam. Hello, Marta," he said, punctuating each name with a nod. "Pleased to meet you. I'm Charles Kenton," he said, holding out his hand to Lois.

"It's so nice to see you!" Marta interjected. "This is my colleague, Lois Aldmann. She's assisting me today."

"Welcome, Lois. It's good to see you too, Marta. I was just speaking with Jon about half an hour ago. He mentioned to me that you would be coming down into the HITS beam line tunnel with a coworker. I also got your message from the administration office."

"Dr. Kenton," asked Adam, "do you have time to have a cup of coffee with us?"

"Sure," said Kenton. He got himself a cup of coffee and joined them. Meanwhile, Marta explained, "Lois, Dr. Charles Kenton is the chief science director of HITS. He is a good friend of Jon's and mine."

"Dr. Kenton," asked Lois, "how did you know where to find us?"

"I called the HITS security unit. They located you here in the break room."

"But how did the security unit know where we were?" asked Lois.

Dr. Kenton replied, "Well, they know where everyone is here in HITS all the time. Surveillance cameras and sensors are located in every section throughout HITS."

"Jon told us that you were going to be starting up the accelerator for a beam line run later today. Is that still on?" asked Marta.

"Yes, we will be operating the beam line in a few hours, so I'll have to get going soon—but we can visit for a little while."

"Lois," asked Kenton, "do you work with Marta in Medical Research?"

"I work with Marta on some projects in Medical Research, and I work on other projects in the Molecular Biology Building. Marta has mentioned these facilities to me several times, and I am eager to come help out here."

Kenton smiled. "Well, what do you think of this place? It's impressive, isn't it?"

"Absolutely, I can't get over the fact that we are more than four hundred feet below ground. And the size of everything is really hard to grasp."

"Most people know that these facilities are far underground as a safety measure. The earth provides a barrier in case of release of radiation. But what a lot of people don't know is that the earth is also needed to provide a shield from incoming cosmic radiation which could affect our experiments."

"Dr. Kenton," said Adam, "just before you came into the room Lois had some questions. Now that you're here I'm off the hook. Her oh-so-easy questions were, 'what does all this mean?' and, 'what is this place for?'"

Kenton smiled and said, "Well, Lois, this place and the QUEST project are each a kind of an observatory in a sense. The difference is that our observatories are not looking into outer space, but what you might call 'inner space'. Instead of examining planets, stars, galaxies and black holes, we are looking into the fabric of matter, space, and time. And although we are looking at the very small, rather than the very large, we are, in a sense, trying to figure out what this universe is made of—from the smallest levels possible in the universe to atoms and how they interact. We also want to know how what goes on at these infinitesimally small levels relates to things in everyday life that we see and touch. What gives objects their color and their feel? Why and how did this universe produce someone like you to ask me these questions? And why and how did it produce someone like me to answer them?"

"Wow, well, what are some of the most interesting things that you are finding, Dr. Kenton?" Lois asked.

"There are so many fascinating research possibilities for us, but some of my favorite areas are the possibility of extra dimensions in the universe, and the search for antimatter during the creation of the universe. We have found evidence for both already, but there's much more work still to be done."

"Adam mentioned something to me about the Higgs Field—that your research here has been looking into that?"

"Yes, our work with the Higgs Field and particle field theory has been very interesting. Dr. Sanborne at QUEST is really working more extensively in that area though with his Macro-STARR."

"What is so interesting about the Higgs Field?"

"The Higgs Field is the key to the mystery of why you and I exist in this universe. You see, the Higgs Field is an invisible field of energy that exists throughout the universe, and is composed of a particle that is called the Higgs Boson particle. Imagine the entire universe as a vast ocean of energy, and that ocean is made of particles of Higgs Bosons. These are very tiny particles, and are very hard to find. They are much smaller than electrons. Now, you and I, these chairs, the Earth and every other thing in this universe have condensed out of this vast ocean of energy. This is because the Higgs Boson particles interact with the vast ocean of energy and cause it to have mass and interact as matter. Did you know that matter is composed mostly of empty space? When you look at anything that looks solid like a mountain or a car or even me—it is actually 99.99999 percent empty space. No matter how solid something seems, this is the nature of matter. It's really hard to grasp, and most people are unaware of this, but most of what we see and experience in this strange universe is an illusion, projected by the hidden energies and particles of the vast ocean of energy—the Higgs Field."

"I've read about something called the 'other worlds theory'—that our universe is not the only one out there, and that there are other possible universes. Is your research related to that? I know it sounds kind of crazy, but it seems related to what you are talking about, doesn't it?"

Glancing at Kenton, Marta said, "Lois, the HITS facility does basic observational physics research. They try to avoid the realm of abstract interpretations."

Kenton noticed Lois's keen interest and answered, "Well, Marta, I think I can shed some light on the concept that Lois is referring to. You're right, Lois, there is a connection. Most people think of the universe as the present state that they experience in their everyday life. But for generations scientists and philosophers have been looking into just what this universe is, and how that is related to our life experience. It has become apparent that the universe we perceive is not the only one that exists. In fact, physicists have found evidence that leads us to postulate that there may be four different types of alternate worlds, parallel worlds, in fact. A recent space probe with very sophisticated instruments for measuring the space in the universe has indicated that our universe is, in fact, infinite in size. The first type of parallel world is one that could exist in an infinite universe like ours. The theory is that, in an infinite universe, another Earth exactly like this one, including you and I, and these chairs, and this sofa, exists somewhere out there in the infinity that is our universe. That type of parallel universe is known as a level one parallel universe."

Kenton continued as he looked down at his cell phone, "The next type of parallel world is classified as level two. It is posited that when our universe was born in the Big Bang, there were many other universes born alongside of our own universe, meaning many simultaneous Big Bangs, not just ours. Kind of like the Fourth of July—each Big Bang creating a parallel universe.

"There are other types of parallel universes possible also. Another type of possible parallel world is based on the concept of superstring theory, the existence of branes, and the existence of other universes attached to these membranes. This is a very abstract possibility. Superstring theory makes a great deal of sense, though it has not been conclusively proven yet. This sort of parallel universe would be classified a level four.

"But perhaps the most interesting of all the possibilities of parallel worlds is what is known as a level three parallel universe. This type of parallel universe derives from the fabric of the micro-universe right here, where the laws of quantum physics rule our present existence. This theory predicates that the space that we occupy is composed of an infinite ocean of copies of ourselves which form infinite parallel worlds. This means that you and I are in a movie playing our world, but there are infinite movies being played, and in each movie we are playing a different role. Reality, Lois, is really more than the one universe you see, but we cannot detect these other possible universes through our ordinary senses. I find the level three parallel universe theory the most intriguing, I must say. This type of parallel world theory was first proposed by Emery Hilcraft and others during the fifties and sixties. It was rejected by the scientific establishment because it was a threat to the status quo, and would have created complete upheaval in the world of theoretical physics."

"I know it sounds kind of out there," Lois said. "It's so strange to think that there is the possibility of another one of me walking around out there somewhere. It's almost impossible to wrap my brain around it. I'll have to give it some more thought tonight, after a few glasses of wine, with a little electronic music to inspire my meditations."

Kenton laughed.

"So, are you doing research into the level three parallel worlds theory?" asked Lois.

"We are not doing direct research into parallel worlds theory at all, but in an indirect way, our research may have something to say about it at some point. If you are going over to QUEST, you will definitely see more specifically related research there. They have an entire facility set up to do research into advanced quantum physics, and one of the things that they are looking into is different quantum states of existence, also known as superpositions."

"Are there practical applications for all this research? I mean, it's really fascinating, but why would anyone fund all this?" Lois asked.

"Good question. Yes, this type of research may be invaluable for the next generation of quantum computers that are currently only theoretically possible. Much of the funding for QUEST has come from very wealthy, major computer companies that are especially interested in that line of research."

They were startled by the sounding of a loud alert signal that persisted for several seconds.

"Don't worry," Kenton said, "you never quite get used to those—but that's a good thing, because it's important to pay full attention to each message."

After the strident tone stopped, the announcement began,

"Attention all staff members inside the Heavy Ion Target Supercollider and QUEST beam line tunnel facilities! All personnel must vacate the accelerator beam tunnels within the hour. Repeat. All personnel must vacate the accelerator beam tunnels within the hour. The accelerator will commence operation within one hundred and twenty minutes. Please prepare to leave the facility immediately. Again, you must leave the accelerator beam line tunnels now. Thank you for your cooperation."

"Okay," Kenton said, "I guess that's our cue."

Marta asked, "Can we still get to QUEST through the HITS tunnel? Do we have enough time to get there?"

"Yes, if you go directly there on the monorail, you should be fine. Just make sure not to take any detours along the way. Adam can escort you through, and then we'll arrange for his pickup later. Is that okay with you, Adam?"

"Sure, Dr. Kenton."

"Good. I'll notify the HITS control room that you are going on the monorail to QUEST."

"So, what would happen if we got stranded in the accelerator tunnel when they are scheduled to operate it?" Lois asked.

"Well, you certainly would not want to be in the tunnel when it's operating! No one could survive that kind of radiation flux. But you will be glad to know that the HITS and QUEST operations management take worker safety very seriously, and they would certainly detect someone in the tunnel, and hold off on scheduled operation until it was all clear. The operations and security offices of the accelerator have surveillance cameras and sensors along the entire sixteen miles of the accelerator ring, and along all of the three miles of the QUEST beam line junction tunnel. The operators would know if anyone was stranded in the tunnel right away. Also, there are emergency exits about every one thousand feet, so you can easily escape through one of those exits too. The operators would not run the accelerator even if you were in one of the emergency exits. On the other hand, it would be extremely embarrassing to be the cause of that kind of delay, so we really never run into a problem!"

Lois laughed. "Yeah, I think I'll avoid that walk of shame! Thanks for the explanation. I feel quite a bit safer!"

Kenton looked at his watch. "On that note, let's get going. Great seeing you, Marta! Please let Jon know I may stop by to see him at QUEST after our proton beam accelerator run. See you later, Adam.

Nice meeting you, Lois!"

"Nice meeting you, too!"

They parted, and Adam led Marta and Lois into the HITS tunnel.

[15]

Down into QUEST

"How is Dr. Kenton going to get back to the HITS control room center? Isn't he going to take the monorail back with us, and continue on to the control room?" Lois asked.

"No, he'll either take one of the electric travel carts back in the opposite direction, or he might grab a bicycle. There are some carts and some bikes stored at the PIXX Detector staging area. A lot of the workers here like the opportunity to exercise. It's kind of amazing to ride a bike through here. You kind of feel like a kid again—riding through a lost world of forgotten tunnels. Anyway, really, don't worry! They won't start up the accelerator until everyone is out—I promise you," Adam said.

They three took their seats in the mini-monorail car, traveling toward the eastern section of the HITS beam line tunnel.

"When we get to the QUEST beam line tunnel junction we'll have to get out and switch to another monorail system that goes over to QUEST," Adam said.

"I haven't had a ride like this since I went to Busch Gardens last year. This is really cool. What a really neat place to work!" Lois said.

Marta smiled in agreement.

Adam nodded, and said, "Yes, it really is, but it's also a bit lonely down here. And of course, it is not without risk."

About fifteen minutes later they reached the QUEST beam line tunnel junction. Adam stopped the monorail car just past the entrance to QUEST. They walked into the junction tunnel and entered another monorail car there. After a short ride, Adam stopped the car.

"Lois," said Adam, "look, this is where the accelerator beam line for HITS splits off into the QUEST beam line tunnel. The operators of HITS have the option to continue to accelerate the particles in the beam pipe around the sixteen miles of loop for HITS, or to transfer the particles off the HITS ring to QUEST. This is how they feed their protons beams to QUEST for their Macro-STARR system."

"How do the magnets know how to divert the particle beams off toward QUEST? It must be a complicated system?"

"It's fascinating. The focusing magnets at the junctions have to be energized very precisely to nudge the protons into the QUEST beam line tunnel. It is all controlled by powerful computers and precise engineering."

"It is fascinating. It took some very smart people build this thing!" Lois said with a laugh.

Marta joined in. "Yeah, Lois, just wait till we get to QUEST. The brain-power is overwhelming!"

Adam checked to make sure Marta and Lois were carrying their emergency breathing units. After a short while, Lois noticed they were traveling downhill. "Why are we descending?" she asked.

Raising his voice over the noise of the monorail, Adam replied, "We have to go down because the QUEST facility is five hundred feet deeper than the HITS accelerator ring. We'll be heading down about nine hundred feet deep into the bedrock."

"Why is QUEST five hundred feet deeper?"

"It has to be at that depth to shield the sensitive electronic equipment from particles from outer space which penetrate the earth. Every second there are trillions of particles from outer space striking the Earth's surface. Some of those particles manage to penetrate the Earth's crust. At a depth of nine hundred feet, there are fewer of these particles to affect the instruments."

"It's kind of scary to be going down this deep underground. I guess you get used to it," Lois said.

"Where are we now, Adam? What part of Long Island is above us?" Marta asked.

"I think about now we're probably under the northeast area of Ridgewood, but I'm just guessing."

After a few moments of silence, Lois noticed that they were no longer traveling downhill. With a sigh of relief, she said, "Finally! We have leveled off! Thank goodness!"

After traveling for a another ten minutes, Adam stopped the monorail car and directed their attention to the maintenance service elevator shaft directly above them. "It's about thirty-five feet in diameter, and goes nine hundred feet straight up to the surface. This is how equipment for QUEST and the beam line tunnel enters the complex. Anything that has to be removed or installed into the complex must be brought into or out of this facility by way of this tunnel. There is really no other way."

"How do they actually get things into or out of this tunnel?"

"It's not easy. There is a huge crane at the surface that is built on a track system. It's all contained within a very large building. They lower things down into the elevator tunnel by way of the crane and cable system. It's tricky because they have to control how much the equipment sways so that it doesn't get damaged by smashing against the wall of the elevator tunnel."

"Once," said Marta, "when I was here, they had a problem with the crane and a piece of equipment was stopped in the tunnel for some time while they repaired the crane."

"They do have problems from time to time, but the crane operators are very savvy. I've seen them solve all sorts of problems," Adam said.

"Has anything ever been dropped from the top into the tunnel?"

"Thankfully, not yet, Lois. Knock on wood!" Adam said, knocking on his head. "Okay, let's continue into QUEST. It may be tempting fate to stand under the service tunnel."

They proceeded east to the entrance of QUEST.

"We're almost there, Lois!" Marta said, turning to look at her friend.

Adam slowed the monorail car down to a crawl as they approached the end of the QUEST beam line tunnel and the access point into the QUEST facility.

They exited the car. Adam walked into a large entrance hallway that led into the facility as Marta and Lois followed. They stopped to read a wall information display dedicated to the QUEST facility.

"Wow," Lois said. "It says here that this facility was built to study the nature of our existence, and that it is the first of its kind in the world!"

"There really is nothing else in the world like the QUEST research facility," Marta said. "This is truly a one-of-a-kind science experiment."

"I have to get back to the HITS facility soon," Adam said, "but you two will have some time here at QUEST on your own. In about an hour you'll have to leave. The facility will be in lockdown and safety mode because they'll be accelerating protons into the Macro-STARR."

They all proceeded further into the QUEST complex.

"I see the beam line pipe has separated and gone in a different direction from us," Lois said.

"Yes," Marta said, "this is where the beam line pipe that is carrying the protons from HITS heads toward the Macro-STARR system which is located further up, deep inside the QUEST complex. We'll see that later when we get to the QUEST research center and main control room."

"Cool," said Lois. "This is a very cool place."

At the lobby of the QUEST complex, the trio again went through the steps of signing forms, showing their identification, and having their dosimeters checked. After the formalities were completed, Lois looked around the lobby with interest. She noticed a very large, brightly colored triangle on the east wall of the lobby, adjacent to the entryway to QUEST.

Lois approached the extraordinary triangle and examined it more closely. Under the word QUEST, which was written above the triangle, were the words spelling out the acronym: Quantum Universe Existential Spectral Time. The words were mind-boggling in and of themselves, but what really captured Lois' attention as she approached the emblem was the image itself. Upon closer inspection, the enormous triangle was much more complex than she had realized from a distance. The larger triangle was composed of many symmetric triangles, which were themselves composed of even more smaller triangles, and so on—a seemingly endless myriad of intricately interwoven, intertwined, and infinitely repeating triangles.

"So," asked Marta, "what do you think?"

Lois took her time responding. "It's amazing. Up close it's hypnotic—mesmerizing. And somehow it feels both very modern and very ancient at the same time. There is even a mystical feel to it, which is not something I would have expected."

"That's a great description. I sometimes think of the logo as a gateway to prepare you for experiencing what is to come when you enter QUEST."

They returned to the desk, where the attendant Alice returned their identification and their dosimeters.

"I'd better head back now," Adam said. "It was a pleasure escorting you through the HITS facility today. I hope you found it interesting and that I answered all your questions to your satisfaction."

"Thanks so much, Adam!" said Marta, as she shook his hand. Holding her hand out, Lois replied, "It was a pleasure to meet you! You were so patient with all my questions, and your answers were very clear and informative. You're a wonderful guide. Thanks again, and I hope that we meet again sometime." They both found themselves grinning at each other as they released their grip.

Marta waited till Adam had walked away, then said, "While you were just busy flirting with Adam, Alice told me Yi Chen is coming to guide us into QUEST. Yi is one of the top scientists here at QUEST. She works with Jon all the time."

Yi Chen arrived shortly, and after a brief exchange of greetings, she led Marta and Lois into the QUEST research facility.

"Yi, this is Lois' first time here," Marta said. "She just saw the HITS accelerator tunnel for the first time. We came by way of the junction tunnel."

"How many people work on the QUEST system here?" Lois asked as Yi steered them past offices.

"Altogether we have about one hundred seventy full and part time employees working in the facility. That includes the physicists who analyze the data in the control room. We also have several professors and grad students who come from all over the world to visit the facility and participate in the experiments here. This project is truly an example of international cooperation. For example, some of the equipment that we use here is manufactured in the national laboratories of other nations."

They continued down the hallway until they reached a large wall of glass.

"This is the control room for QUEST," Yi said. The room was a huge bi-level construction. It was filled with instrumentation and computer monitors of various sizes which were arrayed in all kinds of configurations. Rows of individual workstations were interrupted by larger stations that could accommodate groups of several people. From the observation window, the women could observe a buzz of activity in the two levels. The walls were covered with tremendous flat screen monitors. Abstract, intricate, colorful shifting images filled the screens, like a gigantic modern art installation. The center wall of the complex was occupied by a very large central monitoring display, bordered all around by several smaller monitors.

"I have never have seen so many monitors in one place before," Lois said. "Yi, what are they doing in this room?"

"This is the place where all the data is gathered and analyzed during a Macro-STARR quantum seduction event. A seduction event is what takes place when we receive the accelerated protons from the HITS beam line and the accelerator is energized. The physicists are preparing their instruments right now in preparation for the event, which will take place in about an hour or so."

Marta interrupted, "Oh, I see Jon in there now. Let's go say hello! Do you think that will be okay, Yi? I don't want to disturb him if they are too busy."

"I have to get you both of you out of here in less than one hour because of the experiment, but I think that we can visit for a short while. Let's go in and say hello."

They headed across the room toward Jon, who was apparently involved in an intensely focused conversation with his colleague. As they approached Jon, Yi called out a greeting, "Look Jon, we have some visitors who you may know."

Jon completed his conversation and turned to them. "Hi! How did you make out at the HITS facility today? Is Yi treating you right here at QUEST?"

"Lois is a bit overwhelmed by everything, but I think that she is having a worthwhile experience!" Marta said.

"This place is just astounding," Lois said. "I don't know what I could possibly say to describe these facilities. It kind of reminds me of the movie 'Forbidden Planet'."

"Were the folks at HITS nice to you? I hope they didn't give you a hard time with all their security concerns?"

"Actually, they were really nice to us. I think they were extra helpful because they already know me," Marta said.

"Good, sometimes they can be a bit bureaucratic, and they aren't always so accommodating. They get quite a few visitors. At times, it interferes with their routines. We're all on a rigid schedule, and it can get stressful.

"So, Lois, this is the control center of the QUEST research facility. This is where we look at the data that is generated during an experimental run. We are getting ready for another run in about an hour and we're making last-minute preparations."

"Can I ask what that huge monitoring screen is for?" Lois said.

"That is the main viewing interface for the Macro-STARR-Quantum Superposition Coherence system, which is located further down the hallway from where you just entered this room. I guess you haven't seen it yet, have you?"

"No, I haven't, but I've already heard quite a bit about it. Dr. Kenton met us in the break room near the PIXX Detector, and he was telling us about the theoretical physics related to the Macro-STARR."

Jon looked up and checked the time on the huge clocks that are secured on the front center wall near the master flat screen display. The count-down clock for the next proton beam line run read fifty-five minutes. "If we go quickly I can take you to see the Macro-STARR before the run. We still have a little time."

Jon called out to his staff supervisor, "Tom, I'll be taking my guests into the Macro-STARR for a quick visit, if anything important happens please let me know. I should be back in about twenty minutes."

"Okay, Dr. Sanborne, I'll keep monitoring the systems. If anything comes up, I'll notify you immediately on the intercom. We'll be powering up the focusing electromagnet starters in about fifteen minutes."

"Very good, Tom," said Jon, turning to leave the control room with Lois and Marta.

"Dr. Sanborne, are you going to show them aliens that we captured from another dimension?" Tom called jovially.

Jon turned to Lois and Marta. "Please don't mind Tom. He's a bit of a knucklehead, and probably had a bit too many beers last night with his friends. Let's get going while we still have time!"

Chuckling, Lois said to both Jon and Tom, "I would love to meet some aliens. We could get the History Channel down to interview them!"

They left the control room, and their amusement dissipated, replaced by a more serious mood of awe at the strange majesty of what they were experiencing. They headed left into the large hallway and passed more offices and work areas along the way. "Just a bit more of a walk to get into the Macro-STARR," Jon said.

"Is there a radiation hazard here when the accelerator is operating with the proton beam functioning?" Lois asked.

"Good question, Lois. Luckily, no. The accelerator beam pipe splits off at the beginning of the QUEST facility and travels far enough away from this area to dissipate any radiation hazard. Also, there is lead shielding between the beam pipe and this area to block any radiation hazard that remains. The design engineers of the facility had to do that because any radiation from the HITS beam pipe would have interfered with the sensitive instruments in the control room and the Macro-STARR. Those same special measures that were taken to prevent radiation from interfering with our work also protect us. The quantum universe that we are studying here is exquisitely sensitive to any outside interactions, so we have to be very careful of these potential effects."

They continued forward and the hallway transitioned from a square structure to a cylindrical tunnel. The texture of the walls and ceiling changed, too. Patterned mesh and wire covered the entire surface. The mesh and wire surface was brilliantly burnished and reflective, creating an ambient blue light that was almost neon. As the group neared the entrance to the Macro-STARR, a loud reverberating noise was heard by all. Lois looked up and flinched in an alarmed manner. Jon immediately stopped and held back his friends from entering.

"What the hell was that!" Lois said with a frown on her facc.

"It's Tom, he started up one of the electromagnetic starters. It's nothing serious but when those things activate they make a loud whining sound that dissipates quickly," Jon answered.

"Oh, okay, I guess we're safe then."

"Definitely, now come this way and follow me."

[16]

The Macro-STARR Experience

"Okay, Lois, we're about to enter the Macro-STARR. It's really more awe-inspiring than I could ever describe," Marta said, rather seriously.

"I'm already on overload from everything I've already seen today, but I'm looking forward to this."

The tunnel came to an end. The approach to the Macro-STARR was somewhat darkened, lit only by a brilliant blue radiance emanating from the entryway into the facility.

Lois hesitated when she saw the strange blue brilliance ahead.

Jon motioned them ahead, and intoned, "Take a good look around, Lois. Prepare to be amazed!" Lois entered the Macro-STARR very slowly, walked forward, and looked all around. She turned about gradually, gazing in each direction before turning to the next. She came full circle, and then stopped and looked up. Perplexed, Lois, said, "I can't seem to make out just how big this place is. It is so strange."

Jon and Marta remained silent. Lois' reaction brought back their own memories of the awe they felt the first time they entered this space, and they allowed Lois time and silence to come to terms with her own perceptions. After a few moments, Lois realized that she was gazing upon a space so vast and cavernous that it was almost too enormous to imagine. She stopped struggling to find defining barriers, and began to relax into a sense of wonder.

Marta noticed the shift, and asked, "Tell me, what are your thoughts now. How would you describe what you see?"

"It is just so huge and unfathomable. It's so strange to be in an enclosed space that is so big I can't even tell where it ends. That brilliant, shimmering blue haze that seems to radiate from every direction is unbelievable. It looks like the reflection from the strange mesh and wire wall surface that we saw near the entrance, but it's everywhere. It's beautiful and eerie at the same time. It's all so futuristic, but then those weird metallic angled structures on the floor, ceiling, and walls are reminiscent of ancient geological structures, like stalactites. And those irregular monolithic structures positioned in a geometric pattern remind me of stone circles, or some other mysterious creation of Neolithic peoples. It doesn't make any sense. It's so incongruous and just plain bizarre.

"Jon, what the hell is this place?!" Lois asked, the fear evident on her face. "Is this a military warfare experiment of some kind?"

Jon looked directly at Lois and took her hand. "Lois, this is the Cathedral of the Goddess of Existence. This is the Macro-STARR—the actual facility where we are conducting our research into the fabric of matter and energy, and developing the philosophy of what existence really is. Most people take everything that they see and touch for granted. They never realize that all is not what it seems."

"What on earth do you mean by that?"

"When we measure things, we find out that there is a fundamental problem that crops up when we start to go smaller into the atomic and subatomic scale. This is because everything is composed of particles, and, as physicists know, particles are not just particles they are also waves—waves of potential. What that means is that everything that you think that you see, everything you identify as real and solid, never really existed until that moment when you made an actual measurement of it by looking at it. In actuality, the particles of that item that seemed so solid were spread out all over the place, in constant motion."

"That is so strange, and completely counterintuitive. How can that possibly be?" Lois asked.

"I know that this is very different from what we believe and live by on a day-to-day basis. Even physicists need to believe the floor will be there when they step out of bed in the morning. But perception and reality are not the same thing. Our work in quantum field theory shows us that reality is kind of like a hologram, everything is made up of particles that are both a wave and a particle. What's even stranger is that it is proven that particles can be in more than one place at the same time. So, since we are made up of particles, that implies that *we* can be in more than one place at the same time. Picture this, you and I and Marta, and this Macro-STARR facility, are now in a holographic movie that is playing right here and now. But, at the same time, this movie is only one of infinite holographic movies playing all at the same time, and all in the same place. This is referred to as the many worlds theory in physics. Each holographic movie that we are in is a bit different from all the others. Sometimes, the differences are slight, and sometimes they are profound."

"Wow. I've read about the many worlds theory, and Dr. Kenton was just telling me more about it a little while ago. It seemed so philosophical, almost like a metaphysical reflection, but here in this space I'm astounded by the idea that you are actually doing this research. It's not just an idle pipe dream about abstract ideas."

"What is most amazing to me is that without a conscience observer there would only be an expanding superposition of possibilities in the quantum hologram. There would be no observations, and no reality," Marta said. "It is our minds that put all this flux of energy, particles and waves together into a world that we can understand and be part of."

"Of course, Marta, you are giving us a psychological interpretation of the quantum universe, but don't forget that our minds are also part of this imaginary solid world of particles; therefore, we are intimately connected to this strange realm," Jon said.

"So, just how does this Macro-STARR system work? How do you use it, and what kinds of things are you discovering?" Lois asked.

"We're using this amazing system to examine some of the other quantum states of reality. In terms of the analogy of our existence as one of many quantum holographic movies—we are using the Macro-STARR to take a look into another one of the infinite concurring holographic movies. The one we are exploring right now is, well, it's kind of, metaphorically, 'right next to ours'—so if the conditions are exactly right the Macro-STARR device can get the state of the waves and particles into precisely the proper phase or alignment, and we can make observations into that quantum holographic movie."

"That is truly incredible. I mean it literally stretches the boundaries of what is believable. What kind of mind could have thought up something as complex as this—and what kind of minds could figure out what the mechanics of actually making something like this work?" Lois said, shaking her head slightly.

"Several physicists were thinking about this sort of possibility. One of them was Emery Hilcraft. He worked here at Ridgewood many years ago. Ben Carson was actually his colleague, and they were close friends years ago."

"Ben—who we met at lunch—was friends with Emery Hilcraft? That's the guy we were talking about who disappeared years ago, right?"

"That's correct, Lois. They were buddies. I wonder if we will ever find out what happened to Hilcraft and why. His insight and his scientific innovations in quantum physics were the foundation for this Macro-STARR device. I wonder what he would think if he could see this all now."

"Jon, why are the ceiling and walls of the Macro-STARR Chamber all glowing with this strange blue iridescent light?"

"The entire surface of the Macro-STARR cathedral interior is coated with superconductive material containing vast amounts of silver. There are also special semiconductor materials used in the mesh coating that radiate blue when the Macro-STARR is activated. These materials are known as meta-materials. They were only recently created by the Q-Wave Computer Company. They were created specifically for this system, and they are very expensive."

"Why is silver used?"

"It turns out silver is a miracle metal. It is the most electrically conductive, the most thermally conductive, and the most reflective metal in existence. Without silver this facility could never have been constructed. The way the Macro-STARR facility works is that we generate an ultra-powerful magnetic field with a feed of certain types of subatomic particles in an exact proportion. With some special quantum tweaking of the Higgs Field, which is then saturated, we are able to *seduce* one of the other holographic quantum states. That special quantum state also happens to be our co-location state, or our *superposition*, which is called a *torqka*. That's a kind of simplified explanation of something very complex, but it gives you the general idea."

"I keep wondering when I'm going to wake up. This is science-fiction stuff come true."

"That's a good way to put it, Lois. Even Einstein would have been astounded by this type of science, but he never liked quantum field theory anyway. He always said that God does not roll the dice."

"Jon," said Marta, "don't you think you are rolling dice with this complex equipment? Let's hope you don't roll snake eyes."

"Marta, everything in existence is probability, and the conditions created by the Macro-STARR have a very high probability of accretion, so I'm not too worried about any problems. Over a year of testing has not turned up any anomalies."

"I just worry that with all the energy and complexity of the systems someone will get injured or worse. Garrett Hansen's death weighs on my mind. I wish we knew more about what actually caused his death."

"Don't worry so much, Marta. I have full confidence in the equipment and our staff. I really believe we have thought of every possibility, and prepared for every contingency. We have plans and backup plans. And I am positive that what happened to Garrett had nothing to do with QUEST."

"I wish I were as confident as you are. You know I worry about you," Marta said. Her eyes swelled lightly and her face lined a sorrowful frown. Jon felt her tender-hearted look and gazed back warmly at her.

A loud resonant tone echoed through the vast complex, calling attention to the announcement that followed, "Attention, all staff now present in the HITS and the Macro-STARR facilities, we are now thirty minutes from a proton beam line activation of the Macro-STARR. All personnel must leave the area immediately. Please go to your designated work or safety areas now. A personnel safety audit will begin momentarily. I repeat; please leave the Macro-STARR area now and go to your designated work or safety areas immediately."

"Okay, that's our cue. We'd better head back now. You guys will have to leave QUEST."

Just before they headed into the exit tunnel Lois stopped to take a final look at the cathedral-like structure. With reverence in her voice, she commented, "Damn, this place is amazing and beautiful. I will remember this moment forever. Before I leave here today, I just want to say this is one of the most amazing experiences I have ever had in my entire life, and I want to thank you for that. Not many people ever get the chance to experience anything like this. You could sell tickets to people for this experience. Thank you both so much."

As they exited, Marta said, "Well Lois, you are now my assistant health physicist. I'm certain we'll need your help down here in the future."

"I would be so thrilled if you can get that cleared with my unit supervisor."

"Don't worry, Lois, I can pull some strings. I'll clear it with Dr. Kenyatta," Jon said.

"Perfect! I'll be honored to be a part of the QUEST team!"

Marta put her hand on Jon's arm. "Jon, before I forget, I need to have all of your QUEST employees visit my office over the next few days for their quarterly employee medical evaluations. We will also be doing neurometric testing on everyone, so they should fill out their questionnaires before they come in. I know you have a lot on your mind right now, so I'll send you an email when I get back to the Lab."

"Really, already? It seems like we just did those tests a few weeks ago?"

"Time flies. It has been almost three months. You know how strict the administration is about employee medical evaluations, so make sure you send them down to the Lab, or you'll be in hot water—especially after what happened to Garrett."

"Okay, Marta, they'll all be down in the next few days." Jon took his leave in the hallway near the control room hall window. "This was fun, but I'd better get in there. Just go back to the main lobby, take the elevator to the top, and head out. You know the way, Marta."

"How late will you be here tonight, Jon?" Marta asked.

"I don't know exactly, but probably most of the night, and possibly into the early-morning hours. When these proton beam line runs are generated by the HITS facility we have to be ready to accept them so that we can do our experiments. We can only operate the Macro-STARR when they send us protons for our Higgs Field saturation. So we are really dependent on what they do."

"Yes, I know. Well, maybe I will see you late tonight or tomorrow sometime at your place." Grasping his hand, and looking into his blue eyes with great concern, she said, "I want you to be careful."

"Everything will be fine, Marta! I'll see you tomorrow. Maybe I'll make that clam casino on the grill tomorrow night."

"I can't wait. I'm already looking forward to it," she said, releasing his hand.

As Marta walked back toward the main lobby with Lois, she glanced back at Jon. It was clear that she was still worried about the potential dangers of working with such experimental equipment and high energies.

[17]

The Torqkadrone Launch

Jon entered the main control room for QUEST, and quietly observed the room full of scientists preparing for the proton beam line run, and the activation of the Macro-STARR system. He spotted Ben and VG among the more than twenty-five highly focused scientists who were all busy at their various workstations and system controls. Ben and VG were holding coffee cups, and discussing something, while looking up at the main viewing interface for the Macro-STARR.

Jon approached them. "Hey guys, how did things go today with the focusing magnets?"

"It all went very well," VG said. "Everything is working optimally so far. Ben and I did some resistance testing on the Macro-STARR dipole magnets. They all showed super-conductivity. We measured the magnetic field to be between 120 to 130 microteslas."

"It amazes me that we can generate a magnetic field greater than that of the earth's geomagnetic field itself," Jon said.

"I know. The invention of those tetragonal linear neodymium magnets has changed everything. That and four hundred gigavolts of electricity! The confluence of recent inventions that have made the Macro-STARR possible is a miracle in and of itself," VG said.

"Yeah," Ben said, "without quantum computers none of this would be possible."

"We really are fortunate to be in a time and place where all these factors have come together. Without the quantum computers to control and interact with the dipole magnets, magnacasters and Higgs Field sensors, the system could not work. Okay, let's concentrate now, we only have about twenty minutes until the beam line run and we should expect some issues to crop up! VG, what is the status of the Torqkadrone? Is it all tested and prepped for the quantum coherence seduction?"

"Yes, Jon, Yi Chin is in the Torqkadrone assembly room right now. She and her staff have been preparing it for the journey into the Macro-STARR. It should be all set."

"Let's take a last look at it now, and while we're at it, let's check the display readout data," Jon said.

"Tom, please activate the Torqkadrone monitor, and display it on the big screen," VG said.

"The Torqkadrone monitor is activated, and the sensors are displayed," said Tom, after rapidly entering the commands into his terminal.

Jon, VG, and Ben looked up at the Torqkadrone. Yi and several physicists were busy preparing the device for the upcoming experiment. They were all covered head-to-toe in white, nylon, lint-free, clean-room clothing to avoid contamination of the Torqkadrone's sensitive electronic systems.

"Look at that thing! Damn, it is amazing! Who would ever have thought that we could one day look into another quantum state of existence parallel to our own?" Ben said.

VG nodded in agreement. "The Torqkadrone is a true beauty. We owe thanks to the good people at Q-Wave for their help in creating it."

"Yeah, their technical assistance in developing the integrated quantum computer, and the special detection instruments, was really invaluable," Jon said. "Dr. Kenyatta and I have been invited to have dinner with the inventor and president of Q-Wave Computers soon. He may even tour the facility."

"I still don't understand everything about it. Could you give me another primer on it, Jon? If you don't mind," Ben said.

"No problem. The physics of what is happening here is this: all the matter and energy in our universe, or our quantum state, is not only in our present perceived reality. It simultaneously exists in infinite parallel states. Some theoretical physicists, including your friend, Dr. Hilcraft, had a brilliant insight concerning this multiverse concept. They utilized complex mathematics and theorized that one of the parallel sites of our present quantum state had a very high probability of existing simultaneous to ours. It is not the only other superposition quantum state of course. There are actually infinite other possible parallel quantum states. Each has a version of you and me in it, and all of them are similar to, but different from, our present quantum state. Dr. Hilcraft coined the term *torqka* for the co-location state that is the most probable superposition of our own quantum state. This works the same way as the electron quanta in the atom. Electrons can actually be found at any time, and at any location, around the atom, but there is a higher probability that the electrons will be found at the atomic orbital locations.

That is eerily similar to the torqka state of our present quantum reality. Do you see the similarity between the atomic orbital locations, the quantum many worlds, and the torqka?"

"Think, Ben! I'll give you a hint," VG said. "Think of a tree with repeating patterns in the branches and leaves. Think of the repeating and reiterating patterns in seashells, and even in vegetables. Picture a cauliflower. Are you starting to see the similarities, Ben? The self-similar patterns repeating in infinite regress?"

"You mean a fractal recursion," said Ben. "Is that what this is?"

"Correct, Ben! You nailed it! This is another example of Mother Nature displaying herself in a most elegant, efficient, and exquisitely beautiful flower of recursion."

"So how does the Torqkadrone function, then?" asked Ben.

"I guess you could basically compare it to a kind of satellite which we place into the Macro-STARR system of QUEST while we are receiving a stream of protons delivered from HITS. When the Higgs Field there becomes *saturated* from the protons and the magnetic forces, we achieve a quantum coherence seduction of one of the infinite quantum parallel states. By definition, that state is most likely to be the torqka."

"But that is not the only possible quantum state that could be achieved?" Ben asked.

"Right," Jon said. "That's definitely true, but the torqka is the most likely of the infinite possibilities. Anyway, whichever quantum state we achieve, the Torqkadrone will record data during its quantum excursion, and we analyze and process the data here in our control room."

"How many Macro-STARR quantum seductions have you achieved so far?"

"We've done fifteen different seductions so far, and each one has provided very interesting data."

"Do you always use the Torqkadrone during a quantum seduction, and do you ever put anything else into the Macro-STARR during these seduction events?" Ben asked.

"Yes, we have experimented with sending other items into the Macro-STARR during the quantum seduction event."

"Wow, what kind of data do you get, Jon? I mean can you detect anything interesting about what it is like in another quantum state of reality?"

"I'll show you some of our data after this next test. It really is stunning."

"Okay, everyone!" Tom McGuiness' voice boomed over the PA system. "We are only five minutes from counting down for the activation of the Macro-STARR. All systems have been optimized, and set into automatic mode."

Looking up at the main viewing monitor, they saw Yi give a big thumbs-up, indicating that she and her team had completed their preparation of the Torqkadrone. "Torqkadrone preparation completed. Activating insertion into the Macro-STARR," she announced.

As the control room staff watched in admiration, the highly polished, silver-gray ovoid Torqkadrone slid into the Macro-STARR by way of a specially constructed robotic track. Jon and his team of scientists now focused their attention on various monitoring equipment, but most especially on the main viewing monitor, which displayed the Torqkadrone located in its resting cradle in the Macro-STARR.

Composed entirely of a metal alloy containing titanium, silver, and molybdenum, the Torqkadrone was twelve feet long, seven feet wide at its midpoint, and five and a half feet high. Several small, evenly-spaced, black rectangles covered the upper surface area of the Torqkadrone, and at the top there was a slightly askew, small, jagged metallic structure which gave the impression of a crown.

The countdown clock displayed two minutes until quantum seduction, and the control room buzzed with system readout checks from the expert staff. "Aaron, what is the telemetry function status of the Torqkadrone?" Tom McGuiness yelled out.

Aaron, the control room science technician, responded immediately, "Function indicators show all sensor readings within scheme guidelines. Everything is within parameters, sir!"

At that point, another technician called out, "We have a sequence 912 indication in the Macro-STARR. I am breaking it down now. I'll let you know when it is fully analyzed!"

Yi Chen, who had entered the control room a moment earlier, stood with Tom, watching the main viewing monitor. The Macro-STARR chamber became brighter and brighter. The intense light shifted between shades of blue, indigo, and purple, and continued to oscillate in frequency. Both sound and kinetic vibrations filled the control room. Tom calmed the staff, "Settle down everyone! This is normal resonance during the magnacasters induction. It will demodulate in time."

"What is the status of the 912 indication in the Macro-STARR?" Tom shouted.

One of the technicians shouted back, "912 analyses noted instability. There's a decoherence problem within the Q6-computer and the Higgs Field sensors. The backup Q6–2-computer was automatically activated parallel and has worked through the dephrasing time."

Puzzled, Jon glanced at Tom and Yi, who said, "He is telling us that everything is okay now." She smiled, looked up at the main monitoring screen, and said, "Oh, my God! The protons from HITS are streaming now at twenty million per second!"

"Okay, people! This is it! We are now eleven seconds from quantum seduction. Brace yourselves!" Tom called out.

Every single person in the control room responded by focusing on the main monitor. A sparkling, iridescent blue plasma-haze enveloped the Macro-STARR cathedral. The vibrations in the room steadily increased in a whining wave of sound which reverberated and modulated strangely. People grabbed on to various fixtures in anticipation of the force of the upcoming energy release.

Tom called out, "Here we go-five–four–three–two–one!"

As they witnessed the Torqkadrone in the surreal Macro-STARR chamber, the collective sense of awe at the realization of the nature of the event unfolding before their eyes was palpable.

"What the hell is happening?" asked Ben, as a severe jolt shook the room.

The reverberations were felt elsewhere, too. Staffers in the offices located near the QUEST entry lobby, and scientists working at HITS felt the jolt and the ensuing tremors. The phones in the Ridgewood Site Security Police Force office began to ring with callers reporting the event and wanting information.

In the control room, Jon and his team of scientists watched the main viewing monitor closely. The Torqkadrone was now completely enveloped by a pulsating, shimmering, blue shroud of energy-plasma which obscured it slightly from view. The energy-plasma emanated from the huge geometric metallic monoliths and antennae struts which were located on the ground and ceiling of the Macro-STARR. Held by those oddly earth-like structures, the magnacasters directed a tremendous mix of magnetic forces and subatomic particles at the Torqkadrone device.

After about ten minutes, Jon announced forcefully, "The energy flux in the Macro-STARR is now reaching a critical stage. Be on standby to react to any irregularities immediately!"

At that moment, a sudden burst of energy-plasma was discharged from the Macro-STARR–Torqkadrone matrix, radiating in every direction at the speed of light. Immediately, all movement stopped, as each person in the control room froze, stunned by the intensity of the quantum seduction event.

The spell was broken as suddenly as it had begun, and Jon and the others re-entered their common, perceived world. They seemed to share a sense of significance. Something unique had happened to them a few seconds before.

"Have we detected any phase space yet?" asked Jon.

"No, Dr. Sanborne, not yet, but reactive sensors in the Macro-STARR are showing the presence of a density matrix," Tom answered briskly.

"Well, that's a good sign that we are probably close to a phase space," Yi said.

VG checked his instruments. "I am noting some quantum superposition phase angle integration between the wave functions. This is a very good indication!"

"Excellent!" said Jon, in high spirits. A similar, happy, hopeful, expectant mood was reflected on faces all around the control room.

"Everyone, look at the Torqkadrone!" Yi cried out.

The Torqkadrone was becoming more difficult to make out. The blue plasma shroud had become denser, small lightning bolts flashed through the plasma, and the Torqkadrone itself began to look sort of pixilated and evolving, morphing and transforming.

"I am activating the audio feed of the Torqkadrone sensors, so we can get more data of the evolving wave function coherence," VG said. Sound, generated by the particle flux energies emanating from the blue plasma shroud, filled the room.

"It sounds like a flowing stream of air or water," Ben said. "White noise, full of both some high and low tones. It is surprisingly pleasing to the ear."

"Yes, Ben," VG said. "We call it the melody of the quantum realm."

"It's enchanting, and somehow both invigorating and relaxing. I feel like I've heard this same sound somewhere previously," Ben said. He stared at the image of the Torqkadrone, surrounded completely in a blue haze of energy and plasma, and drifted into a state of relaxed focus. He traveled through memories of his childhood, and pleasant experiences at various junctures in his life. He noticed something subtle and unidentifiable interacting with his coherent conscience reality. He was watching himself walking outdoors in a beautiful mountainous area. His reverie was suddenly shattered by intense pain in his hands. Ben looked at his hands in anguish, and then looked back at the image of the Torqkadrone in its blue plasma cloud. Immediately, he reconnected with the real world again. Now, strangely, as he viewed the Torqkadrone surrounded by the intense blue plasma energy matrix, and heard the sound of the music of the Torqkadrone, he felt no discomfort at all. "What a strange daydream. I guess I am more tired than I thought!" he thought to himself.

Ben said, "I see it, but I don't believe it. What is happening, Jon?"

Watching the distorted image of the Torqkadrone through the intense blue plasma shroud, Jon answered, "Ben, you are witnessing a macroscopic deresolution. The Torqkadrone is starting to enter a phase space or quantum seduction into one of the infinite parallel hologram worlds. We're expecting the torqka state, which is the most probable parallel reality, but we can't be sure that is the one we'll encounter, this is all new science we are discovering here—so expect the unexpected."

"How long does the process take? I mean, for how long will the high-energy flux from the HITS protons flow into the Macro-STARR? At what point does the quantum seduction event complete, and how long does it last?"

"Well, Ben, it's really more of a process than an event. It usually takes several hours for the energy patterns of our present quantum state to become a coherent wave function, and for the energy patterns of the co-location torqka quantum state to interact and align into a coherent quantum ensemble. It is also always possible that this will not happen effectively, and then we won't be able to achieve our goal of a quantum seduction. It's always a nail-biter, but so far, after several experimental events, we have not had any failures."

[18]

Twenty Million per Second

An hour later, things were still proceeding smoothly. Jon sat at his desk in the control room, reviewing the Macro-STARR sensor data. Yi Chin approached. "Jon, so far all of our system checks of the Macro-STARR and the Torqkadrone are virtually perfect, and we are detecting some phase space tunneling. It's currently in a very stable interactive state, our sensors are operating well, and the data quality of the quantum seduction is rather good. I don't see us having any additional problems. It should be just a matter of time now for the quantum ensemble interactions to fully equilibrate and complete."

"Very good, Yi! You and your staff have once again done a great job preparing the Macro-STARR and the Torqkadrone for this latest excursion. I want to go up to the mid-level station room for a while to discuss a few things with Ben, where it's a little quieter. Can you and VG handle things here if we leave now?"

"Sure, Jon. You could use a little break from this place. You guys have had so much going on lately between Dr. Kenyatta and the Environmental Review Committee."

"Great," said Jon. "If any transients or anomalies appear please notify me immediately. I really want this experiment to go well."

Jon called Charlie Kenton as Yi walked away. "Hello, Charlie! Thanks for the proton stream! How are things going at HITS?"

"Hi, Jon. Good to hear from you guys down there. How is your experiment going?"

"Great, Charlie! The proton flux from your HITS accelerator is meeting our goals. Very well done on your part! Please thank your team for us!"

"We plan to operate the accelerator for another nine hours. So far we are having no internal issues, so I anticipate the experiment will go as planned. We did feel some shock vibrations. I assume that was from the Macro-STARR activation, but it didn't cause any structural problem with our systems," Kenton said.

"Yeah, it's a good thing that the ground motion which usually occurs with the initiation of the Higgs Field saturation doesn't last too long."

"Yeah, the HITS accelerator is built to absorb ground motion of that magnitude—no problem here whatsoever. As far as your experiment, how long is it going to run? I'm very interested in seeing some of the data, Jon. Everyone here is very interested in what you are doing. Everyone wants to be a part of such cutting edge, breakthrough science! You know, Jon, there are all kinds of rumors flying around about the project because of the mystery and secrecy surrounding it."

"Why don't you come down here in a week or so? I'll be glad to show you some of our data once it's analyzed and interpolated on the Q-Wave Q6-

supercomputer. It is all pretty amazing stuff, although I must say, there definitely is some mystery to it—even to us!"

"Twenty years ago no theoretical physicist could have even imagined that modern physics would have come up with an experiment that could take a look into what the quantum world was hiding from us. It almost seems like we are in some way playing a game of chess with the gods, doesn't it, Jon? I just hope that the gods don't checkmate us in some unexpected way! There may be some things that we are not able to comprehend yet—in the physics of the quantum realm. You know, Jon, the quantum world does not like to share its secrets, or be observed in any way."

Jon gave a little laugh. "Well, Charlie, I've never thought of it that way. But if you want to use the analogy of playing chess with the gods, then we are sure to win in at least one of the infinite parallel quantum states."

"Yes, but you realize that implies that you will also lose the game in at least one of those alternate realities."

Jon shook his head, as if trying to dislodge the momentary doubt brought on by Charlie's speculations.

"Oh, I forgot. I wanted to give you a heads-up. There was a HITS staff meeting yesterday. Dr. Tonner was there, and he was asking all kinds of questions about our arrangement with QUEST. He doesn't seem to consider QUEST to be a worthy scientific endeavor. He even implied that it is a possible waste of funding."

"He's such an idiot—I wish the administration would get rid of him."

"Don't worry, Jon. I've got your back. I gave Tonner an earful about how the QUEST project is the new frontier of scientific investigation and learning about how the universe works. And you are right,

Jon. Dr. Tonner is an idiot, but he is powerful, and he is not on your side, so be careful with him and the administration. He seems to have it out for you. I've got to go, but let's get together soon and grab a few beers somewhere."

"Sounds great, Charlie. Let's do that soon. Maybe after the data from today's experiment is processed in the next week or so you can come down. We can have a few beers at the mid-level station here at QUEST, and play some good ping-pong. Hell, maybe we'll even go over the data from the latest quantum seduction experiment."

"Sounds good, if you can handle being beaten in the next game of pong," Charlie said.

"Well, you can try, but you haven't done too well in the past. You know that I'm the official champ of the mid-level station," Jon said. His smile could be heard in his voice as he proudly boasted with mock seriousness, "And don't forget, I am the beer cup champion."

"Yeah, yeah. I'll give you a call in a week or so, and we'll do the beer and ping-pong thing. Take care, Jon. Good luck with the experiment!"

* * *

In the Macro-STARR control room, the main monitor viewing screen displayed the Torqkadrone, still enveloped by ever-changing blue plasma. Yi took note of an indicator light that lit up on the control systems console.

"Tom, can you please activate the side B monitor? Display the rate of change values of the cryogenic distribution grid profile of the supermagnets in the magnacasters."

"Sure, Yi! Just give me a few seconds."

Within seconds the B monitor was activated. Tom and Yi examined the cryogenic temperature values of the magnacasters alongside a graphic display of the thermal range distribution of each supermagnet section. "Well, we have a slight issue with the section 104 supermagnet," she said. "The octant subsection is noting temperature range values of minus 271 degrees Celsius to minus 256 degrees Celsius."

VG joined them. "What is the issue here?"

"We have an out-of-range data reading on the number 104 unit supermagnet, sub-octant section of the Z37 magnacasters," Yi said. "Specifically, it is showing an out-of-range value on the high side."

"Yes," VG said, "I see the values are about 7 degrees Celsius on the high side. I think we can rectify that by adjusting the liquid helium feed attenuators. I'll see if I can reconfigure those attenuators right now."

"Okay, VG, give it a try, and I'll keep checking the temperature distribution range on Z37 while you are making the adjustments," Yi said.

Yi and Tom spent the next several minutes focused on intensely monitoring the temperature distribution range. Yi began to feel tired, but she continued to observe the B monitor displaying the cryogenic distribution grid profile data, as well as the main control room monitor showing the Torqkadrone in its blue plasma energy flux. Yi's thoughts about the latest temperature issue were interrupted by a shift in the sounds streaming in from the audio feed of the Torqkadrone sensors. At first, she ignored it, writing it off as a change in her awareness, but as time passed she became convinced that the shift was real. Her attention rapidly refocused on the sound coming from the Torqkadrone audio sensor feed. She stared at the Torqkadrone image on the main monitor and became mesmerized by the beautiful, surreal view of the Torqkadrone, and the enchanting sound of the audio feed. She closed her eyes for several seconds and drifted into a meditative state. In that state of peaceful solitude, her perceptions became enhanced.

Yi abruptly opened her eyes, and she said urgently, "Tom, do you hear that?"

Tom glanced up from his computer monitor to look at Yi, "Do I hear what?"

Yi looked him in the eye. "Listen. Do you hear that sound? It is very weird. I have never heard that sound before."

Tom, hearing the urgency in Yi's voice, stopped what he was doing and rose from his chair. He walked closer to the main control room viewing monitor, and looked carefully at the view of the Torqkadrone. He then looked at the speakers which were broadcasting the sounds from the Torqkadrone. "Yi, I don't hear anything different than what we have been hearing for the past hour or so—ever since we activated the sound sensors on the Torqkadrone."

Yi walked over to the main viewing monitor, stood next to Tom, and looked at the Torqkadrone. She focused on the sound of the audio feed, and said, "I definitely hear something in that sound stream."

"Well, what does it sound like to you, Yi?" asked Tom, in a gentle tone.

"It sounds almost like a voice. I guess that is the only way I can describe it to you."

"You know this control room is really hectic, and we are all a little worn out. Why don't you go take a break and get something to eat? VG and I will take care of things here at this level."

They both continued to look at the main monitor for some time, and then Yi sighed. "Yeah, Tom, I'm going to take you up on your recommendation and get a bite to eat. I'll be back in a half an hour. Make sure you keep an eye on the cryogenic distribution grid profile of the dipole magnets in the magnacasters. We don't want to disappoint Jon!"

Yi walked away reluctantly, still thinking about the strange voice she heard.

[19]

The Mid-Level Station

Jon found Ben working in the room adjacent to the control room. "Ben, let's go up to the mid-level station, take a break and grab a cup of coffee. I also need to check my email, and take care of a few things."

"Sounds great."

In the elevator, Jon asked, "Ben, have you ever been in the mid-level station room?"

"No, but I hear it's a pretty cool place."

"Yeah, it really is a nice place to hang out, relax, or even get some work done. You'll see."

As they exited the elevator, Jon pointed to the left, "Ben, just so you know, the mid-level station room is to the left when you exit the elevator. If you turn right instead, you end up at the equipment service elevator shaft."

"How far is it to the service elevator shaft?"

"About three hundred feet. When you get to the end of the hallway, there is a balcony overlooking the vertical shaft. From there it goes straight down about another five hundred feet to the HITS beam line junction tunnel. That is the way that the giant dipole magnets and magnacasters unit assemblies are brought into QUEST."

"Damn! That must be some view!"

"Yeah, it's impressive. The elevator shaft is thirty-five feet in diameter, and the view is not for the faint of heart, or anyone with a fear of heights. I'll have to show you the view from that balcony sometime after we've had a few beers here."

"Hell, no! I will not go there after we have been drinking!" laughed Ben.

"I was just joking! Anyway, let's go get something to eat."

On the way down the hall in the opposite direction, Jon indicated an exit sign. "The emergency exit stairway runs the entire nine hundred feet from the surface to the QUEST main lobby. This mid-level station is the only thing in-between. If you are ever here in the future, and there is a problem and the elevator is shut down, that stairwell is about the only way out of the facility."

About fifty feet further on, they approached the doorway into the mid-level station. "Here we are. Check this place out!" said Jon, opening the glass door into the station.

"It is a lot bigger than I expected!"

"Yup, it is pretty big. Check this out," Jon said, walking over to a series of switches on the wall. The side walls slowly started to light up in a magnificent array of light and colors.

"Wall holograms! They're tremendous. I've never seen anything like these."

"They are specially manufactured from one of the electronics companies we contract from. It's actually a Canadian company which also produces many of those magnificent, and extremely popular,

3D simulated movies. They produce a line of these broadcast holograms, too, and we were able to install them here in the mid-level station room."

Ben studied the hologram on the south wall. "This is amazing. It's so real, and lifelike. Between the massive size, and the quality of the resolution, I feel like we are actually standing on the side of this mountain—like I could walk right along that ridge, or dive into that cool, inviting lake. I have never seen a hologram this big. And the resolution is unbelievable."

"Check this one out," said Jon, turning toward the north wall.

Ben tore himself away from the hologram, and walked over to the opposite wall. His journey across the room took him from a sunlit mountain range into the dark of a night sky filled with the shimmering glow of planets, stars and galaxies. "Un freaking-believable. This is totally amazing, too. No wonder this place is so popular with the workers here."

After giving Ben a few moments to take in the hologram, Jon said, "Let's go to the kitchen in the back. I'm starving. Are you?"

Jon led the way toward the kitchen area. They passed a sunken lounge, complete with perfectly arranged, comfortable-looking, inviting couches, chairs, and tables.

"What a great place for people to rest up, read, or get some work done."

"It really is. We also have a game area complete with ping-pong and pool tables, board games, bathrooms, showers, and sleeping rooms for layovers when we are pulling all-nighters with some of our experiments with the Macro-STARR."

"How on earth did you get all this into the budget when you built the place?"

"I insisted on it, because when I was working on my post doc at the accelerator at Fermi Labs, there was no place nearby to relax and get together with the other scientists. I convinced the architects of the project to include it. We got it through the review committees, and here it is."

"Very impressive, Jon!"

"Let's see, we have bagels, some assorted sandwiches, frozen pizzas, and donuts on the menu here today. Can I take your order, sir?"

"Okay, be honest with me. How are the frozen pizzas, Jon?"

"They are actually surprisingly good."

"Okay, I'll take a chance on frozen pizza."

"Two frozen pizzas coming up." Jon popped the pizzas into the microwave, and opened the refrigerator. "You want a beer with that?"

"Sure, if you're having one."

"I always make it a point to have a few beers here whether I am working or playing ping-pong."

"Didn't you say to me about hiding your ping-pong paddle somewhere here so no one would find it?"

"Yup, follow me. Here's your beer."

They walked past the service area east of the kitchen, passing bathrooms, sleeping rooms, and a janitor's closet. They came to a narrow hallway that led off to the right. They took the narrow hallway down to a secluded metal door. Jon opened the door for Ben, and waved him inside.

Ben paused in the doorway, exclaiming, "Holy Christ! What is this place? Is that an escape ladder well-tunnel?"

"Yes! Exactly, Ben! That is exactly what it is, and almost no one knows it even exists."

"I have not seen anything like this since I was in the military at a minuteman missile silo in North Dakota back in the early sixties."

"The designers installed this escape ladder tunnel as a backup escape for this area, and I keep my personal ping-pong paddle in here so no one takes it. I'm glad to see that it's still safe and sound here. This paddle is an expensive one, made in Korea, and I don't want some drunken physicist messing around with my personal paddle here."

"Jon, have you ever gone up this escape ladder to the top?"

"Nope, not to the top. But I did go partway up to explore. Actually, I got scared because of the hand ladder. It feels really precarious, so I stopped after going up a ways and came back. Marta thought I was crazy for even doing that."

"Yeah, I can see her point. I definitely would not want to climb four hundred and fifty feet to the surface unless I really had to."

Ben and Jon headed back to the kitchen. They gathered their food and beer and settled down in the sunken living room.

"I can't believe how nice this place is. It's so relaxing and comfortable here that it's hard to believe we are four hundred and fifty feet below the surface of the earth. The holograms create a fantastic mood here. I'm also pretty surprised that the management allows alcohol consumption here," Ben said.

"We have a strict policy here, and the management accepts it. Moderate alcohol consumption is permitted here, but no alcoholic beverages are permitted in the HITS and QUEST facilities. The management is very strict about that rule. Some of our most productive theoretical physics meetings take place here after we relax, play some ping-pong, and have a beer or two. It definitely stimulates your thinking, and it's good to get away from the equipment for a while. Did you know that the famous quantum physicist, Niels Bohr, was a great ping-pong player? We even have a poster of him here on the wall."

"No, I didn't know that. Didn't Niels Bohr come up with the *we collapse the wave function* idea."

"Yes, he did. Another interesting thing about Niels Bohr was that he was actually introduced to the many worlds interpretation of quantum physics in 1959, but he rejected it. He did not like it at all. A young physicist in the military, who was a friend of Emery Hilcraft, met Niels Bohr and introduced him to the concept. Reportedly, Niels Bohr thought that it was 'a stupid idea.' Look how the concepts of quantum physics have changed now. It's amazing to me that even scientists like Niels Bohr could not be open-minded enough to consider just what is really happening in the quantum realm."

"What a story! I'll have to share that with my friends at AES. So, Jon, can you show me some of your data from the Torqkadrone experiments?"

Jon finished his pizza, took a swig of beer, and put his bottle down on the table. He walked over to a shelf located near the game tables, pulled out a wireless keyboard, and sat back down with the keyboard on his lap. "I will show you some of the data from our Torqkadrone experiments now, but I want you to promise me that you will not discuss this with any one."

"Of course. I'll keep this private."

"Good," said Jon sharply.

A large rectangular window opened up in the middle of the north wall hologram of outer space, creating a flat monitor screen which seemed to be suspended among the stars.

"That is so cool."

"Yup. It is an electronic interactive hologram system. We actually have a variety of choices for the holographic image display. The mountains and outer space are two of my personal favorites. The screen view can also be reconfigured into any size that we want here, which is very useful for scientific presentations."

"This must be about nine feet by five feet. The resolution is startling, particularly at that size. Ever think of watching the Super Bowl down here?"

[20]

Many Worlds with Many Lives

Ben watched as Jon navigated through the computer files of the QUEST website, and accessed a password-protected file. Jon then scrolled through several pages of data, and finally said, "Okay, this is some of the data that we have discovered using the Torqkadrone in the quantum coherence seductions. But first I want you to hear this," said Jon, activating the audio system.

The room filled with the surreal sounds of movement. Ben was swept up in a stream of images evoked by the sounds: rushing rivers morphing into ocean waves, giving way to a sandstorm in an isolated desert, resolving into leaves rustling in a gentle breeze—but all in some way beyond natural sounds.

"That is the sound of the hologram that we are now in. You see, Ben, this perceived state of reality is really just a holographic movie. And this movie is really just one of infinite holographic movies all being played at the same time, and in the same place."

"I've heard that analogy before."

"Do you understand it?"

"Well, sort of. Theoretically is one thing, but on a more concrete level it's quite another. What I don't really understand is how all of the infinite quantum states or holographic movies can be going on at the same time. That's hard to wrap my brain around."

"It is because time itself is multidimensional, which means there are infinite addresses to time. Kind of like the many keys on a piano."

"So you are saying that because time has many different locations, simultaneously, things can be going on in many different times at once?"

"Yeah, but one thing we still don't know is if those locations are continuous or discontinuous," Jon said. "Alright, Ben, let me show you what we found in some of our Torqkadrone quantum coherence seductions."

As Jon typed, several images appeared on the holographic monitor. Jon got up and walked over to the wall. "Ben, you are looking at a superposition state of our own spectral time reality. We have recorded endless images like these."

Shaking his head, Ben rose slowly. He walked over to Jon, and looked more closely at the images. "You are saying this is a picture of another world contained within our own reality? Is that right, Jon?"

"Yes, I guess you could call it that—another universe contained within our own reality. But remember this is only one world of infinite other ones. This one is most likely our co-location *torqka* state."

Examining the images, Ben asked, "These look like pictures of a wooded area of some sort. What are these pictures of exactly? Do you know what they are showing?"

"Frankly, we are not quite sure. What we are sure of is that this is a picture of another quantum superposition of this universe. By the way, the Torqkadrone measured the environmental conditions at this location. It found them to be similar to normal, habitable conditions here on Earth. Theoretically, these alternate superposition realities can be much different from our own world in infinite ways."

"Different how?"

"Well, for instance, in one of these parallel worlds there could be an Earth that was hit by a gigantic asteroid which extinguished all life. Or there could be a world where you are the president of the United States, and I am a prison warden. Or even a world where you are the prison warden and I am a prisoner. Every possibility actually happens in these alternate worlds, so to see that image of a world that looks like our own, and is habitable, too, is very interesting."

"This is totally amazing, Jon! What is that gray area near the bottom of that picture?"

"We don't know. It is a mystery to us also right now. We have tried to do computer enhancements to determine what it is, but we haven't come to any conclusions. It definitely is something consistent with that alternate superposition world, though."

"Have you found anything else interesting?" asked Ben.

Jon went back to his keyboard and brought up some different images.

"Well, this will blow your mind. We developed some specially constructed Torqkadrones, and have conducted tests with animals placed into the devices while they are sent into the Macro-STARR for a quantum coherence seduction."

"You're kidding! How were you able to do that?"

"Marta, and some of her colleagues in Medical Research were able to provide us with some laboratory research animals."

"What kinds of animals did you use?"

"Take a look," said Jon, displaying a series of images, "First, we used some Lab mice, and then we used a Lab chimp. It took some time for us to construct a Torqkadrone fitted for the animals properly, but all went fairly well with the experiments."

"How did the chimp react to being sent into a quantum coherence seduction? From the control room it looked very dangerous. It doesn't look like something a living thing could survive."

"I know. But when you analyze the environmental data of the interior of the device during the coherence seduction, it's actually perfectly pleasant inside for the occupant."

"Well, so how did the animals make out after the seduction? Did they all survive?"

"Perfectly well. No deleterious effects at all were noted. After the animals were in quantum seduction for more than seven hours, Marta and her staff did complete medical evaluations. They found no medical anomalies. Take a look at the chimp here," said Jon, displaying two pictures of the chimp during and after the quantum coherence seduction.

"Unbelievable. It looks fine. Uh, so how many people in management here know about this, Jon?"

"Let me put it to you this way: information is shared only on a 'need to know' basis. We are keeping this information very contained, but Dr. Kenyatta is in the loop, as well as several officials in the medical research lab and the administration office."

"Well, I'm honored that you are letting me in on it. It's absolutely amazing stuff. I will definitely keep my mouth shut."

"Thanks, Ben. Now, here's something I think you will find very interesting. This is from the Torqkadrone that we have been preparing for our next Macro-STARR quantum coherence seduction experiment. Take a look at this baby!"

"Holy Cow, Jon! That is a big Torqkadrone! What are you going to do with that one?"

"This Torqkadrone is specially designed to take a human subject into the quantum coherence seduction."

"You have got to be kidding me, Jon! Are you serious?"

"Dead serious, Ben. We have been working on this project for quite some time. We are totally confident that we will be able to use our Macro-STARR equipment to get a human subject into another superposition state of the multi-universe. We have several volunteers trained and ready to go, but we haven't made the final selection yet."

"This is surreal stuff. I definitely want to be there! I will help in any way I can. Just let me know if you need my assistance. I'd love to be a part of that experiment! I can't remember the last time I heard anything so completely mind-blowing."

"Thanks, Ben. You'll be invited to participate when we do that next coherence seduction."

"You said before that this reality we are a part of is a like a holographic movie, inferring that this world that we perceive is not real in some way. What do you mean by that?"

Jon drained the last of his beer, and banged the bottle down on the table. "Let me show you something else very odd. This is an actual data feed from a sensor located on the Torqkadrone. It comes from a special instrument called a particle wave sensor. This device is a kind of probe that can sense and detect structures which measure sizes near the Planck Scale, which you might know, is the smallest scale of measurement in the universe. The Planck Scale measures objects that are many orders of magnitude smaller than an electron. When we look at the smallest things in the world which make up matter, we find something that is very strange. As we look at the smallest bits in the fabric of space-time and matter, we detect things we call Planck Pixels. What is astonishing about this find is that these are not manifested in three dimensions, but rather in only two dimensions of space-time."

"That can't be real, Jon. Are you telling me that the fabric of our universe, at the sub-basement level of structure, is actually in only two dimensions of space-time?"

"Exactly. Look at the picture on the screen. You can almost see it."

Ben looked at the image from the Torqkadrone particle wave sensor, and said, "This will rewrite physics books, if it is true."

"There you have it, Ben. We are living in a world that is a structured fabric in two dimensions which appear to be three dimensions to us, just like a hologram. Think of it this way, Ben. Say that you and I are living in a cartoon that is part of a newspaper. You and I are living and existing in this cartoon world, interacting with all the other cartoon people, and all the cartoon matter that composes the cartoon universe. But what we don't realize is that we are just two-dimensional creatures living in a two-dimensional world, that just appears to be a three-dimensional universe to us in our cartoon world."

"Amazing!"

"It's psychologically humbling, isn't it?"

"Definitely. It sure is a humbling thought. I can conceptualize it, but it's really hard to believe! If this holographic reality is being broadcast like a movie, then where is the information being broadcast from?"

"Good question, Ben! The information that creates this holographic reality is apparently being broadcast from the outer edges of the universe. That is the source of the two-dimensional information."

Rising from his chair, and pointing to the view of outer space displayed in the wall hologram, Jon said, "It is out there, Ben, located way out at the edges of the universe. That is where it exists. That is the source of everything we perceive as real."

Shaking his head in wonder, Ben said, "You know, Jon, the concept of holographic reality was even theorized in some way by physicists in the sixties, including Emery Hilcraft, here at RNL, and Rudy Cohen from MIT. In some of their particle experiments they detected some fuzziness in the structure of the atomic realm. I remember Emery describing it as kind of like enlarging a photograph over and over again and seeing a degradation of the resolution. I remember that the year after Emery came back from visiting his friend in Czechoslovakia he started talking about the possibility of our reality being interpreted as holographic in nature. It was such a radical theory that the mainstream physicists wanted nothing to do with it."

"I know. I've read some of the physics literature of the time. I'm familiar with their research, and also how much they were bashed and marginalized for their theories. I guess it's not surprising, considering that the physicists then were still operating under the Niels Bohr's model. It's a big jump from the idea that there are infinite possible universes in the quantum sea, and when we make an observation *we collapse the wave function* and create *the one* universe that we exist in, to the idea of a multiverse with infinite diverging outcomes for each of the individual universes. They did not fully understand the true implications of quantum theory."

"I don't understand why we can't see and observe any of the other infinite universes in the quantum ocean around us. Why are we locked into this one?"

"Each time we make a measurement, or have any kind of physical interaction within the quantum realm, we are united with all of the collections of the ensemble of our conjoined quantum state. We become our own united quantum universe. If we could see what is going on in the other possible universes, we would see that an infinite number of Ben Carsons would make an infinite number of measurements, or observations, and each at the same time each in a slightly altered way. Over time, these slightly different variations within each universe would then magnify so that each of the infinite individual universes would have totally diverging outcomes. In one universe, Ben Carson is the president of the United States; in another, Ben Carson is a wanted FBI criminal."

Ben chuckled. "Yeah, in another universe I am the winner of the largest lottery jackpot in the history of the world!"

"Yes, Ben, that outcome is out there somewhere. It is definitely out there somewhere. I just hope you split some of the money with me! Listen, Ben, now that I have you here where we can talk privately. I want to ask you a few more things about Dr. Hilcraft and the graphite reactor."

Ben's manner suddenly shifted. He scanned the room quickly, and seemed perturbed.

Jon reached out and put his hand on Ben's arm. "Don't worry, Ben, you and I are totally alone here, four hundred and fifty feet below the surface of the earth. It's eleven o'clock at night. There's no need to worry about anyone hearing our conversation."

Ben seemed to relax slightly. "Okay, Jon, what do you want to know?"

"Well, first off, why do you get so uptight anytime that we talk about the RGR and Emery Hilcraft? What's up with that?"

"I guess you might have already realized that I really don't trust the management here. Ever since Dr. Tonner's arrival, security here has become much more intrusive and aggressive. We have more highly classified, super-secret research projects going on here than ever before, and quite frankly, it scares the hell out of me."

"Yeah, I've also noticed that Dr. Tonner's directives have been more totalitarian, and that the levels and areas of secrecy have been expanding. You've probably seen those black-mirrored unmarked vehicles riding around the Lab. I wonder just what the hell they are they doing here."

"Exactly. I've seen them too—especially at the Molecular Biology Building. There are other large, unmarked vehicles, too."

"Point taken. It can't hurt to be careful, but I can't think of a more isolated space than this one. I wanted to ask you about a few things you talked about when we were in the woods near Bowers Hall. Remember when we were in the Ridgewood Graphite Reactor doing the environmental inspection with the Environmental Review Committee the other day, and I wandered off to a lower level where you found me and tried to help me open a big heavy metal door?"

"Sure. Of course I remember."

"Do you think it's possible that door could be an access to the tunnel that leads over to the subsurface complex of Building 720?"

"I don't know. It's possible. If it is, then it also must be the conduit tunnel that carries the pneumatic tubes that go from the reactor pile to 720."

"That was part of the Hades Project, wasn't it, Ben?"

"Yes, it was part of the Hades Project, which, as far as we could tell, was some kind of black ops military project. Emery was very aggravated with the whole thing, and did not want to be involved with it in any way."

"If we could get into the RGR when no one is around, and get that metal door opened, and find the tunnel with the pneumatic tubes, then we could find out for sure whether that is the tunnel that leads to the subsurface complex at Building 720."

"I think it must be, Jon. It's the only one that I know of."

Jon thought for a moment, and grinned at Ben. "So, Ben, do you have anything planned for tonight?"

"Well, as you know, I was just planning on being here all night, working on the Torqkadrone experiment with you."

"I would really like to find out if that is the Hades conduit tunnel that leads to Building 720. Do you think you could sneak us into the RGR?"

"I could get us in, but I imagine we'd be in deep shit if someone found out. When were you thinking of going there? I only have a few more days with your team before I have to go back to AES."

"What about now?" asked Jon, standing up.

"You're crazy, Jon! It's near midnight, and I'm getting tired. And what about the Torqkadrone experiment? In case you forgot, your experiment is going on right now."

"Oh, don't worry about that. It's going fine. My staff has it operating perfectly. They are more than qualified to take care of it. It's in a stable state now, and will complete in about five hours. Meanwhile, there's not much to do but wait, so now would be a great time to check out the RGR and that conduit tunnel. No one would be there now, that's for sure. We just need to get in, bring some flashlights, and something to get that big metal door open."

"Well, I have to admit, I am pretty curious to know if that is the conduit tunnel. I can definitely get us into the RGR from the southeast utility door entrance, but we'll have to be extremely careful not to attract any attention. I guess it makes sense to try to do it at night. I don't know if there are any alarms, so we'll have to keep a sharp eye out for alarm sensors. In terms of getting the door open, I have a couple heavy-duty pry bars in my car. One of them would probably do the job."

“Perfect, Ben! If we follow the RGR conduit tunnel it will probably get us into the old Building 720 subsurface complex. Now that would be really interesting! Maybe we’ll find some clues about what the military was doing there. I wonder if there’s any chance we’ll get any leads on what happened to Emery. I’ll grab flashlights on the way out. Let’s get going right now.”

“Okay, Jon. I just hope that we don’t get caught in there. You realize that Dr. Tonner would love to have anything he could use against you to disrupt your QUEST project.”

“Don’t worry, Ben. I have friends in high places and, besides, you worry too much.”

They headed out of the mid-level station toward the elevator. Jon was about to push the button to call the elevator when he noticed that one of the elevator indicators was lit up.

“I wonder who the hell could be coming down at this time of night. I doubt they’ll stop here at the mid-level station. It’s probably someone from HITS or QUEST returning from an errand,” he said. But then they heard the subtle change in sound as the elevator began to decelerate. “Hmm, I spoke too soon. I guess we’ll find out who it is.”

They both took a step back from the door as it opened, and its occupant stepped out and greeted Jon. “Hello, Dr. Sanborne. It looks like you gentlemen are working here late tonight.”

“Hello, Officer Kendrick! I did not expect to see anyone here at this hour. What brings you here? It’s very rare to see security here at QUEST.”

“Forgive me, Dr. Sanborne, but we were ordered to check out the premises due to our new security initiative, particularly because we received several complaints about some ground-shaking activity. Is everything here okay, sir?”

"Yes, Officer, everything here is fine. Our QUEST facility does create some localized microseismic activity. Some people may have felt some mild ground shakes above our site here, but they should have been slight and they certainly were benign."

"Very good, sir. Glad to hear everything here is okay. Since everything is fine here, I'll just head down to the QUEST lobby and check in to make sure everything is okay over there. Then I'll be leaving the QUEST site. I hope you don't mind, sir. We're doing this type of security surveillance in every building here at Ridgewood. It's just routine now."

"I don't mind at all, Officer Kendrick. It was a pleasure meeting you. Thanks for your help in making Ridgewood a safe place to work."

"Thank you, Dr. Sanborne," said Kendrick, pressing the button to close the elevator doors.

"Have you ever had uniformed site security police officers visit your QUEST facility before?" Ben asked.

"It's very rare to see them here. I have seen then in other research buildings, and even in parts of the HITS facility, but not in the accelerator sections, and not here at QUEST. This is all part of the ever-increasing surveillance."

"Yeah," Ben said. "I don't like it. It feels like a police state, doesn't it?"

"Yes," Jon said. "Exactly. Well, let's get going, Ben. I think we're going to have a long interesting night ahead of us."

[21]

The Sulov Rocks

Marta returned to Jon's home in Aquebogue exhausted and hungry. After putting in extra hours at work she had stopped in for a short visit with Lois. She opened the freezer and removed a plastic container of lasagna that she and Jon had prepared a week earlier. As it heated in the microwave, she rummaged around until she found the postcard Emery Hilcraft had sent Ben so many years ago. Marta stared at the postcard, admiring the beautiful panicle rock formations and the magnificent, unusual mountain vistas.

She entered Jon's office and sat down at the computer to do a little sleuthing. Marta entered the phrase "famous mountains in Czechoslovakia" in the Google search bar. A long list of results appeared. She scanned and studied each link, but nothing seemed particularly interesting. Her mind wandered, and she realized how very tired she really was. She shook her head a bit to clear it, and typed in "strange rock formations in Czech Republic." Again, a long list of results appeared on the computer monitor. Marta sorted through them one by one and saw nothing that seemed a likely match for her postcard image.

Fighting her exhaustion, she decided to give it one last try, typing "strange rock formations in the Slovak Republic." Just as she was about to give up, something caught her attention. She followed the link and saw a small image that looked promising. Excited, Marta double-clicked on the image. Fantastic photos of abstract mountain pinnacles very similar to the ones in the postcard flashed onto the screen. They were called the Sulov Rocks. Marta compared the pictures of the Sulov Rocks to the postcard picture of the rock formations in the Tatra Mountains. The resemblance was remarkable. In her excitement, she forgot both her hunger and exhaustion, and eagerly devoured the information on the website. She learned that the Sulov Mountains were located in a national forest preserve in the northwest corner of the Slovak Republic, near the borders of both the Czech and Polish Republics. Intrigued, Marta could not stop clicking links, oblivious to the beep of the microwave. She was determined to find out why these strange rock formations were apparently so meaningful to Emery Hilcraft. She stumbled upon a Wikipedia site describing the enigmatic rock formations. The article said the mountains were a highly-revered place of worship in Slovakia, and that they were an integral part of the ancient folklore of the people of Slovakia. The article pinpointed the location of the Sulov Rocks in the Fatra-Tatra area of the Inner Western Carpathian Mountains. Reading on, Marta was elated to discover that modern archaeologists had been studying the area for more than seventy years, and that there had been many fascinating anthropological finds about the ancient people who inhabited the area thousands of years ago. In fact, this specific site was named as the oldest known settlement of the ancient Chalcolithic European culture that existed in areas of Central and Eastern Europe dating back more than seven thousand years ago. The Chalcolithic European culture had established several copper and tin mines in the Sulov Mountains, and they had built several thriving communities there during that ancient time period.

Marta rose and retrieved her lasagna. She returned to the computer and ate as she continued to read. After a bit, she found herself beginning to nod off. She startled at an unusual noise, rubbed her eyes, and got up to find the source of the sound. Listening, she realized the sound seemed to be coming from outside. She opened the front door and stepped out on the porch into the dark, windy night. As she looked around, Marta felt something soft move against her leg. Jon's cat, Onyx, was winding herself around Marta's legs. Glad for the company, she picked Onyx up and gave her a big hug. Onyx let out a friendly meow.

"What were you doing out here tonight, you little devil!" said Marta, as she brought Onyx into the house.

Marta returned to the door, listening carefully. She still heard something in the wind. She stepped outside, closed the door, walked around the south side to the back of the house, and looked around. The wind off the bay gave her a burst of energy, and she found herself walking down to the beach behind Jon's house. The walk to the beach was not long, and soon she was walking on the sandy beach toward the Great Peconic Bay. The water was pickle-green, and the waves reflected the light of the half-moon as they crested. Marta began to relax. She gazed down the length of the beach as it led into the county preserve to the west. The wind blew through the cedar trees and small pitch pines on the slight rise of barrier beach separating the Peconic Bay from the waters of the estuary marsh flats. Marta closed her eyes and took in the aromatic richness of the natural world. She relaxed into a state of comfort and contemplation, and said a small prayer to herself, focusing on hopes of safety and goodwill for Jon and his team at the QUEST project. She felt at one with everything and everyone, united with the universe.

[22]

Into The Depths of Hell

Ben pulled into the parking lot at Building 401. "I think this is the best place to park if we want to be inconspicuous about sneaking into the reactor. This is the Research Support Building, and there are usually several people working in this building at night, so my car won't be noticeable. We are fairly far from the RGR, too."

He pulled into a spot in the western corner of the parking lot near several other cars. Ben popped the trunk and they got out of the car, grabbing the tools they needed to bring with them.

It was dark out, but there were some lights from nearby Lab buildings that they needed to avoid. They walked up a small hill, past the east side of the RGR building, and headed down toward the southeast entrance at the back of the RGR complex.

They approached the utility maintenance door slowly, scanning the area for anyone who might observe them. The area was quiet and dark. Despite his casual attitude, Jon was concerned about being seen, and carefully surveyed the surrounding area.

"Jon, shine your flashlight here on the combination lock, and I'll enter the code."

Jon trained the beam of his flashlight onto the lock, while continuing to scrutinize the area.

"Damn, Jon! It opened! We are in, my friend!"

"Great, you old bastard, I knew you could get us into this place!" said Jon, clapping Ben on the back.

Ben opened the door slowly and quietly to avoid making any detectable disturbance. They stepped inside, and Ben closed the door with equal care.

"Okay, so we'll head to the other side of the reactor maintenance area, and then into the old museum area, and then down to the subsurface areas," said Ben.

"Sounds good?"

"Sure Ben, you know your way around here, and I have no idea where the hell we are right now, so I'll follow your lead," Jon said.

They made their way into the old reactor building, and past the old science museum, by the light of their flashlights. Just past the museum displays that had been used to teach the public about the peaceful use of nuclear power they entered a stairwell and descended several levels. When they reached the bottom, they walked onto another stairwell and headed even further down. Finally, they approached the big metal door they were seeking.

"Here we are, Jon. This is our challenge for tonight. Let's give it a try and see if we can get this thing opened."

"If we find the pneumatic tubes in the tunnel then we're on our way to Building 720 and the carry lab."

Jon pulled on the heavy door handle, while Ben inserted the metal pry bar into the crack of the door opening on the right side of the doorframe. Jon put all his weight into pulling on the door handle, while

Ben got better leverage with the pry bar. The door began to move. The loud screeching noise echoed down the silent halls. Both men stopped, looked around, and listened carefully. Hearing nothing but silence, they returned to their task. Jon continued to pull on the door handle while Ben used a pry bar on the partly opened door. The heavy door squeaked and screeched open grudgingly, finally opening enough to grant them access to the tunnel concealed behind it.

"We did it! I wasn't sure there for a while, but we did it!" Jon said.

"Yes, we did! It pays to have leverage on your side."

"I have to tell you, Ben, especially for an older person you are as strong as a bull. Boy, you are in good shape for your age," Jon said.

"Well, I was a wrestler in college. I try to keep active and healthy. I work out at the RNL gym, all the time. You can't beat the price—it's free."

Ben and Jon shone their flashlights into the tunnel. The dark unknown was now exposed. Ben walked forward into the unknown, pushing aside cobwebs with his pry bar.

"Well, well, well—looks like we hit the jackpot tonight, Jon. Come on in and I'll show you something interesting." Ben's flashlight highlighted something on the left side of the tunnel. "This is it, Jon. We are definitely in the tunnel that leads to Building 720. Look at those pneumatic tubes coming from that conduit running under the floor of the RGR and into this tunnel."

"Wow! There must be at least twenty of them, and with such a wide variety of diameters. Do you think these all run the full length of this tunnel and travel to Building 720?"

"Absolutely, Jon. This tunnel had two purposes for the RGR. It provided an access point to service the pneumatic tubes if they had a problem with them, and it provided an interconnection between Building 720 and the RGR. I vaguely remember some personnel going into this access point from time to time, but I had no idea just what the heck they were doing then. It was off-limits to most of the RGR employees."

"Well, let's get going! We don't want to hang around here in case security comes around. It is getting late."

Ben led the way. The large square cement tunnel was pitched down slightly. They walked northward alongside the pneumatic tubes for several minutes.

"I wonder how long it has been since anyone has been in here, and who last took this tunnel to Building 720? Look at all the crap on the floor from the wall and ceiling deterioration," commented Jon.

"I don't know, but I suspect it was a long while ago. The engineers who were in charge of the RGR decommissioning may have taken a look at it some years ago, but it doesn't appear to have been traveled at all lately," answered Ben.

Ben froze suddenly. The beam from his flashlight shook as he tried to focus on something on the floor in front of him.

"There is something on the floor in front of us and it looks like a body!"

"Are you serious? It can't be!"

Jon pointed his flashlight at the object on the floor, and cautiously approached the object. "Yep, it is a body all right, but fortunately it's made of plastic. It looks like a dummy of some kind. I wonder what the hell it's doing in this tunnel."

"It was probably part of the science display for the museum exhibit. I know there were mannequins there dressed like reactor operators to give the display a more realistic look. Why it's here I have no idea. Only a government worker would do something as stupid this!"

Jon laughed, and they continued on for several more minutes. Eventually, they descended a few steps still in the tunnel and the tunnel became level. They continued on further until they came to a doorway. The door was emblazoned with large and imposing biohazard and radiation danger signs.

"I think we are about to enter the carry lab, Jon. I hope this door is working. It's obviously as old as hell, but look, this biohazard sign appears to be new!"

They stood in front of a large, old, gray metal door. The floor in front of the door was littered with flakes of corroded metal. Ben was astonished to find the door opened on the first try. He looked at Jon, pulled the door wide open, and said, "Welcome to the carry Lab, Jon. I have no idea what's in here. This place had restricted access and security surveillance 24–7, so you can bet they were doing something in here that they didn't want anyone to know about. Let's take a look inside."

They walked through the doorway into Building 720. They stopped and listened carefully to see if they could hear anything.

"I think I hear water dripping somewhere," Jon said.

"Do you smell something weird?" Ben asked.

"Yes. It's terrible. What is that smell?"

"I don't know. Maybe some stored, leftover lab chemicals that they were working with?"

"It's definitely a god-awful smell. I just hope it's not toxic," Jon said.

"It looks like we are in a hallway of some kind here. The pneumatic tubes continue on the other side of the wall. They must travel to some lab area in this building, so let's go forward."

As they continued down the hallway, they walked past numerous doorways that were entrances into office areas. They entered a long-abandoned office and Ben flipped the light switch, with no result.

"I didn't think the power would be on down here. This place hasn't been used for decades."

They walked along further and followed a hallway to their left. It led past many laboratories on each side of the hallway. The labs were mostly empty. Eventually, they came to a lobby which housed several elevators. Jon pushed one of the elevator buttons, and was not surprised when nothing happened.

"It looks like these elevators haven't been used in a long time. This elevator is so much bigger than the others. I wonder what they used it for," Jon said.

Using his flashlight, Ben indicated a stairwell on each side of the lobby. "What will it be Jon, up or down?"

"Let's go down *into the depths of hell,*" said Jon, with a stone-faced stare.

They headed down the staircase next to the elevator bank. They looked around the next level, using their flashlights to probe into the darkness. They saw what appeared to be more offices and labs, and decided to descend another level. As they approached the next level, the smell they had previously noted became more perceptible. They walked out into the room and shone their flashlights around. They came upon a large open area containing old equipment. Wall signs indicated the presence of dangerous radioactive materials.

"Hey, Jon, look at these old full-body radiation scanners."

"They must have about ten of these things here. These are the oldest-looking ones I've ever seen. Why would they have so many of them here?"

"They were used for monitoring radiation levels in human subjects. They are sensitive enough to find trace micro-sieverts of ionizing radiation on, or in, the human body. We had a few of them in the RGR when I worked there," Ben said. "They were manufactured by

New England Research Labs. These look like they were made by the same manufacturer. These were probably some of the first ones ever mass-produced for nuclear workers around the world."

"Hey, look at these! Old biosafety full-body suits. They're really old. Look how they're decomposing."

"Yeah. They are many decades old—some of the earliest manufactured versions. But look here, there are some newer Bio Level Safety 4 suits here, too. Apparently, someone's been down here doing something more recently."

"Ben, there is something really strange here. Check out this wall over here. There are multiple stations with individual glass booths for doing something. Do you have any idea what they could be for?"

Ben studied one of the booths. He thought for a little, and then said, "Outside each booth there are rubber glove access points, and inside the booths there are apparently receiving slots. The booths are all vented to a central manifold exhaust system. So whatever it was they were working with here it must have been a dangerous controlled area of some kind." Ben continued to walk around to each of the booths, shining his flashlight here and there to examine things more closely. He took some time to think things out, and then came to a conclusion. "I think I know what these are. These are the receiving ports from the pneumatic tubes that are running from the RGR. This is where the experimental materials were sent after they were passed through the fission reactor of the RGR."

"Then this is part of the Hades Project," Jon said, sucking in his breath.

"Yes, it is. Technicians here would be in contact with both the Hades Project operators and the RGR plant operators. They would then know just what was being passed through the reactor and how much radiation it had adsorbed. Then, when the capsules came through, they would remove the materials and do their experiments on the exposed materials."

"So the question is what exactly the scientists did with the irritated materials?"

"That is the sixty-four million dollar question isn't it, Jon? I think that the answer to that question is here in this room somewhere. We'll have to find it."

As they proceeded further into the carry lab they found a large puddle of water on the floor.

"Damn, this place is flooded with water. I wonder where it's seeping in from. Did you notice that the smell that we noted before is definitely getting stronger again? It's terrible, and it's starting to get to me. I hope that we don't get exposed to any airborne radioactive contamination particles. I suppose there may even be plutonium particles in the air here."

"It's possible but I'm not too worried about it. It's a chance we'll just have to take, I guess, to find out what's going on here."

"Yeah . . . I guess you're right."

"Look here, Jon. Check this out! There are lab tables here that appear to be for surgical use of some kind. They even have straps on them. Just what the hell were they doing here?"

"Yeah, I see them. There are a lot of them, along with all those sinks and washing stations. And look at all the materials and chemicals that they must have been using on whatever they were studying. There are side rooms full of shelving that must have been stacked with vast amounts of chemical reagents and materials. What the hell were they doing here?"

They continued to explore the huge space. Eventually, they found themselves in a remote corner of the room. They were both shocked and puzzled by what they found there.

"What do you make of this area, Ben? Very weird."

Ben walked around and examined the assemblage

of small concrete cages with metal doors. Some of the cages were stacked three high. “These are containment cages for animals. They must have been doing experiments on animals.”

“Yes, that’s definitely it. They must have been animal cages. You can see that they have floor drains here so they could wash up the area. I wonder what kinds of animals they were doing research on. Some of these are quite large. I wonder if they were using primates,” Jon said. *God, this place is eerie, I wonder what we have gotten ourselves into here.* Continuing past the animal pens, Jon saw something even more puzzling, “Hey, Ben, over here!”

They found themselves exploring several concrete walled rooms with large metal doors. Each metal door had a thick glass window located high up on the door. The hinges to the doors were massive, and each door had a heavy-duty lock. They walked into one of the segmented concrete walled rooms.

“Each room seems to have a toilet, a sink, a bench, and a shelf. They look like prison cells. What could these cells have possibly been used for?” Ben asked.

Jon was shining his flashlight on a wall. “Ben, take a look at this. What does this look like to you?”

“It looks like someone was scribbling on the wall in a foreign language, but I’m not sure which one.”

Jon’s flashlight slipped from his hand and crashed to the floor. Ben nearly jumped out of his skin, but he quickly regained his composure and shone his light on the floor so Jon could retrieve his own flashlight. Fortunately, it still functioned.

“I think I have an idea what these rooms are, but it doesn’t make any sense at all,” Ben said.

“Yeah? What are you thinking? ’Cause I don’t like what I’m thinking.”

“They seem like confinement cells—for people,” Ben said. “First, I thought maybe they had some other purpose, but look at those hinges and the heavy-duty locks on the doors."

"Confinement cells! Why would they have confinement cells here?"

"I don't know, Jon, but how else could you explain them? There is every indication that a person was occupying this area. They probably even had a bed in here. There certainly is enough room for one."

"You don't think that they were doing experiments on human subjects here do you, Ben?"

"I don't know. It doesn't make any sense," said Ben, shaking his head.

Ben began to recall several unusual events he had noticed when he was an assistant operator at the RGR. He had seen evidence of strange biological research being done at Building 720, but he had kept it to himself. He never told a soul. To this day, what he had seen had left a psychological wound in his psyche, but he had not wanted to speak of it until now.

Although they'd each had a long day, and they were getting tired due to the late hour, both Ben and Jon were now perplexed and uneasy. The two men continued to look around a bit more, both hoping for answers and dreading what they might find. They headed westward, further into the carry lab. They saw more labs, and more antique radiation monitoring equipment scattered about. The equipment was rusting and covered with dust, as were the lab tables and sinks. They found a large metallic structure at the end of a narrow hallway. They faced a large metal door which led into the metallic structure, and noticed that a large round duct emerged from the top of the structure and led up into the ceiling. They paused to examine the exterior of this odd corroded metal structure before opening the door to explore the interior. Jon pulled open the door.

"Ugh . . . God, it smells inside this thing! I wonder what the hell is in here," Jon said, using his shirt to cover his nose.

Ben noticed some black debris scattered about on the bottom of the unit. He used his pry bar to stir the debris, while Jon focused the beam of his flashlight on the contents. The unknown material was several inches thick, slightly sticky, and very smelly.

"What the hell is this stuff?" Jon asked.

Something caught Ben's eye, and he retrieved it with the hook. It was a small, deformed, and oddly contorted metallic object. Ben tried to clean it off by rubbing it on his shirt. He then held it out so that Jon could shine his flashlight on it. Spellbound, they studiously examined the blob of metal, trying to discern its significance.

"Oh, my God, I can't believe it, it looks like a—a metal image of a skull and crossbones!"

"Here, Jon, you hold the flashlight and let me take a good look at it."

"Damn, what the hell is this thing? It does look something like a skull and crossbones that has been partly melted. I can't believe it. What the hell were they doing down here?" Ben wondered again.

"This is an incinerator. That black stuff is ashes and soot, and this object was part of something only partly melted in the incinerator. That pipe coming out at the top of it is a vent stack to remove the smoke when it was operating," Jon said.

Suddenly a large drop of liquid dripped onto Jon's head, startling him. He stopped to wipe it off, and suddenly froze with a look of terror on his face.

"What is the matter, Jon?"

"Shh. I hear something. Be still! Don't you hear it?"

"No, I don't hear anything. My hearing is not great," Ben whispered.

Jon grabbed Ben by the arm and quickly pulled him out of the room.

"Somebody is coming, Ben. I hear people coming! Let's get the hell out of here!"

They rushed down the hallway, and back through the carry lab, heading back out the way they had come in.

"Jon, are you sure that you heard people coming?"

"Absolutely sure—damn it!"

They stared at each other in the silence, and listened carefully, but they heard nothing. Several moments passed, and then suddenly they heard distant movement and faint voices yelling out words they couldn't make out.

Jon motioned to Ben, and the two men swiftly made their way past the walled-off rooms, through the area with the surgical tables, and into the large area containing the pneumatic tube glass booths.

[23]

Escape from Hell

Jon signaled to Ben to keep still, and carefully listened for a moment. In the distance, he heard a faint but discernable voice shouting, "This is the Ridgewood National Lab site security police. Whoever you are, we know you are in here! Come on out and give yourselves up! This is a restricted area and you are not permitted in this site!"

Ben looked at Jon and whispered, "What do you think we should do?"

"We have to find a way out of here without being detected. That's our only option. We're screwed if we get caught . . . let's go!"

They raced on until they reached the full-body radiation scanners. They stopped for a moment to catch a breath, and then took off again. The deep fear of being caught by the RNL police motivated them to keep up their pace. They entered the stairwell they had taken down to the carry lab, and paused again to listen for voices.

Winded, but wired, Jon said in a muted voice, "I don't hear anyone now. I wonder where they are."

Equally hushed, Ben replied, "There are ways out of this building other than the tunnel to the RGR. We could try to go out of one of the Building 720 entrances on the surface level. We just have to find one of them."

"Do you know where one is? Have you ever used one before?"

"Yes, back in the sixties. I'm just not sure I know how to get to one from here. I visited this building while it was in operation years ago, but I never came down here."

Ben was considering their best route out of the building undetected, when they were suddenly propelled into movement by the shock of hearing RNL police officers shouting out their commands. Fortunately, the voices sounded more distant than they had previously.

"Let's try to get up to the surface level. Follow me!" said Ben, hurrying up the stairs as softly and noiselessly as possible. He directed his flashlight beam as close to the floor as possible to avoid broadcasting his beam. Jon followed close behind him. They ascended countless stairways. Finally, they arrived at a floor that was more open, and lighter, offering some relief from the utter darkness of the lower levels. It was the first time in a long while they were able to see light that was not from their flashlights. They ran down the hallway, uncertain, but encouraged by the increase in ambient light. They found themselves in a very long hallway lined with several doors which opened to office spaces. Jon frantically moved forward, shining his flashlight around, and peering into one of the nearby offices. Ben followed him into a long-empty office flanked by a bank of windows. Faint lights were visible outside the window. Their exhilaration and renewed hopes that they might escape from their adventure unscathed was abruptly interrupted by the sound of voices nearby. Both men broke into a sweat. Jon focused his light on the window, while they desperately searched for a latch. At last, Ben noticed a dull brass latch partly painted white. He pushed and pulled the latch in a panicked way, but struggled to free the window, which was frozen shut after decades of disuse. With a great heave, the window finally released and opened fully, making a screeching sound.

"Jump out, Ben! Let's go!"

Ben climbed up and paused momentarily on the ledge, outlined by the old paint peeling off the window frame. He disappeared into the dark, and Jon heard a thud as he hit the ground. Jon contorted his body into the geometry of the window frame, and threw himself into the dark night. Jon fell hard and rolled down a small embankment. Coming to a stop, he looked around frantically to determine his location and find Ben. He was relieved to spot Ben's tall figure standing nearby holding his pry bar, ready to defend him from any physical assault.

"Jon, get up! Let's get the hell out of here!"

Ben held out his hand and helped Jon to his feet. They started running from the east side of the silent RGR building. They continued running north, down the gentle slope away from the building. After several minutes, they reached a series of tall, lush cedars. They stopped for a breather under the cover of the trees. It was a quiet and dark night, although several partly-lit research buildings along the roadway glowed faintly, providing just enough light to discern the road running along the north side of the RGR.

"Holy Christ, Ben! For a while there, I thought we were going to get caught for sure. I can't believe that we got out of there so quickly. How the hell do you think they found out that we were there?"

"I don't exactly know, but I suspect that they had the place wired somehow. We apparently tripped an alarm somewhere. Hang out here a minute, nature is calling. I think it's my nerves. Be right back."

"Okay, I'll keep watch, then I'll take a turn, too. I think that this RGR foray has stressed us out!"

Ben disappeared behind some bushes. Jon found himself becoming anxious as the details of their escape started replaying in his mind. He quieted himself, and then the impact of their disconcerting finds at the carry lab hit him full force. For the first time, he really allowed the sense of malevolence that was present in the carry lab to penetrate his consciousness. He muttered quietly, "Just what the hell was that place used for?"

"RNL police! Stay put right where you are! I'm placing you under arrest for breaking and entering. Put your hands up in the air where I can see them . . . NOW!"

The officer's command was followed immediately by a shriek and a thud. Jon spun around to see the officer lying facedown on the ground, apparently unconscious. Ben stood directly behind the fallen officer, his arm extended, pry bar in hand.

They examined the officer and checked his vital signs. "He'll be okay. He's just unconscious. I can feel his pulse," Jon said. "I can't believe you did that. Where did you learn a maneuver like that?"

"I don't know," said Ben, shaking his head. "It was an automatic reaction on my part. I took a good swing at his ankles, and he just fell forward on his face. I think my military training must have helped."

"Let's get the hell out of here, Ben!"

They walked rapidly down the hill, and crossed the road cautiously, looking out for observers. They had walked a little further when they saw the lights of a vehicle approaching from the west.

"Quick Ben, get on the ground now—a car is coming!"

They dropped flat, sheltered from view by a slight depression in the terrain. The vehicle passed by very slowly, but they were not detected.

"I think that was a RNL police cruiser," Ben said.

"Yeah. It was one of their trademark vehicles—an unmarked, midnight blue Chevy Tahoe—with darkened windows," Jon said.

"Do you think they know that we were the ones who broke into the carry lab?"

"Probably not, but I guess we can't be sure, so we'd better be extra cautious when we get back to work. Let's get back to your car and get the hell out of here before they find us."

The adrenaline rush began to wane, and the effects of their long day and the late hour hit them as they headed back to Ben's car in the dark, quiet night. They walked past several lab support buildings, across several grassy fields, and down a path through a small wooded area. They approached the parking lot where they had left Ben's car, and paused at the wood's edge to make sure no police presence awaited them. All was quiet, and nothing seemed out of place. There were still a few other vehicles in the parking lot, so Ben's car was not particularly conspicuous. Much relieved, though still harboring lingering feelings of apprehension, they approached Ben's car. Just two normal scientists working the night shift. Some lights were still on in Building 401. Ben clicked his car door remote transponder, and the men piled into the car like there was gold to be found inside. They were exhausted, but exhilarated, and quite happy to be back in the car and home-free.

Ben pulled out of the parking lot, careful to drive normal doing the speed limit. He headed south onto Tesla Drive. There were no other cars on the roadway, and the Lab seemed asleep.

"I think we should call it a night, Ben. I am totally shot," Jon said.

"Yeah, me too. I shouldn't be doing these things at my age," Ben said.

"What about your experiment?"

"Don't worry about it. I haven't gotten any calls or messages from QUEST, so everything should be fine. I'll check in with them tomorrow to see how the data came in. Um, Ben, can you make any sense of what we saw tonight in the carry lab?"

"It looks like they were doing some type of biomedical research using materials which had been irradiated by sending them through the reactor core. We can only imagine what types of experiments they were doing, and what kinds of subjects they were experimenting on," Ben said as he gave him a petrified look.

"Well, it seems obvious that the experiments were not just limited to animals."

"No. You're right. It was very disturbing to see the possible involvement of human subjects. Although I keep wondering if there is another explanation for what we saw."

"I certainly hope so. If that's what Hilcraft knew was going on, no wonder he didn't want any part of being associated with that kind of crap."

Ben turned into the QUEST parking lot, and pulled up next to Jon's car. "What a night we had. I will never forget this one."

"Yeah, it was a crazy night. I'm going home. You go on home and get some sleep. You need it. I'll give you a call over the weekend, and we can talk over things. I'll get in touch with VG and find out how the experiment went, but I am sure it went well."

"Oh, Jon, one other thing before I leave."

"What's that, Ben?"

"That metal nodule that we found in the incinerator. Would you mind giving it to me? I'd like to have it looked at by my friend Keith. He's an expert in metallurgy. Maybe he can tell us what the hell that thing is."

"Sure Ben, here you go—good idea."

"And get some sleep!" Jon shouted, as Ben motioned to start his car.

Ben drove off to the south, and Jon got into his car, headed toward the main entrance and back to his beach house in Aquebogue. It was a long drive, and he was tired and worn out.

[24]

Targway Proving Ground

"Jon, wake up. Wake up," Marta called, softly insistent.

Jon slept profoundly, like an ancient bolder stuck in the bottom of a remote gully. Marta pulled off the covers, exposing Jon to the cool morning air. She shook his shoulders. "Come on Jon, wake up. It's getting late, and we should get going!"

Jon groaned. "Am I in Aquebogue, or am I on another planet somewhere?"

"Yes, indeed, Jon, you are certainly in Aquebogue! It's Saturday today, and we have a great long weekend ahead of us—so get up and I'll make you a nice breakfast," Marta said. She kissed Jon, and headed into the kitchen to prepare their breakfast.

A few minutes later, Jon entered the kitchen, washed and dressed. He kissed Marta, sat down, and said groggily, "I still haven't woken up fully yet. Wow, what a night!"

"I don't know what time you got home last night, but I do know that it was after two-thirty in the morning. Where were you last night?"

"Well, we were working at QUEST for a while, then we did something that I don't want you to tell anyone about. Not even Lois," said Jon, catching Marta's eye and holding her gaze for a long moment to impress her with the seriousness of his request.

Returning Jon's gaze, Marta said, "I do promise, Jon, but I hope you weren't being bad last night."

"Ben and I broke into the Ridgewood Graphite Reactor last night."

"What! Oh, my God! Did you get caught?"

"Almost, but we were able to escape without anyone finding out who we were."

"Why would you do something like that?"

"Because we wanted to find a way into Building 720. You know, the place where they did the secret experiments that I told you about."

"Well, what did you find? Did you find anything interesting? Anything that indicated what they were using that place for? I can't believe you two did that."

"Yes, we found out a lot of things. I will fill you in about it later, but I could definitely use some food right now. We had some small frozen pizzas at the mid-level station around eleven last night, so I am starved. What time is it now anyway?"

"It's ten-thirty."

"Damn, it's late. Christ, we usually get up before eight on Saturdays."

"Here you go, Jon. I hope you like this," said Marta, placing a plate in front of Jon.

"Cool, Marta! Wow, potato pancakes with kielbasa—what a nice breakfast. Hey, what kind of kielbasa is this? It's skinny, but really delicious!"

"It is called *kabanosy* in Polish. It is a special spicy kielbasa usually served to the Polish royalty. This was said to be a favorite of Pope John Paul II."

"Where did you get this?"

"Here in Riverhead, at Lech's Meats in Polish Town. They don't always have it. It's very popular around holidays."

"I'm so lucky to have you, Marta. You're the best! Is that the same Lech as your uncle Lech?"

"Yes. He is my mother's brother. He came from Poland about fifteen years ago, a few years after my mother and father arrived here. He opened the store soon after."

As they ate, Marta said, "Guess what? I did some Internet research into the picture on that postcard that Ben gave us. I think I found out where it's from."

"Wow. Cool. What did you find out?"

"It took me some time, but it looks like this photo was taken at the Sulov Rocks, which are located in the Tatra Mountains of Slovakia. They are unique and mysterious, and have mystical and spiritual associations."

"In what ways are they so unique?"

"The rocks are very distinct. There are natural towers, spires, and cone shapes. Even more fascinating is the fact that anthropologists have found ancient human settlements there from many different periods, as far back as 5,000 BC. There is even evidence that this was a place of ancient religious ceremonies. Many unique artifacts have been found there, along with symbols that seem to be some kind of hieroglyphs."

"Wow! That is fascinating! I wonder what it was, in particular, that fascinated Dr. Hilcraft about the location."

"I wonder if, in some way, the rock formations inspired his theories on physics. I am going to try to find out more information about these Sulov Rocks," Marta said.

"So, Marta, what do you have planned for today?"

"Well, I was thinking that I should go into the Medical Research building for a little while to finish up a few things. After that, we have the whole weekend to ourselves."

"Good! I think we should get away somewhere. I was thinking about going up to the Catskills for a few nights to do some hiking together. It would be a nice change of pace. How does that sound to you?"

Marta rose, placed her dish in the sink, and put her hands on Jon's shoulders and her face up against his head. "That sounds wonderful. Let's do it!"

"Yeah, with all the excitement from last night, and all the Lab crap going on, I think it will clear my head out. It will be great to have some time together up in the Catskills and maybe do some hiking too."

Marta walked over to the kitchen counter, reached for her laptop and then looked back at Jon and said. "It will be a nice quiet time for us, Jon. We can hike and relax together. Why don't you come with me to the Medical Research building, and I will show you around? You can see my lab animals, and meet Ayu, the Komodo dragon."

"Sure, but we can't stay too long because if we don't head to the Catskills by two o'clock we'll get up there too late."

"I will just clean up here quickly. Let's pack up now, and then we can leave for the Catskills right from the Lab."

Jon rinsed out his coffee cup and put it in the drain board. A small piece of mail near the phone caught his eye. For some reason, he felt compelled to take a closer look at the weird advertisement that Marta had brought in with the mail several days earlier.

Interested in a free trip to Hades?
Call 555-0177-2366.

"Hey, Marta, did you see this piece of mail?"

"I think I brought that in with the mail a few days ago. Strange, isn't it? Are you interested in a free trip to Hades, Jon?"

"No, because Ben and I already took a free trip to Hades last night. The reactor and Building 720 were part of the Hades experiment that Dr. Hilcraft worked on back in the 1960s. This is pretty weird."

"Do you think there is some meaning to this? Maybe a secret code of some kind?"

"It certainly is strange, isn't it? Especially since they capitalized all the letters of the word Hades. Let me give them a call to see if there is anything to this."

Jon picked up the phone and dialed the number on the card. After three rings, a firm voice commanded, "Targway Proving Ground. Please state your security passkey code."

Jon said nothing, and shot Marta a concerned look.

"Please state your external security passkey code now!"

Jon remained silent.

"This is a high-security line. Who is this? Identify yourself now!"

Alarmed, Jon slammed down the phone.

"What happened, Jon? What did you hear? What's the matter? You look terrified. Tell me!"

"Someone answered the phone 'Targway Proving Ground,' and repeatedly asked me for my *security passkey code.* He said it was a high-security line. I have no idea what Targway Proving Ground is."

"What do you think this means, Jon? Was this piece of mail just a coincidence, or is someone trying to pass us some information? Why would someone send a postcard with the phone number of a high-security line?"

"Exactly . . . it's not junk mail. See the postage stamp here on the upper right corner? Obviously, someone is trying to give us some kind of information linking the Hades experiment and Targway Proving Ground. I wonder if Ben knows anything about what the hell the Targway Proving Ground is. More mysteries again. Anyway, we'd better get going. Let's get back to packing. We've got a wonderful long weekend ahead of us."

The ride west from Aquebogue was quiet and pleasant, without the normal workday traffic. They arrived at the Medical Research building and found the parking lot nearly empty.

"Come on, Jon. It will only take me about an hour to get my work done. You can hang out in the lunchroom or library, and then I'll show you the animals."

Marta used her computerized key card to gain access to the building. They walked past the building security guard and exchanged greetings on the way to the medical research library.

Marta left, and Jon walked around the dead-silent library. The large library housed a collection of books, periodicals and documents. Continuing his tour, Jon passed several groups of tables and chairs, and peered into a spacious conference room, complete with a projection screen for seminars. Jon returned to the rows of books and began to browse through them. A collection of books and artifacts pertaining to the history of RNL caught his eye. It was located in a separate display case, and protected by a glass sliding window. He was surprised to find a book that was not of medical science on display. Opening the case, he removed the book, and took it into the conference room. After a brief search for the light switch, he settled down into one of the comfortable plush chairs, and started to read the book. Suddenly, he remembered that he should call VG to check on the completion of the Torqkadrone experiment. He felt somewhat dazed thinking about the adventure and turmoil of the previous night.

"Hello, Jon. I was going to call you. I'm glad you called."

"How did everything go last night?"

"The experiment went very well, Jon. We did have a little data interface incident with some of the information reception from the particle wave sensor, but overall, everything went fine."

"Very good, VG! Please tell everyone they did a great job, and they deserve some good time off after staying up all night. By the way, how late did you guys stay up with the experiment?"

"We completed the coherence seduction fully at around three in the morning. The data telemetry took about another hour or so complete. Yi and I got out of there at about four-thirty, but the others left a little earlier. Tom stayed with us, and the three of us celebrated by having a beer in the mid-level station afterward."

"Where are you now?"

"We are all here in the mid-level station now. After a few drinks we were too tired to leave the site, so we crashed here. I just happened to get up when you called—almost like we are on the same frequency!"

"Again, VG, excellent work! Tell all the team members congratulations on their success. Oh, also, I just want to let you know that Marta and I are away for the weekend, so when I get back early next week I'll go over the data analysis with you and Yi."

"Okay, Jon. Yi and I will be interpolating the data on Monday, so I'll probably see you then. I have to tell you, we found some more of those visual anomalies that we had previously seen in past Torqkadrone visual feeds—but I didn't spend much time studying the data yet, so I don't know what else is in there."

"Very well, my friend. Email me some of the data when you can, and I'll see you early next week. Have a great holiday weekend."

"You guys have a great weekend, too. See you when you get back."

Jon pondered some of the accomplishments of his program, and the wonders of the Macro-STARR, a true masterpiece of technology. He was proud of his efforts, and triumphant in his realization that the chances he took to get the QUEST facility built were paying off richly.

Jon settled back in to his chair and resumed reading the historical material about the Lab. He was surprised to find a great deal of information he had not been aware of concerning the construction of the Lab and its uses during both world wars, before the place became a national lab. He became engrossed in his reading, until several minutes later a queer surreal feeling overcame him. He looked up at the partly closed door to the library, and jostled in his seat. Was someone peering at him through the slight opening between the door and the hinge area? He leapt to his feet, quickly walked over to the door, and flung it open. No one was there, and there were no sounds to indicate that anyone was walking away. Absolutely sure he'd seen something real, he searched throughout the library. Nothing. Dead silent, and not a soul around. Finally, he returned to the conference room and was about to sit down when he heard footsteps approaching. Still spooked, he found his anxiety rising, until he caught sight of Marta at the door.

Marta opened the door and bounced in. She was looking forward to their weekend, and it showed in her movements. "Jon, I am all done with my things. I hope that you found something interesting to read here in this old library."

"Marta, did you come in here a little while ago?"

"No, why do you ask?"

"I thought I heard something in here before."

"You look a little flustered. There is no one around here today. The place is empty. Maybe it's all your stress from last night?"

"Well, I guess I might be a bit on edge from our RGR raid last night. I'm pretty wiped out. How about you drive up to the Catskills, if you don't mind? I could use a little more rest."

"That's fine with me. Let's go see the lab animals now, and then we can head upstate."

"Sure, let's go."

Marta led Jon out of the library and though a series of halls. They headed down a flight of stairs, through another hallway, and into the animal holding area of the Medical Research building. Immediately, they heard the sounds of many animals.

"Wow. Well, if the sounds aren't enough of a clue, you can tell by the smell that there are a lot of animals kept here," Jon said.

"Here are the rat and mouse cages. And there, a little further up, are the rabbit and goat areas."

"I didn't realize you used so many different types of animals for your experiments."

"Yes, we do. It all depends on when you come here, because the types of animals all change from time to time. We do various experiments with the animals but we are careful to be as humane as possible with them at all times. Some experiments are totally noninvasive and arc harmless to them."

"Interesting, it's nice you treat them with respect!"

"Let's continue. I want to show you the primates, and Ayu."

They passed several more cages of animals, including cattle and snakes. Jon walked slowly past the various animals, totally enthralled by what he saw.

"Who takes care of these animals?"

"We have several lab animal keepers who take care of them every day—even on weekends. They feed the animals and clean the cages. They always work in pairs, as a safety precaution. Also, there are cameras monitoring the animals. This way, the animal keepers can monitor the animals all the time, even when they are at home," said Marta, pointing to one of the cameras. "Smile for the camera, Jon. You are being watched."

"Unbelievable. Everywhere we go we are being monitored!"

"Here we go, Jon. These are the primates."

"Wow, these guys are really something," said Jon, staring in wonder. "These are two different types of primates, aren't they—both chimps and baboons?"

"Good observation, Jon!"

"I can't believe this little baboon is using that mirror he's holding to look at my reflection. They look so smart, but I never really realized how damned intelligent they really are."

"Yes, they are very intelligent creatures. When you work around them they start to learn all about you. They know how to get food from you, and how to push your buttons, too! It's pretty amazing to see how close they are to the humans."

Jon approached the baboon, and said, "I wonder what he is thinking now. I wonder what he thinks of me."

The baboon did not face Jon directly, but moved around in his cage and used his mirror to see Jon's reflection from different angles. Jon tore his gaze away from the baboon, and followed Marta as she walked on. "Let's go see Ayu now." They stopped at a locked metal doorway. "This is the special Komodo dragon room. It's a secure area. Anyone who enters must take special precautions because Komodo dragons can be dangerous." As soon as Marta opened the heavy door they heard odd, high-pitched cries.

"Is that sound coming from the Komodo dragon?"

"Yes, that is Ayu. She is concerned that we are in the room with her. That's the sound she makes when she's anxious."

"This is a really big area here for her."

"Komodos require a large habitat cage, otherwise they can harm themselves. We try to make their habitat as natural as possible."

"She is absolutely huge. What does she eat?"

"Komodo dragons will eat any kind of meat. She weighs about three hundred pounds. Can you believe a Komodo dragon can go through up to five sets of teeth in its lifetime? They can live up to fifty years."

"She's amazing to look at. She is staring at me almost like she wants to be friends with me."

Marta laughed. "If I opened the cage, Ayu would pounce on you and eat you in about five minutes. She is very fast, and you could not possibly outrun her. She definitely likes you, though."

"Well, that's a pleasant thought. On that note, I think we'd better get going if we want to get upstate while there's still afternoon light."

"Okay, I'm ready. So let's go."

Jon turned back at the doorway, and said, "See you later, Ayu." As he turned back he had a strange sense of clairvoyance after seeing her face staring at him. It almost seemed like there was some kind of connection between both of them. Something he couldn't explain.

[25]

A Weekend Getaway

When they reached the car, Marta opened the doors with the remote, and Jon relaxed into the passenger seat. "I am very impressed with your lab animals—especially the primates and Ayu. She was very cool. Thanks for the tour, Marta."

"I'm really glad that you finally got to see Ayu. In a few days she's being moved to the RNL Science Museum, and then she is going to the Molecular Biology Building for some time, so if you hadn't seen her now it might have been a while."

"Why would Ayu be going to the Molecular Biology Building?"

"The scientists there use her blood and venom in certain experiments, so we both have partial use of her in our research."

"Interesting. I wonder what experiments they're doing with her."

"I really don't know, but Lois might know."

"We'll have to ask her."

Marta eased onto the Long Island Expressway. "It's a wonderful day to travel. I find it very relaxing when we go up to the Catskills."

"Where do you want to hike this time? We could do Slide or Giant Ledge Mountain again, or maybe some mountain that we haven't tried yet?"

"I think Giant Ledge would be a nice trek for us. We could pack a lunch and maybe try to get to Panther Mountain, too—if we have the energy."

"Okay, that sounds good. Giant Ledge is always a nice mountain to climb. The view from the top ledge is awesome."

Traffic was light, and they made good time on the LIE, and out past New York City, to the Tappan Zee Bridge. "What a great view of the Hudson River today, Marta. Look at those white caps on the river. It must be windy out."

"I can feel the wind blowing the car around the road, but I'm not going to look at the water because it makes me dizzy. I am always nervous driving over this bridge."

"Marta, I want to ask you something, and I hope you don't find it too weird."

"Well, I'm a psychiatrist, so I am used to weird. What's your question, Jon?"

"Okay, I know this sounds strange, but did you ever get a feeling, at times, likc you are in a different world?"

"A different world? Well, what do you mean by a different world?"

Gesturing with his hands, Jon said, "I don't know how to exactly describe it, but what I mean is, we go about our daily lives day after day and month after month. We think about the moment that is in front of us all the time, and occasionally we review our past experiences and relive those memories—both recent and more remote. But occasionally there are those odd times when you think back about your life and your past experiences seem so strange and almost alien to you, and so very far away."

"Strange in what ways? I'm very interested to hear what that means to you."

Gazing out the car window at the scenery, Jon answered, "Well, I know this probably must sound very odd, but what I mean is—it just seems like a different world. It almost seems like the world that we are in now was not part of my past world. It feels like I was in a different world somewhere else. Like we were actors in different plays who were suddenly thrown into a new play together." Jon peered at Marta with a sheepish frown, anxious to hear her response to his thoughts.

Marta glanced at Jon. "I think I understand what you are getting at. It is rare for people to ignore all the distractions of modern life and the media, and plunge more deeply into questions about the nature of reality. It's more common to glide along the surface than to pursue deeper self-realization. My own thoughts have touched on concepts similar to what you are talking about, but I haven't really felt that kind of thing experientially. It really is fascinating, though."

"Have you ever heard of a concept like this before?"

"Yes. There is an unusual psychological condition that is very similar to the paranormal perception you are describing. It's called reduplicative paramnesia."

"That's a mouthful. What is that?"

"Reduplicative paramnesia is the belief that a place or location has been duplicated, existing in two or more places simultaneously."

"Wow, that almost sounds like what I described, doesn't it?"

"Unfortunately, that psychological condition is considered delusional, a form of mental illness."

"Well, I don't think I'm crazy yet, Marta. Although some people think that we are crazy with our work with the QUEST project! Do you think I'm crazy?"

"No, Jon, you certainly are not mentally ill, but I am going to have to give your unique perceptions some additional thought." Gazing out the window, Jon missed the concerned look on her face as she glanced his way.

As they continued along the New York State Thruway and closer to their destination they eased into vacation mode. Marta exited onto Route 28 and headed west into the Catskill Mountains.

"Marta, are you getting tired yet?"

"No, I still have a lot of energy. I'm fine driving."

"Where do you want to stay this time?"

"I checked the Internet before I left my office. I found a hotel-restaurant in Pine Hill that seems like a nice place. From the photos and reviews it looks like a quiet, well-kept retreat. Some celebrities have even stayed there and recommended the place, according to their website."

"You're kidding! Pine Hill!" exclaimed Jon. "That's the village that Emery Hilcraft had a house in, isn't it?"

"Yes, that's the same village. I thought that maybe we could try to find his house to see if it is still there."

"Great idea, Marta! This sounds like fun—a mystery-solving trip and a hiking trek. What could be better?"

"I wonder what Pine Hill is like. We have never been through it before."

"We'll find out in about thirty more miles. I just hope the place is nice, and the food is good. I'm starving."

"Me too, and I am getting a little tired now, after all this driving."

"The mountains are so beautiful today, especially at this time of the day. I love the light at this time of day."

"Yeah, toward sunset the mountains get a beautiful blue hue to them. Maybe that is why the Native Americans named them the Blue Mountains."

Marta and Jon arrived in the village and searched for the inn.

"This is a really tiny, quiet place. It is much smaller then Margaretville," noted Jon. "I don't think there's much more here than the post office and a few stores. I should be very relaxing,"

"Here it is! The Pine Hill Arms Hotel. It looks just like it did on the Internet."

As they exited the car Marta looked around at the surrounding scenery and gazed at the inn. The building was a brown-colored wood-shingled two-storied structure. It looked old and charming, like something one would see on an antique country painting dating back to the early nineteen hundreds. The building had been renovated and had a huge glassed-in greenhouse section extending out the restaurant dining room toward the front of the street.

"This looks like it might be a nice place to have a wedding, doesn't it Jon?"

With a mock frown, Jon asked, "Are you trying to give me a hint?"

They entered the main building, and walked up to the check-in counter, but were greeted only by a friendly yellow Labrador. Petting the Lab, Marta asked, "Where are your parents? Is anyone here?"

As if on cue, an elderly gentleman entered and welcomed them.

"Hi. My name is Jon Sanborne, and this is my fiancée, Marta. We were wondering if you have a room available for the next two nights?"

"Nice to meet you both. I'm Robert Anderson. Welcome to the Pine Hill Arms. My wife Valerie and I have owned and operated this facility for over thirty years. We welcome you here, and hope you have a wonderful stay. Yes, indeed, we have rooms available, and I can certainly help you get checked in. You'll like room number eight. It's upstairs in the building just adjacent to this one."

"Thanks, by the way, what time do you open for dinner tonight?"

"We will be open in about half an hour."

"Great, we'll be down for dinner. See you in a little while."

Jon and Marta headed back to their car, grabbed their bags and walked a short distance into the adjacent building. Jon unlocked the door, and they brought their things inside. Marta put her arms around Jon, and said, "It's very nice here, so very quiet, and look we even have two beds and a couch!"

"I like it too. It looks very comfortable, and I love the quiet here."

They relaxed a little bit and freshened up, and headed down to the restaurant.

After they placed their orders, Marta said, "You must be very worn out from all that nefarious activity you and Ben engaged in last night."

"Yeah, I'm somewhat fried, but considering how late I got to sleep I am not too bad. I'll sleep really well tonight, though."

"Oh, I forgot to ask, you said before that you were reading some material about the history of RNL while you were in the library waiting for me. What were you reading about?"

"Oh yeah, that's right, I did find out some neat things about the history of the Lab. It started as a military base in 1917 to house and train soldiers for the United States, which at that time had no standing army prior to our entry into World War I. After the war, the site was named Camp Ridgewood, and was used to demobilize the units of soldiers and decommission them."

"Lois once told me that her uncle told her that during World War II the site of Camp Ridgewood was also used as a military base, and that they held German prisoners of war there."

"Now that is interesting!" Jon said.

"Here you go, you two." The waitress placed their entrees in front of them.

"This ginger lime chicken looks great," Marta said.

"It does, but I'm glad I ordered the rib-eye steak. It's pretty huge, and I'm starving."

"I'd be happy to come back here, Marta. Oh, not to change the subject, but I have to tell you that some of my workers at QUEST have been complaining about the physical exams that you are requiring them to complete. What is it with all of those unusual tests that you are making them do?"

"As the QUEST team health physician I am required to evaluate your staff of employees and establish a baseline of their health. I have to check for any health-related issues, so I am doing the compulsory medical tests. I have to admit though, that I have pursued a bit of research for some of my own biomedical interests."

"I thought that some of the medical and psychological tests that you were making us do seemed somewhat excessive. For example, what are those tests where you make us look at certain visual images and ask us questions about them for?"

"Those tests are for us to better understand the dynamics and efficiencies of how your brains work. It's called neurometric and psychometric testing."

"Why would you want to do that kind of testing on the QUEST personnel? It doesn't seem relevant."

"It definitely is relevant, Jon. The environment in, and near, the Macro-STARR is a very dynamic place where all kinds of energies and particles are interacting with your bodies. I want to see if there are any measurable biometric effects on you and your employees. Remember that Garrett Hansen died there, and the specific cause of his death is still a mystery."

"That's a very salient point, Marta. I have to agree that it probably is a good idea to do the additional testing. So let me ask you, are you finding any anomalies in your research so far?"

"Nothing conclusive yet, Jon. I don't really expect to find anything, but I'm going to continue on with the testing. When my analysis is complete, you'll be the first to know if I have discovered anything."

They were interrupted by Robert Anderson, as he stopped at their table. "How is your dinner tonight? I hope you two are enjoying the food here."

"The food is exceptional. I love it. This lime ginger chicken is cooked perfectly. I would love to get your recipe for this," Marta said.

"Sure, I will get it to you before you leave. It's really easy to make. We have been serving it here since we opened the place back in the seventies. It's one of our most popular dishes."

"That's quite an accomplishment, having operated this inn since the seventies. You must be proud of this place. It's quiet, comfortable, and charming—and your food is wonderful!" Jon said.

"Why, thank you for your kind words. My wife and I try to do our best to provide a nice experience for anyone visiting this wonderful mountain region. We love it here. If you're so inclined, maybe you could write some comments in our register before you leave."

"Sure. I'd be happy to. Could you tell me, Robert, have you ever heard of a guy named Emery Hilcraft who was from Pine Hill?"

"Emery Hilcraft! I haven't heard that name for a long time. He did live here, but he disappeared many years ago. Why do you ask?"

"Marta and I work at Ridgewood National Lab on Long Island. Emery Hilcraft worked at Ridgewood from the fifties until he disappeared sometime in the nineties."

Anderson nodded. "It was big news around here, where everyone knows each other. People don't just disappear. The New York State Police came nosing around for any clues or evidence. That was a pretty big to-do for a little village like this. Emery had a house here. He came in to eat here from time to time, and we'd chat, but I didn't know him very well. I still remember what he liked to order. It was pretty disturbing when he disappeared."

"What was he like? How would you describe him?" Jon asked.

"As I said, I didn't really know him on a personal level. He seemed like a pretty quiet guy. Years ago, back around when we first opened, he used to come in for dinner with his wife, then later years he started coming in with some friends now and then. Other than that, I can't remember much else about him."

"Do you know where his house was?" Marta asked.

"Sure. Emery's house is a little further west on Rock Water Street. After his disappearance the house was sold. The buyer lived there for a few years, and then died, and the house was never sold again. It's in very poor shape, rundown and overgrown. I'm surprised it's still standing."

"How would we get to the house from here if we wanted to see it?" Jon asked.

"Easy. It's about a fifteen-minute walk from here. Just go west on Main Street 'til you come to an intersection in the road, and then take the left there onto Rock Water Street, and then follow that down toward the end. Emery's house is on the left side. It is very overgrown. If you make it to the small water treatment plant you went too far. That's the source of water for the village."

"Thanks a lot, Robert. Your restaurant is great, and you're a great host. We appreciate the information," Jon said.

"Thank you. Well, I better get back to work, so enjoy your stay. We'll be serving a nice breakfast buffet tomorrow morning if you're interested!"

When Robert had walked away, Marta grinned at Jon, and said, "Let's take a walk by Dr. Hilcraft's old house to see what it looks like!"

"Absolutely, we're both too beat now but we could take a walk to it tomorrow after our hike up Giant Ledge. We'll get an early start on our hike tomorrow."

They finished dinner, and strolled back to their room for an early turn-in, happy, relaxed and excited about their wonderful weekend and their upcoming hike.

The next morning Jon and Marta headed out toward Giant Ledge Mountain. They were both eager to engage in the physical challenge of climbing to the mountain's summit, and looking forward to the fantastic views that would be their reward.

* * *

Tonner was finishing breakfast when the phone rang. He drained his coffee cup, and looked at the caller ID on his phone. The incoming call was from Lieutenant Harmon Reynolds, chief of the Lab police force. He took the call.

"Hello Lt. Reynolds, I understand that we had a security issue at Building 720 the other day."

"Yes, that is correct, sir. Apparently someone broke into Building 720 very early in the morning and set off an alarm. Two of our officers went into the building to investigate."

"Have you identified how the intruders gained access to the building?"

"No, Dr. Tonner. We are not sure yet, but there is some evidence that they may have accessed Building 720 via a connection tunnel from the RGR."

"Do you have any idea who the intruders were? Did the officers see anything of note?"

"They did not find anyone inside the building. But Officer Lutz was assaulted outside the building. He spotted someone on the north side of the building and when he tried to subdue the individual and bring him in for questioning, he was accosted, apparently by an accomplice. Officer Lutz was knocked out, and they got away."

"Do you have any idea what they were doing inside Building 720?"

"We have no idea. They left no trace of their activity."

"Listen, Lt. Reynolds, this is a very serious situation; one that I want dealt with immediately! I want you to find out who broke into 720, and I want those individuals apprehended."

"Sir, we are doing everything we can to find the intruders. We are studying video camera data from the nearby buildings to see if there are any leads."

"Very good, Lt. Reynolds. Keep me informed. I want to know about any and all possible leads. Arrange for additional surveillance on 720 and the RGR immediately. This absolutely cannot happen again. Do I have your understanding?"

"Yes sir, Dr. Tonner, we will find out who these criminals are and they will be apprehended."

[26]

This Enchanting World

Jon and Marta spent most of the morning scaling the mountain, hiking on steep trails, and scrambling up several rock chimneys. They finally reached the top of Giant Ledge after much effort. They walked along a trail that traveled along a steep cliff. There they were greeted by several magnificent views to the north.

"Jon, let's stop here and have our lunch. The view is absolutely fantastic."

Jon grabbed Marta affectionately, hugged her, and said, "God, Marta, we are so lucky to be together here—you and I. Can you think of anything better to do than this?"

They lingered in their embrace, and kissed each other again, absorbing their joy in being together in such beautiful surroundings. They unpacked their lunch and settled on a large bolder and made themselves comfortable. The view was surreal, and they paused to feast on the majesty of nature spread out before them. The breeze whispered through the balsam firs. The lovely sounds were complemented by the fragrance of the firs and damp mosses. An aromatic radiating essence unique to the higher elevations of the Catskills filled the air.

"What a great day, Jon. It's perfect for a fall day, the weather is just right, the sun is shining, and this is heaven."

Jon was silent looking north, and seemed to be in a trance.

"Jon, what are you thinking about now?"

"I'm thinking about how beautiful this place is, about the marvelous views of the mountains to the north, and about my life here with you, here in this universe, and how happy I am."

Marta put her arm around Jon, and they continued to enjoy their journey into the enchanting world before them.

Some hours later, they left the mountain behind them. They stopped for a quick bite and a beer in Margaretville on the way back to the inn. It was dark by the time they got back.

"How are you feeling after that great workout? Wasn't the day wonderful?" Jon asked.

"My feet and legs are a little sore, but overall I feel pretty good. I'd love a glass of wine, though."

"Yeah, I think I have a blister on my left foot, but I made out alright physically. Do you think that you have any energy left to go for a walk to see what Dr. Hilcraft's house looks like?" Jon asked.

"Now? Well, I was thinking I'd like a hot shower, some wine, and then I'd be set for the night, but I guess I can find enough energy for a small walk. I don't want to stay out too long, though."

"Good, Marta. Let's go right away, before we get too tired. Put on a warm sweatshirt because it's cooling down quickly tonight."

They went downstairs, and walked west on Main Street. The street was silent and empty, and the cool mountain air was refreshing. After several minutes they saw the sign for Rock Water Street.

"Look, Jon! That sign shows that there is a Pine Hill Museum down that way to the right. I would like to visit it sometime."

"Next time we stay in the Catskills, let's stay here again, and visit the museum. I love this town. I can see why Dr. Hilcraft had a house in this village. It has a special feel to it."

They turned onto Rock Water Street, and continued on as the road headed up hill.

"Damn, this street gets steep here, but it's kind of cool the way the Village of Pine Hill is built on the side of the mountain. It's nothing like Long Island, that's for sure."

The hill began to level out, and they walked past several houses. Some were surprisingly well-maintained, while a few were old and in poor shape. It was now fully dark, so Jon pulled out his flashlight. He used the flashlight to highlight every house they passed. It was stunningly quiet out. There were no signs of human activity, and woods separated most of the houses from each other. Their autumn nighttime walk had a decidedly ghostly feel.

"Look, Marta! This is probably Dr. Hilcraft's house here on the left. It's so overgrown that you can barely make out the place from the trees."

The deteriorating white exterior of the house glowed faintly in the dim moonlight.

"God, it looks eerie, doesn't it? Almost like someone is inside looking out at us," Marta said.

"Maybe the spirit of Emery Hilcraft is still inside. Let's go check it out up close."

"Okay, but I don't want to stay too long, Jon. This place is scary."

They approached the house, careful not to get entangled by all the overgrown vegetation. It was a moderately large, white, two-story house with big old windows. Years of mountain weather had taken their toll on the house. The gutters had long ago detached from the house and were lying on the ground. The front porch had partially caved in and twisted strangely. And yet, oddly, an ornamental windmill near the porch was working perfectly, catching the mountain wind and making an enchanting sound. They traveled around the right side of the house to the back. Jon ascended the small wooden steps. He directed the beam of his flashlight into the small window and peered inside. He tried the doorknob, twisting and pushing, and abruptly the door opened up. He jumped back, startled.

"Someone is apparently going into this house from time to time."

"What are you doing Jon? We'll get in trouble! Don't go inside!"

"Come on, Marta. Let's check out the house. The spirit of Emery Hilcraft wants us to go inside. I can feel it."

Reluctantly, Marta followed Jon into the silent house. They were accosted by a foul odor. The house was filthy and disorganized. After years of neglect, the interior was as ramshackle as the exterior.

"Look at this kitchen table, Marta. I wonder what happened to it. The cabinets are warped from all the moisture. It's amazing how quickly even the inside of a house can become dilapidated without maintenance. Without the heat on in the winter, the moisture accumulates and freezes and thaws."

"This is the living room in here, Jon. It must have been a very nice room when it was in good shape. Hey, Jon, don't get too far ahead of me. Slow down! You have the flashlight!"

"It's strange how the walls are so bare. It looks like it's been ransacked—probably by kids, I'll bet. Or maybe the relatives of the last owner just came in and took what they wanted and left everything else in shambles. The furniture is just covered with mildew and mold. I wonder how long it has been since Dr. Hilcraft sat on his sofa and relaxed in this room."

"Jon, what is this all over the floor over here?"

Jon shined his flashlight to the spot Marta indicated. "That looks like animal droppings, as if the stench of the mold and mildew were not enough."

"Yuck, that's disgusting. I wonder how animals that size are getting in here."

Jon and Marta continued to explore the ground floor of the old house, identifying a dining room, bedroom, and bathroom which all exhibited similar signs of deterioration, and were all devoid of personal paraphernalia. Then they headed up the stairs. Marta was close behind Jon.

"We really should get going back to our room, Jon. I'm worn out, and this place is dilapidated and dangerous!"

"Just a few more minutes to see the upstairs, okay?"

"Okay, but let's make it quick. We still have to walk back to the inn."

At the top of the stairs they entered into a small hallway. Jon directed his light right, and then left, and headed left down the hall past a small bathroom. Marta was right behind Jon as he turned into the next room, which was obviously a bedroom. As he set foot in the doorway, the silence was pierced by a terrifying sound. Red eyes, belonging to nothing human, glared at them for a split second, but before they could fully comprehend the situation, there was a sudden rush of movement headed right toward them. Jon forcefully pushed Marta to the side and scrambled after her.

"Christ, it's a damn raccoon!" said Jon, as they tumbled into a wooden cabinet and fell to the floor. The raccoon disappeared into the hallway while Jon helped Marta up. "Are you okay? I hope I didn't push you too hard!"

"I'm fine. Well, that was a shock. I can't believe that there was a raccoon in here."

"It scared the hell out of me," said Jon, shining his flashlight around the room, which was occupied by an old bed and bedroom set. "This house is infested with raccoons and other animals getting in somehow. This room is in even worse state of decay than the rest of the house."

"Jon, what's that on the ground near your feet? Something shiny is reflecting the light from your flashlight."

Jon noticed the shimmering item with his flashlight, and picked it up carefully. He examined it closely, rotating it to see it from different angles.

"It's some kind of medallion. It looks like an old large silver coin of some kind. There are some strange symbols on it. Maybe when we hit the dresser cabinet it fell out from under it or something."

"It looks very old to me. The inscriptions on it are so intricate."

A sudden noise from the direction of the stairwell startled them. Jon put the medallion in his back pocket, and they left the room and went to the stairwell. Looking down, they saw light radiating from the ground floor of the house.

"Who do you think it could be?" asked Marta, anxiously.

"I hope it's not the police," Jon answered.

"WHO ARE YOU? WHY ARE YOU IN THIS HOUSE? COME ON DOWN NOW!" It was a woman's voice.

Jon glanced at Marta. The look on his face almost screamed, *"Oh-no, we're in big trouble now!"* Although the woman had not sounded extremely threatening, he decided to play it safe. You just never know. "HELLO! WE ARE ON OUR WAY DOWN NOW. PLEASE DON'T SHOOT!"

They proceeded slowly down the old wooden stairs, which creaked loudly as they descended. Marta peered at Jon and Jon immediately recognized that tense angry scowl. He knew he was in trouble now for not leaving earlier when she wanted and that they had gotten caught red-handed by someone in the house. As they reached the bottom of the stairs, the woman's flashlight shone directly at them. Looking into the light, they could only make out a vaguely human silhouette, nothing more.

"I live down the street. I saw you two walk by a while ago. What are you doing in this house? You're trespassing! You shouldn't be in here!"

Much relieved to have been apprehended by a concerned neighbor rather than the local police, Jon answered, "Ma'am, we are very sorry to have disturbed you. Please allow me to explain why we are here now."

"Please do."

"My name is Jon Sanborne, and this is my fiancée, Marta Padlo. We are visiting from Long Island. We're staying at the inn down the road. We both work at Ridgewood National Lab on Long Island, and have heard a great deal about Dr. Hilcraft. We were speaking with Robert Anderson at the inn, and he told us that this was Hilcraft's house."

"So you broke into Hilcraft's old house in order to sightsee? Why are you so interested in Emery anyway?"

"We work with several people who knew Dr. Hilcraft, and I've learned a lot about him because he was a very well-known researcher at the Lab. We're really curious about his life, his work, and his disappearance. When we found out that his house was right here in this village we felt compelled to take a look at it."

"So you know about Dr. Hilcraft's disappearance?"

"Yes, that's a big part of why we wanted to find out more about his life story. I work with a scientist who was a close friend and colleague of his, and he's told me many things about Dr. Hilcraft that intrigued us. We didn't intend to enter the house, but when we saw that it had obviously been abandoned years ago, we thought it would be harmless."

"When I saw you two walk by I thought you looked like nice young people, but you never know, and I wanted to make sure you weren't going to damage the house. I keep an eye on this house even though it is falling apart. I owe it to Emery; he was a good man."

"So you knew Dr. Hilcraft?"

"Yes, I knew Emery for quite some time. My name is Ariel Fisher. I'm the village librarian here in Pine Hill. Would you two like to continue this conversation over a cup of tea at my place? It's just down the street. It's probably best not to linger here too long. I haven't been inside for a while; the house is really starting to fall apart."

"Tea sounds great, and we'd love to learn more about Dr. Hilcraft and this beautiful village."

"Okay, then follow me. Be careful of the animal droppings on the floor. The raccoons have found their way into the house, and they are not good tenants."

[27]

We All Live on Forever

Marta and Jon followed the older woman down the hill on Rock Water Street. Shortly, they turned up a neat walkway, and Marta commented, "Your home is so beautifully maintained. It's really lovely."

"Thank you, Marta. It's not easy taking care of a house in the mountains. The winters here are very wet and cold, and I'm getting older. There's no stopping time."

Ariel Fisher led them into her living room and switched on the light. "Make yourselves comfortable. I will put some tea on for us and be right back."

"She's really nice," Jon said. "I'm so glad that we didn't get in trouble for sneaking into the house."

"Yes. We were very lucky. I think you've been getting into quite enough trouble lately. What did you do with the thing that you found in the upstairs bedroom?"

"Don't worry. I have it in my back pocket. I'm not going to mention it to Ariel, though."

Marta nodded her head in agreement, and looked around the room. "What a charming house. I love all the antiques."

"That painting on the wall is interesting. It looks like an old hotel or spa."

"It looks like it's from some long gone time, doesn't it?" Marta added.

Ariel returned bearing a lovely serving tray. Scented steam spiraled up from an exquisite porcelain teapot, and a pretty plate was filled with pastries.

"Wow, what a lovely tea. Thank you, Ariel. Your house is just beautiful. I love your antiques, and the wall hangings. We were just talking about this painting. Can you tell us about it?" Marta asked.

"Oh, yes, that's a painting of the Grand Hotel. It was located on Monka Hill in Highmount, which is a few miles west of here. It was constructed in the 1880s, and had more than four hundred rooms."

"It must have been a magnificent place to stay. What happened to it?"

"It burned to the ground in the 1960s and was never rebuilt. Now there is a restaurant on that same location, though. This area of the Catskills once was home to several large resorts. Wealthy New York City residents used to flock to the area in droves to escape the city heat and enjoy the majestic Catskill Mountains. Many of these resorts were built in the late 1800s here, but by the mid-1900s they had declined greatly. A train station in Highmount helped keep the Grand Hotel going longer than many of the surrounding resorts."

"I would never have imagined that. It would be amazing to be able to go back in time to see what it looked like then. It must have been wonderful," Marta said.

"If you are interested, you should visit our Pine Hill Museum. There are many photos, paintings and assorted memorabilia from the many old hotels that once brought so many to the Catskills."

"We are definitely going to do that sometime soon, but unfortunately we have to get back to Long Island tomorrow. We'll have to visit the museum the next time we are up here," Jon said.

"Mrs. Fisher, you told us that you knew Dr. Hilcraft back when he lived in the house down the road. We are very interested in his disappearance. I was wondering what you can tell us about him?" Jon asked, changing the subject rather abruptly.

"Emery was a quiet and pleasant person. He seemed very intelligent. I knew that he worked at a National Laboratory on Long Island. He wasn't around all that much. His wife stayed here in Pine Hill and raised the children, and he came up on the weekends and vacations to be with his family as often as he could. They all loved the Catskills way of life. His wife was from this area and she never wanted to leave, but I guess he couldn't do the work he wanted to up here."

"Do you remember his wife's name?" Marta asked.

"Her name was Susan. The children's names were Sara and Allen."

"Do you know what happened to them?"

"Susan died of some kind of cancer sometime in the nineties. The kids were in their twenties. They were both in college when their mother died. Emery was heartbroken. A few years later Emery just disappeared."

"Do you know anything else about what happened to their children?"

"I know that the son, Allen, went on to graduate school in the field of computers. He was a very gifted student, and last I heard he was very successful in his career at a well-known computer company in the Hudson Valley."

"Do you know the name of the computer company?" Jon asked.

"No, I don't. As far as Sara, the last I remember she went on to be a teacher somewhere near Sydney, New York, but that was a while ago."

"Is there anything else that you can tell us about Emery?" Marta asked.

"No, not really. He had friends who lived in the area that he liked to go hiking with, and he really enjoyed being around his family whenever he came up from Long Island."

Ariel smiled, paused, and continued, "I do remember one time Emery was asked by the rabbi from the local synagogue in Fleischmanns to give a talk on science and philosophy. He and the rabbi were good friends. They used to have speakers come and give lectures there all the time. My husband and I attended that particular lecture. We had no idea what Emery was going to talk about. We were totally spellbound. I think everyonc left the room that night with a thoroughly altered sense of what this world really is and what our perceptions really are. It was very stimulating and philosophical. Amazing. I still remember that night!"

Jon leaned forward. "It must have been completely fascinating. Dr. Hilcraft's work was groundbreaking and very controversial. It is spellbinding stuff. Do you remember any specific thing that Dr. Hilcraft said? I know it's been a long time but I'm very interested in what he might have discussed."

Ariel sat still for a moment, and then spoke as if in a trance. "The only specific thing I seem to remember is that he discussed something about how *in some way, we all live on forever into eternity in this universe.*" She sighed, and seemed both moved and comforted by the thought.

After chatting more about the area, Marta said, "Jon we really should get going. We have to leave early tomorrow morning."

Jon rose. "Thank you so much, Mrs. Fisher, for your wonderful hospitality and the fascinating conversation. Do you mind if I give you my name and phone number in case you come across any more information about Dr. Hilcraft?"

"No, not at all, Jon. I'll let you and Marta know if I find out anything more about Emery or his children. I would love to know what happened to him. It's been a long time, but many of us were concerned about him, and distressed at his disappearance. I only hope that he has found peace in his life wherever he is now."

Jon and Ariel exchanged contact information, and Ariel walked them to the door. "Next time you two are up this way give me a call before you come. You will be welcome to come have dinner with me."

"Thank you, that would be lovely," Marta said.

They walked out into the cool early fall air of the Catskills and headed back to their room at the Pine Hill Arms Hotel. The sky was blanketed with stars. The starlight was so bright that they were surrounded by a silky, surreal glow.

"What a day we had today, Marta. What a day in this strange universe."

Too tired to talk, Marta took Jon's hand, and they made their way back to their room.

[28]

East on Route 28

Well-rested, they got an early start back to Long Island the next morning. After stopping at a diner in Phoenicia for breakfast, they got back onto Route 28, and headed toward Kingston and the New York State Thruway.

Jon drove. "The mountains look especially enchanting today, Marta. Look at that cliff on that ridge over to the right. It's huge."

"Yes, that's a big one. I really love all the cliffs around here. Did you notice the hawks flying around the mountains this morning? They're magnificent."

"I think some of the birds we've seen are turkey vultures, not hawks. They look very similar. You can tell them apart by the darkness around the inner wings of the vultures. Also, the hawks have a reddish tail."

Marta retrieved the medallion they had found in Hilcraft's house, and studied it. "Jon, this medallion you found is very interesting and strange. Have you looked at it yet?"

"Not very carefully. I was going to look at it tonight after we get back from our trip."

"It looks so old, so ancient. I wonder how old it is."

"I am thinking of taking it to the Patchogue Coin Shop next week if I have time. I'd like them to take a look at it."

Marta continued to examine the coin. "One side of the medallion shows a very mystical looking figure surrounded by some strange symbols, and the other side displays some sort of intricate triangle and some additional markings. It's obviously very old. It's pretty worn."

"It's weird how it must have fallen out from under that wooden dresser. If we hadn't been terrorized by that raccoon and banged into the dresser, that coin might have been stuck in there forever. Strange how things happen in life."

"Maybe we were meant to find it, Jon. Perhaps it was a quantum event."

"Yeah, maybe Emery guided us there for a reason," said Jon, not quite believing his own words.

"Do you think that it belonged to him?"

"It may have, but I don't know if we'll ever know that."

"Oh Marta, isn't that drug trial with Dr. Haslinger taking place next week?"

"Yes. Are you going to take part in the study?"

"I definitely want to be a participant! After all, it is open to the public. I already filled out my application, and they should have received my required medical exams. I think VG may participate in the trial, too."

"I don't know if you should take part in this medical trial, Jon."

"Why not, Marta? It seems like it is going to be a really interesting experience. I have read all of the reference material on it, and it does not seem like a big deal. Besides, it will be like attending a party with a lot of interesting people."

"Jon, they are going to be giving out test doses of the LSD isomer, Pegasus, to the participants. It's a trial, which means the effects are still being evaluated."

"I read in the application that the Pegasus LSD isomer has been studied for several years as a pain management drug, and that it only has limited intoxicating effects that are well tolerated. It clearly stated that there are no known short-term or long-term side effects from the drug, and I'll be helping out in the study, so what is the big deal?"

"Well, that's true. Pegasus has been studied for quite some time for pain management, but I'm still reluctant to see you take part in this study."

"Marta, you are going to be there to assist Dr. Haslinger, aren't you?"

"Lois and I, and several other researchers, will be present to help out in the evaluation of the test subjects."

"Well, I'm looking forward to it. Please don't worry about me. I bet there will be many people there that I can have interesting conservations with."

"Yes, several scientists and physicists will be there. We have some subjects who are visiting from other parts of the country, and even from Europe."

"Great, Marta! It is going to be a neat event. Oh, by the way, how did your shooting practice go the other day?"

"It went very well. Lois's uncle came to visit from Albany, and he gave our Eastern Women's Rifle Team some special professional shooting lessons. He spent several years in the military as a Special Forces team member, and now is a captain in the Emergency Services Unit of the New York State Police. He is very knowledgeable about weapons care, maintenance, shooting styles and techniques. Lois talked him into volunteering to give us a series of lectures on gun safety, shooting and weapons care and we really benefited from his trainings. We've already had a few sessions, and he'll be coming back for a few more. We are all very excited, because we've been invited to meet with his fellow Emergency Service team members for a joint shooting competition in a few months. We are all practicing a lot, and with the extra instruction we're improving a good deal, so it is going to be a fun competition."

"Do you think that your team has a chance to beat the New York State Emergency Services team?"

"Not a chance if they shoot like Lois's uncle. He is an unbelievable shot, and completely undisturbed by the stress of competition. The rest of his team is probably just as good, and we really don't care if we lose the competition. What's important is that we improve and have a good time."

"What is Lois's uncle's name?"

"His name is Jason Adams. He's a captain in Troop G, headquartered in Albany. If you like, I'll let you know next time he comes up. I can invite you to visit our team training, and you can meet him. You can even join the weapons training. I'm sure the team won't object."

"That sounds great. I'd like to meet him and your fellow team members, and it would be fun to do some shooting, too. I'll bring my nine-millimeter carbine rifle down and blow off a few clips. I haven't done it in a while and it will be good to shoot some."

"Jon, we just passed the exit for Woodstock, have you ever been to Woodstock? I have heard so much about it with all the hippie folklore. In Europe, people are fascinated by it. Kind of like your cowboys and Indians urban legends, too."

"Yes. It's a very colorful little town. There are some nice art galleries, bookstores, and restaurants, and a great summer stock theater. The name still draws tourists, which helps the town thrive, but actually the concert "Woodstock" was not in Woodstock at all. The concert was in Bethel, New York, which is about forty miles from Woodstock. My sister Margaret actually went to it. She told me all about it. She saw Jimi Hendrix play there."

"That's so cool. I wonder what it would have been like to be there and experience that time, all avant-garde music and art, and the anti-establishment counterculture."

"And don't forget the psychedelic drugs!"

[29]

Uninvited Visitors

They took a short break at a coffee shop off of the thruway, and then continued on their trip home. After several hours of driving, they arrived at Jon's beach house. They grabbed their bags, and Jon took out his key to open the front door.

"Damn, Marta! The door isn't locked. I wonder if I forgot to lock the door when we left."

"I don't think so, Jon. I'm sure you locked the door."

They entered the house warily. Marta immediately flew her hands to her face in shock at what she saw. "Oh, my God," Jon exclaimed as he reeled back. "Look at this place! Someone's completely ransacked this house!"

"It's a mess! Who would do something like this? How did they get in? This is going to take forever to clean up, why would someone do this?"

"I don't know, but I have my suspicions," said Jon, glancing at Marta.

"What! Who do you think would do this to you?"

"Somehow I think that Dr. Tonner and the RNL police had something to do with this! Who else would want to break into my house? It could have been some local thieves, but I seriously doubt it because it doesn't look like anything valuable was taken."

"You're right. It doesn't look like anything was stolen, but it certainly looks like someone was searching for something. Why on earth do you suspect Tonner? What's going on, Jon?"

"I'm afraid that they somehow suspect that Ben and I broke into the graphite reactor, and they are trying to look for evidence against us."

"Maybe they think you took something from the graphite reactor and they are looking for it."

"The only thing we took was a small, partly melted, metal nodule that we found inside something that looked like an incinerator down in 720. Ben has it. I don't really think it was anything important. We couldn't figure out what it was, so Ben is going to have it examined by a friend of his who is a metallurgist. He thought his friend might be able to determine what it is."

"If they did do this, Tonner is obviously very concerned that you found out something during your break-in, and they are more than a little pissed about it. What did you guys find there anyway, Jon? What is it about that place that would cause them to come after you?"

"I want you to keep this very quiet. Don't tell anyone, not even Lois."

"What did you find there? Tell me!"

"We got into the reactor from the south maintenance entrance because Ben still had the code to the door, and it still worked. We made our way into Building 720 by way of an underground service tunnel. When we got into Building 720 it was a terrible mess, all wet and corroded. It was awful. Most of the old equipment had been removed, but there were still some things left from when they used to do their secret experiments there decades ago."

"What secret experiments were they doing there? Did you find out anything?"

"Yes. We came across some very strange and puzzling things. Ben told me these secret experiments were part of something called the Hades Project, a secret project funded by the military. We found a series of labs down in the massive underground complex, and one of them contained the receiving ports for the pneumatic tubes that were used to send radioactive samples through the graphite reactor core."

"What else did you find? Anything else interesting?"

"Yes, we went further into the lower levels of the complex, and we found a lab that apparently did experiments on animals. There were animal holding pens, cages, dissecting tables, and other associated lab equipment. What was most disturbing was that we found several confinement cells that seemed to be designed to hold human subjects."

"WHAT! HUMAN SUBJECTS! Are you sure? That is unbelievable. Maybe they were for large animals, or some other use!"

"I know it sounds crazy, but we could find no other explanation for what we found. Those were definitely holding cells for human subjects. They were outfitted with toilets and sinks. Animals don't use toilets and sinks, Marta."

"God, Jon! This is really scary, and now with our house being broken into . . . I am totally terrified!"

"Marta, there is one more thing that I have to tell you—and really, you can't tell anyone."

"I can't believe you kept all this other stuff from me all weekend. What else could you have possibly left out, Jon?"

"Ben told me that since Dr. Hilcraft worked on the graphite reactor he was required to be involved in the research at Building 720. They needed his involvement to send samples through the reactor core to the carry lab. Ben said that Hilcraft hated working on the project, and had conflicts with the management of 720. He suspects that this conflict might have had something to do with Hilcraft's disappearance."

"Really? That is very troubling, but it makes perfect sense, doesn't it?"

"Yes, it does make sense. We are going to have to be really careful in the future, because we may be on their radar now. I'll bet Tonner is in real deep with the Black Ops military-funded programs. We can only wonder what the hell they have going on now here at RNL."

Marta put her arms around Jon. "I am very worried now. What do you think we should do?"

"Don't worry, Marta. Everything will be alright. They really don't have anything on us now, and they are probably groping for answers, hoping one of us will panic and make a mistake. They are probably concerned that they'll be exposed. Just be cool, and we'll continue as if everything is normal. I wonder if they are becoming concerned because we are close to finding out what happened to Dr. Hilcraft. Or are they more worried that we might be learning about some of the *awful things* that have gone on at the Lab? Anyway, let's just get our bags in from the car, clean up the mess, and relax a bit. Then I'll give Ben a call to see if anything interesting has happened to him. Let's let the police know that our house was broken into."

Jon and Marta spent the next hour straightening out the house. Finally, when things were somewhat back to normal, they sat on the couch to relax. Marta couldn't stop fidgeting, and finally stood up, saying, "Jon, I want to take out some firearms and place them in accessible places in case we have any trouble. Is that alright with you?"

"Sure, Marta. Go ahead if it makes you feel safer. Just let me know what you are putting out and where you are putting it."

"Okay, I'll put my Beretta 9-millimeter pistol in the kitchen cabinet above the phone. And I'll put my 20-gauge pistol grip shotgun here in the hallway closet. Is that okay with you?"

"Damn, Marta, you mean business! Hell hath no fury like a woman scorned! I would hate to be the idiot who breaks into this house and meets up with you!"

"You can bet your ass on that one!" Marta said proudly, in her lush Slavic accent.

"You know what, Marta, I'll take out my 9-millimeter carbine Hi-Point, and keep it in the bedroom. I think we'll be fine, but just in case we get a visitor at night, it will be good to know we are prepared!"

"Good. I'll feel a lot safer, and sleep better with that in reach."

Marta headed into the kitchen to prepare dinner, and Jon picked up the phone and called Ben.

"Hello, Jon, how was your trip up to the Catskills?"

"Wonderful! We had a great time. We stayed in a great place. It was really nice, very quiet and charming, and the food was fantastic. We climbed a mountain, and took in some amazing views. It was great to get away. We also met up with someone who lived right down the street from Emery Hilcraft's old place in Pine Hill. After meeting under some unusual circumstances, she actually invited us over to have a cup of tea. We had a nice chitchat. I'll fill you in on that when we see each other. Unfortunately, the end of our trip was not so great. When we got back we found out that the house had been broken into. The place was completely ransacked and we just finished getting everything back in place."

"Really? That's awful! Sorry to hear that your return home was disrupted like that. Did they take anything?"

"Well, that's one of the strange things about it. We couldn't find anything missing, and we have no idea who would have done something like this. Although I have an uneasy suspicion that Dr. Tonner and his security police thugs may have been involved."

"That's a possibility, Jon. They may suspect that the incident at Building 720 had something to do with us."

"That's what I'm wondering about. I was wondering if you had any kind of incident yourself."

"No, things have been pretty quiet here at my house with my wife and me the past few days."

"Good, glad to hear that. As they say, no news is good news. So, guess what, we actually located Hilcraft's house there in Pine Hill. It's still standing, but it is in terrible shape. Marta and I found a way into the old place and we searched around a bit. I have a lot to tell you about what we found out up there in the Catskills."

"Great, Jon. I can't wait to hear about it. Oh, by the way, my friend the metallurgist checked out that metal nodule that we found in that incinerator at 720."

"Really! Great, what did he have to say about it? I'm anxious to hear."

"Okay, but you're not going to believe it."

"Well, tell me anyway!" Jon exclaimed.

"According to him, it turned out to be a partly melted World War II military metal."

"That is strange, but I guess that certainly could be the case since RNL was the site of a military base during World War II."

"No, Jon, it turned out to be a German World War II Death Head metal pin also known as a *Totenkopf.*"

"You mean it was a copy of a German World War II medal?"

"No, Jon, he said that it was an original, genuine, authentic German Totenkopf medal—most likely that of a special Nazi SS brigade known as the SS-Totenkopfverbande, which translates as the Death Head's Unit. The Death's Head Unit was an independent unit within the SS ranks. It was one of the most malicious and feared units in the SS."

"What the hell is going on? How the hell would an original authentic German SS Death Head medal get into an incinerator that was inside the Building 720 subcomplex? This is crazy, isn't it, Ben?"

"Exactly! My friend, who happens to be a World War II history buff, said that the SS-Totenkopfverbande was involved in the massacres of thousands of Jews and non-Jews in Eastern Europe. They operated the concentration camps, and were also involved in several massacres of US Army troops during the Allied invasion of Europe."

"Wow, Ben! That is totally weird and strange! This whole thing is getting more and more unbelievable."

"Yes, it is. Hey do you want that melted medal pin back? I kind of want to keep it as a memento."

"You keep it, Ben."

"Thanks. I'll keep it as a souvenir of that night we got into 720—and got out alive too!"

"Yeah, what a night that was! Okay, I'll see you in a few days at QUEST. I'm going to invite Charlie Kenton down to be with us when we review the data from the last experiment."

"Sure, that will be fine with me. I'm anxious to go over the data, too. I can't wait to find out what the hell the Torqkadrone discovered on its latest excursion."

"Definitely! Me, too! Okay, Ben, I'll catch up with you later, man."

"Hey, Jon, one more thing."

"What's that?"

"You and Marta be careful with yourselves, seeing that someone got into your home."

"Don't worry, Ben. We've already started taking countermeasures on that issue."

"Very well, Jon. You two take care."

Jon put the phone down, and looked around the house. A chill ran through his body as it hit him how vulnerable they really were.

[30]

The Disease from the Woods

After dinner Jon and Marta settled in for the evening. Jon sat in his favorite recliner, and Marta sat on the couch with Onyx snuggled up against her. They had their laptops out, and were checking emails and work updates they might have missed during their trip.

Suddenly, they heard a thud near the front door. They both froze momentarily. Onyx darted into the hallway. Marta jumped up and grabbed her Beretta from the kitchen cabinet. Silently, she hid against the wall next to the front door, while Jon looked out the front window near the door.

"I don't see anything," he said quietly.

Again they heard another sound near the front door. This time it was louder. Marta positioned her pistol prepared to propel multiple rounds of slugs into an unwelcome intruder. Jon unlocked the door and opened it swiftly. A middle-aged woman stood stock-still in the doorway. She was clearly shocked and terrified.

"Please, don't shoot me! Please, don't shoot! I'm your neighbor!"

Jon pushed Marta's pistol arm down toward the ground. "Oh, my God! We are so sorry that we scared you like this. Please come on in here and sit down. I'm so sorry."

Jon took his neighbor's arm and escorted her over to the couch. Jon assisted her as she sat down slowly. Jon and Marta sat down, too, and for a few moments they all sat in stunned silence.

Marta broke the ice. "You must be very troubled with what you just witnessed. I assure you these are not our normal security measures. We just got home from a trip this afternoon, and found that the house had been broken into and ransacked. We didn't hear you knock at the front door, and we were concerned that the prowler was back again."

The woman was beginning to recover. She explained, "I just want you to know that I did push the lighted doorbell, but you didn't answer the door."

Jon sighed. "Sorry about that. My name is Jon and my fiancée here is Marta. Unfortunately, our doorbell is not working. We should have had a sign up to knock on the door. What brought you here tonight? Has there been other trouble in the neighborhood?"

"No, not that I've heard of. I understand how you must feel very vulnerable and violated. It's a terrible thing. I guess now that I don't have a gun pointed at me, I'll introduce myself. My name is Jeanne Gassert. I came by today because I'm volunteering to raise awareness about Cray's disease. I was going house to house in the neighborhood today educating everyone about the disease, and looking for volunteers and donations to the Cray's Disease Association."

"Cray's disease! I'm somewhat familiar with that illness. I participated in a study at a nearby hospital with several patients who had Cray's disease. It's a very unusual disease, and can be so debilitating. Do you know someone affected by it?" Marta asked.

"Yes, it is a terrible illness. Unfortunately, my daughter contracted it several years ago. She suffered a great deal."

"How did she get it? I've heard of it, but I don't know anything much about it," Jon said.

"She got bitten by a tick on her back when she was hiking in the woods, but didn't realize it. Over the course of several weeks she got very ill, and became bedridden."

"What were her symptoms?" Marta asked.

"Well, it started like the flu with a headache, and then there was the numbness all over her body. Later, she developed encephalomyelitis, which got worse, until she could no longer function properly and was bedridden. She lost her sense of smell and taste and had severe concentration problems."

"That is terrible! I never realized that Cray's disease could be so serious. Is it a viral infection?" Jon asked.

"Cray's disease," Marta interjected, "is caused by a spirochetal bacterium, *torellgelius flaturni*, which infects the body by way of tick bite. Cray's disease can infect multiple body systems including the brain, heart, and really any other organ of the body. Tell me, Mrs. Gassert, how is your daughter doing now? Did she get proper treatment?"

"Thank God, she is doing much better now, although she still has some relapses now and then. But, overall, she is doing better. Luckily, she found a doctor who recognized her illness and knew how to treat it properly. He treated her for several months with very powerful antibiotics, which worked well. She is now back to work and doing much better."

"Long Island has a very high number of cases of tick-borne illnesses, and Cray's disease is one of the worst," Marta said. "If untreated, it causes lesions in the brain with accompanying neuro-psychiatric symptoms. This is very similar to the spirochetal diseases syphilis and leptospirosis but Cray's disease is much more virulent and potent."

"Marta, you have a lot of expertise in this! Would you be willing to assist our Cray's disease support group?"

"Certainly, my time is limited, but we'll see if we can work something out."

"We'll be having one of our meetings soon. It would be great if you could come to that meeting and introduce yourself. Then we could take it from there. We meet every first Tuesday of the month at the Aquebogue Community Center."

"Very good. I will mark it on my calendar. It's good that your organization is taking on Cray's disease. It is a terrible illness that afflicts our community."

"Here, before you leave let us make a donation to your group now," Jon said, taking out his wallet.

As Jeanne Gassert left the house, Jon turned to Marta. "Damn, I never realized that there was another dangerous tick-borne disease prevalent in this area. Has it always been around this locale?"

"No, Cray's didn't show up as a substantial concern around here until the 1970s. Many early cases of the disease went unrecognized, and patients suffered tremendously. It was a real shame because, if treated properly early in its course, the disease doesn't cause much of a problem."

"Maybe I'll attend that meeting with you, if I am not booked doing something else."

They settled back into their previous positions on the sofa and the recliner. Onyx returned to snuggle with Marta, her new best friend. But neither of them could really relax. They were both wondering what the real reason for the break-in was and who was behind it. Marta only managed to sleep at all that night because she had her 9-millimeter pistol and Jon by her side.

[31]

The Standing Stones

They both awoke feeling somewhat refreshed and renewed. After breakfast they took a walk on the county preserve beach which was near their house. They walked the entire long curved beach and discussed their wonderful trip. Clouds skittered across the sky in the gusting wind, and the green waves shimmered, reflecting the light of the changing sun.

"Look, Jon! Our friend the moon is up in the sky today smiling at us. Let's honor her, the Goddess in her crone aspect, and all the beauty of this magnificent beach, by building a stone monument."

With the sounds of the wind and the waves hitting the beach in the background Jon said, "It is a gorgeous waning moon—so bright up in the sky—especially for daytime. Okay, I'll help you gather some beach rocks for your shrine."

Marta and Jon scoured the beach and collected a large handful of flat rocks. Slowly and carefully, Marta constructed a foot-high rock tower on the beach.

They walked back several feet and gazed at her creation, which was framed by the water and moon in the background.

"Let's take a few moments to meditate on this magnificent moment right now."

Contentedly and quietly, Jon joined Marta in a moment of meditation—moving into a solitary and yet shared experience of eternity and harmony.

"What do you think, Jon. Do you think that it is complete?"

"Yes, Marta, I think that the universe has accepted your offering and now the gods of nature are content."

Marta took Jon's hand, and they both looked into the wind and water on their beautiful beach. They were filled with a sense of magic and majesty. Looking at the waning moon, Marta said, "She doesn't have much time left before she leaves us."

"She will always be here with us, Marta, always."

"Jon," asked Marta, gazing past the waning moon into the depths of the light blue sky, "do you think that there are other life forms out there in the universe?"

"Absolutely, Marta, there is no doubt in my mind."

"How can you be so sure?"

"Because this vast universe is infinite in size, and since there are infinite planets and moons out there in the universe, there is no doubt that somewhere out there other lifeforms exist."

"That does sound probable when you use that logic."

"Not only are there other life forms out there, but there has to be *another one of you and another one of I out there somewhere.* I am sure of that."

"How could you possibly come to that conclusion?"

"Because we humans are basically a collection of particles. A very special, complex collection of particles, but still we are essentially just an arrangement of particles. And therefore, out there somewhere in the infinity of the universe, there has to be another collection of particles that is just the same. In other words, somewhere out there, there exists an exact copy of each one of us. In fact, I'll bet you that there is a copy of me out there somewhere right this moment walking around thinking that he is the real Jon Sanborne, and that I am just a copy of him."

"What a strange notion! I really don't hope that you're right about that."

"Well, I'm absolutely sure that is the case, whether we like it or not."

"I'm not so sure on that one, but I'll have to give it some more thought."

They continued their stroll along the shore, enjoying every moment of the lovely morning. After they walked back toward the house, Marta peered back to the rock memorial they had left down the beach. Jon, while holding Marta's hand, also looked back toward the standing stones. They could vaguely make out the shape of the little monument in the distance. Marta commented, "I wonder how long it will last," and they both turned to walk on in a peaceful and reflective, if ambivalent, mood.

Back at the house, Jon called Ben. "How is your morning going?"

"Very good, Jon. I am just taking care of a few things around the house. I'm going to start painting my garage soon."

"Hey, don't do too much today! Take the afternoon off and have a few beers."

"Yeah, maybe I will."

"Ben, I won't take up too much of your time, but I just wanted to ask you if you've ever heard of a place called Targway Proving Ground?"

"Uh. Targway? Yeah. What do you want to know about Targway?"

Stunned, Jon exclaimed, "You do! What exactly is it?"

"Targway Proving Ground is a secret military installation located in the northeast of Nevada. It is rumored to be the primary test facility in the nation for biological weaponry. I happen to know about it because when I was in the military in the early sixties I had a friend who was sent there on duty. He said that it was a very high-security facility, and pointed out that it is never mentioned in any way in the press. They try to keep it quiet and out of the public eye. Targway is where most of the nerve gas was stored and tested before they destroyed it when we made that treaty with the Russians." Ben took a deep breath, "I believe that Dr. Tonner may have come from Targway before he became security director of Ridgewood. I'm actually pretty sure about that."

"What! Are you sure that Tonner came from Targway?"

"I'm pretty confident that's where he worked before he came here to screw up this place. Why are you asking about it anyway?"

"This is pretty strange. I received a piece of mail several days ago. I thought it was junk mail. It said something like, 'Interested in a trip to Hades? Call this number.' When I called the phone number listed, they answered, 'Targway Proving Ground' and asked for a security key code. I really didn't know what to make of it, but it kind of spooked me. Especially since it had the word 'Hades' on it. Especially given our recent adventures. Strange, isn't it?"

"Very strange, Jon. It almost sounds like someone sent you that piece of mail for a reason."

"What could that reason be?"

"Well, if this is not just some weird coincidence, then they are intentionally giving you a link between the Hades experiment and Targway Proving Ground."

"Yeah, and since Tonner came from Targway, then there is a link involving him in there too."

"Exactly, Jon. That's just what I was thinking. Was there anything else written on that piece of mail?"

"No, what I told you is all that was written on it."

"I wonder who would send out something like that? For some reason, someone who knows you wants you to have this information."

"I wish I knew, but I have no idea right now. Alright, well I won't take up any more of your time. I know that you have to get back to your painting. I'm going to head out to the Patchogue Coin Shop as soon as I get off the phone. Let me know if you come up with anything about all this."

"Why are you going to a coin shop?"

"It's a long story. I'll fill you in when I see you tomorrow at QUEST."

"Okay. See you tomorrow. Enjoy your trip to Patchogue."

"Thanks for the info. You take care."

Jon hung up the phone and grabbed his coat. "Marta, I'm going to take that medallion to the coin shop in Patchogue. Do you want to come take a ride?"

"No, you go ahead. I need to call Lois, and I want to put up a pot of mushroom beef soup for dinner tonight."

"I should be back in a few hours. If VG calls tell him to get me on my cell."

"Okay, Sweetie, I'll see you later. Be careful driving."

"Lock the door after me, and don't forget to keep it locked," said Jon, with a quick parting kiss.

Jon headed west, enjoying his long drive through the Pine Barrens and over the glacial highlands of Hampton Bays. Just as he started to relax, he noticed his inspection sticker and remembered that it had expired. He muttered to himself, "I better get that done soon. The last thing I need is a ticket!"

He drove through the downtown area of Patchogue and was amazed at how much major reconstruction had taken place there since his last visit. He passed several blocks of old time brick-faced buildings rising into the sky that were new but still somehow gave a feeling of years' past heritage and charm. He passed a few interesting ethnic restaurants, shops, and brew houses, and thought it would have been neat to hang out there with Marta if she'd come along. He nabbed a parking spot right near the coin shop, and went inside. The staff was busy with other customers, so he spent a few minutes examining the coins and metallic artifacts displayed in the antique-looking glass cases that lined the walls. The owner had the shop for over thirty-five years and had seen everything in his career, including coins from throughout the world.

"Hello, sir. I recognize you, but I don't remember your name," Jon said.

"I'm Anthony, the owner of this thriving establishment."

"Hi, Anthony. I'm Jon. I live out east, so I don't get here all that often, but I bought some Morgan silver dollars from you a while back. I like to collect some old coins from time to time."

"How can I assist you today?"

"I found this old medallion a while ago. I have no idea what it is, and I was wondering if you could take a look at it and see if you can tell me anything about it," Jon said, taking the coin from his pocket and placing it on the velvet pad on the counter.

"Let's see. What do we have here?" Anthony examined the coin carefully. Then he took out his loop and again examined the medallion even more carefully. "It's apparently old, very old, maybe even ancient, and it's definitely quite worn. On this side there is a raised impression of what appears to be a feminine image surrounded by abstract markings. And on this side there is the triangle that has lines radiating from it. Did you look at this under magnification? When you look into the triangle, it is completely composed of smaller and smaller triangles. I also see flow lines that emanate from the central area of the coin out to the edges to give a shimmering effect. The medallion is obviously handmade, and seems to be composed of an alloy of very high grade pure silver mixed with some gold."

"Wow! Do you have any idea how old this coin is, and where it could have come from?"

"It definitely appears to be of European or Southern European origin. There are no apparent characteristics of Asian influence, but I have been wrong before. As far as the age of the coin, it looks very old. I don't know for sure, but if I was to guess I would say it is somewhere between seven hundred and a thousand years old. But as I said, that is a guess."

"Wow! That's amazing!"

"So, Jon, tell me, where did you really get this medallion? This looks like something that would be found in a museum somewhere."

Jon answered with a nervous grin, "I actually got this medallion at a yard sale in upstate New York, in Margaretville."

Anthony obviously had his doubts, but discretion was highly valued in his trade. "So, what would you like to do with this coin then, Jon? Would you like to sell it?"

"No, I'm not looking to sell it. It has sentimental value to me. My fiancée actually found it at the yard sale. We bought it and plan on mounting it on the wall in the living room."

"Oh, too bad. I know someone who might be interested in purchasing it from you. He's a professor of archaeology at Stony Brook. I know he'd love to take a look at this, and he might be able to tell you much more about it."

"Really! That sounds interesting. Could you arrange it?"

"Sure, I could do that. I deal with him all the time. He's a member of our numismatic association. I could give him a call now to set up a meeting to have it examined. I know he would be very interested in it."

"Sure, why don't you do that! I'll take a look around the shop while you call."

Anthony returned a few minutes later. "Professor Nicolaides is available now if you can make it to his office."

"Tell him I'll be there shortly. I just need to know where his office is."

"Very good. I'll let him know you're coming."

"Okay, Jon, do you know how to get to Stony Brook University? Professor Nicolaides is located in the Social and Behavioral Sciences Building. The Anthropology Department is on the fifth floor, and he's in room 549. He'll be waiting for you. He's very interested in seeing what you've got."

"Okay, no problem. I often go to events at the Staller Center, and that's right on the other side of the parking garage there. Thank you so much for your help today. It was a real pleasure seeing you again."

"No problem, Jon. Give me a call and let me know what the professor thinks about the coin. I'm very interested myself in finding out just what you got. It certainly is unusual."

"I'll let you know! Thanks again!"

[32]

The Goddess Siva

Jon noticed a police car pass by as he jumped into his car, and again remembered his expired inspection sticker. He drove north to Stony Brook, and parked in the parking garage. Some years previously he had participated in a Particle Physics Conference which took place at the Javits Lecture Center, so he had walked by the Social and Behavioral Science Building several times. Jon bypassed the elevator and headed for the stairs, ever eager to get a little more exercise. While climbing up the stairs, he had a bit of a spell. It was hard to describe later, but he needed to take a short rest, and felt somewhat confused. He grabbed the handrail, and tried to shake off the weird disassociation from reality he was experiencing. Time seemed to stand still. At one point, he felt that his body seemed to move from where he was to a vortex of matter outside of himself. It was as if he was looking at himself from elsewhere in space, and yet he still felt as if he were in the stairwell. His perceptions didn't make any sense to him, as he saw himself observing several other spaces simultaneously. Was he in the stairwell? Or outdoors in the woods somewhere? Where in the woods? He had no idea, but the place seemed familiar. It was a beautiful and peaceful place. He heard voices, and then suddenly the episode passed, and he was standing in the stairwell, gripping the banister, his head clearing as two young college students passed him on their way downstairs. He watched them pass by, regained his composure, and then continued up the stairs. Was it just a daydream? Psychological fallout from his overly busy schedule? But deep inside, he felt that this was something different. Something extraordinary had happened. He made a mental note of it, but carried on with the task at hand in a normal mind frame.

The Anthropology Department walls were home to several displays depicting ancient human species, and included some human skulls. He read the information under one of the displays: *"Homo Habilis, the "Handy Man," was the first human ancestor. Homo Habilis lived between 1.4 to 2.3 million years ago and made tools that enhanced his ability to survive."*

Jon remembered learning about the early hominids in the physical anthropology course he took in college. He recalled the sense of wonder and adventure he experienced during those college years as he learned so many fascinating things about the world. It was so exciting then!

Professor Nicolaides' door was open. Jon tapped on it, and entered slowly. The thin, middle-aged, graying man who was sitting at his desk working rose to greet him.

"Hello, Professor Nicolaides. I'm Jon Sanborne. Anthony said you'd be interested in looking at my medallion."

"Oh, yes, Anthony is a good friend of mine. Thanks for coming over. It's good to meet you," Nicolaides said, as they shook hands.

"I was just looking at the displays in the hallway. It's been a while but I remembered that human ancestor from when I took physical anthropology as an undergrad at RPI. I have always been fascinated by human evolution, and how far we have come in terms of intelligence and civilization," Jon said.

"Yes, human evolution is fascinating. My specialty is the study of the early and later Neolithic peoples in Europe and Asia."

"That's something I don't know much about, but I really enjoyed anthropology. It's an interesting way to learn about ourselves and our past."

"Definitely. I've been studying it for quite a number of years and I still find it intriguing."

Jon pulled the medallion out of his pocket and placed it in front of the professor. They were both quite still as they gazed at this intriguing piece of antiquity in the harsh, modern lights of Professor Nicolaides' office.

"Anthony told me that this medallion seemed very special. He said he has never seen anything like it. He very rarely calls me on these things, so it must be significant. May I examine it?"

"Of course. That's why I'm here! I hope you can tell me something about it."

The professor opened his desk drawer, removed a pair of thin, white gloves, and put them on. He gingerly placed the medallion on a soft white cloth, and slid over a stand which held a magnifying glass and a strong light. He spent several minutes examining one side of the coin, and then gently turned it over and then studied the other side. He then brought over another piece of equipment that looked like a microscope. He placed the coin onto the viewing surface of the instrument. He looked into the viewing tube, and adjusted several knobs to improve his view of the intricate details of the coin. From his practiced movements, it was obvious to Jon that the professor was highly experienced at this kind of examination.

Meanwhile, Jon explored the room. He noticed several displays of ancient Greek and Roman coins and artifacts mounted on the walls.

"Professor Nicolaides, I suppose you have traveled to Greece and Italy?"

"I travel to Greece quite a bit, but I don't get to Italy as much. I have family in Greece. Have you ever been to Greece?"

Still gazing at one of the ancient artifacts on the wall, Jon answered, "No I haven't, but I would love to visit Santorini one day."

"Santorini is really a beautiful place to vacation. Do you know it was the site of an ancient volcano?"

"Maybe my fiancée and I will get married there someday. She'd like that!"

The professor turned off the power on the microscope, and put the coin back onto the white cloth. "This medallion is truly amazing. I almost don't believe it, but I think I know what this is. If I am right, it is a very rare find. Tell me, where did you get this?"

Jon was nervous, but answered smoothly, "My fiancée and I purchased it at a yard sale when we were upstate a few days ago."

"Really! Well, it looks like you were very, very lucky. If this is what I think it is, it will be worth an awful lot of money."

"Are you serious?"

"Yes, very serious. This coin seems to be a rare artifact from the people who inhabited northeastern Europe about nine thousand years ago. At that time they were mining copper and tin, and we see examples of the production of some of the very earliest bronze artifacts. Rarely, they also mined silver and gold. These early Bronze Age people who inhabited that area are known as the Eneolithic and Chalcolithic People."

"This is unbelievable, Professor. Do you have any idea of the meaning of the symbols on the medallion?"

"We can only speculate about some of it, but I can tell you something about the female figure here."

"Really? What can you tell me?"

The professor's face glowed with excitement. "This is what is so amazing about the coin. First of all, the medallion is in fantastic shape considering its age. The next notable thing about the coin is that it is made of a silver-gold ore. It looks like it's probably about a nine-to-one ratio of silver to gold, which is sometimes known as electrum. Also, note that the coin is almost perfectly round. This is not the usual case for medallions from this time period. But the most stunning thing about this piece is this image of the goddess Siva. Impressions of Siva are very rare on the artifacts that we have recovered from that time period."

"I have never heard of that goddess before. Is anything known about her?"

"Siva was the ancient goddess of the Chalcolithic tribes that inhabited the Carpathian Mountain region of northeastern Europe. Not all that much is known about the Chalcolithic peoples, but we do know that they had a fairly vibrant civilization and worshiped several gods. Siva was one of their deities. I think I have a picture of her here somewhere."

After some searching the professor located the image. "Here it is. This is an artist's rendering of her image."

"Wow, she is beautiful. No wonder they worshiped her! What else can you tell me about the goddess—as far as her meaning?"

"Well, according to what we know, Siva was the Goddess of Living, Being and Existence. In other words, she represented life and reality."

"Those are good things to worship," Jon said.

"There is some debate in the academic community as to the relationship between the goddess Siva and the Indian goddess Shiva. Some feel that they may be the same goddess worshiped in two separate cultures, but a bit differently. There is now a new theory that Siva was the first established goddess in that macro-region, or the more ancient one, and that the Indian people actually adopted the goddess Siva, renamed her, and remade her as Shiva. This, of course, is a very controversial theory. Indian Shiva proponents totally reject this idea, but there is some recent evidence to support the view that Shiva is actually the goddess Siva.

"Totally fascinating, Professor. Tell me, have you ever heard of the Sulov Rocks in Slovakia?"

"Of course, the Sulov Rock region is an area that was inhabited by the Chalcolithic peoples. Some of our best archaeological evidence has come from that region specifically. How did you know about the Sulov Rock region? Not many people know about the link between that area and the Chalcolithic People."

Jon hesitated, with a blank expression on his face.

Professor Nicolaides found himself becoming wary. He realized that he did not trust Jon, and became concerned that the medallion may have been obtained illicitly. "Jon, I know several experts in the field who would do anything to get a chance to study this rare find. How about we set up an arrangement with you so that we can have this item studied for a period of time?"

"Arrangement? What do you mean?" Jon asked.

"I'm talking about a monetary arrangement, Jon!"

"Um, I don't think that is possible at this time, Professor."

Jon grabbed the medallion and placed it in his pocket, saying, "Thanks so much for you expertise, Professor. It's getting late, and I have to get going."

Professor Nicolaides hurried after Jon. "Wait, Jon. Wait! Our department can offer you a handsome sum of money for that medallion. We have museums that would love to have it in their collection! I am sure that we could negotiate a financial settlement for that coin. Please consider the sale of your medallion! You must! This find is far too important to vanish into obscurity. It must be studied!"

Jon walked rapidly down the hallway, as the professor followed him and tried to convince him to give up his possession. Nicolaides was still calling after Jon as he headed down the stairs.

Somewhat unnerved, Jon left the Stony Brook campus, completely unaware that he was being followed by a midnight blue SUV. The driver of the SUV artfully stayed several car lengths behind. Eventually, Jon pulled off the Long Island Expressway to grab a cup of coffee at one of the gas stations on the service road. On returning to his car with his coffee, he noticed the midnight blue SUV with darkened windows parked alongside the edge of the parking lot. His skin prickled, and he did a double-take, realizing that the vehicle was familiar to him. He had buckled in, and was taking a moment to enjoy his coffee, when suddenly his cell phone rang. Startled, Jon answered the call.

"Hello, Jon. Dr. Kenyatta here. Sorry to bother you on this nice day, but something important just came up. I hope I'm not interrupting anything."

"No, not at all, Dr. Kenyatta. I'm just coming back from Stony Brook, sitting in my car having a cup of coffee."

"Okay, good then. I just got a call from the Local 9 News television station. They want to visit the QUEST facility and do a story on your work down there. They would like to interview you. Will that be alright with you and your team? I hope you can fit them in soon. It's important that we have favorable press coverage here at Ridgewood, and an interesting TV story would be a good thing—especially for future funding."

"Sure, no problem, Dr. Kenyatta. I'll call VG and Yi Chin to let them know. I definitely think that they should be present for the filming. When are they planning to come down?"

"They want to come first thing tomorrow morning. Will that be alright with you on your end?"

"That should be fine. When I get home I'll call the others and let them know that they are going to be TV stars."

"Excellent, Jon! I'm so excited! This is really good for us. Make sure you take them into the Macro-STARR facility. That will really blow their minds."

"Oh, I'll definitely show them the Macro-STARR. They'll never be the same afterward!"

"Maybe they'll want you to star in a science-fiction series after they film your facility."

"If they do, they'll have to pay me big money, and I'll have to have a hot-looking co-star alongside me."

"You're funny, Jon! I always get a kick out of your humor. Good luck tomorrow. Oh, one other thing—the president of Q-Wave Computers is coming for a visit next week. I expect he may also want to tour your facility. I'm scheduling a dinner meeting with him and his entourage, and he wants you to join us. He's really looking forward to meeting you and discussing your research."

"Wow, that's great Dr. Kenyatta! I definitely want to meet him and his associates. Let me know the date and time and I will be there."

"Oh, Jon, about that interview, I was thinking that maybe we should avoid using the name Macro-STARR. I think it sounds a little too much like a military experiment, and that might scare the public. Do you have another name for it, perhaps?"

"Yeah, actually I do. I nicknamed it the SIVATRON!"

Kenyatta thought for a moment, and then said, "Superb! How did you come up with that name?"

"It's a philosophical thing that would take some time to explain."

"Very well. It doesn't sound particularly threatening. Let's go with that. One other thing: I suggest that when you explain QUEST to the public on TV that you don't make it too complicated. Just tell them why it's important and worthwhile. Don't scare them with any of the parallel worlds stuff."

"Good idea, Dr. Kenyatta. I'll remember that."

"Great, see you tomorrow morning at nine. I'll bring the crew over myself. I want to be there to show support."

"Thanks. I'll be there. See you then."

The dark blue SUV was gone. There was no sign of it, as if it had never existed. Jon felt uneasy. Ever since the foray into the reactor and Building 720, he'd had several experiences of feeling that he was being watched. He started the car and continued home, looking forward to telling Marta about the medallion.

Jon pulled up his driveway, got out of the car and instantly sensed the delightful aroma emanating from Marta's cooking.

"Hey, darling, I'm home! What smells so good in here?" he asked, with a lingering hug.

"I thought I'd surprise you with a special recipe from my aunt. Take a look," Marta said. She led Jon toward the stove, and pulled the lid off the pot. "This is a mushroom-onion soup made with twelve beef bones and a lot of sage. You're going to love this!"

"It looks outrageous. I can't wait to have some. The smell is tantalizing me."

"It's almost done. Just a little while longer. Meanwhile, you can tell me about your trip to the coin shop."

"Well, I ended up making a trip to Stony Brook University to have the medallion examined. The coin shop owner knew a professor there, and sent me over. The professor knew exactly what it is, and guess what?"

"What?"

"It's worth a lot of money, and it may be nearly ten thousand years old."

"Are you serious, Jon? I knew it was old."

"Yes! Totally serious. He was hot under the collar to arrange a purchase for it, either for his department, or a museum somewhere, so they could study it."

"My God! I wonder where Hilcraft got that thing."

"Yeah, I thought about that, too. Remember Ben told us that Hilcraft went on a trip to Slovakia back in the seventies, and he showed us that postcard that he got from Hilcraft that displayed the Sulov Rocks?"

"Of course. How is that relevant?"

"The professor told me that the medallion came from an ancient tribe of people. They were known as the Chalcolithic People, and had a well-established settlement around the Sulov Rocks."

"You're kidding. The Chalcolithic People—I read about them online, and I told you about them and the Sulov Rocks."

"That's the connection . . . don't you see! Hilcraft somehow came into possession of the medallion during his visit to the Sulov Rocks!"

"That does make sense. What does the medallion mean? Did the professor say anything about that?"

Jon pulled out the medallion and showed Marta the image of the goddess Siva.

"He said the female figure is an image of the goddess Siva, who is known as the Goddess of Existence, Living, and Being, or in other words, life and reality."

"How strange! Do you remember that Ben said that after Hilcraft's trip he changed? That he thought differently, and his philosophy and even his scientific theories changed. I wonder what happened there."

They both stared at the medallion, lost in reflection.

"Apparently," said Jon, "he developed a relationship with the Goddess of Existence. I wonder where he is now. I'm sure he's out there somewhere. We just have to find him."

After dinner, Jon and Marta relaxed in their living room. Hot tea and great music set the mood.

"That soup was totally delicious. You are a true master chef. I'm sure your aunt would have been proud of your rendition. I'm so glad you made a big pot. I can't wait for leftovers!"

"Thanks, honey. That is quite a compliment. My aunt probably would have made it better, but I thought you'd like it. Oh, Jon! I forgot to tell you about the conservation that I had with Lois today."

"What about?"

"Lois was talking with a colleague in Medical Research who knows something about Helen Dunne—you know, the woman who had a friendship with Dr. Hilcraft."

"Really, what did she have to say about her?"

"She is going to try to find out for us where Helen Dunne lives."

"Great! If we find out where she lives we'll get in touch with her. Maybe she can offer us some information on Hilcraft."

"Lois said that the woman told her that Helen is really nice, and that she retired a while ago, but still comes to Ridgewood to visit every now and then."

"Cool. I'm looking forward to talking to her."

"She knew Ben, too. So we may want to bring Ben so she feels more comfortable talking about the past."

"Good idea. We'll ask Ben when we get her contact info. Oh, guess what—Kenyatta called me today. I have a TV interview tomorrow morning at nine, so I have to head in early tomorrow. I have to call Yi and VG to let them know, and then I want to get a little extra rest. How about if I grab us a couple of glasses of wine, and we head to bed early?"

"That's exciting. You'd better call them now. They may want to get some nice clothes together for TV. Do you have something nice to wear? Is the interview going to be at QUEST?"

"Yeah. Dr. Kenyatta is going to be there. He really wants us to show off the place and get good press coverage. You know, to boost public support and f-u-n-d-i-n-g."

"That is going to be so neat. I can't wait to see it on TV."

"I just hope that it all goes off well."

"Is Tonner going to be there too?"

"I certainly hope not, but with him you never know."

"Well, good luck with it," said Marta, adding with a devilish look, "I'll be in the bedroom in a little while to show you my little surprise."

"Surprise? What kind of surprise?" Jon quipped.

"You'll see!" said Marta with a giggle.

[33]

The QUEST TV Studio

Upon arriving at QUEST, Jon was stunned to see a crowd of people standing around. TV cameras and other associated electronic equipment jammed up the area, making it difficult to navigate through. He steered his way past the mob and found VG and Yi Chin talking in the hallway that led to the control room.

"Hey, guys, what's going on? Are you ready for all the excitement today?"

Yi laughed. "Welcome to the QUEST TV studio, Jon. It looks like you're about to become a star."

VG added, "Thanks for giving us a heads-up on this. I hope they don't take up the entire morning. We've really got a lot going on today."

"Sorry to drag you guys into this, but Dr. Kenyatta really want us to show the place off to its best, and give them a nice story about our research project. He wants good publicity, so we have to give them some good shots."

"Where are they going to do the interview?" asked Yi.

"I'd like them to do part of the interview in the QUEST control room, and then take them into the Sivatron, show them the immensity of the place, and stun the hell out of them."

"Sivatron? You mean the Macro-STARR?" asked VG, perplexed.

"We're going to call it the Sivatron because Dr. Kenyatta thought that it sounded too much like a military project and that we'd scare the public. And besides, I kind of like the name Sivatron anyway. So let's refer to it as the Sivatron from now on—if that's okay with you guys?"

"Sure, it has a sci-fi sound to it," said Yi.

"Fine with me, Jon. The name reminds me of the Indian goddess Shiva," added VG.

Jon stared at VG, pointed right at him, and said, "What a coincidence! I'll tell you about that some other time."

Jon felt someone poke him in the side, and whirled around. "Are you Dr. Jon Sanborne?" inquired a woman's voice, smooth and polished.

He saw a beautiful woman who looked vaguely familiar to him. "Yes, I am. What can I do for you?"

"Oh, good, Dr. Sanborne. We are all set up and ready to do the interview with you. I'm Holly Schneiderman, the reporter with Local 9 News who will be conducting the interview. Are you guys ready to go?"

"Yes, of course, Holly. I'd like to have two of my scientists with me for the interview. Is that okay with you guys?"

"Sure, Dr. Sanborne. However you want to do it is fine with us. Why don't you take us where you want to do the interview? We'll start there."

"Very good. Follow me."

Kenyatta watched from the back of the room, smiling like a contented cat, as the TV crew set up in the QUEST control room. Work virtually stopped as other

QUEST workers watched the goings-on and chatted in excitement. Jon spotted Ben, who gave him a thumbs-up for good luck. The control room looked strange under the bright lights.

Through the lens the main viewing monitor created a backdrop for the interview. Smaller monitors oscillated with abstract images creating a somewhat surreal and futuristic setting.

"Holly Schneiderman here today at Ridgewood National Lab, right here in Ridgewood, Long Island, New York. We are at the site of one of the most interesting physics experiments in the world. I am standing in the control room of the amazing QUEST research facility. This facility is located nine hundred feet below the surface of the earth. I'm standing next to the director of QUEST, Dr. Jon Sanborne. Dr. Sanborne, please tell us what this facility is used for, and why it is located nine hundred feet below the surface of the earth?"

Jon was surprised to realize he was completely at ease. "So nice to be with you and your TV audience, Holly. Thanks for visiting. This facility is an advanced particle physics research laboratory, and we are studying the very small things that make up you and me, and all that you see in the universe. We are trying to find out just how and why matter acts the way it does at the smallest levels possible, and what happens to these small particles when they interact with other sources of energy. This facility is nine hundred feet below the surface for two reasons. First, our experimental equipment is very sensitive, hundreds of feet of earth are necessary to filter out most of the cosmic rays that strike the surface of the earth so they don't interfere with our research results."

"And the second reason, Dr. Sanborne?"

"We also need this facility to be buried deep below the surface because when we activate the many high-powered electronic supermagnet systems here there is a tremendous amount of electromagnetic radiation generated. The same way that the hundreds of feet of earth shelter our equipment from the sun's radiation, the earth also shelters people on the surface from the energy that is generated down here. Conducting these experiments this far below the surface of the earth, under high security, keeps it safe and secure and harmless to the public."

"Dr. Sanborne, there has been a lot of speculation about other aspects of your research here. One matter for speculation is whether your research is being conducted for military or civilian use. Can you clarify this issue up for the viewers?"

"Certainly, I'm glad that you brought this up. Everything that we do here at QUEST and at the Sivatron, which I will show you later, is done exclusively for basic science research into the micro-universe. There is no military involvement in any way with our research."

"Dr. Sanborne, most of our viewers have probably heard something about your QUEST facility and about the exorbitant costs involved. Can you tell us why your research is important? Will it actually have any beneficial effects on our daily lives?"

"Excellent question, Holly! The research that we are doing here is simply amazing. We are now getting the first look at what is going on at the microscopic levels of the universe. We are looking at what is known at the *quantum level*. You see, Holly, reality is really a strange, mystical world where things are quite different than what we think they are. When we look into the tiniest levels of what makes up everything in the universe we see things that are extraordinarily weird and strange—even to scientists like us who are used to some very strange things."

"Strange? In what ways, Dr. Sanborne?"

"Well, one example is that when we look at particles at the smallest levels we don't just see particles in this universe, we see particles in other quantum states at the same time, or what we call superpositions. These superpositions are really particles that are in their own separate distinct individual universes."

"Wow! That is strange!"

"What is really interesting is that we are actually for the first time opening up a line of communication with those other particles in their own distinct and separate universes."

"How many other particle universes are out there, Dr. Sanborne?"

"This is one of the strange bits, Holly. There are an infinite number of other particle universes. And to answer your question about the benefits to the individuals out there wondering if this research will help them. Well, many scientific challenges had to be overcome in order to get these systems operating. And many breakthroughs were produced in creating this facility. For example, some of the most powerful quantum computers ever constructed in the world were created for this project. That's an example of technology being generated here that will benefit everyone. Another example of a crossover in technology which will benefit everyone, is the development of new types of supermagnets. These supermagnets are already improving everyday life. For instance, the new supermagnets have already been used to improve medical scanning devices that save lives every day."

"Dr. Sanborne, what are your thoughts about the future of this project? How long into the future do you expect the QUEST systems to continue operation? Can you tell us anything about how you expect the project to be used in the future?"

"The QUEST system, including the Sivatron, has already been in operation for over a year. We are receiving amazing data results from our experimental runs. We are planning to take the new experiments to much higher energy levels, and we anticipate new breakthrough discoveries into the mysteries of the quantum realm. We expect to publish our new discoveries in several research papers, which will be shared with the public right on the Ridgewood website if anyone is interested in learning more."

Holly signaled the camera crew to stop filming. "Okay, we're ready to go over to the Sivatron facility and do some filming there."

Jon, Yi, and VG led the crew toward the Sivatron complex. As they entered the tunnel area near the Sivatron several members of the television crew commented on the blue translucent mesh material on the walls and ceiling. Jon overheard one crew member say, "This place is like an alien world!"

The crew followed the QUEST team to the Torqkadrone staging area. The crew was obviously awestruck.

Jon called for everyone's attention. "Please be very careful not to touch or brush up against anything."

Taking in the enormity and strangeness of the cavernous interior, Holly exclaimed, "Wow! This is like something from a sci-fi movie. I don't know if I could ever really describe this to someone who hadn't seen it with their own eyes."

Jon turned, and looking Holly right in the eye, he intoned, "This is the place where the Goddess of Existence tells us her secrets, Holly. This is the place where the infinity of existential reality meets our comprehension."

Holly noticed Jon's intense gaze, and responded, "That's very poetic, and somehow sort of comforting, too. I can't believe how huge this place is, and the blue iridescences everywhere. I'm nearly overcome by the strangest feelings. And what are all those strange structures on the floor and ceiling?"

"What do you feel, Holly? Tell me."

"It's hard to describe. I feel almost like I have experienced this before in some way. It's not an unpleasant feeling, just strange and hard to describe. Everything is so weird and wonderful, but I feel somehow soothed and relaxed. It's almost like a homecoming."

Jon smiled. "I think I understand. Several of us have had a similar experience. It's hard to comprehend; something here seems to generate a sense of self-realization. Maybe it's a psychological effect, but one way or another it's real and many of us have felt it."

Holly suddenly shifted out of her reverie. "Okay, well let's get on with the filming, and continue our interview. This will look so awesome on TV!"

As Holly interviewed Jon, some of the crew filmed the surreal surroundings in the imposing cathedral, while others filmed Holly conversing with Jon with the splendor of the Sivatron as their backdrop. Finally, Holly wrapped up, "Well, thank you very much, Dr. Sanborne, for telling our viewers today just what is going on deep below the earth here at the QUEST facility at Ridgewood National Laboratory, in Ridgewood, New York. At this amazing, one-of-a-kind place, right in our own backyard, scientists are fulfilling the dreams of science and searching for the fundamentals of what makes up our very universe."

The crew director shook Jon's hand energetically. "What a great story! Can't wait 'til we get it on the air tonight! This is going to be hot. Great job, Holly! Fantastic interview, Dr. Sanborne!"

"Thanks! We're really happy to get some good press coverage that showcases what we do here."

"Okay guys, let's get packed up and get going. We've got another interview to get to. Let's go!" called out the production director. As the crew packed up their equipment, Jon and Holly headed back toward the control room. Holly stopped outside the control room and said, "I just want to thank you again for accommodating us all today. I know we must have totally messed up your work schedule this morning."

"No big deal, Holly. We're thrilled to get some good publicity for what we do here. You're a great reporter. I was very impressed with the questions you asked."

"So listen, I'd love to learn more about this place in the future. Could we do lunch sometime? You could tell me more about what you're doing here," Holly said as she pressed her card into Jon's hand.

"Uh, yeah—sure. It will be a pleasure."

"Great! Give me a call. I can't wait to meet!" Holly said, as the crew approached on their way out. She gave Jon a quick look back as she headed toward the elevators with the rest of the crew.

Jon turned to enter the control room, and saw Ben and Dr. Kenyatta. Slightly flustered, he realized that they had witnessed his exchange with Holly.

Ben grinned at him. "You keep doing things like that and you are going to get in real trouble with a certain psychiatrist we know."

"Ha, ha, ha. I'm sure that she just wants to know more about the research we're doing here. Maybe she's thinking of doing a series of stories."

"Well done, Jon!" said Kenyatta. Ignoring the exchange between Jon and Ben, he clapped Jon on the shoulder. "We need more press coverage like this. I'm sure this will help generate interest in our projects, and increase our future funding."

"Thanks. It seemed okay, but I just hope that I didn't make it too complicated for the average Joe."

"No, no. It went very well. You came across very well, and you were relaxed and informative. I'm quite pleased."

Yi approached, and said to Jon, quietly, in his ear, "We have the data results back from the Torqkadrone run."

Jon's face lit up. "I'll be in the control room in a little while. Can you get it ready?"

"The data is in! We're going to go over some of our data from our latest quantum seduction. Dr. Kenyatta, would you like to join us in the control room since you're here?"

"I'd love to, but unfortunately I'm already behind schedule," answered Kenyatta, glancing at his watch.

[34]

The Infinitrum

Jon, Ben, Yi, and VG had gathered in the control room and asked non-senior staff to leave the room. Charlie Kenton joined them for a private review of the data.

"Dr. Kenton, do you know Ben?" asked Jon.

"Sure, Ben has helped us out with some projects at HITS. Ben's a fixture around here. Ben, you've worked here at the Lab longer than anyone else, haven't you?"

"Not quite, Charlie. There's one other guy on site who has a few years on me—can't think of his name right now."

"Yi, you can start the data review. VG, please do me a favor. Close and lock the door, and alert the reception desk that we are not to be disturbed until further notice," Jon directed. "Everyone, please remember that what we are about to see here is to be kept in the strictest confidentiality. Go ahead, Yi."

Yi hit a few keys on her keyboard, and all at once all the room monitors were filled with images.

"A few days ago we started our latest quantum seduction experiment using the Torqkadrone and the Sivatron. Charlie, that's our new name for the Macro-STARR."

Yi displayed various images of the Torqkadrone and the Sivatron on the main monitor.

"Now, take a look at the main monitor. This is the view inside the Sivatron. This is an actual video feed of what went on within this structure during our last experiment, which used the feed flow of protons from your HITS facility, roughly twenty million per second, and the immense power from our supermagnets and magnacasters within the Sivatron structure itself. After a period of time, a state of quantum gravity was achieved, and within this plasma flux a gateway was opened into the quantum multiverse."

Charlie Kenton had never observed such a recording before, and the stunned expression on his face betrayed his struggle to comprehend what he was seeing.

"Now, let me direct your attention to the left monitor. We have developed several different types of Torqkadrones. The most complex version, the VX, is displayed here. This Torqkadronc is inserted into the Sivatron during the plasma flux. It has the ability to not only enter into this state of quantum gravity, but also to become part of the superposition density matrix. You can actually see it go into a de-resolution state inside the Sivatron in this visual."

Kenton blurted out, "What you're saying is that the Torqkadrone becomes part of the quantum superposition matrix! Is that right, Jon?"

"Yes, Charlie! What we have successfully achieved is that the Torqkadrone then essentially becomes a virtual entity in the infinite possible superpositions. Of course, this happens all at the same time and all at the same place—right here in the Sivatron. The Torqkadrone device then acts as a satellite and has the ability to scan these parallel worlds and record data from these alternate states of reality." Glancing at Yi, Jon signaled, "Okay, Yi, put some of the data up on the monitors."

Images appeared on all the monitors simultaneously.

Jon continued, "Displayed here is a very small sampling of the visual data feeds that the Torqkadrone recorded during its many worlds quantum excursion."

"These images are deformed, aren't they? I can't seem to make anything out," commented Kenton.

"Correct! That's because the data was recorded in the different quantum states that the Torqkadrone occupied during the course of the experiment. That has been the problem with other less complex experiments by physicists throughout the world who have attempted quantum world superposition exploration. The quantum multiverse does not like to have itself looked at. It seems that Mother Nature wants to keep her secrets from us. She has not shown us her other faces . . . until now!"

Yi typed a few commands into her computer and the images began to resolve slowly into a coherent visual image.

"What we are looking at here, for the first time ever, is an image of the infinite parallel worlds that exist right here, in this same time and place that we ourselves occupy."

Some of the monitor images displayed visual graphics that appeared typical of a city street with tall magnificent structures that were commonplace of a modern city. Others looked vastly different with alien structures and artifacts not recognizable to a human on earth. The images changed every so often, replaced by new ones that reflected the bizarre newly discovered parallel worlds.

"We call it the *Infinitrum.* The Infinitrum is the place where any possibility that you can think of, any possibility that you can't think of, or any possibility that no one could ever think of, exists simultaneously with our own existence. These parallel worlds exist only atomic distances away from us, but we can't see them. We can't usually interact with them at all, but NOW using the Sivatron, we've established a link to those other parallel worlds."

Astonished, Charlie rose from his chair and walked closer to the monitors, observing with intense concentration. "My God! Jon, this is absolutely astonishing! How many people know about this?"

"Only a minimum here at Ridgewood know about this aspect of our research. Those who need to know have been informed, including Dr. Kenyatta."

"Why do some of the images look similar if this is different parallel worlds of reality?"

"What you are looking at is only a small fraction of the trillions of visual images that we have processed and observed. If you were to see much more of them you would start to realize the changing states of the individual parallel worlds. Over time, small changes within each universe start to amplify, and eventually create dramatically different worlds. In one universe, there is a version of you as you are now, and in the other infinite parallel worlds there are versions of you that are totally dissimilar. There are even universes where you don't exist anymore, or were never were born at all."

Kenton took hold of the edge of a nearby desk for support. He searched Jon's face, asking, "Can this be real? Are these visual images actually real parallel worlds? Maybe this is just a kind of simulation? A virtual replication generated by your computers that is tricking us?"

"No, Charlie, these images are very real. Not only have we received data from the quantum multiverse, and opened up a line of communication, but we have also exchanged matter from our universe with the other parallel worlds."

"What?"

"We have experimented with sending inanimate objects, and even living beings, into the other parallel worlds."

"That is crazy! How is that even possible?"

"The Q-Wave Q6 quantum supercomputer is able to interact with the Sivatron system that interpolates the data received. That enables us to align the quantum information of our universe with the information structures of the infinite other parallel worlds. We can thank the good people at Q-Wave for this amazing breakthrough, enabled by their latest technology."

"Kenyatta told me some Q-Wave executives will bc visiting you. Now I know why. But this is just not believable."

"Q-Wave gave us millions to fund to our research, with the agreement of technology sharing rights, so they will be getting a lot back in return. Our data will help them engineer new, more powerful quantum supercomputers in the future. Kenyatta said they want to meet me during their visit, and invited me to a dinner meeting with them. It should be interesting."

"Damn! I wish I could go, too! That will be fascinating!" replied Charlie with enthusiasm.

"Jon, you know this could get you a Nobel Prize? When are you going to go public on this? This will changc the world forever!"

"I don't know, Charlie. I don't think that the world is ready to accept proof of the multiverse concept yet. Let's keep this quiet for a while. We don't fully understand everything yet about these alternate worlds."

"These kinds of breakthroughs have happened before, and society had to adapt and accept it. Just like when they realized that the world was round and not flat, or that the universe is ever-expanding."

"Good point, Charlie. Eventually it will be accepted, but it will require a real shift in our understanding of who and what we really are."

"Yeah, that's why we have religions."

"I totally agree, Charlie—people always need something to believe in."

After Kenton left, Jon and his staff spent the next few hours poring over the data from the Torqkadrone excursion, cross-checking it with their supercomputer systems, and cataloguing the information for use in their next experimental runs.

That afternoon Yi approached Jon, and said, "The fabrication team is nearing completion of the latest version of the VX Torqkadrone for the next planned quantum seduction. Would you like to take a look at it?"

"Sure, Yi. Let's see it."

They walked further into the depths of their subterranean complex and entered the Torqkadrone design and construction complex. Yi brought Jon over to one of several Torqkadrones that were in the process of being constructed by highly-skilled design engineers. The room buzzed with activity as several workers dressed in bright-white, clean-room uniforms embellished with the QUEST project's distinctive triangle emblem, carried on with their tasks.

Bright overhead lights lit up this Torqkadrone. It was right in the center of the huge room, as if on display. The highly polished, silver-gray entity almost glowed. Surreal reflections of the room radiated from its alien-looking, elongated body.

"This is it, Jon! It's fully complete—though it still needs to have an equilibration analysis. What do you think of her?"

Jon caressed the bright, elegant, silver-gray surface. "Wow! What a beautiful beast. I love it! It's totally amazing. How big is she?"

"The VX2B is sixteen feet long, eight feet wide, and seven feet high. The radial telemetry crown adds roughly another two feet to its height. Like all the others, it's composed entirely out of an alloy containing titanium, silver and molybdenum, and specially cast in a poured mold."

"It's very impressive, Yi! When will you complete all your systems checks on it?"

"In the next few days. So far we haven't detected any critical anomalies."

"Fantastic! Is it all we hoped for?"

"Yes, Jon. It is fully capable of carrying a human occupant, and is actually quite comfortable. This version also has the most sophisticated telemetry interface yet, and multiple compensation drivers for additional safety."

"Excellent work! This will be our greatest challenge yet, but I anticipate everything will work out well. Just think of the implications of what we will learn about this weird and wonderful universe."

"Jon, are you willing to take your chances inside this thing during a quantum seduction? Without test runs I am somewhat apprehensive about going to this next level."

Jon walked slowly around the vehicle, feeling its surface. He peered at Yi and asked, "Give me your honest opinion. You know that I have the highest respect for your expertise. Do you think that we are ready for the next level of quantum seduction experiments—involving us conscience observers into the Infinitrum?"

Yi took her time to answer. Finally, nodding her head, she said, "Yes. I really think that we are fully prepared and ready to go the next level. We've been successful with each of our mission goals, and even I am astonished at the success that we have demonstrated. But you are going to have to ask yourself if the risk is worth the possible rewards. Something could go wrong. You know that with the complexity of these electromagnetic systems there is no sure thing."

"Well, I'll think about it a bit more, but as of now, I'm ready to go for it. I really want to know what is out there in this unbelievable multiverse of infinite realities. Besides, if I do go for it, it is only because the universe is allowing me inside to see what's there. Maybe it's ironic, but it's the universe herself that has created a world that has enabled me to delve into her secrets and realize her infinite splendor of possibilities."

Looking at Jon, Yi contemplated the significance of his words and of her own existence in this universe.

[35]

Red Lights Flashing

Jon left QUEST and headed for his car after a satisfying day. The day had gone almost perfectly. He'd had a successful television interview in the morning, and enjoyed a rousing end-of-the-day ping-pong match with Charlie Kenton at the Mid-Level Station. Driving through the woods near QUEST a chill ran down his spine as he realized that he was being followed by one of the midnight blue vehicles driven by the Ridgewood Police. Jon tried to shake off the uncomfortable feeling. He headed toward the main gate as if unaware of the police presence behind him, but managed to catch a glimpse of the SUV in his mirrors every now and then. His stomach sank as he saw the police lights come on. Reluctantly, Jon pulled over onto the side of the road. The area was a remote, heavily wooded part of the Ridgewood property. Jon remembered that he had not yet gotten his car inspected.

One of the officers headed over to Jon's window while the other approached the passenger side of his car. Jon rolled his window down and greeted the officer, "Hello, Officer Kendrick, isn't it?"

"Hello, Dr. Sanborne. Yes. This is my partner, Lieutenant Harmon Reynolds."

"Very nice to meet you again, Officer Kendrick, and you too, Lieutenant Reynolds. Nice day today, isn't it?"

The officers glared coldly at Jon.

"Do you mind if I ask why you pulled me over today?"

Glancing at Lieutenant Reynolds, Officer Kendrick said, "Dr. Sanborne, I'm going to ask you to step out of your vehicle and walk over to the passenger side onto the shoulder of the road for a minute, sir."

Jon was taken aback. "Why would you want me to do that, Officer?"

"We just want to ask you a few questions, sir."

On either side of his car, each officer now had one hand placed on top of his own firearm. They were both staring him down. Jon got out, and walked over to the passenger side of the car, careful not to make any sudden moves. The officers stood, one on each side of him, and began to ask him a series of questions.

"Dr. Sanborne, where were you the night of Friday, October the fourth, at approximately one in the morning?" Lieutenant Reynolds said, his face just inches away from Jon's.

"I have no idea. I'll have to think, Lieutenant. Uh, I believe I was working late on an experiment at QUEST that night. Why do you ask, Lieutenant?"

Reynolds glared at Jon, then responded, "One of the buildings here on site was broken into and vandalized that night. We are looking for any information on just what happened that night. One of our officers was accosted while investigating the disturbance, and we are going to make sure to find the guy who did it. Would you happen to have any information about that incident, Dr. Sanborne?"

"No, Lieutenant, I really don't know anything about it."

"Who were you working with that night? Can anyone verify that you were working at QUEST that night?"

"Yes, certainly Lieutenant, I was working with a group of people that night. One of the people who I was working with was Ben Carson. We were working with a whole team of others, too. We were involved with a very technical experiment using a streaming energy source from HITS, so we had to stay into the early morning hours of that Saturday morning."

"Dr. Sanborne, have you ever been in the RGR Building or Building 720 complex previously?"

"Yes, just recently I took part in the ERC inspection of the graphite reactor as part of the agreement with the state and local environmental agencies. We were reviewing any lingering issues that remained pertaining to past spills and storage issues from the reactor."

"The ERC committee? I've never heard of any ERC committee. What the hell is that?"

"The Environmental Review Committee, Lieutenant. Dr. Kenyatta assembled the committee, and asked me and Ben Carson to participate. I hope that clarifies that issue for your understanding."

As well as speaking like a drill sergeant, Reynolds used his height and bulk to intimidate. "So you claim that this Ben Carson was working with you last Friday night late into Saturday morning along with others in your QUEST facility. Is that correct?"

"That is correct. We were all working late into the night last Friday at QUEST."

Suddenly, in one smooth motion, Reynolds pulled out his baton and pinned Jon's neck against the side of the car. Jon was unable to speak or move.

"You listen, and you listen good, Sanborne. We are going to check up on your information, and if we find anything out of line with what you claim, you'll be lab animal meat. You got that?" Reynolds emphasized his point by pressing harder on his baton for several seconds. When he released Jon, Jon slid to the ground, gasping for air. Kendrick threw a piece of paper at Jon and jeered, "Here's your ticket, *sir.* Your vehicle is uninspected!"

As they left Jon writhing on the ground gasping for breath, Reynolds sneered, "And don't forget to have a nice day, *sir.*"

It took Jon several seconds to get to his knees, and several more to recover enough to stand up. He noticed that the small pen magnet gun that Jim Morris had given him in the magnet shop had fallen out of his pocket. Fighting dizziness, he reached over and picked it up. He looked at it for quite a while, and as if in slow motion he put it back into his pocket. Finally, he stumbled to his car in shock. He had never imagined he would be a victim of police brutality. He looked at the ticket Kendrick had thrown at him, thinking, *What a bunch of Nazis thugs! Tonner's probably behind this crap! How could this Lab have gotten so infested with this corruption! I better let Ben know what's going on, they might go after him, too!* After several moments he turned the key in the ignition and headed home.

On the long ride home Jon calmed down and regained his composure, but he became more and more furious about the abuse of power and the undercurrent of evil at the Lab that most people knew nothing about.

Later that night, Jon told Marta all about his terrible experience with the Ridgewood Police.

"Jon, I can't believe that they would do that to you. Why do you think they would do something so violent like that?"

"I'm not sure, but I think that they are very concerned that Ben and I had found out their dirty secrets about the Ridgewood Graphite Reactor and the Hades Project. Especially about the bad things that went on inside the subsurface complex at 720. Those creeps are probably the ones responsible for breaking into our house when we went upstate a few days ago."

"Unfortunately, I think you're probably right and that's why they are threatening you. You two may have stumbled across some terrible secrets, and they are sending you a message. What a bunch of evil pricks!"

"Don't worry Marta, one way or another they will get what is coming to them. I guarantee you that! I'm going to call Ben now to let him know. Ben and I are going to have to think out a plan to get these guys—especially that bastard Tonner."

"Why don't you go to Kenyatta and tell him what you found out?"

"I am thinking about that, but what if he knows about it already and he's allied with Tonner? I really don't think so, though. I think Kenyatta is a good guy, so I may take a chance and approach him if I have to. But I would also not be surprised if Kenyatta already knows about a lot of the bad things that went on here decades ago, and maybe even some of the stuff going on now! I guess I'll try to feel him out a little more before deciding what to do."

"Maybe that's best. On another note, remember I told you Lois told me her coworker had some information about Helen Dunne. Well, today her coworker gave her Helen's home address, and I got it from Lois."

"That is amazing! Where does she live?"

"She lives on Sound Shore Road in Laurel, near the Long Island Sound somewhere. I have the address written down. Maybe we can find it sometime."

"We should do that soon. We really have to thank Lois for helping us out with this!"

"Actually, Lois wants to come too. She is very interested in finding out more about Hilcraft. She completely flipped out when I told her what you found during your adventure with Ben the other night."

"Sure, that's fine with me. I just hope Helen opens up and tells us about her past with Hilcraft. I bet we'll find out a lot about the unscrupulous things that were going on at Ridgewood. Let's go pay her a visit in a few days after the Haslinger LSD Isomer study is done."

"That's tomorrow, Jon! Did you forget already? You have so much going on that you are starting to forget about some important things. I think you'd better slow down a bit."

"Yeah, I know. I've got a lot going on, but I'm really looking forward to taking part in the study. It's very interesting. What time should I be where tomorrow?"

"We are all going to meet at the Lab rec grounds—by the ball fields in the late afternoon. They're going to have the area all set up with picnic tables and chairs. There'll be trailers and tents set up with special monitoring equipment. Dr. Haslinger wanted a relaxed environment so that the participants can enjoy their experience. There will be about twenty medical people there, and about forty subjects taking the Pegasus LSD isomer."

"Great! I know a bunch of other scientists who are going to be there to take part in the study too. It's almost going to be like a party without the drinking."

"We've been getting everything set up. Dr. Haslinger has gone over everything with us in great detail, so everything should go off very smoothly. And, of course, there won't be any alcohol, but the dose of Pegasus will definitely induce intoxication for a few hours."

"How long will the study go on for?"

"At least eight hours, considering we have to perform all the before and after neurometric and psychometric evaluations on the participants. Dr. Haslinger and his staff will go over all that information at the start of the study. I'll drive us home after it is over, and other volunteers will be there to help drive anyone home who did not arrange for a pickup."

"Oh good, Marta. Let's go in your car because after those thugs assaulted me today, they gave me a ticket for having an uninspected vehicle."

"You've got to be kidding! I've been telling you to get that car inspected. I only hope that those bastards get their butts kicked in one day!"

"When bad people do bad things long enough, bad things catch up to them."

"I certainly hope so. They could have injured you severely. I'll have to give you one of my physicals tonight and make sure everything is in top working condition."

"That sounds like fun! But I think that I will have to perform a physical exam on you too."

Marta laughed. "Okay, Jon. You have my permission. Jon, who were the officers who pulled you over and gave you that ticket? I wonder if I know them. Some of them go to our shooting range to practice."

"Kendrick was the one who gave me the ticket, and the one who shoved his stick in my throat was a Lieutenant named Reynolds."

"Reynolds! Was he a big African-American man who looked like a football player?"

"Yep, that was him, along with that other jerk, Kendrick."

"I know those guys. I've seen them shooting at the range. They're arrogant, egotistical, rude jerks. And neither one can shoot."

"That sounds like them alright. That Reynolds dude seems like a real nasty guy."

"They both seem evil to me. We'll have to be more careful from now on, since we are on their surveillance list."

"Absolutely, and please tell Lois to keep quiet about 720 and Hilcraft. We don't want to get her into any trouble either. And I think that from now on we better be careful what we say over the phone. It could be bugged. I keep thinking of that strange response I got when I called that Targway Proving Ground phone number. This situation could be broader than we think and involve the military—who knows."

Marta cuddled up to Jon affectionately, and said, "I never thought of that, but you're right—we have to be more careful about what we say and do. I just hope that nothing bad happens. I'm worried, Jon."

"It's going to be okay, Marta. Everything will be fine. Eventually these bad players will get caught up in their own evil schemes. I'm going to call Ben and let him know about my experience today. I wonder if anything eventful happened to him. I hope he's alright."

[36]

The Pegasus LSD Isomer Study

Elsewhere, hours later, a phone conversation took place that Jon could never have imagined.

"Hello, Dr. Tonner! I'm surprised that you are calling me this late into the evening. What's on your mind at this time of the night?" Kenyatta said.

"I understand that you were notified about the recent breach in security that took place at the graphite reactor and Building 720?"

"Yes, Dr. Tonner. I have been apprised of the situation. I was also notified by the central offices that there was an unusual event that took place involving Targway."

"Good then! I have alerted the Lab police to track every movement of the individuals in question and take preemptive measures when necessary to stop any more meddling and interference. I also got clearance from central offices for several of their agents to be assigned here temporarily. They'll be looking into the disturbance and are authorized to take any appropriate actions necessary."

"Very good, Dr. Tonner, I totally concur. Unfortunately, several individuals here have crossed the line. Conventional methods are no longer suitable to resolve the disruption that has occurred. Please keep me informed of any further developments."

"Indeed, I will, Dr. Kenyatta. Will you be speaking with the director about this soon?"

"Yes, of course, Dr. Tonner. I don't have to remind you to keep this quiet. I do not want anyone to know about this unless it is absolutely essential. I hope you understand."

"I totally agree. I'll meet up with you in the next week or so as things progress. Take care, Dr. Kenyatta, and sorry to disturb you and your family at this late hour."

Kenyatta hung up the phone and paced the room, with a look of concern.

* * *

Marta and Jon drove down a little-used road at the Lab to a very remote section of the Lab's property.

"I hadn't ever been in this area until we started setting up for the Pegasus study a few weeks ago. It's so remote and heavily wooded," Marta commented.

"Yeah, I think the Lab owns more than five-thousand acres of woodlands and meadows, including the headwaters of the Paumanok River, which is over on the northern side of the property."

"The Paumanok River! This far west? The Paumanok is in Riverhead and Calverton; are the headwaters really this far away?"

"There is actually a story to that. The headwater area here on site was basically swampland around the time of World War I. The Army had soldiers dig out a main drainage canal through the swampland, which drained into the headwaters of the Paumanok

River, making this the most western part of the Paumanok River. The Lab's wastewater treatment plant now discharges into this part of the river."

"It's such a remote area that I was kind of surprised to see some other vehicles scattered around the other day when I was helping set up for the study."

"Sometimes you will see some RVs and campers scattered about here. Some retirees are allowed by special permit to come and camp out on the Lab grounds. I think that they limit them to two nights of camping twice a year."

"That sounds like fun. Do they have to pay a fee to the Lab for camping here?"

"The Lab officials tried to charge a fee, but the alumni association used their political influence to stop them. They're very politically powerful!"

"They seem like a very active group. I see them often in Bowers Hall attending lectures and concerts. Maybe when you and I retire we'll get a camper and come camp out here."

"I'd love to get a camper, but I'd much rather go up to the Catskills or to a National Park than come back to where I worked!"

"Well, you never know about the future. You may miss this place more than you think."

"We'll see about that. I certainly would not miss some of the people here—like that asshole, Tonner, and his goons dressed up as cops!"

"I don't think he is going to last here."

"I hope you're right about that!"

Jon and Marta arrived at the recreational fields, where the study was set up. Several acres of large open fields were surrounded by woods full of pitch pines and large oaks. A number of paths led through the woods to other grounds. Several long, white, aluminum trailers, large tents, and canopies dotted the fields. Lines of brightly colored flags were suspended from poles, adding color and creating a festive atmosphere. In the center of the field, surrounded by the trailers and tents, there was a large carpeted area, covered by a huge nylon canopy. A Buddha and some other wooden totems and icons were arrayed around the carpeted area.

"Wow! This place is all set up for a party today," Jon said enthusiastically.

"Haslinger wants everyone to take the time to enjoy their experience. He's really nice. You'll like him."

"He's from Germany, right?"

"Yeah, he's from Aachen, Germany, which is to the west, near the Netherlands. He's a neurologist. He was at the Darmstadt Medical School in Germany until he immigrated to the United States about fifteen years ago, when he was invited into a research program run by the military at Northgate Army Medical Center in Kansas. He spent some time there before he came to Ridgewood about seven years ago. The research program he set up here is becoming world-renowned."

"So he's a real leader in his field."

"Yes, he is, but he's just a pretty regular guy. He loves to joke around, too. I think that you will really like him. I'll definitely introduce you sometime during the study today. I've told him all about you, and he's very interested in meeting you."

"Cool! I'm really looking forward to all this."

"Oh look! There's Lois. She's helping today. I think she'll be driving some people home later, too. I'd better get to work. Why don't you go mingle with some of the other participants?" suggested Marta, pointing toward the carpeted area under the canopy.

"Okay, Marta, you do what you have to do, and I'll get to know some of the other guinea pigs."

Marta grabbed Jon's hand, and gave it a quick squeeze before rushing off toward Lois.

Under the canopy, Jon saw several people chatting near tables laden with food and drink.

"Hi! Welcome to the Pegasus Isomer Study. My name is Janice. We're going to get started soon. In the meantime, relax and make yourself at home. Name tags are on that table. Please keep your tag on for the duration of the study. Help yourself to any refreshments you'd like, and let me know if there's anything you need."

Jon got his name tag, and helped himself to a root beer and some mixed nuts.

A familiar voice called out, "Hey Jon! Glad you're here today, buddy! At least there's someone here I know." Tom McGuiness, Jon's colleague from QUEST, clapped him on the back.

"Hey, Tom! Good to see you, man! I thought you might be here. Where's VG? Is he coming?"

"Nah. He couldn't make it. I think he had to visit his father."

"Aw. That's too bad. I bet he'd love this. He's such a cerebral dude. We'll have to rib him endlessly about missing it."

"Don't worry. I'll get him. Goofing on him is one of my favorite sports."

Realizing that most of the participants were already filling the seats, and that Haslinger was about to speak, they scurried to find seats.

A graying, middle-aged man tested the microphone at the podium. His German accent was noticeable, but easy to understand. "Will everyone please take your seat. We are about to get started," he said. The crowd quieted, and Haslinger continued, "First, I would like to thank you all for volunteering your time and efforts to assist us with this unique preliminary study of the pharmacological drug candidate known as Pegasus. I'm so glad to welcome you all here on this beautiful day. We are lucky that the weather has fully cooperated, and nature is greeting us so beautifully. Let us thank that higher power that is looking out for us.

"So let me give you a little background. When I first proposed this study at a meeting with Ridgewood's director and Dr. Kenyatta they stared at me blankly and then started laughing. They truly thought that I was joking. When they finally understood that I was dead serious they stopped laughing. I'm not sure how to describe the changes in their faces. Stone-cold. Shock? Disbelief?"

The audience roared with laughter as the various participants envisioned the stunned looks on the faces of two of the most powerful officials at the Lab. Haslinger waited for the laughter to diminish, and continued, "To make a long story short, I am a doctor of neurology who has been studying, for quite a while, the issue of pain, and the perception of it, in the human subject. My staff and I have studied many different chemical candidates, and how they chemically operate in the relief of different forms of pain in humans and animals. About a year ago, we started studying a new class of pain management drugs that are quite similar in structure to the drug Lysergic Acid Diethylamide. These drugs have very powerful pain abatement properties. Of course, this chemical is also known as LSD, the psychedelic drug that was widely in use for recreational purposes during the sixties and seventies. Our version of the drug is altered very slightly from the form that was used as a psychedelic compound. Interestingly, we were only able to produce this variant form of LSD in our laboratory due to a totally new technique of molecular alteration called transformative molecularization. This is a complex process that involves the bombardment of a chemical substance in a computer-controlled magnetic field. Pegasus, this particular version, or isomer, of LSD has been found to have very powerful pain management properties. Some of you will receive that drug today. Please note that although Pegasus does not have the full intoxicating effects of LSD it does induce a very unique form of intoxication.

"Today we have three different groups of participants in this pilot study. Some of you do not have any profound pain issues who will be given Pegasus. Another group of participants who do suffer more profound pain from a variety of ailments will also be given Pegasus to see how they evaluate the pain relieving properties of the substance. And then there will be a control group. If you are in the control group you will receive a placebo rather than receiving Pegasus. All participants will be asked to perform certain neurometric and psychometric tests along with some unique brain scans. All these tests are totally noninvasive. They will not cause any harm or discomfort to you. I did want to take questions at this time, but unfortunately we are short on time, so I'll ask you to direct your questions to the medical staff who will be working with you. Just keep in mind that this is not an official double blind study but rather an informal guidance investigation."

"Before we begin, I just want you all to hear a short statement from one of our patients about why this research is important to the quality of her life. Amy?"

Amy, an attractive, middle-aged, brunette, approached the podium and began speaking nervously. "My name is Amy Litton, and I just want to tell everyone here that I am a patient in Dr. Haslinger's clinic. I suffer from severe migraines and cluster headaches. When I get these headaches they can last for hours, day after day. It gets so bad that I just want to put my head into a vise and squeeze it until the pain stops. I've tried everything, both over-the-counter and prescription, and so far nothing has been really effective. When I have these headaches my life is on hold. I cannot be a productive person, and it's hard to be a compassionate, patient mom, or empathetic friend, because the pain is so overwhelming. My life is not my own. Because of this research, and the cooperation of volunteers, I believe that better treatments for those of us who suffer extreme, debilitating pain is just around the corner. Again, I thank you all for coming and volunteering. You have my profound gratitude, and give me hope."

Haslinger returned as Amy left the stage. "Okay, everyone! Let's get this show on the road. Study groups will meet in the trailers. Please go to your study group area as indicated by the signs over to your right."

"I'm in Group A, Tom. How about you?" Jon asked.

"Group A, too."

Jon and Tom headed to the appropriate trailer. Three members of the staff were seated behind a table, and several other workers greeted the participants as they entered the trailer.

"Welcome to the Group A study area. Let me check your name tags, and then we can give you your test dose. Jon Sanborne and Tom McGuiness . . . Group A. Good. You're in the right place! We dilute the dose in a beverage. Any preferences, guys?"

"Do you have ginger ale?" asked Tom.

"Sure thing. How about you?"

"How about seltzer, lemon-flavored?" Jon requested.

Tom and Jon waited until they both received their doses, and then held up their effervescent plastic cups for a toast. "For science, and helping out those in pain!" Jon toasted.

"I'll drink to that! Bottoms up!" Tom said.

"You can now enjoy your time here over in the center canopy area. Help yourselves to refreshments, relax, and mingle with the other participants. We just ask you not to wander off, as we will need to see you at specific intervals for our testing," said the attendant, disposing of their cups.

They returned to the central area, and settled down on comfortable plastic lawn chairs near a small group of participants engaged in lively discussion.

"Hello, Dr. Sanborne!"

"Hi. I don't believe I recognize you. Have we met before?"

At that moment, Kenyatta approached and addressed Jon. "Hello, I see you've already met Dr. Thorstrum."

"No, Dr. Kenyatta, we just sat down, and we haven't officially met yet."

"Let me introduce myself to you and your friend. I'm Max Thorstrum. I'm here as a visiting scientist from the University of Toronto. I'm in theoretical physics. I'm working on the Gravity Wave Detector here at Ridgewood."

"I've heard about that. It sounds very interesting. How's it going?"

"Well, let's just say that we have a lot of work ahead of us, but things are going well overall."

"You fellows enjoy your time here. I'll be back to check in later," said Kenyatta, as he left.

"Tell me Dr. Sanborne—" began Thorstrum.

"Please call me Jon. And this is my friend and colleague, Tom McGuiness."

"Nice meeting you too, Tom. I've been hearing about your QUEST project for quite some time. I understand that you have been working up the power levels of the magnetic fields and you have been achieving superposition seduction. Is that correct?"

Suddenly, Jon felt really strange. He stopped to reflect on his feelings, and asked, "Tom, do you feel strange now? I think I'm starting to feel the effects of the Pegasus."

"Yeah. Kind of. It's weird."

"Max, what group are you in today? Are you also taking the Pegasus drug too?" Jon asked.

"Yes, Jon I'm in Group B. I have also taken the Pegasus drug and I'm an official pain management patient. I have very bad arthritis. I thought maybe the drug could help me with my pain issue."

"Do you feel the effects of the drug now, Max?"

Smiling, Max said, "I'm feeling something right now. Remember that Ricky Nelson song from the seventies? *I went to a garden party . . . da . . . da . . . da.*"

"I wonder exactly how this stuff interacts with our biochemistry," Tom mused.

"Marta said that it has an effect on the serotonin receptors in the brain. Let's ask someone," said Jon, rising from his chair.

Jon scanned the canopied area looking for one of the medical volunteers, and quickly spotted one clearly identified as a member of the medical team wearing an orange T-shirt that all the medical volunteers were wearing. He waved to her, and she approached.

"Hi, my name is Sandy. Can I help you?"

"Hi, Sandy. We just have a few questions for you. I think we're starting to feel the effects of the Pegasus chemical. Can you tell us about how it works and the effects that it will have on our bodies?"

"And our minds, too!" added Tom, giggling.

"Sure. When taken orally the chemical starts to enter the brain cells within about twenty minutes, and the effects are first felt. Typically, one will feel a slight rush of energy. You may notice some changes in perception, too. These shifts in perception can include the auditory and visual systems of the brain. Your sense of time and awareness may be heightened. A relaxed, reflective state, which Dr. Haslinger refers to as *galactic-radiance,* is commonly perceived. It is also at this point that the very powerful pain mitigation effects of the drug start to take effect."

"Well, I think we're starting to feel the full effects now. So, what is the theory on how Pegasus works? Do they know what the actual biochemical processes are?" Jon asked.

"We think that the molecule in Pegasus binds to certain protein-coupled receptors in the brain. There seems to be an antagonistic effect that increases certain other chemicals in the brain which are known to interfere with pain sensation. Indirectly, this also produces a mildly intoxicating effect similar to LSD, although more muted, and somewhat different. Tell me, how are you all feeling now?"

"Pretty relaxed! Time feels like it's passing very slowly right now. See those colorful flags, blowing in the wind . . . I feel like those colors are part of my body. I feel great, though! I feel like I could easily run a mile without stopping!" Tom answered, grinning happily.

Thorstrum was smiling like the Cheshire cat. "It's amazing. All of my arthritis pain is completely gone. I feel something very, very mild that's almost like dizziness, but it's not really uncomfortable. Colors are so intense. The color of your orange shirt is so bright that it's almost like I'm tasting and smelling it as well as seeing it. All my senses seem heightened. There is a wonderful aroma in the air that I hadn't noticed before. I think it's the pine trees—and things keep popping up in my head—crystal-clear memories from my childhood, interesting thoughts, and observations. It's all very amazing, and it's so wonderful to be free of pain."

"That must be such a relief. How 'bout you, Jon? Feeling fine?" asked Tom, smirking.

"I feel really good. It's weird, but really cool. My whole body just feels great, somehow supercharged with vitality and energy. I could run that mile with you, Tom, and whoop your ass. And my senses feel like they're superpowered now. I can hear everything.

I can pick up the conversations of people who are all the way over there. And like you two said—the colors—wow. I feel like I'm being physically touched by colors around us, the sky, the trees are like moving me, and at the same time they all seem to blend into one giant, multimedia, kaleidoscopic movie. And maybe most amazing is I can visualize anything that I want inside my brain—anything at all—and surprisingly, my ability to think seems to be enhanced in a bizarre way, like if I took a test now I would do better than normal."

"Excellent, gentleman, just try to remember all these experiences and please record them in the survey that will be handed out after the study is ending. Soon, you will be asked to participate in medical tests inside the designated trailers but until then enjoy your unique experiences and I will check on you all later."

After Sandy left, Jon turned back to Thorstrum.

"So, Max, you were asking about the issue of our energy level tests at our QUEST, and I never got to answer. Yeah, we've been increasing the energy levels of the systems over the past few months, and—drumroll, please—we have obtained quantum superposition seduction," Jon said.

"That is so cool. Do you worry at all about having problems with your supermagnet systems in the quantum gravity flux? Those electromagnetic integrated components are so complex and intricate it could be very dangerous, especially if there were any problems with the cooling system, like that cooling system explosion that occurred at CERN during their early runs."

"I'm surprised you know so much about our setup. Yeah, it is potentially very dangerous with the liquid helium cooling systems and the proton beam magnacaster inductors, but so far all of our preventative measures have paid off royally."

"I know you did extensive metal fatigue testing with Phosglow. We use Phosglow, too. There's nothing better for finding defective metal housings in the cooling systems. It's just so very damn toxic though. You know there are rumors that one of your researchers may have been overcome with that chemical? Whatever happened with that anyway?"

"Nothing at all. He hardly used the stuff, and we religiously follow all health and safety procedures. The medical report confirmed that his death was most likely caused by an undetected underlying medical condition. It sucks. He was a great guy, and a good friend," Jon replied, obviously brought down by the turn in conversation.

The uncomfortable silence was broken shortly as Sandy returned. "Okay, guys! I'll be taking you each for some medical tests now. Who's first?"

Tom jumped up enthusiastically. "I'll go this round. See you guys in a few—and don't drink any beer 'til I get back."

"So sorry to hear about your friend and coworker, Jon," said Max. "I know the loss must have been really difficult for you and your crew. The physics lab also has some potentially dangerous components. We all have to be really careful, especially working with such high voltage. One of our workers was burned very severely by an arc flash. I don't think he will ever work with us again."

"Yeah. It's crazy. But we make health and safety our greatest priority, and we run routine malfunction mitigation simulations all the time, including evacuation preparations."

"Hey, Jon, I been reading about the theory that your work is based on, and I noticed that the foundational theory of your work was taken from some of Emery Hilcraft's research."

"You know about Hilcraft and his work?"

"I've been very interested in his theories for a long time. I was completely taken with his view of our universe as a projection of information from the future to the past, which is essentially an infinite mathematical structure in nature."

"Me, too! I hardly know anyone who really understands his concepts and just how advanced his ideas were. You know he also believed that what we do in the future has an effect in the past?"

"Yup, one more of his theories that is just now finally becoming recognized as possible. He certainly was a genius, ahead of his time. I wonder whatever happened to him. He seems to have just fallen off the radar."

"I don't know, but I've been looking into his past, and there are a lot of *strange events* that happened to him while he worked here. Perhaps someday we'll find out just what happened to him."

"Jon, I'm going to be frank with you concerning your research here at QUEST—if you don't mind. Dr. Kenyatta filled me in on just what you and your team are working toward now in your current research, and it's actually very concerning to me."

"Really? Concerning? In what way?"

"Well, from what I hear, you're now trying to not only study the effects of the superpositions in their respective parallel universes, but you are actually attempting to interact matter from our universe into the other quantum parallel universes. Is that right, Jon?"

"Yes, something like that, Max."

"And I also understand that you have built a device that is used to transpose or interrelate with one or several of the other parallel worlds in the particle wave field—part of that many worlds theory."

Thanks to the effects of Pegasus, Jon was less defensive than he might have been. "That is also somewhat correct, but you sound like it's problematic in some way, and that is just not the case. Everything we are doing at QUEST is based on predictive science. We've been taking the research in a step-by-step approach right from day one."

"Well, would you mind explaining to me just what that Torqkadrone is, and how you use the Sivatron, or the Macro-STARR, or whatever you call it?"

"The Torqkadrone system can be thought of as similar to a probe or a satellite-type device that is inserted into the quantum gravity flux generated by the proton feed, which we receive from the Heavy Ion Target Supercollider. During that time alternate quantum states are unlocked, which gives us an opportunity to create interaction between our universe and the other infinite parallel worlds. We call it a *quantum excursion*, and so far we have had many test interactions with other quantum states of reality with no adverse effects."

"But, Jon, have you thought of the possible complications? There are potentially really serious consequences. Just think of the adverse paradoxical implications!"

"Such as what, Max? We have run computer simulations on the possible effects and outcomes, and we have not encountered any complications."

"Okay, I'll tell you a few that come to mind. With this drug in my system, I can literally visualize some of these issues. How about the problem with *quantum entanglement*, have you considered that? Let's just do a little mind experiment here. Say a human interacted in a parallel quantum universe, the information of his structure would then flow from this universe toward that other universe—that information would be entangled into that other parallel world. Who knows what effect that would have on the information of that human being in this universe. You get the picture?"

Jon said nothing and stared, expressionless, at Thorstrum as he continued to express his concerns.

"Now consider all of the other theoretical parallel worlds out there only atomic distances away from our own universe. Each one has a Jon Sanborne in them theoretically, and each Jon Sanborne has a unique and distinct physical form, personality, and perceptions. Just consider the effects of causing your physical form to interact in these other parallel worlds. Just who is which Jon Sanborne in what universe? What I am saying, Jon, is what will happen to your perception in these other universes? What will you think you are? And what will become of your consciousness in whatever quantum state you are in? Will you still perceive reality or will you lose your understanding of reality? Think about this, Jon. There is a postulated term in physics for this conundrum—it's called the *mirror butterfly paradox*. Dr. Kenyatta and I are concerned about where you are going with this research. We're both alarmed that in your passion for your work you may do something dangerous. You're a very bright scientist with a great future ahead of you. Take my advice and proceed slowly. Don't take any unreasonable risks with your QUEST research. There is too much at stake, both personally, and in terms of your fascinating research. I'm completely awestruck by the work you're doing down there. Can I visit, and get a tour with you one day soon?"

Jon remained uncharacteristically unperturbed. "Max, maybe our experiments will define just what consciousness and perception are in this abstract flux of the particle wave field that we call reality."

Max was startled by that comment. Jon's reply struck him as both scientific and philosophical, and rang with some unsettling truth.

"Anytime you want to visit us, I'll be happy to show you around personally," Jon continued. "I know you'll be blown away by the pure science aspect of it."

"Guys, I'm sorry to interrupt again. Who will it be this time?" Sandy interrupted.

Thorstrum rose. "Jon, I'll look for you later, but if I don't see you—take care of yourself—and good luck with your research. Please think about what we spoke about!"

"Certainly, Max. I appreciate your opinions. Call me when you want to visit."

"I'll definitely do that. Take care of yourself."

Jon watched Max head toward the medical research trailers. It felt as if he and Max were part of a remote dream, perhaps somewhere else, some other time. He began to relax and contemplate their conversation. Lost in his thoughts and the ambient drug-induced glow, Jon sank into a state of pleasure and content. He found himself observing, *breathing in*, all the activity taking place around him: the background scenery, the brilliant colors, a symphony of sounds. As he pondered a mathematical problem he had been struggling with in his research, he found himself falling into deeper and deeper states of concentration. He traveled into that mystical place where reality is perception and thoughts exist as real—virtual reality.

"Jon, I brought someone here to meet you!" Marta said, gently shaking his shoulder.

"Oh. Hi. Uh, I guess I was drifting off a little," Jon said sheepishly, rubbing the top of his head.

"Dr. Haslinger wants to meet you!"

Jon jumped up and held out his hand. "I'm very happy to meet you, Dr. Haslinger. Marta has told me a lot about you and your research."

Haslinger welcomed Jon warmly. "The pleasure is all mine, Dr. Sanborne. Marta has told me much about you and your work here at Ridgewood. Tell me, Jon, how are you feeling after your test dose of the Pegasus isomer?"

"Well, I'm definitely feeling its effects. It's really interesting and kind of a strange experience."

"Have you noticed some visual, perceptual, or cognitive changes?"

"Yes, definitely! I can easily get more deeply into my thoughts very quickly and efficiently. Very interesting effects! What is it about the drug that creates this mental clarity and stimulation?"

"Frankly, we are not totally sure. Normally, during the human perception experience, the brain is exposed to about eleven million bits of information per second from the senses. But we have found out that the brain can only take in and process about two hundred bits of this information per second. We have discovered that, like the molecule LSD, the Pegasus molecule has the effect of allowing more information to be processed in certain parts of the brain—especially in the frontal cortex and limbic structures. Although our research here is focused primarily on pain mitigation, it will also help us find out more how Pegasus works in the brain. Of course, as a study participant, you will receive a report of our research results when we have it completed."

"Have you created any other LSD isomers that do not have any intoxicating effects?"

"Yes, we have, but unfortunately they do not have the pain reduction capabilities either. We hope this study will help us determine the nature of that connection. Once we know more about how the chemical is actually working, we may be able to determine whether or not it is possible to separate out the intoxication from the pain mitigation."

"Thank for that information," Jon said.

"Marta told me that you two are engaged, and are going to marry in the near future. You are a lucky man, Jon. Marta is a very beautiful and smart woman. I wish you two good luck and happiness in your future together."

"Thanks, Dr. Haslinger. That is so sweet of you to say," said Marta, grinning.

"I know how lucky I am to have such a wonderful woman. I expect we'll be tying the knot before too long!"

Haslinger surveyed the area. "I must get back to the medical staff now, but it was great meeting you, Jon. I'm sure we will be seeing each other again."

"I'm sure we will, Dr. Haslinger. The pleasure was all mine."

"Bye, Jon. I'll check on you in a while," said Marta, giving him a quick peck on the cheek.

Jon sat back, and returned to his previous state as his thoughts spiraled into themselves. He drifted back up to the surface as Tom returned noisily.

"So, how was it Tom? What did you have to do with the testing?"

"No big deal at all. First, she asked a bunch of questions about my state of mind and how I felt. And then she did some of the usual medical checks like blood pressure, temperature, and heart rate. Then they gave me a bunch of psychometric tests. One was kind of challenging. I had to name as many words as I could think of starting with the letter R. They were timing me. When I started to run out of them I was grasping at straws and came up with the word Romulan. The tech gave me the strangest look, so I just looked right back at her and said, 'Hey, that's a real word!' We both had a pretty good chuckle over that."

"Cool. What other tests did they do?"

"There was one really weird set of tests where I had to look at a series of pictures that looked similar—and then she asked me which of the pictures were different from the others. There were a whole series of tests like that. Finally, they performed a series of brain scans on my head by using two different types of scanners. I have never seen anything like those before."

"I guess they'll be coming for me soon. I'm still feeling the effects of the Pegasus. How about you?"

"Oh yeah. Me too. It's very relaxing though, pretty nice actually!"

"Lois is over there talking to Dr. Kenyatta. She's been hanging out with him for quite a while there."

"Are they friends?"

"Yeah, Marta mentioned that somehow Kenyatta is friends with Lois's family. They get together sometimes."

"Huh. I wonder what that rent-a-cop is doing here," Tom said. A Ridgewood officer was heading over to Kenyatta and Lois.

"Shit! It's that thug Kendrick who I had an encounter with the other day. Him and his associate, Lieutenant 'Prick' Reynolds."

Jon and Tom watched discreetly as Kendrick spoke with Lois and Kenyatta.

"I wonder what they are talking about over there."

"I don't know, but I just hope that Lois is not too friendly with Kendrick and his pack of rats in the police force."

Even under the influence of the Pegasus, Jon could not maintain his feeling of tranquility and well-being as he watched Lois laugh and joke with Kendrick. He felt stirrings of suspicion as he flashed upon recent events like the intrusion into his home, and the roughing up he experienced.

[37]

Project Red Field

Wiped out by the effects of the drug, and a day full of social interactions, Jon relaxed while Marta helped wrap things up at the end of the experiment. Among the last to leave, they finally headed home at eleven that night. Jon sank into bed gratefully, reveling in the cool evening air and sound of the bay lapping at the shoreline. He had the best sleep ever: restful, restorative, and deep. And his dreams were intense and reflective.

The next evening, after they had each returned home from work and had a pleasant dinner together, Marta asked about the location of the medallion.

"The goddess Siva medallion—I have it on top of my desk in my office room, near my computer."

"Really? Someone could steal it! It's worth a lot of money and—especially after that break-in—I think you should find someplace much safer for it."

"Yeah, you're right, but I'm definitely not going to sell the thing. It's far too valuable to me because of the connection to Hilcraft. You know there's something about it, though—when you hold it in your hand, it gives you a calming ethereal feeling."

"Jon, it seems you're developing a strong emotional attachment to the Siva medallion. This is a characteristic of Essentialism."

"What's Essentialism?"

"It's the idea that objects are more than their physical properties. Psychologists find this a very common form of human expression among cultures."

Jon gave Marta a serious and confused look, sensing something unusual between his perceived connections to the Siva medallion.

Changing the subject, Marta asked, "Do you still want to go tonight with Lois and me to try and find Helen Dunne's house in Laurel or are you too tired after working all day? Do you still feel any effects of the Pegasus?"

"Actually, I feel real good now. I'll definitely go with you guys. But I have to say, and it may sound silly, I'm kind of concerned about Lois going with us."

"Concerned? Why? Lois is helping us out, and she is very intrigued by the whole Hilcraft mystery."

"I know, but how do you know that she won't leak information to Tonner and his police hoodlums? You know how people chitchat and mention things."

"Why would you say something like that, Jon? Lois is our friend. I know she would never do anything like that."

"I saw her talking to Kendrick and Kenyatta yesterday right before I had to go in for my medical tests. Lois and Kendrick looked very friendly. It definitely got me concerned. More than concerned!"

"Jon, you know you sound paranoid. It's probably because you were intoxicated by the drug. Kenyatta is personal friends with Lois's family, and Kendrick probably just went over because he had some police business there. I certainly wouldn't worry about it at all. Lois is one of my very best friends, and she is very honest, and a good person, and I know she hates the Ridgewood Police herself. She's even had some altercations with some of them at the shooting range when they mouthed off to her."

"You're probably right. I'm just a bit worried that Tonner and his evil conscripts are looking for anything to go after us on because they know that we have found out some interesting things about Hilcraft and the troubles he experienced at the Lab. On top of that he absolutely hates our QUEST research, too. We also don't know who else is involved in the sinister projects that went on in the past here. Who knows if any of that stuff is still going on? Remember what happened when I called the Targway Proving Ground number! This is getting complicated, so we have to be careful of any outsiders."

"I totally agree with that, Jon. But I really don't think Lois would tell anyone about what we found out. I'm going to tell her to be very careful not to speak to anyone about our Hilcraft information. I won't even tell her about what you and Ben found out concerning the graphite reactor and Building 720."

"Good, Marta! That makes me feel a little better. When do you want to go to find Helen Dunne's house? It's already getting late."

"We should leave now. I'll call Lois, and tell her we're leaving to come pick her up."

Lois came right out and jumped into the back seat as soon as Marta pulled into her driveway. They drove through the backwoods pine barrens of Manorville and Wading River and headed to the hamlet of Laurel, hoping to find Helen Dunne's house.

As they traveled east on Sound Avenue past the farms in Northville, Marta commented, "It's so nice to see that there are still pristine farm lands left here. Long Island is becoming so overdeveloped now. There are housing developments, shopping centers, and McMansions everywhere. It's sad."

"It really is nice to still have farmlands and open space around here," Lois added. "It's too bad so much of that farmland has been saturated with toxic chemicals that are now contaminating our water table. Still, it is beautiful. As we travel toward Laurel we'll pass a farm that has a fenced-in area with a bunch of animals. They even have some llamas and donkeys there. I stopped there on a bike ride once and hung out with them for a while. It's really a beautiful area, and such a relief from the overdevelopment on so much of Long Island."

"Let's all go biking together sometime. Lois, you can bring your bike out to our house. We'll all bike to Bay Boulevard in Jamesport, and then go north toward Northville. We could even travel up to Long Island Sound at Iron Pier Beach. How's that sound?"

"Let's set a date in the next few weeks. As we get into November it may get too cold. We can grab a burger or a bowl of chowder at the Riverhead Grill or the Rendezvous for lunch when we head back," said Lois, enthusiastically.

"How's that sound, Jon?"

"Sounds great—let's do it!"

"Marta, you're going to turn left up ahead, and then make a right onto Sound Shore Road, so get ready to slow down."

"I think that Helen's house should be right around here—over on the left—according to my friend."

"Wow! We're right on the bluffs of Long Island Sound. The view must be incredible!" Marta said.

"Here it is! Let's park over here in front of the house," Lois said.

As they walked up the sidewalk toward the front door of the ranch-style home, which was painted gray with white trim, Lois said quietly, "Nice house, it must be worth a lot of money here on the Sound."

"I hope this is the right house, and she's willing to talk to us about Hilcraft. We don't know how she's going to react," Jon fretted.

Marta took command, and knocked on the door sharply. After waiting a few moments she knocked again, more forcefully. Meanwhile, Lois looked around and noticed a car parked in the driveway.

"There's a car parked over on the other side of the two-car driveway so someone must be at home," she said.

Marta headed over to the right side of the house. Jon followed her. "Hey! What are you doing?"

"Maybe she is in the backyard, so let's go take a look."

"Okay, but don't be too forward! You don't want to freak her out."

They walked over to the east side of the house, and opened the gate tentatively.

"Look, there's a lady over by the shed. I wonder if it's Helen Dunne."

"God! Will you look at the view here! Right on the cliff overlooking the Long Island Sound. What a gorgeous place to live," Jon said.

"Yeah, we must be at least a hundred feet above the beach. It's magnificent," Lois said.

Marta called out in a friendly voice as they approached the woman, who was kneeling down by one of the garden beds. The woman turned toward them and slowly rose to her feet, staring at them.

"Hello. We're sorry if we startled you. We tried the front door and there was no answer, but we saw the car in the driveway," Marta said.

"Hi. I'm just pulling out some of my dried-up tomato plants. How can I help you?"

"My name is Marta, and this is my fiancé Jon, and my friend Lois. We all work together at the Ridgewood National Lab. We're hoping to find Helen Dunne."

The woman brushed the dirt off her knees, and took off her gardening gloves. Silent and expressionless, she looked them over for several moments. "I'm Helen Dunne. Why would you be looking for me?"

"Jon, why don't you explain?" Marta said.

"I'm so glad to meet you, Helen. I know you don't know me, but I work with Ben Carson at the Lab, and he mentioned you to me."

"Ben Carson! I worked with him for many years. It's been a long time. How is Ben doing?"

"Ben is doing well. Lately he has been working with me on my research project at QUEST."

"QUEST? That sounds like quite an amazing project from what I read in The Isotope newsletter. But what on earth does that have to do with me?"

"Well, actually, we wanted to talk with you about Emery Hilcraft."

The sun was setting, and Helen's blonde hair glinted in the final rays of the day, as she placed her gardening tools in the shed. "Yes, I knew Emery. We were very close friends for a long time. Emery and Ben were close, too, and we all worked on several projects together. Why do you want to know about Emery?"

"I got interested in Hilcraft's theories when I was planning the QUEST research years ago. At some point I started to look into his past. I was intrigued to find out that he disappeared many years ago without a trace. Recently, Ben and I came across some things that made us wonder about Dr. Hilcraft's troubled relationship with Ridgewood—particularly concerning the Hades Project that took place at the graphite reactor and Building 720."

Helen automatically scanned her yard. "It's getting a bit chilly. Let's continue this discussion inside." They followed Helen into her den overlooking the backyard and the Long Island Sound.

"I really don't know if I should say much about Emery, since I really don't know any of you. It's hard to know who to trust these days," said Helen, with a sigh. She was so well-spoken and articulate that her intelligence was already obvious.

Marta reached into her pocket and pulls out the photo of Helen, Ben, and Hilcraft from a physics conference they had attended together at Princeton in the sixties. She handed it to Helen. Helen studied the photo.

"Where on earth did you get this photo? I can't believe it—look at all of us. We were so young—Emery, Ben—what a time that was! We had so much fun together."

"Ben found that photo in his office and gave it to me. Here, why don't you keep it for a while? I'm sure that Ben won't mind," Jon said.

"Thank you so much. It brings back wonderful memories of a time long ago. I'll give it back to Ben myself. I haven't seen him in a few years. I'd like to see him again."

"It's been a long time now since Emery and I had worked together. We shared many experiences there together at the Lab. He's been gone so long now."

"Do you know what happened to him?"

"I'm not sure exactly, but I'll tell you what I do know. I have to say that I've been a bit reluctant to say anything to anyone about what I know, but maybe it's time now. Why don't you first tell me what you know about Emery?"

"Well, I don't know too much, but Ben told me a lot about how Emery had problems with the management of the graphite reactor in the sixties when it was still operating. I also know that he disappeared in the early nineties, and that they searched for him here on Long Island and in the Catskills, but never found him."

"That's right. It was very strange. I remember having lunch with him at Bowers Hall over the weeks before he disappeared, and getting the impression that there was trouble. He told me that his friend, Ken—Tompkins, I think—yes, Kenneth Tompkins, he had also worked in Building 720—had told Emery that his life was in danger because of what he knew about what was going on there. Ken had protested many times over the years about what they were doing. He told Emery that he had received death threats, and he warned Emery that he was on their list of people to 'deal with,' since he also knew enough to expose the goings-on at Building 720 and the Hades Project."

"Ben told me what he knew about the Hades Project," Jon said. "He told me that it was used to send biological samples through the graphite reactor and then on to 720 for research. Helen, do you know what was going on at 720, and who was in charge of it?"

"Why, it was nothing more than a military black ops secret biological warfare research project. The military took over the reactor early after its completion in the late 1940s and secretly militarized it. For cover some non-military research was still done at the RGR, but the military uses were prioritized. What went on at the massive underground subterranean complex at 720 was really shocking! Emery had told me about it many years earlier, when he was the chief operator at the reactor. He said that after World War II, when the Lab was still Camp Ridgewood, they had many remaining German prisoners confined there. Most of the prisoners were returned to Germany, but there were some prisoners from a certain Nazi SS brigade who were not released. These were some of the Nazi SS elite who had committed some of the worst war crimes. They were sent here by the personal order of General Christopher Mays. He personally ordered, secretly, of course, that members of this Nazi SS brigade be used as test subjects in biological weapons testing. They were transported to the Targway Proving Ground out in Nevada, and kept in an on-site military prison. They were brought to Ridgewood and other test labs when necessary, and used as human guinea pigs."

"What! German Nazi SS bioweapon test guinea pigs! Christ! That's amazing!"

"Yes, but there is much more to this story. Later in the sixties they started a new test research program code-named Project Red Field, which took place partly at Ridgewood and partly somewhere else."

"What the hell was Project Red Field? Do you know what that other location was?"

"Project Red Field was a program to develop a germ warfare agent that could be used to infect the enemy soldiers by using an insect vector to deliver the agent. The agent was developed jointly at Ridgewood, using the Hades Project, and at Lab 257 on Gull Island—right here, off the coast of the tip of Long Island. The Vietnam War was really heating up, and the military command was calling for a germ warfare agent that could be dropped off in the jungles of Vietnam to help counter the communist threat. That is why its development was prioritized."

"I can't believe that they would do something like that right here at Ridgewood."

"They did whatever the hell they wanted. There was no real congressional oversight, or monitoring of any kind."

Jon, Marta, and Lois were all unnerved by these revelations. Even Jon, who had seen the evidence, had trouble hearing this confirmation of his suspicions, and believing that something so disturbing had taken place at the very Lab where he worked.

"I know this next part sounds even more like fiction, but it's not—and it's what really upset Emery the most. The bioweapons scientists settled on using a mutated version of the Spirochete disease leptospirosis that was created right here on Long Island using the Hades Project and Lab 257. This version of the disease was extremely virulent, and it was specifically designed to attack the central nervous system of the host enemy. The idea was to attack the brain stem and render the victim unable to function in a wartime theater. But they were running short of Nazi prisoners, so they recruited domestic volunteers from prisons across the country by providing the prisoners with illicit drugs such as heroin and cocaine as a reward. Needless to say, they did not have a shortage of volunteers, but they discovered that, if left untreated, the disease killed more than half of the test subjects. The next step was to get better data on the effects of the disease as far as the epidemiology and progression of the disease. A doctor, and I use the term loosely, named Howard Shellbrook was running Project Red Field. Emery despised Shellbrook from the beginning, but at one point he learned that Shellbrook ordered the intentional release of the disease, which was now code-named "Red Deer Disease" into the fauna of eastern Long Island. The idea was to track the progress of the disease into the human population. Within months, Project Red Field had started to inflict terrible damage. Emery went ballistic. He contacted several high-ranking military officers he had been friendly with, but unfortunately that move backfired. He was immediately transferred and from that point on he was under constant surveillance from those involved in the black ops projects.

"Several months later Dr. Tonner came over from Targway and took over for Shellbrook. By this time, the Hades Project was shut down and 720 was being deactivated and moved over to the Molecular Biology Building. Hilcraft was moved over to some of the AES projects and he was out of the oversight of the military directors. But they were probably still worried that he would one day expose the terrible things that had gone on at 720, the Hades project and even Lab 257. I suspect they were especially afraid that he would expose Project Red Field. By this time, Red Deer Disease had become endemic on eastern Long Island. Its spread into the human population had accelerated, by way of deer ticks and field mice, which were the reservoir for the disease. Now known as Cray's disease, Red Deer Disease has spread throughout Long Island, the United States, and Canada."

Storming around the room, Jon could barely contain his fury, as Helen finished her story.

"What the hell has Ridgewood become! A death manufacturing plant for killing indiscriminant people! Helen, are you completely sure that what you are telling us is accurate? It can't be!"

"Absolutely! Yes, I am absolutely sure. And I have to say that I wonder what might still be going on at the Molecular Biology Lab. I would not be surprised if their secret biological warfare experiments are still going on there to this day."

"Lois," said Jon, "you work at the Molecular Biology Lab sometimes. Have you ever seen anything that looks like biowarfare experiments going on there?"

"I'm only permitted in a small part of the Molecular Biology Building; most of the lab is strictly off limits to normal operations personnel. I never suspected anything, but in retrospect I've seen some things that seemed kind of shady—like trucks with biohazard signage bringing things into and out of the building—including some large liquid tank trucks which I thought were odd."

Helen interrupted, "I forgot to mention one other thing. It's about Shellbrook. It's puzzling—and rather hideous. About two years after Emery disappeared, Shellbrook was found dead in his house. He had been butchered to death, and his body was found cut up into many pieces."

"Are you serious?"

"Yes, totally."

"Wow!" said Jon, sitting down, stunned.

Silence filled the room for several seconds.

Finally, Jon took a deep breath and broke the silence.

"There are a few other puzzling things concerning Dr. Hilcraft that I would like to ask you about, if you don't mind."

"Sure, Jon. I'll tell you what I know."

"Ben found a postcard that Dr. Hilcraft had sent him from his visit to Slovakia. The postcard showed a picture of a place known as the Sulov Rocks. Do you know anything about that place?"

"Oh, the Sulov Rocks. Yes, I do know something about them."

Helen sat back in her chair, put her head back, and closed her eyes.

"Emery was a theoretical physicist who took his work and his research very seriously. You may know he had been doing personal research on the strangeness of the quantum realm. He had published several papers on that topic. One of them was on the many worlds theory of quantum physics. He was totally fascinated by the implications of the quantum world. He tried to make sense of it in the everyday world that we all experience. You see, he had first thought that the world that we all live in is predictable and objective, and that with enough time and mathematical examination of the quantum reality we should be able to make sense of it—at least in some esoteric way. Emery was invited by his friend, Tomek, who also worked at the Lab, to visit his home country of Slovakia. He went there for several weeks that summer. He had a wonderful time, and when he got back home he told me that the trip to the Sulov Mountains had a profound impact on his life and way of thinking. He said that in some strange, mystical, spiritual way his trip, and particularly his time there in the mountains, had altered his perception of reality.

"Emery also told me about an ancient tribe of people who inhabited that area there many thousands of years ago. He talked about their ancient writings and petroglyphs that were found on metallic and stone artifacts. The strange writing had been analyzed by anthropologists, scientists and mystics for many years—an odd assortment of individuals dedicated to deciphering these voices from the past. He was introduced to some of those researchers at an institute located in those mountains. I remember him telling me that the researchers there had begun to unravel the religion or philosophy of that ancient culture. Some of the scientists think that it was the first known established religious philosophy in the world, and that it was a very advanced belief system. Some even feel that it bordered on science, and may have been the precursor of Hinduism and Buddhism. The researchers translated this ancient belief system about the universe and our existence as the *Time/Space/Mind Culture.*

"Emery returned from his trip thinking very differently about the reality that we live in. His experience there altered his view of quantum mechanics, too. He began to realize that our world, the reality that we live in, is not an objective world at all, but is simply a subjective perceived reality. He returned believing something that he would never even have considered previously—that our *consciousness* plays a major role in what we experience as reality."

"That is so totally strange," mused Jon.

"When we saw the photo of the Sulov Rocks on that postcard they struck us as stunningly beautiful, and somehow meaningful and important," Marta said.

Lois looked lost in her own thoughts, mesmerized by what she had learned in the conversations.

"Do you know what ever happened to Tomek?" Jon asked.

"Tomek went to work at a few different physics labs across the country, until he settled at an electronics company in upstate New York somewhere several years ago."

"Not long ago Marta and I met a woman who lived near Dr. Hilcraft's family home in Pine Hill. Her name is Ariel Fischer. She mentioned that Dr. Hilcraft had discussed the idea that we all live on in some way forever. Did he ever discuss those ideas with you?"

"Oh, yes. Sure. Through his understanding of science Emery came to the same conclusions that philosophers have come to through the ages. Namely, that the world that we see and feel is just an illusion. It really doesn't exist at all, at least not in the way we think it does. Bringing his brilliant mind and knowledge of quantum physics to the question, he hypothesized that our state of reality is one of an infinite number of interwoven realities. He called this 'quantum immortality,' and this related to his many worlds theory of quantum mechanics. He theorized that even when this reality construct ceases in our perceived death, we still exist in other parallel realities, so we continue to live on and on into infinity."

"Wow. That is really something to think about," Jon said.

Marta gently nudged Jon. She held out her hand to Helen. "We've taken so much of your time already. I hope we haven't intruded too much, or overstayed our welcome."

Jon and Lois rose and shook Helen's hand in turn.

"Helen, thank you so much for sharing what you know with us. You gave us so much to think about. I can't believe the terrible things that occurred at

Ridgewood. I'm also awed to hear firsthand about Dr. Hilcraft's theories. Again, thanks so much, and I hope we didn't disturb you too much."

"Well, I should thank you too. I'm glad to get this information out. I have been keeping it inside my head for so long. It's really a relief. I only hope that things have improved there, but I'm not sure about that. Emery's disappearance was a terrible blow. I'm glad that you and your friends are investigating it, and maybe you'll get lucky and find out what happened to him. Please do keep me informed. I'm very glad that you stopped by to see me."

"It was certainly our pleasure to have met you. If we find out anything about Emery I will definitely let you know."

"Thanks so much, and please stop by again sometime. Here's my phone number. Just give me a call before you come. It's good to talk about Emery. We had a special relationship—one that I will never forget. And when you see Ben, please tell him to get in touch with me. I'd like to get together with him sometime soon, too."

"Sure, Helen! I'll see Ben this week. I'll give him your phone number, and let him know you'd like to hear from him. I know he'll be very interested in hearing what we talked about."

Helen walked them to the car, and Jon, Marta, and Lois drove off into the darkening end of the day. The car was quiet as they were all deeply engrossed in their own thoughts.

[38]

The Road to Gull Island

The next day found Ben driving around the Lab on various errands. It was a beautiful day, and he was enjoying the admiring glances as he tooled around in his Stingray. He had pulled into the post office parking lot and was approaching the building when he was startled by a strange noise. He turned to see an unusual dark blue tanker truck driving by very slowly. His mood soured when he noticed the biohazard sign on the back of the truck. He entered the post office muttering to himself, *What the hell is that truck doing here? I've never seen anything like that here before.* He checked his mail, dropped off a package, and returned to his car. Driving his mint white 'Vette, with its stunning red interior, on this gorgeous sunny day lifted his mood again, and he decided to take the long way back to QUEST. This was heaven on earth.

As he passed the Molecular Biology Building, Ben noticed the same dark blue unmarked liquid tanker truck idling at the service entrance. Several men in black uniforms surrounded the truck, and several more stood by, observing the area. Intrigued, Ben pulled onto the shoulder of the roadway to see what was going on. While pretending to read his newspaper, he noted that several of the guards had gun holsters on their belts. *Wow, these guys aren't playing around. There is something really bad going on here!*

Impulsively, Ben decided to follow the truck as it pulled out. He followed the truck off the Ridgewood site and south toward the Long Island Expressway. Ben was shocked to see the truck exit and head east on the expressway. *Why the hell would this tanker truck be headed east?* Even more intrigued, Ben continued to follow the truck from a discreet distance. He followed the truck all the way out to the eastern tip of Long Island's North Fork. Finally, the truck slowed down and entered the high-security entrance of the Gull Island Animal Disease Laboratory at Orient Point.

Ben pulled over onto the side of the roadway and intently spied on the action there. He couldn't see very well, but observed several more men in black uniforms as they came out and inspected the truck. He caught a strange glint of bright light, and realized they were using mirrors to inspect the undercarriage of the truck. He suddenly squinted to make out the objects that several of the guards were holding, and exclaimed out loud, *Christ! Those are M-16 rifles! What's in that damned truck?*

After some time, the truck and several other vehicles were loaded onto the ferry that would cross several miles of the Long Island Sound to arrive at Gull Island, the site of the animal disease laboratory. *Oh, my God, wait 'til Jon hears about this! This will blow his mind! What the hell could possibly be in that tanker truck? What the hell is going on?*

The powerful engine of Ben's car roared as he revved it. He made a sharp U-turn back onto the road and headed back west toward Ridgewood. Passing the entrance to Orient Point State Park, Ben did not notice the unmarked black SUV parked facing the roadway. The driver of the SUV pulled out and followed Ben as he traveled west. The SUV was occupied by two of the guards dressed in black unmarked uniforms.

"Call Tonner and let him know what we found. Tell him we're going to continue to observe him for now, and that we will proceed to institute the procedure when his car is unoccupied and the opportunity presents itself," one of the guards in the SUV said.

"Okay, I'll let him know. Just don't let him get too far ahead. He can easily outrun us in that car."

"Don't worry about that. I'm very good at this."

As perplexed and upset as he was by what he had seen, Ben still enjoyed his ride back to the Lab, taking in all the rural sights. The North Fork of Long Island was always a beautiful place for a ride, but it was especially beautiful today. As he passed Riverhead, Ben became more eager to let Jon know what he had seen. He took out his cell phone and called. Jon was not available, so he left him a message and hung up as he hit the relatively deserted section of roadway that cut through the Pine Barrens in Manorville. He threw himself into the thrill of the ride, and watched the speedometer soar to ninety miles per hour. The engine purred like a kitten. Spotting a police vehicle riding in the opposite direction, Ben slowed back down to sixty. He decided to head back to his home in Eastport, take the rest of the day off, and enjoy the rest of his great ride.

Ben drove up to his house, pulled into the driveway, and headed into his house. Moments later, the black SUV drove by slowly, circled the block, and again scouted out the house.

"Okay, we'll take a little ride and make the move later when it's dark out. I'll let command know what's going on."

"Good, it will be real easy to sting this dude. This is going to work out just fine."

[39]

The Inverted Mask

Later on that day, as afternoon turned into evening and the early fall coolness seeped in from the sky, Jon and Marta sat down to dinner at home. After dinner, Marta gazed out the large picture window and watched the waves on the bay.

"Jon, I want to go over a few things about the Pegasus study."

"Great! How did the study go? Did you learn anything interesting or useful?"

"Yes, definitely. But first I want to do a little extra follow-up—just a few questions—and I want you to perform a few tests for me if you don't mind."

"Okay. Sure."

"Okay, well, first look at these pictures."

"Oh, these pictures? I've seen these before."

"Look at all the pictures here on these pages and think about them for a while. Then tell me anything that you notice about them. Take your time here."

After staring at the series of pictures intently for some while, Jon said, "Well, several of these are different from the others."

"Are you sure Jon? Take another look, and tell me if you are positive about the difference in the pictures."

Again, Jon studied the pictures, taking his time. "I am absolutely positive that some of the pictures of masks are inverted backward from the rest that are not inverted."

Focused on the pictures, Jon missed the change on Marta's face. She seemed somewhat perplexed.

"Look, Marta, this picture, this picture, and this picture are inverted masks, meaning that they are backward or concave, so we are looking at the interior of the mask and not the front of the mask. These other masks are not inverted, so we see the convex side to the mask. Isn't it obvious to you, Marta? It certainly is to me!"

"Something strange is going on here. If I were to give this test to a large group of people, very, very few would be able to distinguish between any of these pictures of the masks. For some reason, you are able to distinguish between the concave and convex pictures of the masks quite easily. The only people who can distinguish between the inverted pictures of the masks are people who took LSD or have certain brain dysfunction syndromes. Why is it that you can clearly see the difference in the pictures of the masks?"

"Well, I took Pegasus, which is an isomer of LSD, so why is that a surprise?"

"The Pegasus isomer does not generally cause this syndrome and when I gave you this neurometric test previously—several weeks before you took the Pegasus drug—you also noticed the difference in the masks. I wonder why."

"I guess I'm just one of the exceptions here."

"No, it's not just that. Something *strange* is clearly going on here! Here, let me show you something else too that is strange."

Marta pulled some papers out of her briefcase.

"These are the results of the brain scan that was performed on you during the study. Compare them to these results of the scan I performed on you several weeks earlier. Look at them—they're identical!"

"So what's the problem?"

"Well—uh—well, they are both abnormal! See here. Look at this region of the brain. Your brain here shows very unusual activity in the pineal gland, along with an increased presence of the brain chemical N-Dimethyltryptamine. No other participants in the Pegasus Isomer Study group showed any of this activity except for Tom McGuiness—although Tom's is of lesser intensity then yours."

"Wow, that is weird!"

"Yes, very weird. And there is more to this. I checked all of the neurometric and psychometric tests that I previously performed on all of your QUEST team scientists. What do you think I found?"

"Do I want to know this?"

"They all showed the same brain abnormalities as you, and they all were able to detect the differences in the inverted mask psychometric tests too, just like you. So, Jon, what this shows me is that there is something going on with the QUEST equipment and your bodies. Something that is interacting somehow with your neurological and biochemical systems, causing these apparent strange brain abnormalities."

"Why the pineal gland? Why would it have an effect there?"

"I don't know, but you might be interested to know that the pineal gland is the part of the brain that is associated with the perception of God."

"God!"

"Yes. That is where the cognitive perception of God or a divine being is manifested in the brain whenever someone is praying or meditating about divinity."

"Wow. Do you think this is something serious? Should we be concerned about this abnormal activity in our brains?"

Marta was again lost in the waves outside the window. Her face was solemn, and her voice betrayed her concern. "I don't know what to make of it, but I am going to continue to monitor all of the QUEST employees closely. I'll consult with Dr. Haslinger on this immediately, and maybe he will have some insight into this mystery."

[40]

The Evil Into the Night

When it was fully dark outside a black SUV approached the sleeping neighborhood they had scouted out earlier that day.

"Alright. We are just a short distance away from the subject's house. We'll park over there in the brush near the recharge basin, approach the house on foot, and institute the procedure. Stay low and quiet."

"Absolutely."

"You have everything necessary for the procedure?"

"All set."

"Be careful with that stuff . . . it's deadly."

"Don't worry. I've done this before. I know what I'm doing."

"Do you ever wonder how they even invented something like this?"

"I don't know how they make it. I just know this comes from Targway, but they don't let us know too much about it. You know that!"

"Yeah, we're better off not knowing. I'll stay back and cover you—just in case we have any trouble with the target."

"This dude has no idea what's about to happen to him."

The first agent pulled out a red flashlight to illuminate a small metal box that the other agent held open. He put on a pair of tightly fitting surgical gloves, and very carefully opened a small compartment labeled with the skull and crossbones emblem. He pulled out a black nylon glove and placed it on his left hand over the surgical glove he had already put on. He then used his right hand, which was also protected by a surgical glove, to pull off a thin layer of plastic film that covered the palm and fingers of the black glove.

"Okay. It's activated now. I'm ready. Let's go."

The gloved agent led the way with the other agent following close behind. Both men used their red nighttime flashlights to make their way toward Ben's beautiful white 'Vette—not making a sound.

The leading agent carefully placed the black-gloved hand onto the driver's-side door handle. He gripped the handle several times, transferring the toxin in the black glove onto the car door handle. Finally, he stepped back from the car and joined his partner. He grinned with pride and quietly gloated, "This turkey will definitely be cooked. Too bad for him!"

The two quickly proceeded back to the SUV and disappeared into the night.

* * *

Yesterday's bright sun had given way to some daybreak clouds the next morning, but it was still a beautiful day. The kind of crisp cool day that awakens the spirit. Ben approached the QUEST facility just as he had many times before. He parked and slowly exited his cherished white '66 'Vette Stingray. As he walked toward the main entrance he suddenly stopped, turned, took a long last look at his beloved car, and then, rather oddly, he picked up his right hand and slowly looked at it. Frowning, he used his left hand to rub a sudden soreness in his right hand. He entered QUEST still rubbing his right hand, looking concerned and fatigued.

An hour later Jon received a call on his cell phone just after driving past the guard gate on his way to work. He wanted to ignore the call, but something piqued his intuition. Realizing he rarely received calls at this time of the day, Jon pulled over onto the side of the entrance road and answered his phone.

"Jon! Jon! This is VG. Something awful has happened!"

"What's the matter, VG? What's going on, man?"

"It's Ben! He came in here earlier. He started to act unusual and then he fell to the floor and started shaking and went into convulsions. It was terrible. Jon!"

"Where is he now?"

"The paramedics rushed him out of here. They took him to the on-site clinic. I don't know if he's there, or if they've shipped him off to the hospital already."

"Do you know what happened to him?"

"I have no idea. I was told that he came in the main entrance and took the elevator down, and when he entered the main hallway he fell to the ground and started shaking violently. There was blood leaking out of his nose and mouth."

"Oh, my God! Listen, I'm heading to the medical clinic right now. Cancel all activities today at QUEST. I'll let everyone know what's going on with Ben after I find out, okay?"

"Okay, Jon, we'll say some prayers for him here."

Jon sped toward the clinic, which was located in the Medical Research building. He rushed past several people and made his way to the clinic admissions counter. He spotted some staff members and called out loudly, "Do you have any information on Ben Carson?"

"Sir, please take a seat and we will get you that information as soon as we can."

Jon spun around as a hand on his shoulder pulled him hard. Marta's eyes were full of tears.

"Jon, come follow me! There is apparently little time left. Quickly!"

Jon followed Marta into the hallway past various medical treatment rooms and into the emergency room, where Ben was attended by several doctors and nurses. Ben lay, bare-chested, on the examination table. Blood was dripping from his mouth. A nurse wiped away both the blood and the intense sweat dripping off his forehead. Ben's graying red hair was soaked with his own perspiration, and his body drooped lifelessly on the table. Jon could not take his eyes off Ben's blue eyes, which were wide open but seemed lifeless. But after some seconds Ben stirred slightly as he slowly moved his head. He seemed to look at Jon for a few seconds in recognition, but then collapsed back onto the table with an unchanging, permanent stare.

Jon brushed the tears from his cheeks as the attending doctor addressed him, "I'm truly sorry. We did everything we could." He placed his hand on Jon's shoulder for a moment, and walked away.

Marta grabbed Jon's hand and held it close to her body. She hugged him tightly, and whispered, "Jon, I'm so sorry."

Through his grief and shock, Jon was drawn to something strange about Ben's right hand, which was hanging off the table. "Marta! Take a look at Ben's right hand! His right hand! Look at it! What is that bloody lesion? And what's wrong with his fingers and palm?"

Marta examined Ben's lifeless hand for a few seconds. "My God, his hand is swollen and traumatized. I wonder what happened to it?" She examined Ben's arm, too. "These are strange skin lesions here, also. I've never seen anything like this. The skin is just dissolving away. I don't know what could have caused this. I'll have the doctor here do a biopsy on it. Maybe this had something to do with his death?" she said.

"Make sure you don't touch it! Make sure that everyone here knows not to go near it!" Jon yelled. The staff turned and stared at Jon in frightened silence.

Marta said, "You're right. I'll warn everyone here to be careful and avoid exposure to whatever this is. We'll get to the bottom of it, Jon. We'll find out just what happed to our friend Ben."

Jon continued to look at his good pal for quite some time in a timeless, disheartened sorrow. Marta stayed with him and stroked his arm affectionately. Finally, he put his head down and turned away slowly, with Marta by his side. Tears ran down both their faces as they left the room.

[41]

The Autopsy Report

A few weeks later, Marta checked her email at home and called out to Jon, "My doctor friend in the medical clinic just emailed me a copy of the autopsy report on Ben. I was just reviewing it. There are some very unusual findings."

Jon took his cup of coffee from the kitchen counter and slowly entered the living room. "What did it have to say?"

"The report said that Ben had somehow been exposed to a variety of potent biotoxins of unknown origin, which caused his arteries and veins to weaken and hemorrhage. They concluded that this contributed to his death. They listed the exact cause of death as intracranial hemorrhages and acute renal failure."

"Biotoxins! How the hell would Ben have been exposed to biotoxins?"

"The pathology report states that disseminated intravascular coagulation had caused a hemorrhagic diathesis in the subject's cardiovascular system. Also noted on the subject's right hand were large hyperemic lesions that appear associated with the subject's systemic insult. The pathologist made an interesting aside here in the margin that says that one of the toxins seems to be associated with the disease *lonomism*."

"Lonomism? What the hell is that?"

"Lonomism is a very rare South American disease that is caused by a large caterpillar. When touched the caterpillar has very sharp hairs that discharge a very potent toxin into the victim. It's generally very deadly. Only recently has an antitoxin been discovered to mitigate the effects of the toxin and it is not always successful. Jon, this is so weird. I don't know what to make of this. Lois told me a while back that they were doing medical research on these caterpillars in the Biochemistry Building a few years ago."

Jon and Marta stared at each other for a few seconds in silence. Jon stood still like a statue as an uncomfortable premonition of fear entered his senses. The hair on the back of Marta's neck prickled as a sudden rush of cold ran down her spine.

"Jon, remember when Garrett Hansen died a while ago and you gave me that copy of his autopsy report."

"Yeah. What about it?"

"Well, that report also noted that he had been exposed to an unidentified biotoxin. Do you remember? Kenyatta gave you a copy of the report and you gave it to me to look at. Do you remember that?"

"Do you think that there is an association between Ben and Garrett?"

"Well, it seems plausible to me after what happened to Ben."

Jon joined Marta on the sofa, and they both stared out the living room window at the waves on the bay.

"God!" Jon blurted out. "These thugs are such bastards! How could they do something like this? Why would they want to harm Garrett?"

"Maybe they wanted to shut down QUEST by creating a controversy. You know that Tonner hates QUEST."

"That's true. He hates our research with a passion, and he doesn't much like me either. But to do something like that you would have to be psychotic!"

Jon put his head in his hand, and mumbled, "He was such a good person. Why would they want to kill someone like him?"

Marta leaned over, put her chin on Jon's shoulder, and caressed his face. "Jon, you have to be careful. I'm very worried now. The break-in, and now the similarities between Garrett and Ben—this doesn't seem like a coincidence. They might go after you next."

"We must have found out something that they are very concerned about. Something they would kill for! This is very serious business. Tonner and his military neo-cons have turned Ridgewood into a bioweapons killing research center. Typical fascists, they don't seem to give a rat's ass about anyone. Once they get started they grow out of control. We're going to have to think up a way around them. I think I have an idea of what we could do next!"

Marta jumped as the phone rang. Jon reached for the phone.

"Jon, this is VG. I just want you to know that we are all set up for our next run. Dr. Kenton just called and told us that HITS will be running in about two hours and we are preparing to receive their protons for another quantum seduction experiment."

"Okay, VG. I'll be there in thirty minutes or so. Make sure you guys pre-test the side B magnacasters in the Sivatron. Those were the ones that were giving us trouble last time with the helium cooling equalization systems."

"Already done, Jon."

"Okay, thanks. See you in a little bit."

Jon hung up and turned to Marta, "I have to go. I don't know when the experiment will be complete, but I should be back sometime tomorrow morning if all goes well."

Marta hugged Jon tightly. "Jon, I want you to be extra careful today. I'm really worried. I want you home alive and well. I love you, Jon, and I can't bear the thought of something happening to you!"

Jon hugged Marta lovingly, kissed her gently, and uttered softly, "I love you too, Marta. I'll always be here by your side."

With tears on her cheeks, Marta gave Jon a soft, wistful smile.

They gazed into each other's eyes, and after a few seconds Jon gently brushed away Marta's tears. Drawing away slowly, he said, "I'm sorry, honey. I have to go now. Don't worry. Everything will work out alright. Trust me on that."

"Call me later!"

Jon left, and Marta paced the room for a while. She felt helpless to protect Jon, and at a loss about what to do to keep him safe. She sat down, and looked to the waves for comfort.

[42]

The Amazing VX2B

Jon pulled into the lot at QUEST, surprised to see Ben's Corvette was still there. He slowly walked by the car, touched its hood softly, and started to reach for the door handle, but his hand stopped, just inches from the handle, as he was overcome with memories of the good times and adventures he had shared with Ben. Somewhere in the back of his mind he noticed that the handle appeared dull and out of place on Ben's meticulously maintained car. He regained his composure and headed into QUEST.

"Hey, VG, has anyone from the police or medical examiner's office called or come by to ask about Ben's car? I mean, it's just been sitting there for a few weeks now. You'd think that they would have made arrangements to have his car brought back to his residence, or to the County Crime Lab, to have the car analyzed—especially due to the nature of Ben's death."

"Not that I know of, Jon. We haven't been contacted by anyone concerning Ben's car. It's kind of weird, isn't it?"

Jon looked at VG stridently, and said pointedly, "Make sure that no one here goes into that car—or anywhere near it, for that matter!"

Startled by Jon's intensity, VG responded, with an odd look on his face, "Okay, Jon, I'll warn everyone here to stay away from Ben's car! I'll tell them that the police are coming to check out the car as evidence."

"Good, VG. Good. Listen, after things have settled down a bit maybe you, me, Marta, and a few others should go visit his wife and daughter. I think she would appreciate that. She was a mess at Ben's wake. She's devastated. It's a damn terrible thing that happened to Ben. I'm still sick over it."

"Jon, didn't the medical staff find out unusual things about Ben's death?"

"Yes, they did, and Marta is looking into it fully. I'll let you know what she finds out . . . if anything."

"You know that there are rumors that Ben's death was no accident, and not normal in any sense. Can you tell me anything else about it? We're sort of getting nervous around here. Is something going on?"

"VG, at this point just try to get all the QUEST employees relaxed and focused on running our upcoming experiments. Please trust me on this. I'm looking into all this very carefully. I have several things going on now that I don't want to get into concerning Ben and Garrett. But I assure you this will all be dealt with properly." VG was somewhat comforted by Jon's confident, reassuring air.

Some hours later, VG returned.

"Okay, we have about an hour before HITS sends us our stream of protons. Everything is going very well in the control room and all monitored systems show optimal telemetry."

"How is the Sivatron operating? Are the Higgs Field sensors interfacing properly with the Q-Wave Q6? You know the last run we had that stability decoherence issue. Is that checking out okay?"

"Yi's staff has been looking into that over the past few weeks. They thought they solved that problem by replacing the dielectric sensors on the magnacaster modules. It checks out okay now on the power-up assessments we have run."

"Good and how about the Torqkadrone?"

"Look over to the side C monitor; you'll get a look at it when I activate the interior camera here. Just give me a few seconds—ah, there it is. Take a good look at it."

"Holy shit! You've got the VX2B Torqkadrone in the pre-launch station quad. Is it really ready for operation? I know that Yi and her team had been testing it out for a while, but I didn't think it would be available so soon."

"I knew you would be blown away by it. It is fully tested and operational for this next quantum seduction experiment. Isn't it beautiful, Jon?"

"God, she's gorgeous! Look at her! That elegant, iridescent body! Do I have time to take a look at her close up now, or are you guys busy doing the pre-engagement sequences?"

"You have a little time to check it out. I'll let Yi know that you are coming down. I know she'll be proud to show it off to you."

"Great, VG! I'm totally impressed with you guys getting everything so prepared. After this run we will have to celebrate the fruits of our labor with a party. You guys are awesome! I'll be back in a little while. Hold off on any of the quadrapole broadcast magnet startups 'til I come back. I just want us to make sure we check out their cryogenic thermal cycle before we run today."

"We've taken readings on the helium chillers, and they have all consistently measured two degrees above absolute zero Kelvin. So there is no indication of any problems there."

"Okay, I can see you have everything in control. I'll be back shortly."

"Okay, Jon, I'll get everyone all set for the countdown sequence."

Upon entering the Torqkadrone prep area, Jon was totally overwhelmed by the sight of the beautiful, glistening, silvery-gray surface of the VX2B Torqkadrone. Finally, he noticed Yi, as she stood next to the craft, broadcasting a radiant smile. He thought she looked like a model showing off the newest vehicle at a car show or, maybe more accurately, like a parent showing off her new baby.

"Well, Jon, what do you think?"

Jon ran his hand across the smooth hard surface of the test vehicle very slowly and carefully. He walked around the entire length of the magnificent structure.

"Gorgeous, Yi, truly gorgeous. Is it ready to enter the multiverse? Will it be able handle the magnetic flux and electromagnetic stresses from within the Sivatron? What is your honest opinion?"

Yi smiled and said, "Yes, it's ready to go! Everything is fully operational, stress-tested, and certified for use. Of course, we should have it perform an experimental test run in an actual quantum seduction before we would have an occupant inside. At least, that is my opinion."

Jon stared at the beautiful, gray beast. Smiling, he again walked slowly around the craft, touching its surface intermittently.

Yi used a device in her hand to open the hatch to the Torqkadrone.

Jon stopped to admire the interior.

"Go ahead, Jon! You can get inside and check it out."

Jon did not wait to be asked a second time. He quickly pulled himself in, settled into one of the two seats inside the vehicle, and checked out the intricate and sophisticated dark gray interior. Peering around the interior he noted four small visual monitors in front of him. The monitors were surrounded by a multitude of toggle switches and push relays, all lighted by neon-blue luminescence.

"During a quantum seduction, of course, the craft will operate totally on Programmed Telemetry Interactive Format, so there would be no need for operator adjustments. This is how we have been *fading* the other Torqkadrones into the Infinitrum."

"Yi, it's amazing that even though I am inside I can still see through the front of the vehicle."

"Yes, this is a remarkable composite metamaterial we are using. We actually stole the secret to this composite meta-window from the advanced military design center in Arlington, Virginia. It gives the craft a forward view outside of the vehicle while sitting inside using the principle of *slow light.*"

"Well, it definitely is an engineering wonder! When I first saw the plans for this I was totally awestruck, but sitting in it and feeling it now is even more unbelievable," said Jon, as he got out of the Torqkadrone.

"This is what QUEST is all about. All of the science and theory that everyone has put into this project for so long, all the efforts of the physicists past and present are now coming to fruition. We are truly entering a new paradigm of science. We are going to discover just what reality really is, and maybe what we really are."

"Well, Jon," said Yi, "I only hope that you find what you are looking for."

Jon was caught off guard by Yi's remark, and there was silence for some seconds, as they exchanged an indescribable look.

The intercom interrupted their thoughts.

"Dr. Sanborne, please report to the main lobby. Dr. Sanborne, we have an important message for you here in the main lobby. Please report to the main lobby as soon as possible."

"I wonder what it could be. I never get messages like that when I'm down here. You guys go on and get ready for the pre-launch sequencing. I'm going to see who's contacting me. It must be important. I should be back in the control room shortly."

"See you there."

[43]

Unexpected Visitors

In the main lobby, Jon was greeted immediately by Alice. "Jon, you've got a message from Dr. Kenyatta here. He wants to have a quick meeting with you up in the mid-level station right away. It sounded important."

"Oh crap, Alice! We're running an experiment here in a little while, and I really should be there when it starts."

"He's there now, and he's waiting for you."

"Do you know if Tonner is there, too?"

"That I don't know, but you're going to find out soon enough."

"Okay, Alice, wish me luck! God, I hate this bureaucratic bullshit."

Alice chuckled as Jon walked over to the elevator, muttering to himself. In no better mood, he got off the elevator, and headed to the mid-level station hallway. As he passed the emergency stairwell he thought he saw something black out of the corner of his eye. Glancing back, he was surprised to see a man dressed in black emerging from the stairwell.

Jon opened the door into the mid-level station, and was surprised to see the room was only dimly lit.

"Hello, Dr. Sanborne. So glad you could join us today."

Jon did not recognize the voice. He peered into the darkness, and called out, "Hello, is Dr. Kenyatta here?"

Instantaneously, the lights blared on, and Jon saw three men dressed in black clothing. "Dr. Kenyatta couldn't make it here today, but that doesn't matter," said one man, derisively.

"I was told Dr. Kenyatta asked me to meet him here. What's going on? Who are you guys?"

"There is no meeting today, Dr. Sanborne. But you'll be coming with us now."

When it sank in that there was no meeting and this was some sort of setup, Jon's heart began to race and he broke into a sweat. He noticed that all three men were carrying guns, and that their black clothing was some kind of unmarked, paramilitary uniform.

"Where are we going? Who are you working for?" shouted Jon, as the men moved toward him.

Jon turned and bolted from the room into the hallway. As he ran toward the elevators he saw the man he had glimpsed before, in the same black uniform, still standing in the hallway near the emergency stairwell. The man noticed Jon, and began to reach for his side arm. Jon crashed into him, knocking him to the ground, and the gun fell from his hand and skittered away toward the wall. Jon saw the gun slide away as if in slow motion. He was about to lunge for the gun, but instead took off into the elevator lobby as he heard footsteps approaching from behind. He knew there was no time to wait for an elevator, but that was not his intent. He pushed the call buttons to confuse his pursuers, and headed down the hallway toward the equipment service tunnel. He realized an escape down the vertical wall-mount ladder would be dangerous, but it was his only option now.

Jon reached the balcony at the end of the hallway, and was in full view of the massive equipment service tunnel, when his pursuers caught sight of him.

"Stop right there or we'll shoot!"

Ignoring them, Jon scrambled over the balcony and grabbed onto one of the wall-mounted hand rungs. His foot slipped as he reached for a lower rung and for a moment he dangled in midair, gripping only the top rung with his hands. Looking down the vertical precipice he was almost overcome with panic, but on hearing the armed men approach, he gained an unexpected sense of composure and focus. On pure adrenaline, Jon managed to swing into position and find his foothold. He began the long descent down the vertical shaft. He did not allow himself to think about the dangers of climbing down a four hundred fifty-foot shaft into the HITS junction tunnel, and was elated to think he'd escaped from the clutches of these sinister agents.

Several seconds later, Jon was shocked and dismayed to realize that he was being followed down the ladder. He picked up his pace, but again lost his footing. His body swayed back and forth for a short time, while the man above him gained on him. Jon regained his footing and continued his descent with renewed vigor. Hearing shouts, Jon glanced down and realized that the rest of his pursuers had regrouped at the bottom of the tunnel. Between a rock and a hard place, Jon stalled for a moment. All of a sudden, he felt a vibration in his hands, and then a larger rumble. Soon, the entire nine hundred-foot deep tunnel started to oscillate and shudder. He suddenly realized that the disturbance was due to

HITS sending the stream of protons down the junction tunnel to QUEST. A quick look up showed that the thug who was following him was frozen in place. He was obviously confused by the unexpected shaking as it continued on for several minutes. As it subsided, a deafening bang reverberated throughout the tunnel. Jon smelled the gunpowder, and realized that the man above him was attempting to shoot him then and there, on the ladder.

"Dr. Sanborne, stop where you are! It's no use trying to escape! You won't make it out alive!" the agent above him shouted.

At that very instant, many miles away, back in Aquebogue, an ancient medallion lay on a wooden desk in Jon's house. It began to vibrate slowly, and then more and more powerfully. No one was there to witness the spectacular sight as brilliant, iridescent light radiated out in all directions. A strange, whirling vortex of sound also filled the room.

Trapped, both above and below, Jon considered his options. The shaking started up again, with even greater force, and Jon struggled to maintain his grip on the ladder's rungs.

And miles away, yet somehow entangled here and in this moment, the medallion released a translucent powerful pulse of energy. It spread through the beach house, permeated its walls, and broadcast out into the atmosphere in all directions. As the energy dissipated into the universe, the medallion slowly faded away from sight and became invisible.

Jon heard the unique sounds being generated by the QUEST experiment down below and realized that the pulse wave from the Torqkadrone deresolution into the Infinitrum was about to take place. Quickly, he grabbed on tight to the hand ladder in anticipation of the force effects. Suddenly, there was a flash of electromagnetic energy that seemed to last forever. During this wave pulse Jon closed his eyes, and received in his mind a vision of himself inside the Torqkadrone, looking out at the scientists who were launching the Torqkadrone craft. From this perspective, the images of the scientists and their equipment start to visually fade into a strange, decaying, pixilated landscape where they no longer looked human. These bizarre humanoid statues, frozen in movement, with grotesque expressions on their faces, slowly drifted away from him.

Jon struggled to maintain both his composure, and his grip on the ladder, but he was determined to survive. Again, he saw himself inside the Torqkadrone, now traveling through an eerie vortex of abstract pixilated structures, deformed and evolving in shape. There appeared to be faces out there, looking back at him, looking into his mind, but he was not sure what to make of this experience. Suddenly, he was brought back to his sanity, back to the present world, as the pulse wave from the Torqkadrone launch finally stopped. He again realized his precarious situation. He was trapped on the service tunnel ladder, four hundred feet above the HITS junction tunnel.

Jon looked up and saw the light at the top of the tunnel five hundred feet above him, and felt momentarily blinded and woozy. He refocused, realizing that the villain above him had also survived the pulse wave, although he was still recovering. Jon looked around in desperation, contemplated his options, and realized that he still had the magnetic shooter that his friend Jim Morris had given him. He groped for the shooter, and, with the reckless abandon born of desperation, he headed up the ladder toward the black-clad agent.

At first, the still-stunned agent did not realize that Jon was moving toward him, but as his mind cleared and he saw Jon coming closer, he reached for his gun. Jon was ready. The agent did not recognize the small, pen-like object Jon held as a threat. He took aim at Jon, but Jon activated the magnetic shooter first. Instantly, with terrific force, the projectile penetrated the body of his pursuer entirely. It killed him instantly, ejecting a spray of blood and tissue into the tunnel air. The body fell to the bottom of the HITS junction tunnel. The thud echoed throughout the cavernous space. Jon saw everything in slow motion as the body floated to the ground. The echo of the thud rang in his mind, and for a second he did not fully comprehend what had happened. He heard cursing and shouting, and gunshots.

From below the words rang out, "You are going to die for this!" Jon wasted no time in taking advantage of the improved situation. He raced up the ladder to the mid-level station balcony. Scanning the area, he saw no one, and felt a rush of elation. His first thought was to warn Marta.

Checking the elevator display, Jon saw that he had just seconds to spare. He ran for the stairs, but heard voices in the stairwell. He panicked momentarily, but then took off at full speed toward the mid-level station. The room was empty. He headed for the kitchen, grabbed the biggest knife he could find, and ran toward his secret hiding place. His heart nearly stopped when he heard faint sounds coming from somewhere near the entrance of the mid-level station, and he moved quickly and quietly toward the back of the station. He turned down a dark, small, and nondescript hallway which led toward the narrow escape tunnel. Jon opened the hatch, scrambled inside, turned on the lights, and closed the hatch behind him quietly. *Four hundred and fifty feet to go—I have to get out of here—I have to warn Marta—she was right to be scared. Christ—if I have any luck at all, those bastards won't know about this tunnel. I'm not even sure where the hell I'll surface.*

Exhausted, but running on adrenaline and his need to get to Marta, Jon kept climbing with sure determination. Upon reaching the end of the tunnel, he precariously grabbed at the hatch to the surface. The hatch did not open easily. Struggling to open the hatch Jon nearly lost his balance, and he was overcome with vertigo as it hit him that there was nothing but four hundred and fifty feet of air between him and the bottom of the tunnel. He closed his eyes for several seconds, breathed deeply, and regained his sense of balance. After several attempts Jon managed to open the hatch.

Jon climbed out of the vertical tunnel, took in the fresh air, and surveyed his surroundings. He was in the middle of a pitch pine forest, but he wasn't sure quite where he was. He pulled out his phone and quickly called Marta, worried about her safety. Jon anxiously waited to hear Marta's voice, but the call went to voicemail. He dialed again. *Damn it! Answer the phone! God, I hope she's okay.* Frustrated, scared, and tired, Jon paused for a breath, and to consider his next moves. He noticed a slightly worn pathway nearby and decided to follow it. *Marta, you were so right—God, I hope you're alright—what the hell have I gotten us into?*

[44]

A Trip to the Molecular Biology Lab

After hiking on the unfamiliar path for nearly half an hour Jon spotted buildings in the distance. He stopped and peered through the trees, trying to get his bearings. *Okay, that's the wastewater treatment plant—I'm not too far from Medical Research—I'm coming, Marta—Stay safe, darling—Stay safe!*

Jon headed down a fire access trail that he had hiked on previously until he came to a paved roadway. *Maybe I'll get lucky and get a ride from someone passing by.* He continued walking down the road for several minutes, periodically pulling out his cell phone and trying to get through to Marta. *Answer the damn phone already.* He looked up from his phone at the sound of an approaching vehicle. *Damn it all! Okay, act normal.* A dark blue SUV neared. Jon did his best to avoid looking at the SUV and act like he was out walking for an exercise break. Much to his dismay, the vehicle began to slow down, and then came to a full stop. The dark-tinted window retracted.

"Hello, Dr. Sanborne, it looks like you're out getting some fresh air today."

Jon played it casual. "Hello, Officer Kendrick. Yeah, it's a good day to get out and get some exercise."

"You look like you're in a hurry. Are you headed somewhere?"

"No, not really, just taking a nice relaxing walk. You should try it sometime yourself."

"Dr. Sanborne, it just so happens that we have a message for you."

"Really?"

"Someone is looking for you."

"Who is that?"

The darkened rear window descended. Jon's heart sank when he saw Marta, looking more terrified than he had ever seen her. Before he could utter a sound, he realized that Lieutenant Reynolds was holding a gun to Marta's head, and smiling coyly.

"Dr. Sanborne, get into the vehicle now if you want her to live!"

Jon opened the door reluctantly and sat next to Marta. "Are you okay?" he asked.

Tears in her eyes, and terror on her face, she gave him a slight nod.

Disgusted, Jon barked out, "What is it you want? Why are you doing this? Let Marta go! She has nothing to do with any of this!"

Reynolds smacked Jon in the head with his gun. Blood trickled down the side of his face from the impact. "Dr. Sanborne, I advise you to keep your mouth shut. Any more trouble from either of you and you'll both get a bullet. I have no problem pumping one into each of you right now! You got that? Now, we're just going to take a little ride, and pay a visit to a special friend."

At that last remark both Kendrick and Reynolds laughed.

Reynolds was clearly enjoying tormenting them. Like a small boy with a toy pistol, he pointed the gun at Marta and Jon alternately.

The SUV approached the high-security entrance of the Molecular Biology Building. Kendrick stopped and idled for several seconds. The garage door opened up and Kendrick drove in. The large automatic door shut, and Kendrick turned off the ignition and got out of the SUV. Pistol in hand, he opened up Jon's door, and said, icily, "Get out, Dr. Sanborne, and don't try anything stupid."

Jon and Marta got out, while the officers kept their pistols trained on them. Kendrick and Reynolds took positions behind Jon and Marta, their pistols out, forcing Jon and Marta forward. They traveled through a doorway and into a large open room which was filled with a strange odor and odd noises. Walking ahead, they arrived at a well-lit area with large animal cages of various sizes holding different research animals, until they stopped at one of the largest cages.

Marta screamed in terror. "Oh my God, Jon, its Ayu, the Komodo dragon!"

Holy Christ! What are these bastards planning to do with us?

Reynolds jammed his pistol into Marta's back, "Shut up, bitch!"

Jon swiveled around and punched Reynolds square in the face, drawing blood. Kendrick whipped out his baton and sent Jon reeling to the ground with a blow to the head. He pulled himself up, and growled, "You pricks are going to get what's coming to you! I promise you that!"

Another voice intervened, "Oh really, Dr. Sanborne? I beg to differ. It looks like you are the one who is going to get what's coming to you. You and your lovely-ass girlfriend, Dr. Padlo. You really don't seem to know when to leave well enough alone."

Jon knew that voice, that slight British accent. He turned, stunned, but somehow not completely surprised, to see Tonner gloating over their capture. Disgusted at the sight of Tonner, Jon replied, "I always thought there was something really wrong with you! You evil bastard!"

"Just keep your bloody mouth shut! There's little time left on this earth for you and you're boo now! You and your *pal* Ben had to keep sticking your noses where they don't belong—interfering in our business here, not understanding just how *dangerous* that was. Now it's all catching up to you. You should have used your brains and realized that you were messing with a higher authority—one that wouldn't tolerate that kind of bullshit!"

Marta yelled out, "Dr. Tonner, how could you get involved with such terrible people. Don't you realize what you are doing?"

"Shut up, you stupid little bitch! I work for an organization that pushes buttons to kill people all over the globe every day. I couldn't give a rat's ass about you or your smartass boyfriend. We do what we have to do to keep peace in the world!"

"You killed Ben, you bastard! Why would you kill a good person like him! Are you and your pathetic Nazi organization that inhuman, to kill someone who would help out anyone anytime?" yelled Jon. "He was a father and he was a military veteran, too—someone who cared about his country, who served his time and his government. You're a fucking monster, you and your police state thugs!"

"Alright, you two, I've heard enough socio-psychological interrelationship bullshit from you both. Now I'm only going to say this once, and if you don't do as ordered, Reynolds here will placc a bullet into both your asses rather quickly. Do you understand?"

Marta folded her hands together, closed her eyes, and began to pray. And suddenly she flashed back to a childhood conversation with her mother about the horrors their family experienced during World War II. Her mother had told her the story about how her late great-uncle was taken out of his house by Nazi SS soldiers, marched into his barn, and shot in the head because he was considered a threat. She opened her eyes, hugged Jon tightly, and rested her head on his chest. The situation appeared completely hopeless to both of them. Jon held Marta tightly, pouring all his love into the embrace.

"Well, well, you two. How very touching. Dr. Sanborne, open the cage door now, and step inside the cage! Dr. Padlo, you are to follow Dr. Sanborne into the cage. I wouldn't dream of separating such lovebirds."

At that moment, a security officer wearing a black uniform and baseball-style cap inserted an access card into the reader at the back entrance of the Molecular Biology Building, and the door unlocked. The officer walked through the garage area, past the SUV, and approached the interior door into the large animal containment area.

Reynolds and Kendrick both forcefully used their pistols to prompt Jon and Marta into the cage. Jon ached to wipe the sick grins off their faces. Eyeing Marta, Reynolds said, "Ayu is going to get a good fresh meat meal today. Don't you think, Dr. Padlo?"

Kendrick shoved his pistol into Jon's side, and forced him toward the cage. Jon looked directly into Ayu's eyes. Her teeth were huge and venomous, and the high-pitched whine she emitted was nerve-wracking.

"Tonner, if you think you can get away with this you are not just evil, you're insane!"

"No, Dr. Sanborne, everyone will read the newspaper in the near future and feel really sad about the story of a beautiful Ridgewood psychiatry professor who was showing her boyfriend one of her research animals. They got too close to the large lizard and both ended up being eaten by the beast—what a tragedy. Besides, everyone already knows that you're a weirdo theoretical physicist who spends his time down in a gigantic underground experimental dungeon, nine hundred feet below the surface, strewn with hundreds of electro-magnets, costing billions to look for the *unknown worlds . . . somewhere.* When they find out that you both ended up being lizard food it will all seem to make sense to them.

"Now open the cage door and give Ayu a big kiss. Go ahead, Dr. Sanborne. Now! I'm giving you five seconds to get in *now* or Kendrick and Reynolds will kill Marta first!"

Realizing there were no other options, Jon moved slowly to open the locking mechanisms on the cage door. Jon released the final clasp and the door was free to swing open. Ayu was right near the door, whining excitedly in anticipation of a live animal feeding.

Marta was watching Jon, desperately trying to think of a way to stall, when she was suddenly blinded by a flash of light that had a triangular appearance. As her eyes adjusted to the flash, she discerned the silhouette of a human figure approaching, dressed in black, and holding something in hand.

Jon took advantage of the ensuing confusion, as Tonner and his men clearly had not expected company. He slammed the cage door wide open, and swiftly jumped away from the opening. The quick movement and the crash of the door frightened Ayu into a full aggression. She lunged forward, straight toward Tonner.

"Shoot! Damn it, shoot! Shoot the damned thing now!" shouted Tonner.

Tonner's agitated movements and aggressive tone further incited Ayu. She grabbed Tonner by the arm, pounced on top of him, and used her powerful jaws to pound his body against the floor, while her enormous claws dug deeply into his torso.

Kendrick and Reynolds had quickly turned back, but could not shoot for fear of shooting Tonner. Tonner shrilled out an unearthly howl as the dragon repeatedly ripped into him, spewing blood everywhere. Kendrick moved to shoot but immediately heard a loud bang, and felt the pain of a bullet rip into his side. He instantly fell to the floor in intense pain as his gun was flung loose by his side.

Marta grabbed Kendrick's gun and aimed it at Reynolds, shouting, "If you move, I'll kill you dead!"

Reynolds froze momentarily, but then he twitched forward, lifting his pistol. Before he could squeeze the trigger another shot ripped through the air and he crumpled to the floor, still holding his own pistol. Jon aggressively kicked the pistol away. He felt for a pulse, wiped the sweat from his forehead, and stood up.

"He's dead," he said.

Marta pulled Jon away and walked him a safe distance away from the precarious Komodo dragon. They hugged quickly as the mysterious stranger approached them.

"Who are you? What's going on here?" Marta asked.

The stranger pulled off her cap, shaking her short blonde hair loose. "I was afraid I was too late! Thank God you are both alright!"

"My God, Lois! How did you know we were here? How did you know we were in trouble?" Marta rushed up to Lois and hugged her, laughing and crying at the same time.

Lois beamed at them. "You have a guardian angel looking out after you! I was contacted by Dr. Haslinger about an hour ago. He told me that you were going to be taken into the research animal holding area by Tonner and some of his henchmen."

"I don't understand," Marta said. "Why would Haslinger notify you? And where did you get that gun? I've never seen you with a Glock pistol before. What's going on? I'm totally confused."

Lois looked sheepish. "Ah, well, I have a secret that I've been keeping from you for a long time. I'm actually a New York State Police agent working undercover."

"You're what?!"

"It's a long story. I'm sorry that I had to keep it secret from you, but I had people to protect, including you and Jon. I only wish that I could have helped Ben, but I guess no one had any idea that these sick thugs were going to kill him too."

"You mean you don't really work for Ridgewood, you work for the New York State Police?"

"Well, I'm working for Ridgewood National Lab now, but only undercover. And yes, I'm actually a detective. I would love to keep this job, though. I was asked to volunteer for this secret mission because of my previous background in laboratory research, and because I have a bachelor's degree in biochemistry. They needed someone to play the part of a researcher at a national lab in order to investigate a rogue agency gone bad."

"Unit 411, please respond on the 781! What is your status?"

Pulling her police transmitter out of her pocket, Lois replied, "Copy that. This is 411. I'm located in the back area of the Biochemistry Building. Suspects are down and incapacitated."

"Copy that. Ambulance is on its way with backups and should arrive shortly."

"Roger 411 and out."

"What's going on now? Will everything be okay? What about the other corrupt police here—and the thing with the Hades Project and the Targway people?" asked Marta.

"Don't worry. That is all being dealt with as we speak. In a few minutes this place will be crawling with state police and FBI agents. I'd guess that right about now the joint task force will be entering the main gate with a full inspection warrant to comb through this place. I expect there will be several arrests."

"So, let me get this straight. Dr. Haslinger was our friend who alerted you to the danger we were in?" Jon asked.

"Yes, both Dr. Haslinger and Dr. Kenyatta were doing everything they could to put an end to evil activities that have been going on here unchecked for decades. They were the ones who started the process of getting the corrupt military officials investigated. It wasn't easy because the corruption was embedded deep into the system. But they pulled the right strings, and alerted the administrative officials of the New York State Police, who opened up a dialogue with high-level military contacts. Eventually, a special unit was formed to infiltrate Ridgewood. They learned about the sick things that had gone on here in the past. I was then assigned to the task force, and that's how I became the biochemistry research scientist that you all know."

"Wow what a story! Is your name really Lois?"

"Yes! My name really is Lois, but my last name was changed to protect my new identity. I have to say that I had a real hard time trying to keep all this from you."

"Well, you certainly had us fooled for a long time," Jon said.

"No wonder you're the best shooter on our rifle team!" Marta said.

The terrifying sounds of Ayu feasting on her prey reached them as they paused in their conversation.

"Oh, God! What a mess! I don't think I've ever seen so much blood. It looks like Ayu is going to devour every bit of that monster," Lois said. "The funny thing is, I don't mind at all."

"Yeah, it looks like Tonner is the victim of his own evil scheming. You live by the sword, and you die by the sword," Jon said brazenly. "That could have been us. I would have been a lot more disturbed at his fate before he tried to feed us to Ayu."

Suddenly, several New York State Police officers rushed into the area. Lois directed them toward Kendrick, who lay injured and semi-conscious on the floor. She instructed them to place Kendrick under arrest and to exercise extreme caution in getting Ayu back into her cage. Then she turned to Marta and Jon and said, "I have to work with my team here and secure this place. Why don't you guys go outside and someone from the task force will be there to debrief you shortly."

Lois looked at her friends and with a moving tone said, "I'm so glad you're both okay. After this is all over, we'll have to get together and celebrate somewhere. I have so much more to tell you!"

"Lois, I'm so glad we're friends—you saved our lives! I had no idea you were my guardian angel," Marta said, shedding some tears.

"Let's have a beach party at our place after everything's settled down. We'll have some brewskis and I'll make my clam casino," Jon said, grinning.

Lois smiled back at her friends and then rushed off to help the team of officers who had converged in the area around them.

[45]

Resolution

Marta and Jon went out to the parking lot, which was abuzz with activity from uniformed and non-uniformed police officials walking about conducting their investigation. The police had set up a centralized command center there. As they approached the command center an officer asked them to identify themselves. They responded, and were cleared to enter the area.

"Look Marta! Kenyatta and Haslinger are over there talking with the police!"

At that moment, Kenyatta caught sight of them. "My God! I'm so glad to see that you both made it out of there alive!"

Marta hugged Haslinger while Kenyatta grabbed Jon by his shoulders and looked directly into his eyes, "I was so worried that something bad was going to happen to you during this investigation. I just prayed that things would work out alright. I'm so glad that God answered my prayers. You don't have anything else to worry about anymore. It's all over. You and Marta are heroes, and I'm going to see to it that you are treated as heroes! Thank you, Jon!"

Jon nodded his head. "I'm so glad it's all over, Dr. Kenyatta. Thanks for all your help. You're really a great person! I'm so glad that there are people in this world like you and Dr. Haslinger!"

In that everlasting moment both felt the warmth and radiance of friendship and a sense of goodness.

As the joint state and federal investigation continued on over the next several hours, Kendrick was eventually taken out on a stretcher, and placed into an ambulance. He was incarcerated, along with many others who were involved in the dark, evil projects of Ridgewood's past. Ayu, the Komodo dragon, was captured and put back into her holding pen, and the bodies of Reynolds and Tonner were removed, at least what was left of Tonner. Many other corrupt Ridgewood officials were rounded up, arrested, and removed handcuffed by the state police.

The Lab now had a new, worthy feeling to it, one that had not been there for quite some time. Gone was the evil that had possessed it for so long. Life and research at the Lab now had the chance to continue on as normal, as was intended when Ridgewood first became a national lab, shortly after World War II. But only with time would the remaining immoral spirits of the past leave the cold recesses of the place for good—especially Building 720, where hidden secrets still remained.

[46]

Test Subjects

Several weeks later, Marta and Jon enjoyed a cool, breezy early November morning walk along Peconic Bay. They watched the seagulls hover above the surf like white kites. The view of their house in the distance seemed almost surreal through the lingering fog. They walked along the beach and gazed out into the sea and fog, losing themselves in the infinite obscurity where the fog and reflection of the sea became one.

They returned home, and Marta began to make lunch. Jon sat nearby, leafing through one of Hilcraft's books, *Particle Field Theory: Insights into the Unknown.*

"Oh, I forgot to tell you! I was talking with Dr. Kenyatta. He told me that the investigation into the bioweapons research that was done at Ridgewood is proceeding along very well," Jon said.

"You mean what they were doing at the Hades Project, and what Tonner was running at the Molecular Biology Building?"

"Yeah. He mentioned that the Pentagon's Office of Internal Affairs is cooperating with the investigation, and that the local politicians are now getting involved too."

"Well, it's about time they recognized what a terrible, misguided project it was. I wonder how many other similar black ops projects are going on elsewhere."

"Kenyatta told me that there are secret negotiations taking place in Albany with the New York State Police, the governor's office, the FBI, and the US Army Intelligence Office. They're the ones that work with the CIA on funding these dreadful projects."

"Wow! Could you imagine being a fly on the wall inside that room? I can't believe that there is nothing in the newspapers about the joint task force raid that they conducted on the Lab, or these negotiations."

"Well, it's a very touchy subject. The military doesn't want anyone to know the true story behind Cray's disease and its link with Ridgewood."

"Can you imagine if the people on Long Island found out that all those people who contracted Cray's disease over the past decades were suffering from a disease that was created by a black ops military project that took place right here at Ridgewood? And that they intentionally released the disease into the environment to study its effects?" said Marta, shaking her head.

"They're very afraid of that. That's why this is all being kept hush-hush. But Dr. Kenyatta told me that the military officials admitted that what went on with the Hades Project and the other bioweapons stuff was well beyond the scope of their directive. They admit that they failed to oversee it properly, and they want to reshape the future of their secret bioweapons programs."

"If you ask me, I think they're full of *govna*! That means 'shit' in Polish, in case you didn't know. You know very well that they knew about everything that was going on, and they were happy to fund it fully for many decades."

"I totally agree, Marta! I mean, what they did with those Nazi prisoners of war and US civilian prisoners as test subjects was totally inhumane and just plain evil."

"Don't forget about those other secret CIA experiments that were done all over the USA back in the forties, fifties, and sixties. Like their psychic-driving experiments. I guess they failed to oversee that properly too!"

A cloud passed over Jon's face. "I have something else to tell you. Kenyatta also said that many of those German prisoners who were used as test subjects in the bioweapons testing were buried in the Park Course woods by those odd-looking brick structures."

"No! Oh, my God! I have walked in that woods so many times—by myself, and also with Lois. I always wondered how those structures got into that woods and thought how beautiful the wildflowers are that blanket the area there."

"Kenyatta told me that the German government and our government will be conducting joint forensic remains excavations in the near future. They are going to use a cover story to hide the real story of what happened to those prisoners from the public."

"It's very sad how a government can become so wrapped up in psychotic fear during times of war that they justify doing such inhumane things. Even though those Nazi officers committed terrible atrocities during the war, they were still human beings. It reminds me of what took place in Poland at Katyn. During the Russian invasion and occupation of Poland, Stalin's army captured twenty-three thousand Polish officers, executed them, and left them in mass graves there. I will never forget the overwhelming sadness I experienced when I visited the memorial site when I was a young girl. It's strange how German soldiers were the ones who discovered the mass graves of the Polish officers and reported that atrocity to the world."

Jon held Marta tenderly. "I'm so sorry. That must have been awful time for you. I remember hearing about the massacre at Katyn in a history class in college. History is full of brutality that cannot reasonably be explained by any rational, thinking human."

Marta shook off her sadness. "Well, anyway, we have to be very thankful for the end of all this horror at Ridgewood. It's amazing how Dr. Haslinger and Dr. Kenyatta helped put an end to so many decades of evil. I will really miss working with Lois. She became one of my best friends. Jon, why are you smiling?"

Grinning, Jon said, "Marta, I have to tell you something that gave me a laugh when I was chatting with Kenyatta the other day. He asked me for the details of what really happened to Tonner that day."

"Okay, and what did you tell him?"

"I said, 'Well, Dr. Kenyatta, Dr. Tonner lost his head!' I couldn't help myself. Then I burst out laughing. Of course, Kenyatta didn't really get it. I think he thought it was a post-traumatic stress reaction. So I told him all the details he could handle."

"What did he say after you told him that Ayu ripped off Tonner's head?"

"He was shocked. He just looked down, shook his head and said, 'You've got to be kidding me!'"

The phone rang, breaking into their conservation.

A mature feminine voice was on the line. "This is Ariel Fisher—from Pine Hill. I met you and your fiancée up here about two months ago. Do you remember me?"

"Yes, of course I remember you! Marta and I really enjoyed speaking with you. You were so gracious to us. Thank you again for sharing so much with us about Dr. Hilcraft and his family. It was fascinating!"

"It was my pleasure, Dr. Sanborne."

"Please, call me Jon."

"Okay, Jon. I'm calling because something happened the other day, and I thought you'd be interested in hearing about it."

"I'm interested already!"

"The other day when I went to pick up my mail from the post office, the postmaster mentioned a conversation she had with the postmaster in Turnwood. Turnwood is about thirty miles from here. Anyway, she said that the Turnwood postmaster told her that a woman came into her post office and wanted to have her mailbox moved to the other side of the street because it kept getting hit by passing trucks. The postmaster gave the woman a form to fill out, and asked for proof of identification. When the postmaster noticed that the name on the form was not the name she associated with that address, she asked the woman about it. The woman explained that she had come in to make the change for her father. Then, when the postmaster checked the woman's identification, she noticed something that really got her attention."

"What was that, Ariel?"

"The name on her driver's license was Sara Hilcraft."

"Sara Hilcraft! Isn't she Emery's daughter?" exclaimed Jon, motioning frantically to Marta.

Jon put her on the speakerphone and Marta moved closer to better hear the conversation.

"Hi, Ariel! It's me, Marta. Is it okay if we use the speakerphone so I can hear too?"

"Hello, Marta. Of course it's okay."

"Did you find out something about Dr. Hilcraft's daughter?"

"Yes, indeed! I suppose it is possible that could be a different Sara Hilcraft, but that really doesn't seem likely."

"Were you, by any chance, able to get the address of that mailbox?" Jon asked eagerly.

"I certainly did! It's in a very remote section of the Catskills, southwest of here."

"Wow! This is truly amazing! Can I possibly get that address from you? I'd love to drive up to Turnwood and check out that house to see if it could be Emery's house."

"Yes, Jon, I'll give you the address, but only on one condition."

"What's that?"

"That I go with you, and that you promise me that you will keep the sanctity of Emery Hilcraft's privacy a secret from anyone else and you will show Emery all the respect that he deserves."

"Of course! We certainly will not let anyone else know about this, and we will definitely show Emery all the respect and privacy that he merits. After reading his books and studying his research papers over all these past years, I almost feel like I'm part of his family."

"That makes me feel a lot better. I'm very concerned that someone else may find out about his secret life and somehow cause trouble."

"If Emery is still alive, I think he would be really happy to learn about QUEST and all the work that we're doing. We are using many of his theories in our research into the quantum realm. I'm sure he'd be proud that his ideas and insights have been so critical in our exploration of this strange universe. I also think he'd be very relieved to hear about some of the recent news from Ridgewood."

"Yes, I agree. I think he would be happy to hear about your research work and all about QUEST. Knowing Emery, I think he would definitely like you two. When are you thinking of coming up to the Catskills?"

"How about this weekend? Would that be good for you?"

"Yes, that's fine with me. Just give me a call the day before to confirm and please stop here at my house and pick me up, if you don't mind, and we'll all go together. You realize, of course, that Emery has chosen to seclude himself from his past life for a purpose, so if we do meet him it will definitely be a bit of a shock. Hopefully, when he sees that I'm with you that will lessen any uneasiness that he may hold inside."

"Yes, I totally understand. In fact, I think I know why he isolated himself for so long."

"Really? What gives you that idea?"

"I'll fill you in when we see you. It turns out that we found out some important information about Emery's past here. A lot has happened here at Ridgewood recently. I have lots to tell you when we see you this weekend."

They said their good-byes and Jon hung up the phone. He gazed at Marta. She moved closer and put her arm around him. Together they shared a few moments of silent contemplation staring out at the fog-shrouded bay.

[47]

The Cabin in the Windy Woods

Jon and Marta picked up Ariel and traveled through a very remote section of the Catskill Mountains toward the hamlet of Turnwood. They journeyed past the high peaks of the Beverkill Range and made their way onto a roadway that led toward Hilcraft's secluded residence.

Jon drove slowly up the gravel driveway, which had a slight incline. The driveway curved to the left past a large boulder and then straightened out and continued on a good distance. Finally, they saw some wooden buildings ahead through the leafless trees. Jon pulled up near the buildings, rolled down his car window, shut off the engine, and stopped to listen carefully. The wind rustled through the trees and filled the woods with mesmerizing white noise. All the windows appeared to be dark. Several birds sitting on the roof of the house suddenly ascended into the gray cloudy sky.

"It doesn't look like anyone's around," Jon muttered.

"There's no car in the driveway, but there could be one in the garage," Ariel said.

Marta opened her door and got out. "Let's look around a little."

The gray, single-story, rectangular cabin with simple white trim blended into the autumn woods. The house also had a wooden porch that wrapped around two sides of the house.

"It looks really well-maintained," Jon said.

"And really quite isolated," Marta added.

As they walked up the wooden stairs, Jon heard something that caught his attention. He looked around and spotted a large, ground-mounted windmill. The blades were rotating rapidly, catching the cool mountain air.

On the porch, Ariel opened the storm door and knocked on the wooden entry door several times. All three held their breath as they listened for even the hint of a sound. There was no answer. Ariel knocked even harder. Her knock conveyed a sense of command that would brook no denial. Still no answer. Ariel released the storm door and peered inside through one of the windows on the porch. "I think I can see the living room area inside but I don't see anyone inside the place."

"Let's go look around back," Jon said.

They walked around the back of the cabin, and were awed by a series of abstract monolithic structures arrayed on the back lawn near the contour of the woods.

"I wonder if those are meant to be some kind of art or some kind of spiritual creation," Marta said. "Somehow it makes me feel like I'm in a cathedral."

At the back of the house they walked up a few stairs and onto a wooden deck. They passed by a metal fire pit and wooden chairs as they approached a sliding glass door. Ariel knocked on the glass. There was no response from inside.

"Oh, that sound! What beautiful wind chimes," Marta said.

"They're exquisite. They give the wind another voice," Jon said.

The sound of the chimes shifted and called their attention to the increase in the wind even before they noticed the increased movement of the tree branches all around them.

Ariel glanced through the slider again, and gave the door a try. To her surprise, the door slid open. They were all astonished, and unsure about how to proceed next.

"Let's go inside," said Ariel, "but be very careful not to disturb anything, okay?"

"Hello, is anyone around? Is anyone here?" Ariel called out.

"Hello, is anyone here?" she called out again, after a few seconds.

"I guess no one's home," Marta said.

"Well, this cabin is very well-kept, and clean, and it appears that it's been used recently. Look over at the wood stove. There's a fresh pile of wood and a pair of shoes near the stove."

"There's no significant dust on the counters either," Marta said, running her hand along the kitchen counter.

Ariel opened up the refrigerator and peered inside. "There's some food in here, and it looks pretty fresh, so apparently someone does live here."

"Yeah, but is that someone Dr. Hilcraft?" said Jon, clearly frustrated.

Jon began to explore the adjacent living room. He walked over to a bookcase and began to examine the books. "Well, whoever lives here likes to read science books and good literature."

Jon pulled one of the books off the shelf and opened it to the page where a bookmark had been left. He read out loud:

All the world's a stage,
And all the men and women merely players;
They have their exits and their entrances,
And one man in his time plays many parts,
His acts being seven ages.

"That's from Shakespeare's *As You Like It*—Act 2, Scene 7, I believe," said Ariel, with an odd expression on her face.

"Well done, Ariel! That's exactly right. You can tell you're a librarian."

"Those words seems somewhat fitting, don't they?" Marta said.

Just then, they were spooked by a tremendous series of sounds from outside. Ariel and Marta ran to the door and looked all about outside. The wind was howling, and the trees danced wildly. The clouds had thickened rapidly, and the sky was darkening.

"What do you think that was?" Marta asked.

"It sounded like a tree falling," Ariel answered.

Jon continued examining the bookshelves. He spotted a bound paper booklet, and reached for it. He glanced at the cover of the notebook, and was instantly astonished. He was totally absorbed as he turned the pages of the notebook one by one. He put the notebook aside, and continued to search throughout the bookcase. Finally, he found some other items that piqued his interest. After some time he reopened the bound report he had set aside. He studied it keenly, reading some pages quickly, while lingering over others. His bewilderment was written all over his face.

"Jon, what are you reading?" Marta's voice finally penetrated his consciousness.

"Did you two find what caused the noise outside?"

"It seems to have been a huge branch that fell to the ground. Thank goodness no one was under it. It could have killed someone," Ariel said.

"The wind is really gusting out there now. I think a storm is coming," Marta added.

"Did you see anyone out there, or check out the garage?"

"There's a car in the garage, but no one's around anywhere. We thought we saw something near the border of the woods, out back near a hiking path, but when we checked it out we didn't find anything on the path. It didn't seem a good idea to stay out in the woods any longer with these winds picking up," Ariel said.

"We really should get going. This place is giving me the creeps," Marta said.

With a devilish look, Jon said, "I've just found out something totally amazing."

"What did you find out? And what's that you're holding?" Marta asked.

"This is the annual financial report for Q-Wave Computer Company. I found it here in this bookcase."

"That's the computer company that funded a large part of your QUEST research facility, isn't it, Jon?"

"Yes! And all of our computers at QUEST are manufactured especially for us by Q-Wave. They practically invented quantum computing."

"That's some coincidence, but what did you find that is so interesting?"

"This is so great! Well, if you look here on page 139, under the Board of Directors, you will find someone listed as Evan Hilden."

"What! Are you sure? That's the guy who is supposed to live here!"

"Yes! And not only that, look here under the Senior Management Section, below the Board of Directors.

There you will see the names Alan Hilden and Peter Tomek."

"So this is Emery's house then?"

"Yes! Yes, I would say so, at least one of his residences. This is probably a cabin that he likes to come to from time to time to relax and experience the great wilderness here."

"But I'm confused. So, Evan Hilden is supposed to be Emery, but who are Alan Hilden and Peter Tomek? I've never heard of them," Ariel inquired.

"I bet Alan Hilden must be Emery's son. Apparently he changed his name to Hilden, too, to protect his father's identity," Marta said.

"And Peter Tomek? Who is he, and how does he come into the picture?"

"Peter Tomek was a physicist who worked with Emery back in the sixties at Ridgewood. They were very close friends. Apparently they stayed friends and Peter works with Emery at Q-Wave Computer Company," Jon said.

"So, according to this company report, Emery is top management at Q-Wave Computer Company," Marta said.

"Hah! Not only that, he's the largest shareholder of the company! He's the damned owner of the company!"

Ariel smiled, shaking her head. "I'm totally astounded! You know, I have to tell you, there is a small shop located toward the very end of the Village of Margaretville that has a small sign on the door that says Q-Wave CC on the door. I always wondered just what that place was."

* * *

In the windy woods, not far from the cabin, a man walked west on a path. He engaged his hiking poles with agility as he marched energetically toward the cabin. As the hiker took a turn by a boulder he spotted something through the trees and froze. He stared at his driveway, shocked to see an unoccupied car parked there. He stood out in the windy, blustery woods and contemplated this unexpected turn of events.

* * *

Inside the cabin, Marta asked Jon, "What are those other documents that you found in the bookcase?"

"Hah! Check this out! I also found this in Hilcraft's bookcase. It's a copy of a research brief that describes the purpose and construction of our QUEST project, complete with a copy of the construction plans and layout. It looks like Emery's been interested in QUEST for quite some time!"

"Jon, I really think we should be going now. It's not right to invade the privacy of this cabin, and we've been here a long time now. Don't you think?" Ariel said.

"Okay, Ariel. Let me put these items back carefully so no one knows that we were here. Then we'll get going."

As Jon moved to replace the items he had removed from the bookcase, a folded piece of paper fell to the floor. He picked it up and instinctively unfolded it. It was a map of some kind. He sat back down, shocked. He held the paper out to Marta. "Look at this! This is a map of the state of Nevada, and look what's highlighted here in the upper northeast corner of the state?"

"What is it, Jon? What does this mean?"

"Someone highlighted the location of Targway Proving Ground with a neon green magic marker."

"It must have been Emery! Jon, remember when you got that card in the mail that said something like 'interested in a trip to Hades'—and when you called the phone number on the card!"

"Maybe it was Emery who sent that card to help me make the link between the Hades Project and Targway?"

A strong gust of wind rattled the windows of the cabin.

"We really must go now! We've been here much too long already," Ariel said as she sternly ushered them toward the door.

Jon stopped to stare into a side room that they passed as something inside caught his eye. He paused in the doorway and then walked to the desk, where he gazed at a small metallic statue of the goddess Siva, dressed in her elegant dark blue and white shroud. Jon reached for the image of the goddess, held her up in the air near a window and stared at her. She glowed as she captured the stray strands of light which broke through the blustery sky.

"What is it, Jon? What are you holding?" Ariel asked.

Jon, lost in a time outside of time, did not answer as he continued to marvel in reverence at the beautiful figurine in his hand.

Marta put her hand onto Ariel's shoulder and said softly with a raised eyebrow, "She's the goddess Siva, the mother of all Existence."

As Jon placed the statue back down onto the wooden desk he noticed a thick bound book which had been left right at the center of the desk. He reached for it, and read the title to himself, "The Existence Hypothesis and Quantum Eternity."

Underneath the title, in smaller print, was the author's name: Emery Hilcraft.

Jon opened the book, quickly scanned some of the pages, and then flipped to the last paragraph. He said slowly and methodically, "Well, it appears that Emery has completed his life's work, and set all his ideas out here in this book, the final chapter of his life in this universe. I'm sure that he wanted us to find it. And somehow here we are."

Marta grabbed Jon's arm. "Jon! Let's go now; Ariel really wants us out of the house now!"

Jon allowed Marta to lead him away from the desk, taking a final glance back at the book and the statue. Once they exited the house, Ariel took a last look to make sure things were back in place, and slid the glass door shut.

* * *

The movement of the three trespassers was carefully monitored through a pair of small, but powerful, hiker's binoculars. The hiker focused on their faces intently as they neared their car. He lowered the binoculars and eyes full of images and feelings now peered out through the windy woods. He looked up into the sky and pondered—It's been a long, long time, hasn't it?—as gusts of wind blew by.

[48]

Unusual Clouds

"This has been some weekend so far," Marta said the next day.

"Boy, this creek looks like it's close to flooding. Sometimes they are so dry up here," Marta said.

"There's been a decent amount of rain these past few months. You can see some erosion at the creek's edges. I heard that a few of the houses alongside of the creek have even flooded this year."

"I noticed that. I'm glad that the road is leveling out here in Oliverea. That last part of Slide Mountain Road was really steep! It's a little nerve-wracking."

"It's definitely a steep, rugged road. Many of the back roads here are pretty rugged, and the rain and snow do a number on them."

"It's all very beautiful here. I love traveling on these back mountain roads, even when they're a little intense. There's a special boundlessness in this mountain forest. The shapes of the mountains, the colors of the trees and rock faces . . . it's hard to describe, but it feels like they cast a spell on me."

"They are beautiful. There's something mystical here, too. I noticed it the first time I ever came up here, when I was in college. I know this might sound odd, but I've felt called back here ever since."

Jon navigated onto Route 28 and pulled into the post office parking lot. "I'm just going to stop at the Big Indian Post Office to mail something out," he said. "I'll be right back."

"What do you have to mail?"

"It's just a postcard to an old friend. It shouldn't take more than a few minutes."

Marta's gaze followed Jon into the lonely, little post office, and then wandered to the surrounding mountain ridges. A strong gust of wind rattled the car. She grabbed her sweatshirt, wrapped it around her shoulders, and stepped out of the car, noting the chill in the air; she reflected that it would soon be Thanksgiving.

The cool, clean air was refreshing, and it helped her relax. She stretched out her muscles, tired after the day's activities. Scanning the horizon, she noticed some very peculiar cloud shapes just over a mountain ridge to the southwest. Peering into the sky to observe the unique clouds she was temporarily blinded by the sun radiating brilliantly in the velvet blue sky. Chilly, she climbed back into the car, slammed the door shut, and settled in.

Noticing an odd reflection on the dashboard in front of her, she searched for the source of the bright reflection. Stunned, Marta reached down and picked up a silvery round object. *My God! It's the Siva Medallion Jon found in Hilcraft's house in Pine Hill. How the hell did this thing get into the car—and why is it on the floor of the car now?*

Jon jerked open the car door and paused to notice the unusual cloud formation in the sky to the southwest. He stared at it for several seconds, then got into the car, thinking he'd never seen anything like those clouds before.

"Nice people here, very friendly. Are you okay? You look a bit flustered."

"Jon! Look what I just found!" The medallion caught the sun's rays as Marta held it out to Jon.

"Where did you find that!"

"Right here on the floor mat. I stepped outside to get some fresh air and stretch my legs. When I got back into the car it was just sitting there on the floor, reflecting sunlight all over the car. The light caught my eye, so I looked for the source. I was completely stunned to realize it was the medallion!"

"You're just goofing with me, right? Aren't you? You took that off my desk some time ago."

"No, Jon! I absolutely did not do that! I'm not kidding you. I found it right here just before you got back to the car."

"This is so strange. I was looking for it a while ago and I couldn't locate it. The last time I saw it, it was on my desk in my office."

They stared quietly at each other, both sensing something strange in the moment they had just experienced together. Something they had felt before.

Jon smiled, took the medallion from Marta, and contemplated the beautiful, mystical face of the goddess Siva. "She is very special to me. I feel that we are somehow connected. Thank you for finding her!"

He placed the medallion onto the console, turned the key in the ignition, and headed onto Route 28. The position of the medallion almost gave the impression that the goddess was looking back at Jon.

"It's starting to get cold. There's a real chill in the air," Jon said.

"I noticed that when I got out to stretch my legs at the post office."

Jon swung the car onto Route 28. At that exact moment in time, a huge tractor-trailer truck was also barreling down Route 28 a few miles further to the east. Ahead of Jon and Marta's car, it was traveling in the opposite direction. The truck was traveling very fast, and the driver of the truck was very tired, finding it hard to concentrate on the road.

"Marta, could you put on the radio and try and get us a weather report?"

"Sure, just a minute," said Marta, fumbling with the controls to the car radio.

"You can try News 77 out of Kingston. They give a weather report on the sevens, so one should be coming up soon."

As Marta searched for the station, a brief musical jingle caught their attention. It was followed by a commercial, and then the very clear voice of a female radio anchor announced, "This is the Weather Watch Forecast now with 77 Radio chief forecaster Mike Thomas. Mike, what do we have coming up this afternoon? Can you give us a picture of what's going on out there?"

"Right now, Stacy, it's about forty-six in our eastern suburbs, forty-four in Kingston, and around forty-one degrees in the central sections of the Catskills. These temperatures are a bit cooler than normal for this time of the year. This afternoon we will have a continuation of the nice cool, dry conditions. Some increasing clouds come into the picture later in the evening, along with a few possible stray showers. Tonight, expect continued colder-than-normal conditions, along with a bit of a breeze and lows dipping down near the freezing mark. It's going to be a chilly Sunday, with some clouds and sunshine in the forecast. Monday looks to be a mix of sun and clouds along with cooler weather. We'll see increasing clouds over here on Tuesday as a weather disturbance tries to move in and we may even get some of the first snow showers of the season in the mountains to our west. There you have it, Stacy.

We'll have more about the coming week's weather later in the broadcast. Now go on everyone! Get out there and enjoy the beautiful sunshine for the rest of the day."

"Thank you, Mike. Now in other news around Kingston today, there's new information surrounding the murder mystery in Ulster County of a forty-five-year-old woman who was found dead in her home in Kingston . . ."

Marta turned off the radio. "It sounds like we're going to have some more nice cool weather coming our way tonight."

"Yeah, it feels good. Maybe after dinner we'll go for a little walk around Pine Hill, and get a great look at those beautiful stars up there in the sky."

"That sounds great! It's amazing how much more clearly we can see the stars in the mountains than we can on Long Island."

The massive tractor-trailer truck was fast approaching Jon's car, picking up speed, heading downhill as it neared them. The truck wandered into the oncoming lane slightly, now less than one mile away, rounding a curve in the highway and coming on fast.

With a sultry gaze, Marta said, "Oh, Jon, I forgot to tell you that I packed something very special that you are going to love. You'd better not fall asleep until I put it on later. I picked it out especially for you, and I do know that you love to—"

Jon startled, opened his eyes wide, as if he had seen a ghost, and then hit the brakes hard, slowing down quickly enough to just be able to take the nearby exit onto another highway which headed north.

Marta yelled out as she was thrown back in her seat. "Jon, what are you doing? Are you crazy?"

"I'm going to take you somewhere really special—somewhere you have never been before. It's not too far away, and I think you'll really find it intriguing and beautiful."

"Wow, well I guess there's nothing like a little spontaneity. You scared the heck out of me. What is this place?"

"I can't tell you. You'll just have to experience it yourself."

Jon glanced at the Siva medallion resting on his center console.

The speeding tractor-trailer passed the spot on Route 28 where Jon had turned off the road. The driver had momentarily nodded off and drifted into the eastbound lane. Up ahead, another driver heading east witnessed the truck's transgression and desperately blared his horn, warning the truck to get back into the westbound lane. The driver of the tractor-trailer snapped out of his stupor and quickly swung his truck back into the correct lane. The car and the truck passed each other safely, but the occupants of both vehicles were stunned and shaken.

The driver of the car whispered to his wife and daughter, "My, God! We would have been killed if we had been here just a few seconds earlier!" None of them ever forgot how they felt at that moment.

Jon began to relax as he drove along the scenic road. He drove north past huge rock walls and imposing boulders that seemed poised to roll down into the road at any moment. After about fifteen miles, he turned right onto another highway heading east. They were now at a much higher altitude. They passed by several large mountain peaks that were somehow reminiscent of gothic cathedrals. Then, as they passed through the sleepy town of Tannersville, Jon said, "Okay, Marta, the place I'm taking you to is just a few miles away now."

"I've never been on this highway before. Actually, I'm pretty sure I've never been this far north in the Catskills."

"Yeah, I know that I've never taken you this far north before, but I've always wanted to. The northern Catskills have a different look to them than the southern Catskills, but they are both uniquely beautiful. This road gets very steep up ahead so we'll have to be careful. We're going to park in a small parking area that is near a ledge with great views. Then we'll take a short hike to a very special spot. I know you're going to absolutely love it."

"I can't wait to see it! You know me, I love surprises."

[49]

Transcendence Through the Multiverse

Jon parked the car in the small lot, and they started their hike into the woods. They hiked up a steep embankment alongside a rapidly flowing stream.

"What a roar! This stream is really powerful!"

"Wait 'til you see what's farther up ahead. I'm not going to give it away. I want you to see it for yourself."

They hiked farther on the winding, uphill trail and passed by large boulders covered with plush, brilliant, moist, green moss.

"Boy, it's getting slippery here. Everything is so damp," Marta said.

"The mist here is beautiful, and on a hot day it's amazing how it cools the air. It adds a special mystique to this area, which has inspired many famous poets and authors over the many past decades."

"Hmm. Wow, the sounds here are amazing! The rush of this river is so magnificent and hypnotic. It's so relaxing and transcendent, too. It seems to be getting louder. I can't wait to see what's up ahead."

"Just a little farther and we'll be there!"

They scrambled uphill, carefully placing their feet for maximum traction on the moist ground, which was sometimes rocky and sometimes soft enough to sink into. Their path zigzagged between and around large, round, sculpted boulders.

Marta stopped to catch her breath. "The air here is amazing. I feel like I'm breathing in the whole forest with each breath."

"The moisture in the air makes these woods even more aromatic than some of the surrounding areas. Just watch your step because it gets steep and slippery in this next section."

"Okay, I will! It's so lovely, and somewhat different from other places we've hiked before."

They continued climbing for a few more minutes as the constant roar became stronger and more powerful. It drew them closer, like a lantern in the distance leading through an enchanted forest.

"One more march up, and we'll be there!"

"I can't wait!" answered Marta, stopping for a few more moments to breathe deeply and take in the beauty all around her.

They walked on for a few minutes more. Suddenly, Jon grabbed Marta's hands and beamed a broad smile at her, "We've reached our destination, Hun. Come on forward and see my surprise."

Marta stepped off the path and entered a grand opening in the forest. Roaring, cascading sounds permeated the area and echoed throughout the naturally constructed rock amphitheater that had been carved out by the falling waters of the creek they had walked along on the way up. Marta was amazed to see that the tremendous waterfall before her was composed of two separate series of falls. She looked up, and way up high she could see how the waterfall formed from a stream falling over a rock cliff nearly two hundred feet high into a large upper pool of water. That water then overflowed from the upper pool and fell another hundred feet into the magnificent lower rock pool that lay before them. Bathed in the misty air and effervescent sounds, Marta felt a tremendous sense of joy wash over her.

Jon placed his arm around Marta, and their hearts soared as they shared the experience of the astounding beauty of this natural wonder.

"I don't think that I have ever seen anything more beautiful in my entire life. What is this place called?"

"This is Kaaterskill Falls. It's one of the most spectacular natural sites in the eastern United States."

"My God! It's amazing! How high are the falls?"

"Both of them together are almost three hundred feet high. The upper falls is the larger of the two. These falls are actually one of America's oldest tourist attractions."

"They're absolutely stunning. I could stay here all day and just admire them."

"Countless artists, writers, and poets have come here over the past two hundred years. They came searching for inspiration, and left with some of their most creative works after experiencing this awesome site. I don't think anyone leaves here unaffected by the majesty of this place."

Marta faced Jon and gazed deeply into his eyes. "I'm so happy that you brought me here today. Let's never, ever forget this beautiful moment," she said, reaching over to gently kiss him.

Jon took her into his arms, and said, "This experience will be in our minds and hearts forever, my beautiful Marta. It's the special moments like this that define our very lives. We were meant to be here, together, now. This is the entire meaning of our existence, to experience this beautiful universe with conscious realization. There is nothing else in life that really matters other than these moments together."

Together, they stood in silence and entered into a meditative state. Their minds clear of all uncertainty; they entered the realm of interconnected eternity. In that instant, they were perfectly unified within their spiritual reality. They were always meant to be together . . . *there forever.*

Jon opened his eyes, smiled, and gently removed his arm from Marta's shoulders, reaching for his pocket. Marta watched as he retrieved an object from his pocket and held it out for her to see.

"The Siva medallion! Why did you bring it here to the waterfall?"

"I don't know, Marta. I've been thinking. Well, *maybe*—we should give it back to the spirits of the universe somehow. Maybe it's not right for us to keep her to ourselves," Jon said, gazing at his beautiful goddess before him.

"So what are you thinking of doing with her?"

"What do you think we should do with our goddess friend?" Jon asked. His mixed emotions played out across his face as he waited for Marta's reply.

Then, simultaneously, they both smiled at each other and turned as one to contemplate the magnificent pool of turbulent water at the foot of the waterfall. The brilliant medallion was secure between Jon's fingers. He held it up before them, and in the solitude of that beautiful place, they each took in the inspiration of the medallion for the last time. After a few moments, Marta touched the Siva medallion in farewell. Then, as if in slow motion, Jon tossed the beloved medallion toward the effervescent pool of water. The medallion shimmered as it flew through the air. It entered the water with a slight splash, and disappeared into the watery realm beneath the falls.

Jon and Marta lingered after witnessing the medallion's descent into the tumultuous waters.

Suddenly, the air was filled with an unearthly sound that seemed to resonate through the entire forest.

"Jon, what on earth do you think that is?"

"I don't know. I've never heard anything like it!"

"What do you think is causing it?"

"Maybe it's the wind or something?"

As they stood in the clearing by the falls, enveloped in sound, they were both at once struck by an overwhelming feeling of transcendence. In this place and time reality was different, and they felt utterly removed from the ordinary events of life they had previously experienced. Somehow, it felt as if time itself had been suspended.

The forest wind began to pick up around them. Marta wrapped her arms around Jon and looked at him lovingly. "I'm so glad you've given our goddess friend back to the spirits of the universe here in this pool. I think Emery would have wanted you to do that."

"Yeah, I think somehow, someway, Emery influenced us to journey here to experience this beautiful place together, and to bring his special goddess back to her home and her future destiny." Jon suddenly looked up with a very odd look on his face.

"What are you looking at, Jon? You almost look as if you've had a premonition. What are you thinking?"

Jon remained silent for a few moments, staring into the sky. Finally, he turned away from his visions and smiled at Marta. "I see other worlds out there—infinite other worlds out there! Don't you see them, Marta?"

"What do you see in those other worlds? Jon, tell me! What's out there?"

Jon grinned happily. "I see you and me together forever in this beautiful world that no words can describe, and in all the other universes that are out there, too. I love you, Marta! We'll always be together, you and I!"

Teary-eyed, Marta hugged Jon tightly, "Oh Jon, I love you so much, too. I am yours in this universe, and in any other universe out there, too. We are meant to be together, always and forever!"

They embraced lovingly in that eternal point in time in that universe, and their true fate and purpose became evident to them in that everlasting moment of love. They realized that the universe they had both strived so hard to understand through science had always been within their consciousness, waiting to be revealed. That moment of revelation had come, and now they were destined to continue their journey into the multiverse with true love uniting them as one.

A Note from the Author and Special Thanks

People in ancient times looked out into the nighttime sky in wonderment at the majesty of the universe before them and tried to make sense of just what this world was. These people searched for answers about how this universe could have come about and how they were somehow a part of it. Many cultures developed religions, philosophies, and superstitions to help them cope with the environment around them and the troubles that they faced in their everyday lives. Later, when superstition was replaced by science and they started to gain a better understanding of their universe they truly realized that *reality was far stranger and richer than they first thought.*

Today, scientific discovery and technology has advanced to unimaginable levels and the scientific achievements and accomplishments have been stunning. In just the past five hundred years our society has gone from believing that the Earth was the center of the solar system to realizing that our universe is a vast, complex, and seemingly endless structure much more weird and wonderful than they could have ever imagined.

In the past hundred years, scientists have produced astonishing new theories that help us better understand what makes up the matter that we see on Earth and the things that extend infinitely far out into the cosmos. Some of these scientists have become popular household names, such as Sir Isaac Newton and Albert Einstein, but there are many others who have escaped the limelight and disappeared into obscurity.

I myself have been on a journey of discovery ever since I became interested in science when I was young. I studied science in college and was lucky to gain employment in a career in science. I have been educated by many in the field of science and also inspired by them to write this science-fiction story.

I want to share with you some of my favorite scientists who have inspired me in the writing of this story and give them special thanks.

One of them was Hugh Everett III, a physicist who developed the now recognized many worlds interpretation of quantum physics. Everett was one of those scientists who faded into obscurity after his untimely death at the age of 51 in 1982. But over the past few decades, his outlandish theory that we live in a universe of infinite parallel worlds all here at the same time, hidden from us, has gained much respect and admiration. He was a brilliant scientist and mathematician who studied quantum physics, which is the science of what takes place at the atomic and subatomic levels. Everett deserves to be recognized as one of the apex pioneers of making sense of our strange quantum world. I would encourage all readers to visit the Hugh Everett Wikipedia page and read all about his life and his amazing research.

In my book, *The Inverted Mask*, I utilize the many worlds theory as a backdrop throughout the story. I also incorporate the concept of quantum immortality. This concept refers to the subjective conscience experience of living on and on into eternity. Everett himself contemplated this paradoxical possibility by postulating that his consciousness is bound at each branching of the infinite parallel worlds to follow whichever path leads to continued conscience realization. We all have to thank Hugh Everett for presenting us with his insightful research and theories—stimulating our intuitions.

Another physicist who educated me in the study of quantum physics and totally inspired me to write my book was Dr. Max Tegmark. Tegmark is a Swedish-American cosmologist, professor at the Massachusetts Institute of Technology, and scientific director of the Foundational Questions Institute. Tegmark has many academic achievements and contributed much to the study of cosmology, the study of the universe. Tegmark is also a leading theorist of quantum physics and has uncovered many insights into the subject of the many worlds theory and quantum suicide, which is a corollary to quantum immortality.

Years ago, when I first became interested in the subject of quantum physics, I was introduced to Tegmark's work by reading some of his articles in scientific journals. One of these was the article "Parallel Universes," which he wrote for the May 2003 issue of Scientific American. In this brilliant article, Tegmark postulates that there are at least four levels of parallel universes. In my book, I also refer to these four levels when the characters Marta and Lois meet Dr. Charles Kenton in the PIXX Detector of the Heavy Ion Target Supercollider.

Tegmark recently wrote a landmark book, *Our Mathematical Universe*, that embodies his quest for the ultimate nature of reality. I would encourage all readers of my book to get a copy of Tegmark's book and check it out, especially if you are interested in many of the topics my sci-fi novel integrated, such as the many worlds theory.

Tegmark was gracious in allowing me to use one of the cartoons that he uses in his lectures and articles. The cartoon below is a representation of the split that occurs based on the possible outcomes for each action, forming parallel realities, according to Everett's many worlds interpretation.

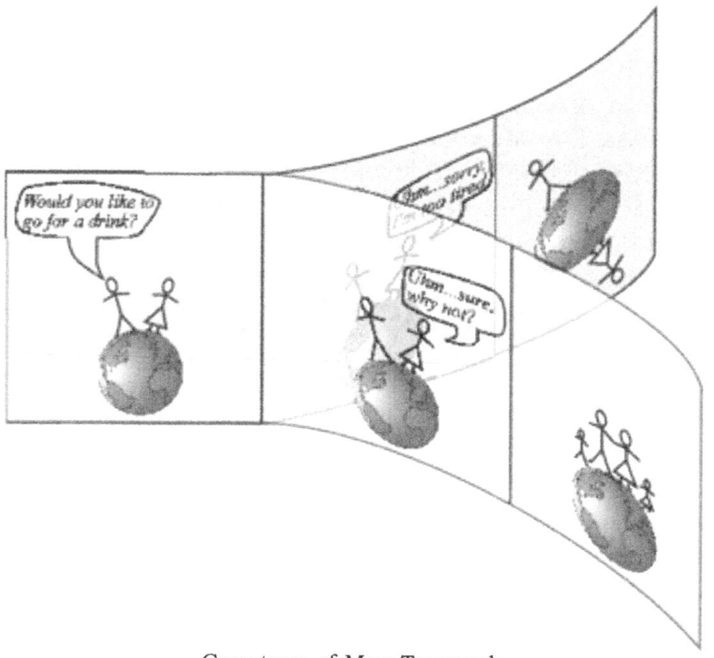

Courtesy of Max Tegmark

In my book, there is a fictitious physicist who writes a fictitious novel entitled *The Existence Hypothesis and Quantum Eternity.* Well, if any real-life physicist could ever write such a novel it would probably be Dr. Max Tegmark. Or maybe in one of the alternate parallel universes Hugh Everett is still alive and writes this novel. I only wish that I could read that book sometime in this universe! Tegmark also has an outstanding website full of articles, videos, and other excellent resources.

Another well-respected physicist who promotes the many worlds theory and who also inspired me is Dr. Frank Tipler, a professor of physics at Tulane University. I first found Tipler's ideas featured on some science shows on television that brought up the question "are there parallel universes?" Tipler does an excellent job in rationalizing this strange, abstract concept in his broadcast interviews and in his books and published research papers. You can go on Tipler's excellent website and find his books and published peer-reviewed research papers there. Tipler also discusses the concept of God in much of his work, which brings an interesting angle to the discussion. In my book, I too brought up the subject of God in several discussions. I don't consider myself a religious man, but I do think that in some sense I am spiritual.

I came across the work of Dr. Thomas Campbell when I was researching science videos on the web for my book. After I listened to several of his interviews, I definitely learned much about the subject of quantum physics and its relationship to our perceived universe. Campbell is a physicist and a consultant for several government agencies. Campbell's work unifies science and philosophy, physics and metaphysics, mind and matter, and the purpose and meaning of our existence. Campbell wrote a trilogy of books entitled *My Big TOE*. TOE stands for his Theory of Everything. Campbell's salient point throughout his work is that we live in a subjective reality and that reality is not objective at all. You can find all about Campbell and his work on his superb website. Campbell's ideas definitely stimulated me in the writing of my book.

Lastly, I would like to thank the Science Channel, History Channel, PBS, and The National Geographic Channel for their fine science program broadcasting. There is so much other garbage programming on television that is withering the mental state of many people in this country who get addicted to junk programming. It's really good that people can still turn on the TV and navigate to those fine stations and find something that will teach them about life, reality, and themselves.

This book took me on a journey into my own mind and the mind of the universe. It included many of my own experiences that I came across in my career and life. I tried to create an entertaining story that embodied the new concepts of modern science and which reflected, just what is this conscience experience of reality?

Please visit my web site at THEINVERTEDMASK.COM for updates, information and comments.

Photo of Izzy Doroski (center) with two of his colleagues while stationed at a well-known national laboratory in 1997

About the Author

Isidore (Izzy) Doroski was born and raised in New York, on eastern Long Island. After receiving his bachelor's of science in biology at State University of New York at Cortland, Izzy attained certification as a wastewater treatment operator. His early employment included a job as a research scientist in neurophysiology and working for a municipality in the field of wastewater treatment. For most of his career, Izzy worked at an environmental regulatory agency as a senior environmental health scientist, protecting public health through environmental regulation enforcement.

Throughout his thirty-four-year career, Izzy's profession took him to many fascinating locations, including several nuclear reactors, energy storage and production facilities and chemical manufacturing plants. He also participated in emergency response situations. Some of the inspiration for this book comes from the full year Izzy spent stationed at a well-known national laboratory, monitoring a radiation leak from their onsite nuclear facility.

Izzy Doroski has always had a deep passion for science and continues to study the hidden mysteries of this unique universe. He has lectured at town halls, schools, and colleges on the subject of energy and alternate energy. In his spare time, Izzy loves to hike, bike, and play guitar and synthesizer. One of his favorite pastimes is hiking in the Catskill Mountains of New York. Izzy's passion for science, as well as the beauty of eastern Long Island and the Catskills, were inspirational in the writing of this book.

Made in the USA
Middletown, DE
17 December 2019